Praise for
American Omens

"In *American Omens,* Travis Thrasher is at the top of his game, imagining the future with the eyes of a seasoned novelist penning th̲ ̲ ̲ ̲ ̲ ̲ ̲ ̲ ̲ ̲ ̲ estined to write. As fresh and relevant as *Left B̲ ̲ ̲ ̲ ̲* ̲ ̲ ̲ ̲ ̲ ̲ ̲ ̲ears ago, *American Omens* may be the firs̲ ̲ ̲ ̲ ̲ ̲ ̲ ̲ ̲ ̲ ̲ ̲ secuted church from this writer. We can o̲ ̲

   —JERRY B. JENKINS, ̲ ̲ ̲ ̲ ̲ ̲ ̲ ̲ ̲ ̲ ̲ ̲ ̲ ̲ ̲ ̲ ̲ ̲ .or
    of the *Left Behind* n̲ ̲

"Thrasher's outdone himself with this multilayered story of ultimate stakes. Written with deft and obvious passion, *American Omens* is a thrilling, eerie sci-fi that feels far closer to reality than fiction."

   —TOSCA LEE, *New York Times* best-selling author

"*American Omens* is, simply put, stunning. Stunning in the delivery of story that grabs you from the first paragraph. Take caution: it will root you where you stand until you finish the first chapter. Then you'll be reluctant to wait longer to start on the rest. And it's stunning in the quality of prose—vivid images and great dialogue. Travis Thrasher has written a novel that will take you on a roller coaster to unexpected places. When you finish, aside from wishing there was more, you'll have a disturbing sense of where the future is headed."

   —SIGMUND BROUWER, author of the Christy Award's
   2015 Book of the Year *Thief of Glory*

AMERICAN
OMENS

TRAVIS
THRASHER

THE COMING FIGHT FOR FAITH

AMERICAN
OMENS

A NOVEL

MULTNOMAH

AMERICAN OMENS

Scripture quotations and paraphrases are taken from the following versions: The Holy Bible, New Living Translation, copyright © 1996, 2004, 2007, 2013, 2015 by Tyndale House Foundation. Used by permission of Tyndale House Publishers Inc., Carol Stream, Illinois 60188. All rights reserved. The Message. Copyright © by Eugene H. Peterson 1993, 1994, 1995, 1996, 2000, 2001, 2002. Used by permission of NavPress. All rights reserved. Represented by Tyndale House Publishers Inc. The Holy Bible, New International Version®, NIV®. Copyright © 1973, 1978, 1984 by Biblica Inc.® Used by permission. All rights reserved worldwide.

Trade Paperback ISBN 978-0-7352-9178-2
eBook ISBN 978-0-7352-9179-9

Cover design by Mark D. Ford

Published in the United States by Multnomah, an imprint of the Crown Publishing Group, a division of Penguin Random House LLC, New York.

MULTNOMAH® and its mountain colophon are registered trademarks of Penguin Random House LLC.

Library of Congress Cataloging-in-Publication Data
Names: Thrasher, Travis, 1971- author.
Title: American omens : the coming fight for faith : a novel / by Travis Thrasher.
Description: First edition. | New York : Multnomah, 2019.
Identifiers: LCCN 2018035324 | ISBN 9780735291782 (trade paperback) | ISBN 9780735291799 (ebook)
Subjects: | BISAC: FICTION / Christian / Futuristic. | FICTION / Christian / Suspense. | FICTION / Suspense. | GSAFD: Christian fiction. | Suspense fiction.
Classification: LCC PS3570.H6925 A83 2019 | DDC 813/.54—dc23
LC record available at https://lccn.loc.gov/2018035324

Printed in the United States of America
2019—First Edition

10 9 8 7 6 5 4 3 2 1

To Barry Smith, for making God known

Another kind of religious leader must arise among us.
He must be of the old prophet type, a man who has seen
visions of God and has heard a voice from the Throne.
When he comes (and I pray there will be not one but
many), he will stand in flat contradiction to everything
our smirking, smooth civilization holds dear.

—A. W. TOZER

Don't believe what you hear, don't believe what you see
If you just close your eyes you can feel the enemy

—U2

If you're going through hell, keep going.

—WINSTON CHURCHILL

Prologue

The spiderweb cracks in the windshield made it easy to spot the old Chevy SUV in the parking lot. Jon Dowland stood next to the car and examined the black duct tape that covered a hole the size of his fist on the passenger side. One of the shots he'd fired last night had obviously connected, but it hadn't stopped the driver from disappearing once again. Even though the Chevy looked abandoned, Dowland knew the man wasn't likely to be far away.

The morning sun began to leak out over the Indiana countryside. Dowland had forgotten how bleak the Midwest could be in winter. The wind was cold and cut through him as he walked toward the motel sitting right next to the gas station and former truck stop in the middle of nowhere. In one of those dingy rooms, the man he'd been hunting was probably wide awake, wasting his time by praying. This little game had been interesting for the last few months, but Dowland was done with it now. Nearly getting run down on an Indiana highway by some lunatic calling himself the Reckoner had used up what little patience he had.

It took only two hundred dollars to bribe the bored and pimply-faced kid behind the front desk to give him a room number. A simple direct exchange, or DE, that took two seconds. Dowland could have shown his FBI credentials, but he never did that. If anybody came around asking, which wasn't likely here of all places, he didn't want the FBI to be a part of any conversation. Only a few people knew what Dowland was doing, and nobody knew his present location. If he was arrested or shot dead for some reason, no one could find anything on his SYNAPSYS. It'd be blank, requiring official approval to exorcise the personal data.

He found the door on the second story, stood there for a moment to look and listen for anybody nearby or in the parking lot below, then took out his customized Beretta just before kicking down the door. They no longer made doors with locks that got old and could be so easily broken, but in this run-down motel built decades ago, Dowland felt like the star of an eighties action movie. Sure enough, nobody was in bed asleep. The covers looked untouched, with an assortment of files and papers spread out on them. The man traveling under a handful of aliases was sitting in a chair next to the table with a laptop computer open beside another set of file folders. It had been a while since Dowland had seen anybody working on one of those archaic devices.

Aiming the firearm directly at the man, Dowland nudged the door back to close it, and when it wouldn't stay put, he took the other chair and propped it against the door. The man in the motel room held his hands up, his fingers outstretched and his eyes open wide. One corner of the glasses he wore was held together with masking tape.

"No, no, no. Hold on. Just wait. Just wait a minute!" he shouted to Dowland.

The target was out of breath and looked as if he hadn't slept in a week. He started to stand up, but Dowland shook his head to make the man stay put.

"Please, I'm not armed. I can't do anything," he said.

"You can mow a man down on the side of the road, can't you?"

Along with his black eye, bruised jaw, and cut lip, Dowland nursed a shoulder injury from diving for cover to avoid the car yesterday. Good thing the mostly useless arm was his left arm, the one he didn't need to shoot his gun.

A quick scan of all the papers confirmed what Dowland already knew. This was indeed the man he'd been hunting all this time.

"Clemente on," Dowland said, stating the name to turn on the man's SYNAPSYS as he held the barrels of the Beretta against his head. "Contact info."

The customized box the size of his hand appeared to his right. The information on the augmented interface was further proof.

Robert Vasquez. I've finally found you.

The SYNAPSYS showed the various code names this nutjob had used during the last few years. Dowland knew the background on Vasquez—from his resignation three years ago as an Arizona senator amid allegations of sexual misconduct and fraud to his incarceration last year for vandalizing a town hall with graffiti. The latter offense had been Vasquez's own doing, but the controversy that had ended his career in Congress was orchestrated by the same group paying Dowland's salary. Vasquez had never shied away from his personal faith, and after years of being told to remain quiet, he eventually had pushed things too far.

No one could have imagined that he was the Reckoner, the one responsible for creating a group to deliver lies and spin stories and incite trouble in the name of Christianity. Dowland had been tracking down members of this group for the last two years and had been ordered a few months ago to take out their leader. Finally, two days ago he got a golden tip about where the man was hiding.

"You don't have to point that at me," Vasquez said. "I'm not dangerous."

"So why are you calling yourself the Reckoner?" Dowland asked.

Vasquez didn't flinch at the mention of the name. He merely shook his head. "That's not me."

"Of course not. And you don't have any connections to all these operations in your files, right? Like Operation Bulls on Parade, where you created chaos in downtown Chicago by unleashing those cows. Or Operation Panic. Or how about Operation Black Waters?"

"I didn't say I had nothing to do with those," Vasquez stated. "But I'm not the Reckoner."

Robert Vasquez was a typical fifty-two-year-old man in every way. He was one of the last guys anybody could imagine suddenly abandoning a successful career in politics to start being vocal about his views on Christianity.

Nobody rises from the dead, buddy. You're going to learn that soon enough.

"Who knows you're here?" Dowland's eyes scanned the walls and the contents of the room.

"Nobody. Not a single soul."

"None of your little frat brothers and sisters? Nobody in your playgroup?"

"It was better for no one to know I'm here."

For the first time since Dowland had stepped over the state line into Indiana, something didn't seem quite right. The way Vasquez was claiming he wasn't the Reckoner and the few items he had in the room with him . . .

"I've been trying to find you for months," Dowland said, the gun now at his side but still ready for any surprise. "How'd you elude me in Philadelphia?"

"That wasn't me."

Once again Vasquez's demeanor made him seem believable.

This man has made telling lies a life mission. He's mastered it.

"You've been waiting for someone," Dowland said. "Who?"

Vasquez gave him a solemn smile. "You, Mr. Dowland. I knew you'd find me eventually."

Staying in this motel so close to where Dowland had found him last night . . . His SYNAPSYS still on and easily accessed . . . Nothing in his files with more information on the Reckoner . . .

For a second Dowland caught a glimpse of himself in the mirror on the wall facing the bed. He resembled a boxer after a fight.

"Just tell me," Dowland said as he let out a tired sigh. "Are you the one behind everything? We're going to find out soon enough after we scour all your data."

"I just told you I'm not."

"Okay, fine. Get your science project together and come with me." Dowland aimed the gun at him again. "We're heading back to Chicago."

"You're being controlled. And you're as expendable to them as the rest of us are."

"Nobody controls me."

"There is freedom in letting go," Vasquez said, "in finally admitting you can't do everything on your own."

"You guys never turn off the switch, do you? Meeting in secret and delivering your clandestine messages."

"We're not the only ones who meet in secret, Mr. Dowland."

He didn't like hearing this guy mutter his name. Dowland stepped closer to the man, close enough to press the Beretta to his temple again.

"I know one thing about control in this world," Dowland said. "I have it in my hand right now."

"The Lord's prophet is warning the rest of us. There is still time but not much. You must listen to me. Hear me out—"

"I had a grandmother who talked crazy just like you. Nobody could tell whether it was the religion or the senility talking. I think it was the vodka she had stashed away."

Sweat covered Vasquez's forehead, and his body odor was strong from spending a week running and hiding.

"I know you think I'm crazy, and that's fine, but you're holding a gun to the head of a normal, decent American who's done nothing wrong. Do you think that maybe—possibly—you didn't happen to find me, but rather you were led out here for a reason?"

"And what reason is that?"

"The Reckoner wants you. You have a specific purpose. That's what he's been told."

Dowland gritted his teeth, then chuckled the same way he might curse. "I want you to tell me right now, this very instant. What are you doing all the way out here? And where's the Reckoner?"

"We've done this to ourselves," the shaky voice said. "We've turned our backs on God, and He's had enough."

Dowland jammed the gun even harder against the idiot's skull. "There's only one god in your life, and he's standing right in front of you. But you're right about one thing. He has had enough."

Dowland fired the shot without further thought. This was going to be done either on the side of an Indiana country road or in this room. It didn't matter. He'd heard enough from this guy. Now it was done. Two more shots made sure of that.

With the body crumpled on the floor beside him, Dowland leaned over and picked up a series of large photographs. After looking at half a dozen, he felt his stomach twist.

There's no way they know all this.

He knew he couldn't leave anything behind in this room. He also knew that things were much worse than any of them had imagined.

Apparently the Reckoner hadn't been lying at his last public announcement when he declared, *"All will be revealed soon."* The faces of the men and women in those pictures were the revelations he was talking about. Dowland needed to know how much proof they had.

And whether or not this corpse was indeed the Reckoner.

While he was piling the belongings onto the bed, a handwritten note slipped out of a stack of papers. Dowland scanned it.

Abraham approached him and said, "Will you sweep away both the righteous and the wicked?" —Genesis 18:23

He let the piece of paper gently drop down onto the dead man. Dowland could only shake his head and curse as he thought about his father. Vasquez had been as deluded as his grandmother, thinking this world still contained both the righteous and the wicked.

The only righteous thing left in this world was being honest about its absence.

ONE

Blackbird

1.

The building loomed above the other towers, pointing toward the heavens, daring to outshine the stars. Inside the mile of floors that composed Incen Tower, night and day didn't matter, nor did sunrise and sunset. The Chicago structure contained its own universe, controlled by mankind and operated by machines. Three hundred stories could make anyone believe in the impossible.

On the 118th floor at the start of the workday, a young woman walked in the midst of the restless crowd that poured into the main atrium from the three stairless escalators that resembled multicolored waterfalls. As always and exactly on time, Cheyenne Burne headed toward Bistro #4. Even though all ten places selling coffee in the atrium had robots serving the same brand, she liked Henry at the fourth counter in the center. She swore he made her morning drink just a little better than the other machines. Plus, she liked the witty things he said each day. They resembled sayings in fortune cookies.

"Good morning, Miss Burne," his cheery voice with a British accent said.

Henry wasn't fully functional. Only half of him stood in place at the counter, swiveling back and forth with metal arms that extended, poured, and mixed. He knew people from ten feet away, and they could even utter what coffee they wanted into their SYNAPSYSes an hour before leaving their apartments. Cheyenne no longer had to do that. She always got the same order, so Henry knew not to ask.

"Did you have a good weekend?" he inquired.

"I worked."

"That means you loved your weekend since you love your work."

Cheyenne grinned. *He's always trying to be ironic.* "Certain aspects, yes," she said and then tried to be ironic back. "Just climbing the corporate ladder."

He picked up the sarcasm and made his smile bigger. There had been no attempt to make Henry or the other baristas look lifelike. Instead, Henry resembled a puppet, with only eyes and a grin that changed sizes. His personality, however, was what gave him character. Each encounter helped develop Henry's knowledge of and relationship with her. Even the most minor and insignificant detail from an interaction was recorded and could be recalled at a later date.

If only guys had even half of those abilities.

Henry handed her the coffee. "Remember, Miss Burne, that 'the higher up you go, the more mistakes you are allowed. Right at the top, if you make enough of them, it's considered to be your style.'"

"That's a great insight, Henry."

"That's a quote from the legendary dancer Fred Astaire."

She laughed and said goodbye to the robot. His wit always reminded her of why she loved her work and why it was never ending.

The genius isn't the machinery. It's the programming.

Enough human beings looked like plastic-and-celluloid creations, so there was no reason for robots to keep up with the Joneses. The great leap was the intelligence that was being built and modified and advanced, an intelligence she specialized in and refused to call artificial. In her mind it was a new form of art. Trying to replicate in algorithms the way neurons in the brain used their synapses wasn't merely complex; some days—most days, in fact—it felt almost absurd.

Yet that's what they said twenty years ago about putting technology in people's heads. Before people ever knew what a SYNAPSYS was.

The coffee was perfection, tasting like vanilla initially, then morphing into a Columbian Supremo caramel in her mouth. It was never too hot, yet it would retain its temperature in the disposable cup. As she headed across the glass walkway that was playing an old music video, she had to have a few sips before getting on the 7:33 a.m. I Elevator going to the PASK offices.

The ingenuity of her morning java reminded her that every great invention, no matter how big or small it was, came from someone asking for and wanting more. *What will these ingredients taste like if I put them all together?*

How can I improve something as simple as coffee? Is there a way to make more out of this staple drink humans take for granted?

That was how she had approached her work in algorithms from the very first days she began to play with them. Could they be expanded and modified? Could something as complex as human emotions be sown into technology? Those questions had been answered over the years with a resounding yes.

The figure underneath her heels looked like a clown in distorted colors, with a thin white face and red lips, until it panned back to reveal the ruffled collar and the hat of a Pierrot. Normally Cheyenne didn't pay attention to the background music or even the accompanying retro videos that filled the atrium floor, but this morning she couldn't avoid it. She knew David Bowie simply by the voice. She couldn't remember hearing this song, but the lyrics made her feel as if a stranger's fingernails were scraping against her neck.

"I never did anything out of the blue."

It was just another morning and another short walk to the offices, and yet for some reason everything about this day felt a bit off kilter, like this song and the video. Cheyenne didn't know why she was feeling this way. Last night and the past weekend hadn't been unusual. There was no reason for her to feel low, and her body monitor gave her all the usual levels, yet she felt as if she were approaching a barrier and impasse. Not in this building but rather in her life.

As she passed Bistro #2, she smiled at the familiar stranger who stood there with his coffee in hand, watching the crowd flow by like a river after a rainfall. He looked like any other businessman, always wearing a suit and fashionable tie, always well groomed, always politely acknowledging her with a friendly smile and either a nod or a raise of his cup. Today, however, the dark-haired man began to walk next to her, something he had never done before.

"Good morning, Cheyenne," he said.

She didn't slow down—she couldn't afford to do that—but she did turn her head in surprise.

"You speak English?"

"Have you ever heard me speak Korean?" he asked without the slightest accent.

A quarter of the occupants of Incen Tower were foreign, with a majority of them being Koreans who didn't speak English. She had lumped this man in with that group, though she deeply resented when others did that to her.

"I've never heard you speak."

"That's because you've never spoken to me." His tone was more playful than condescending.

"You haven't either."

"There's a pecking order, Cheyenne. I'm not on the upper level. I don't get to take the I Elevator." He continued without either of them breaking stride. "I have a note to give you," he said.

"You don't strike me as a secret admirer," Cheyenne said, smiling.

"The note is from your father."

This made her stop, causing the woman behind her to bump into her and almost sending both of them to the ground. Cheyenne stood there, no longer with a smile but with a desire to know what was going on. The stranger now looked completely different, as if shrouded in a shadow.

"My father went missing more than a year ago," she said. "If this is some kind of sales pitch, I will get your license revoked as fast as I can."

The steady eyes and chiseled face remained steadfast in their expression. "Can we talk away from the crowd?"

She nodded and followed him to one of the fountains in the atrium. The water changed colors as it bloomed. Cheyenne recalled walking by one of these fountains ten years ago when she was seventeen and already being recruited by Acatour. Her father had taken her to Chicago, where they had been able to witness the grandeur of the new Incen Tower together. Despite the modern-day wonders of technology, including elevators that soared to the clouds without any semblance of motion, she had most enjoyed watching the rainbow of hues and patterns in the water and had stared at them for a long time. Long enough for her father to put his arm around her and whisper in her ear, *"One day you're going to live here."*

Perhaps he prophesied it, or perhaps he put the ambition in her heart and soul. Her father used to have that sort of power over her until she realized she was not powerless and needed to break free.

"Your father gave me very specific instructions," the man told Cheyenne.

"Who are you? How do you know him?"

"My name is Hoon. I met Keith—your father—at a critical moment in my life. He helped me."

She couldn't help looking above Hoon's head at one of the rows of long escalators slithering up the side of the building like tentacles. The view never looked the same, the tower having been designed to resemble an ever-shifting maze. There were kiosks with Seis to give directions or even escort people to their destination. And all around, everywhere a person looked, security watched and monitored every single soul stepping foot in the building. This included the guards in their uniforms, who carried guns at their sides, and the stationary police monitors—robots that functioned in the same way as the servers in the coffee shops.

Then there were also the men and women dressed in business attire who carefully guarded the premises undercover. Cheyenne knew about these gun-toting people because she had a higher-level clearance than most around her.

"He gave me exact instructions in case certain circumstances occurred," Hoon said.

"Have you seen him? Where is he?"

Hoon's eyes scanned around them in such a way nobody could tell he was looking out. "I haven't seen him in five months. I've only received a few messages, all instant and evaporating upon being read. Nothing via his SYNAP-SYS. But he stayed connected. Once a week I would get a notification from him to let me know things were still okay. But it's been two weeks now since I've heard from him."

"Are you one of them?" she asked. "Are you one of those followers?"
You are, aren't you?

"Who I am is of no concern to you. My story doesn't cross paths with yours except for this." Hoon handed her a square piece of paper, a note that had been tightly folded. "I didn't read this, as Mr. Burne requested. He said if two weeks passed and I hadn't heard from him, I was to give this to you."

She was almost afraid to hold it, as if it might suddenly burst into flames, or maybe someone would come and grab it out of her hand so she could never read it. Cheyenne was afraid to read the words inside. Were they long or short, loving or hateful, approachable or preaching?

"Mr. Hoon—"

"Just Hoon, with two *o*'s."

"Hoon—where do you work? What company?"

"I work for your father."

"You what? For my father? Doing what?"

"Well, for one, I keep tabs on you."

Her palm buzzed, and she looked to see the time. "I'm late."

"I know you have to go. That's why I'm making this short."

The light note in her hand felt so foreign, so unreal.

"What should I do?" she asked.

"Read that and do whatever it says."

He began to walk away, but she clutched his forearm to make him stay. Just for another moment.

"Your contact info—," she began.

"I don't share it."

"Then will I be able to reach you somehow?"

He shook his head. "No. But I won't be far away. I'm never far away."

She could only laugh, and as she did, the man gave her a questioning glance.

"Are you trying to be like Clarence?" Cheyenne asked. "The angel from *It's a Wonderful Life*?"

"No," he stated. "I've never seen that film."

Her comment was a joke, but his reply didn't treat it that way.

"It was my father's favorite. He would get teary eyed every time he watched it."

"If anybody is the angel, it's your father. Be careful, Cheyenne."

With those words the man in the suit stepped into the steady stream of other suits and vanished, as if swallowed up by a sea monster. Cheyenne held the note, her hand quivering. She rushed to the escalator that would take her to the I Elevator.

2.

The eyes and ears of Acatour were everywhere, so Cheyenne wouldn't dare even attempt to read the note after arriving at her office. Soldiers were stationed at the entrance to Incen Tower, and more guarded the elevators leading to the upper floors. She had grown used to seeing them in their bulletproof gear, their machine guns slung over their shoulders. Once she stepped off onto the 248th floor, home to the PASK division in Acatour, she knew eyes were on her just as they were on every other employee entering. Hidden devices scanned for anything unusual on her, while others made sure her data matched her SYNAP-SYS. Big Brother was indeed here, but he wasn't as ominous as George Orwell had made him out to be. The watchful eyes followed her as she reached the front hall, where one of half a dozen women with the title of Advisor would be standing there behind a glass reception desk.

"I still remember when they were called receptionists," her father had told her once after visiting her on the floor, the result of a rare invitation he had received from PASK. "They'd be sitting behind a counter or desk, smiling and answering phone calls and making you sign in. Now you have runway models taller than I am who don't really greet you but simply let you walk by."

"And here I thought women had finally progressed enough to no longer be pretty signposts for men to pass," Cheyenne had replied.

Her father's summary had been mostly true, though occasionally, like this morning, a welcoming personality might be standing by the glass doors to the PASK offices. Missy was a friendly soul and as welcoming as the sunrise she seldom saw outside the building. Yet as Cheyenne approached her, the advisor didn't look like her usual self. No smile, no morning story, no laughter.

"Kaede wants to see you immediately."

Most people, including Missy, pronounced the VP's name as "Katie," but Cheyenne knew it was actually pronounced "Kah-eh-deh." Cheyenne waited to see if there was a punch line for the joke, but none came. As the glass door slid open, she waited, stunned that an executive wanted to meet with her at the start of the day. Especially Vice President Kaede Nakajima. The last time Cheyenne had spoken with Kaede was an awkward exchange in the restroom at a holiday dinner last year.

"Did she say why?" Cheyenne asked.

Missy shook her head, showing no emotion. Cheyenne gave her a polite smile, then proceeded to her space, evaluating the short interaction with Missy faster than one of her algorithms might.

It's obviously serious. Missy doesn't know anything, of course. Does she fear what's about to happen? Or is Missy concerned about what her superiors will think if she shows any sort of emotion?

It wasn't as though Cheyenne went out for drinks in the evening with Missy or regularly shared polite conversation with her. She didn't have much of a relationship with anybody at PASK other than Dina, her tech analyst. There had been Malek, of course, but he had been gone for six months, a very long and frustrating six months. After being fired from PASK, Malek had suddenly disappeared.

Just like Dad.

As with Malek, she knew that once Acatour made a decision like that, it was final and foolproof. The decision had come from the upper levels of management in Acatour and had been communicated to PASK, which made PASK look really, *really* bad. Whatever her dear, beloved Malek had done, it had been serious. But as far as her father was concerned, there was no reason for his disappearance, at least none she could discover.

Officially, Cheyenne had worked for the PASK division of Acatour for five years, but they had actually started training her when she was still a junior in high school. Many of the people working in this division had no clue what PASK stood for. Founded forty years ago, in 1998, by the legendary Jackson Heyford, the company originally carried the cumbersome name of Programming America's Systems & Keys, Inc. As it grew more successful, the name was changed to PASK, and with the introduction of SYNAPSYS and digital identities in 2025, PASK triumphed, and devices such as phones and computers suddenly became secondary in the market.

When she officially joined the company, moving to the Incen building and being given a desk on this floor, another brilliant young university graduate, Sef Malek, also joined the company. She was amazed how quickly he navigated data and how he could manipulate algorithms. It seemed as if his right hand was working on one project while his left hand was working on another, yet somehow his brain could do both. Even so, Malek claimed he had only half of the talent she did.

"You're the most gifted programmer here," Malek once told her, though she believed he was just saying that because he had a crush on her.

CEO Heyford never used such a crude word as *programmer*. He labeled the divisions of the company with amusing names a third-grade boy might have come up with, names such as Astronauts and Spies. Cheyenne and Malek worked in the Architects division, a title she loved to hear.

So far nothing about this morning had been normal, starting with the stranger handing her a note supposedly from her father, and now this.

They have to be related.

Nobody at PASK knew about her father's disappearance, at least not that she was aware of. That might have changed for some reason.

Arriving at her desk, Cheyenne set her coffee on the surface and then waved her hand over the right glass eye. Usually the system popped up immediately, showing four virtual-reality screens she had aligned with her SYNAPSYS. Some people preferred to use only a couple of screens, while others, like Malek, enjoyed working off a dozen interfaces. At least Malek used to enjoy this. She couldn't see any screens, so she tried a few more times but without success.

"Dina, is your system running?" Cheyenne asked.

"Yes. No glitches."

Cheyenne liked to call Dina her partner instead of assistant, but that's what Dina regularly did for her—assisted with any needs that the work spawned. There was usually enough work for half a dozen people, so Dina was always busy.

"My screens are not coming up. Do you know if there's a problem?"

"No. Let me check."

Dina was no-nonsense and socially awkward, but she was a machine when it came to her work. If such a thing as cyborgs existed, the first person Cheyenne would suspect to be one was forty-year-old Dina. Cheyenne didn't know anything about Dina's personal life or if she even had one. All she knew was that Dina sometimes acted before Cheyenne could even speak, and Dina was absolutely trustworthy.

"Your system is nowhere to be found," Dina said as she quickly walked over to Cheyenne's desk, wearing shoes that didn't match. "I was just finishing my cereal in the break room."

"I'm sorry to disturb your breakfast." Cheyenne kept swiping and holding her hand out over the sensor on her desk.

"It was my *break.* I had breakfast two hours ago."

Looking up at the analyst, Cheyenne noted how extra curly her frizzy hair looked. Dina fulfilled only the minimum requirements about daily appearance, just enough that the front offices wouldn't reprimand her about it again. She would have easily fit in with the casual work environment Cheyenne had read about from two and three decades ago when the tech world had exploded.

The petite woman scanned the glass eye, and instantly all six of her stations showed up in front of them. "Mine are there," Dina said. "Let me see if I can manually get yours to come up."

As Dina's hand moved and typed in the air, Cheyenne glanced around the office. Nobody could be seen at the desks nearby. "Where is everybody?"

"There was a large meeting in the conference room. I assumed you were in it."

"What was the meeting for?"

"I thought it was a cake-cutting or work-relations sort of thing. The very things I avoid like a virus."

"Nakajima wants to meet with me."

Dina stopped concentrating on the electronic screens in front of her and looked at Cheyenne. "Why?"

"I don't know. I was hoping you might have an idea."

This time it was Dina who glanced around the silent office.

"They wouldn't tell me if they were going to fire you," she whispered.

Most people wouldn't go directly there in their thought process, but Dina did. And considering what had happened to the equally talented Malek, they knew anything could happen to anybody.

"When is your meeting?" Dina asked.

"Now."

"They took you off the system. That's exactly what they did with Malek."

Another scan of the office didn't reveal anybody. She was looking for the big guys in the flak jackets. Seeing them in an office meant someone had a gun or a bomb or someone needed to be escorted out of the tower.

As Cheyenne went to pick up her coffee, the note she had slipped inside her tiny pants pocket fell on the ground. Dina scooped it up and looked at it.

"What's this?"

"It's a love letter from an admirer," Cheyenne said, which wasn't a lie.

Dina grinned and gave her back the note.

"Listen, I need to go to the meeting before she comes to find me," Cheyenne said. "Stay in touch the best way possible."

This was their way of saying to keep the communication open outside of the PASK lines, though Cheyenne never really knew when the company was watching and listening to her and when it wasn't. Her whole life was basically inside the walls of this building, a building Acatour owned, meaning they could be surveilling her twenty-four hours a day.

"If they force you to leave, what am I going to do?" Dina asked.

"You're going to help me."

"Help you do what?"

"Help me figure out what in the world's happening."

3.

Halfway down the hallway, past familiar walls with photos showing off PASK's global success through the years, Cheyenne heard an unfamiliar voice call her name. Her full name, one nobody here knew. She stopped and turned around, then glanced into the two offices next to her. Nothing.

"Cheyenne Myst Burne," the man said again.

Her father had told her that Myst stood for *mystery,* and that's what Cheyenne had been to them. Or at least to her father. This wonderful, beautiful mystery, according to him. A mystery her mother never pursued since she had left when Cheyenne was a little girl.

The voice spoke again, slowly and carefully, sounding smart and thoughtful.

"Do not overthink and analyze the situation you're about to encounter," he said. "Just act and don't react. Deal with the road in front of you and the door that's about to open."

He's talking through my SYNAPSYS. But that was impossible because she would have to authorize it, and she hadn't given any new authorizations in the last six months. Nobody—not the most notorious hackers out there, not the government, and not even Acatour—could break into an individual's SYNAPSYS. It was scientifically impossible.

"Who is this?" she asked.

"This is your wake-up call, Cheyenne. You've been sleeping your whole life, dreaming those dreams. The alarm clock is about to go off, and there won't be any way to press the Snooze button. So just keep walking. Keep breathing. And maybe start believing."

She continued looking around, but she couldn't see anybody.

"Who is this?" she asked again, then tried a few more times. But the voice remained silent.

She hadn't imagined the voice. It was real, just like not being able to log in to the system, and just like the somber look on Missy's face, and just like Hoon giving her a note from her father.

She knew she needed to read it. She needed to read it now.

4.

The all-watching eye couldn't follow her into the restroom. At least that's what Cheyenne believed. After making sure nobody was in the black-and-white bathroom that had been recently remodeled for no reason, she entered a stall and shut the door behind her.

Her hands shook as she unfolded the letter. The handwriting was unmistakable. Her father had an elegant and deliberate signature, and immediately she knew this note had indeed been penned by him. Before reading one word, she closed her eyes and exhaled to calm herself.

> *Dear Cheyenne,*
>
> *If you're reading this in your office, don't continue. You are in danger and must get out of the building as fast as you can. Save the rest of my comments for later.*

She didn't have to think twice. Cheyenne refolded the note and slipped it inside her pants pocket.

Twenty feet after she exited the restroom, Vice President Nakajima's assistant walked up beside her, looking down with a big grin.

"Right this way, Miss Burne."

With a shaved head and a square rock for a face, the man looked more like a bodyguard, which everybody understood to be the fact. Nakajima was fiercely private and handled most of her affairs herself, including setting up phone calls and meetings and sending messages. The assistant was there in case someone who didn't like the VP decided to do something about it. Quite a few people fit in that category.

"I really need to get back to my office before—"

The man's hand didn't merely latch on to her arm. It locked on like a robot's appendage. He guided her down the hall and didn't let go. When they reached the office, Cheyenne watched the glass door open in front of her, and she thought of the words Malek had repeated over and over to her: *"Don't ever trust her. Not a bit."*

Seconds after she took a handful of steps into the ordinary and average-sized office, bare enough to resemble one belonging to a newly hired manager, the door slid shut behind her, and the glass turned to frost. Nobody could see them now. The vice president stood behind her desk, and several screens were lit up on the black countertop.

"Sit down." Her voice carried a slight accent.

So much for any pleasantries or early-morning small talk.

The chair was less comfortable than the ones in the conference room. Cheyenne had a theory about this office and had confided in Malek about it. She concluded that the vice president had several offices in multiple areas in the building and that they were all a simple means to an end: to project power and authority and to never display any sort of emotion or life outside the company. Nobody knew if Kaede Nakajima was married or had children or anything else remotely personal about her. No official information was online anywhere, and the speculation included everything from her being a Japanese spy to her being a proxy for someone else running their division.

"I was awakened this morning by a surprising call," Nakajima said as she still stood at her desk. "Our CEO called me personally, something that never happens. Mr. Heyford had some rather unfortunate news to share with me."

Nakajima tapped on several of the screens and moved them to show Cheyenne.

"All the national news outlets have it. Progress, Divisional, Foxnet. Mr. Heyford doesn't know what their sources were, but they're validated by the information and the pictures. They're damaging, to say the least."

The words and images in the news feeds seemed to attack Cheyenne at once. The image of her father shocked her. The photos of him were recent. She had never seen him with his gray hair so long or his beard so unkempt. In one shot he carried a backpack, as a drifter might, and was looking over his shoulder as if monitoring who might be following him. Another showed him at a seedy motel. Then another set of pictures showed items that supposedly belonged to Keith Burne, including an assortment of automatic rifles, bomb-making materials, and confiscated letters written by him. According to the news these letters contained "hateful and racist" content.

In the middle of all the materials, one item stood out: her father's worn leather Bible.

"Hate Crimes Linked to Missing Businessman," one headline read. "Former Fortune 500 Exec Turns Rogue," another declared. The last one she read contained all the information she needed: "Suspect Identified in High-Level Hate Crimes; Missing and at Large. Reward Posted."

Under one of the recent pictures, her father's name was spelled out clearly.

"By the look on your face, I gather you didn't catch up on the morning news feeds. It's a lot to read, of course, but I'll show you the reason Mr. Heyford called me." Nakajima tapped and expanded a paragraph in one of the articles. The words grew as big as the VP's hands.

> Keith Burne's only daughter is Cheyenne Burne, a technology expert at the venerable Acatour corporation, who both works and lives in the Incen Tower.

For a moment Cheyenne forgot to breathe, her mind moving faster than the elevators ascending and descending this building.

"Every article mentions you in some way," Nakajima said. "I was amused at the variety of descriptions they had for your title, especially since we don't like to officially give titles to our employees. 'Technology expert.' If they only understood what PASK's most talented architect knew."

The last comment was both a question and a threat to Cheyenne, and she didn't like being cornered and questioned and accused.

"You're wrong," Cheyenne told Nakajima.

"Excuse me?"

"I said you're wrong. Sef Malek is PASK's most talented architect."

"He *was* talented, but he never could approach your abilities. Malek had this wonderfully quirky charisma, one that caught your attention, did it not? But he also had a knack for snooping around in business that wasn't his."

"Why did you fire him?"

The smooth and porcelainlike face didn't move, but Nakajima's lips began to twist in a way that reminded Cheyenne of a worm on a fishhook. "Have you had any contact with your father in the last week?"

Cheyenne wondered if the guy downstairs really was a friend of her father's.

The note is real. It's more real than that image of the Bible, which could have been easily fabricated and manipulated.

"I haven't seen or heard from my father in more than a year."

"What happened to him?" Nakajima asked.

"You know as much as I do. He went missing."

"After quitting his job, correct? After supposedly having some kind of divine experience and suddenly professing vitriol hidden in the sweet perfume of Jesus Christ. Does that sound familiar?"

"I don't know exactly why my father quit his job," Cheyenne said.

This was the first lie, but it wasn't a full-fledged, bold-faced one. Her father had told her about finding God and having a new outlook on life, but his words hadn't made any sense to her. It had been as if he'd gone to Tibet and climbed Mount Everest and then had tried to talk to her about it while speaking in Tibetan.

"A man like your father, as deluded as he most certainly happens to be, would contact his one and only beloved daughter." Nakajima leaned over the desk and glared at her. "I bet he's spoken with you recently. We're already checking records."

"I'm sure you did that before I even woke up, and I know you didn't find anything because there's nothing to find."

"Obviously you can see the problem this has created."

Cheyenne stood up. She was taller than the vice president, so she liked this position better. "I have had no contact with my father in a year, so I have no idea if any of these things they're saying are true. But my father doesn't know how to make bombs. He doesn't own automatic rifles. How could he even find one? They've been outlawed for years."

"So are drugs, yet even something as dangerous as I-Murse can easily be obtained."

"*My father* and *hate* do not belong in the same sentence," Cheyenne said.

"Sit down." Nakajima swiped off the screens.

"I can already see where this is heading. Malek certainly disappeared for doing far less."

"Do you know what your 'buddy' did?"

Cheyenne stayed quiet for the moment, despite the anger and adrenaline racing through her.

"The problem is that you have participated in many more campaigns and have been presented with much more sensitive material than Malek would ever dream of having contact with. You, the lovable Cheyenne Burne, were our golden child who could do no wrong."

You're jealous and have always been jealous, and it still looks ugly after all this time.

"Your work in the last year—"

"Is confidential," Cheyenne interrupted. "I've always known that, and I still do."

"Then surely you can see our current impasse."

"I haven't done anything wrong." Cheyenne turned around and headed to the glass door. It remained shut.

Nakajima circled her desk like a wild animal moving toward its prey. "You can't simply *walk* out of this office. Or merely gather your belongings and be on your merry way. This is not *The Wizard of Oz.*"

Cheyenne turned. "Open this door now. I know my rights. I can blink and send a message to the authorities on our floor. If you want a national public relations nightmare on your hands, just try to keep me in this office."

A glimmer of hesitation could be spotted in Nakajima's eyes. A very rare sight indeed. But she quickly hid it by displaying her smug grin again. "Those authorities you talk about receive their salaries from the same people who pay yours."

"That's fine, but my friends at Divisional News would love to hear about my firing. Since I'm a hot commodity in national headlines, the so-called groundbreaking tech person in the company, people will kill to interview me." She deliberately stressed the word *kill.*

Again Nakajima seemed to be weighing her options.

"Open the door," Cheyenne said.

"What do you think is out there anyway?" the vice president asked as the glass door slid open.

My father. And I'm going to find him.

5.

The glow of the orange numbers on the wall showed the slow passage of time. Even though a voice out of nowhere had told her to wake up and to keep moving, Cheyenne wasn't moving at all. She remained stuck on the hard leather couch she seldom sat on, one of the expensive and stylized pieces she had purchased after starting work at PASK and earning a salary she couldn't have ever imagined making in her life. Just like the figures that increased in her account every week, the fancy furniture couldn't fill the void inside, nor could it provide the comfort she had felt as a child living with her father.

Now her job and income were suddenly . . . gone. Just like the voice she'd heard in her head earlier this day.

Who was talking to me, and how'd they get inside to do that?

That was the number one question she had after the hundreds of questions she had about her father, such as where was he, and what was he doing, and what sort of danger could he be in, and would she ever see him again? They had unfinished business, to say the least. As her mind kept returning to their last encounter, she stopped herself, ending the movie before it began, turning off the images and sounds and forcing herself not to go there, not now. Not after everything that had happened today.

Outside her apartment door stood two uniformed security men, making sure she didn't leave and nobody came in. After forcing her way out of Nakajima's office through threats, Cheyenne had been greeted with another set of men wearing uniforms and carrying sidearms, ones who were so courteous as to usher her out of her own office. At least she was able to see Dina one more time and tell her she would find a way to be in touch, knowing her assistant understood it would be in a way that nobody could hear or read or intercept. As the men told her to gather her personal belongings and leave the building, once again Cheyenne had forced the issue.

"I don't know who you report to, but you can tell them I'm not leaving *right now*. I can't vacate my place in five minutes."

When the two men, brawny and acting the part of bullies, tried to intimidate and frighten her, Cheyenne didn't back down. That only made her more defiant.

"Neither of you has any security clearance whatsoever, so get out of my way, and tell those above you that I will leave first thing in the morning. Or else you will have every single person who hates this company at your doorstep demanding an explanation. Do you understand?"

If the two men Cheyenne left outside the PASK offices had had tails, they would have been tucked between their legs. They knew enough to realize they had to leave her alone. Cheyenne wasn't the enemy, at least not yet, and she was using one of the two assets she had for the moment: her ability either to speak out or remain silent. PASK and all those higher-ups wanted her silence.

I'm also holding something far more valuable: information.

The world would be very interested in and even outraged at the experiments she had been conducting the last year. She could share a lot with others.

This could lead to potential dangers down the road. Actually, it could be the moment she walked out of this building. At least here she was still protected by the number of people around her and all the security and watching eyes. Outside in the real world of sorts—the kind with a sun that moved up and down instead of endless elevators every day—she wouldn't be as safe. She would be on her own in every way, and like a wounded pup that's fallen away from the pack, she would be vulnerable.

"There are people in control," Malek once told her. "Not the government but higher-ups. A small group that controls everything. And Jackson Heyford's one of them."

Malek had never been one for conspiracy theories, but in the last few months of working for PASK, he had started saying things like that. And he had told her that he had the information to back up the claims. But before he could show her, Malek was gone.

"Do not overthink and analyze the situation you're about to encounter," the voice had said to her. *"Deal with the road in front of you and the door that's about to open."*

She kept telling herself that was what she needed to do.

So get up and start. Move and begin to make plans to leave.

Before doing anything, however, Cheyenne had to finish reading her father's note. But as if she were frozen in her seat, which came from fear and shock, she didn't want to open the letter again. Yet she had to. Especially in the confines of her home, a place the government forbade any human monitoring.

They've broken a lot of laws, so I wouldn't be surprised if they were breaking this one too.

Cheyenne finally went over to her backpack, which was full of her important things, dug into it, and took out the note.

Okay. Here we go.

6.

Under the small curved reading light by her bed, Cheyenne cupped the piece of paper close to her eyes so that if there was a watching device somewhere, the people monitoring it wouldn't be able to read what it said.

> *Dear Cheyenne,*
>
> *If you're reading this in your office, don't continue. You are in danger and must get out of the building as fast as you can. Save the rest of my comments for later.*
>
> *I know it's been a long time since you've heard from me, and I'm sorry about that. I'm also sorry that this is the way you're finally hearing from me again. So much has happened, Cheyenne, things that I want to, that I truly hope to be able to tell you, even if it has to be in heaven. And don't roll your eyes when I say that. I mean it with all my heart.*
>
> *A year ago when we last spoke, a conversation I deeply regret having gone wrong, I had the same spirit the apostle Peter had in John 13:37. He was eager to serve Jesus and said he would even die for Him, but Peter was so impatient and didn't understand the bigger picture. He would later, of course, but God had to take him through some difficult times before Peter fully comprehended what it meant to be a disciple. I think I understand; at least I know more now than I did when we last spoke.*
>
> *I'm here to help you—to warn you and also to connect you with someone. But I realize this note might be read or stolen or might not*

ever reach you. So I have to speak in code. We shared our own language when you were a little girl, so this will be easy for you.

There was something that I began to admire and even love later in my life. Something you said that you could never quite understand and something that I even attempted to help you appreciate. Think of this single word.

There is a man with this nickname. He is near the place you always wanted to settle down in. A local will know of him. He loves microbreweries and stout beer. Look for him so he can find you. When he trusts that you are who you say you are, he'll tell you everything he knows.

There are more words to come. But not now. Not like this.

My song of the day is "Blackbird" by the Beatles. Please listen.

Please know I love you.

I vow to tell you these three words again in person one day.

Daddy

She folded the note and stood up beside her made bed. Perhaps other women would have to wipe tears from their cheeks but not Cheyenne. She was still trying to process everything instead of becoming all emotional. She was analyzing the mystery he had presented her. And perhaps burying the other stuff he had written to her.

Moving to the blacked-out windows of her apartment, Cheyenne called out to open the blinds. Of course, there weren't actual blinds, nor was there any sort of glass or a window that could open. Not on the 194th floor of the Incen Tower. The glass was actually a powerfully clear material made in Germany, something that had a technical name but was basically superglass. It couldn't be broken and was also pliable enough to work within the grand structure of this skyscraper. As the tinted windows became clear, she could see the dark night outside.

Cheyenne moved to the edge of the glass and looked down. Chicago looked like golden snowflakes so far below her. It felt as if the city was as far away as her father.

"Indy, play 'Blackbird,'" she said, talking to her LC.

The term "Life Companion" always amused her, since a companion was someone you snuggled with on the couch or spooned in bed or cooked eggs with after waking up. Her father told her that people used to call it "Siri," based on the popular intelligent personal assistant Apple had created. But now those so-called Siris were everywhere, so they needed to be categorized. A Life Companion was the artificial intelligence inside an individual's SYNAPSYS, and perhaps nobody in the world knew more about the intricacies involved with this than Cheyenne herself.

The nickname Indy was short for Indiana Jones, one of her childhood heroes because the movie character had been her father's hero too. So much of her life came back to this monumental figure, one she sometimes wanted and other times needed to chip away at and even break away from. It was dangerous to have heroes. At least real live ones.

As the song began to play throughout her apartment, Cheyenne looked at the walls, listening with her full attention to the song. It was the Beatles; this much she knew. But she couldn't remember hearing it before. The tune was simple and intimate, sung as though the singer were sitting across from her. Just an acoustic guitar and a tapping, as if something were wrong with the audio.

That's a foot tapping. Just like Dad used to do.

She thought of the way he had signed the note. Cheyenne hadn't called him Daddy in a long time, but deep in her heart, that's what he would always be. Hearing from her father made him become Daddy again, at least in this private moment where nobody else could hear, where darkness waited outside her apartment and the rest of the world lived so far below.

"Blackbird fly into the light of the dark black night."

Her father hadn't written only to connect with her. He had given her specific instructions. Tomorrow she would follow his advice.

Tomorrow she would figure out how to fly.

TWO

We Are Accidents Waiting to Happen

1.

"You have to give me your gun."

Dowland laughed at the idea. The guy looking down at him by the doorway leading to the pool surely had to be a former World League wrestler who now provided security in his work hours and ate lots of fried foods in his free time. Being big and bulky only meant the security guy wouldn't be able to chase Dowland if he had to and wouldn't be able to hop back up after getting kicked in the gut.

"You'll have to take it off me," Dowland said.

"Let him in, Manny," a voice commanded from a speaker somewhere on the security guard.

So Manny did, moving aside and opening the wrought-iron door. The Miami sun was hot and bright, and Dowland hadn't stopped sweating since stepping off the private plane. As he walked toward a sprawling pool in the shape of a flower, he squinted even though he was wearing sunglasses. His head hadn't stopped throbbing since his phone had yanked him out of bed at a quarter of three this morning. Dowland was old school when it came to his technology, choosing to carry an actual phone he could initiate or receive calls on. Anything more was too much. Anything more meant he might be easy to find. Especially if his SYNAPSYS was turned on.

The ones calling could reach him, and that was the point. They could tell him a car would pick him up and take him to a chartered plane. That's all they told him and all he knew. Dowland knew enough, however, to recognize this sort of meeting was unusual. He was skipping the gatekeepers this time.

Dowland had no idea why and wouldn't ask. But he kept his compact SIG Sauer pistol nestled in his waistband. Just in case something went wrong.

A hundred tanned, beautiful people could have been mingling poolside, and there still would have been plenty of room to walk around, but Dowland could see only one figure in white sitting underneath an umbrella. No guards were in sight. No ladies lounging on any of the dozen chairs in the sun. No children frolicking in the clear water of the pool. Dowland walked over to the umbrella and discovered a man probably in his seventies wearing what appeared to be linen pajamas. A glass of ice water rested in front of him.

"Forgive me for not standing," the man told Dowland as he offered to shake hands. "Please, sit."

As Dowland sat on a lounge chair, his button-down shirt clung to his back like a sopping towel. The man across from him had about as much hair on his eyebrows and earlobes as he had on his head. The deep wrinkles on his face were prominent in the clear light of midday. He resembled a fair-colored prune.

"My name is Mel Bohmer," he said. "Can I get you anything to drink?"

Dowland didn't need to know Mel's name, but he could think of about a hundred things this little fella could get him to drink.

"Water would be fine," he said, glancing out to the violent ocean waves battering the breakwater on the beach.

Bohmer gave him a gentle nod and a knowing smile but didn't move or react to the request.

"See all that sand?" Bohmer pointed toward the oceanfront. "All of it—every single rock and mineral—came from me. I would tell you how much I paid for it, but that's not only showing off. It's belittling. And as a younger man, I used to hate when people did that to me."

"Why am I here?" Dowland asked.

"To talk. In person."

"I guess I should rephrase it. Why am I here with you?"

Mel smiled. "You're a man of action. Savage, if you ask me. The others respect it. But the situation has grown—*mutated* perhaps is the better word—into something precarious. I wanted you to hear the gravity of the matter, not from someone delivering the message but from the one describing it."

Dowland didn't say anything. There wasn't anything to say. He heard footsteps approaching behind him and turned to see a stunning dark-skinned woman carrying a glass of water.

"Can I get you anything else?" she asked Dowland in an accent that sounded British.

"No, thanks."

Once again the old guy grinned.

"What's that about?" Dowland asked.

"Two chances, my young man. Two offers. Still you simply pass."

"Not quite following you."

Bohmer nodded and then crossed his spotted, gaunt hands and placed them in his lap. He watched as Dowland wiped his forehead.

"Do you like warm weather?"

Dowland drank half of his water in a gulp. "I prefer being told why I'm here in Miami sweating like a pig."

"No nonsense. All business. Ah, I love it. I miss men like you. I'm surrounded by eternal party people. So politically correct. Sculpted and in shape and bored with life. Bored. Can you believe that? In a place like this?"

Dowland didn't say anything, perhaps to stress the point of being bored himself.

"I pretend, Mr. Dowland. I feign being old and bored. This isn't my primary home, so I am honestly a bit at a loss in this place. We are both outsiders sitting on the edge of the country near the expanse of the Atlantic Ocean. And both of us just want to get home. Is that right?"

"I haven't been home in some time," Dowland said.

"Your home—your *true* home—where is that again?"

"Park City."

"Ah yes. I own a vacation house up there. Remarkable place. Wish my legs allowed me to ski."

"Wish my job allowed me to ski," Dowland said.

"Good topic," Bohmer said. "Your job is exactly why I'm speaking to you today."

"Where is Hall?"

"This conversation is above your boss's pay grade."

Dowland laughed. "Either I just got a very nice promotion, or I was giving Hall way too much respect."

"How about both, Mr. Dowland?"

With a grin on his cracked and chapped lips, Bohmer tapped the table to turn on the display. An assortment of images was scattered on the screen next to them. The man cleared his throat.

"Did you know I used to be a movie producer? Years ago. Back when there was still some money to be made in Hollywood. Back when we made movies on actual film."

"Is that how you earned your money?" Dowland asked.

Bohmer cursed. "That's the only time in my life I *lost* money. And I wasn't happy, believe me. You know the tired movie cliché of giving a character 'one last job'? You know the kind. In movies like *Unforgiven* and *Heat* and even *The Wild Bunch*. One last job. That's all. Then the hero will retire. Just one more job."

Dowland glanced at the pool and felt tempted to jump in.

"So, Mr. Dowland. How would you like to be in one of those movies?"

"I don't act," he said without the slightest smile.

Bohmer laughed. "Ah, but you act every day. Right now, for instance, you're surely doing your best to conceal your disgust with this place and my pool and my life. Perhaps my air of indifference. Of course you don't act for a living. But what if I made this particular job that I want to talk about your last?"

Dowland studied one of the images on the table. The man in the photo could barely be distinguished. Same went for four other pictures he looked at. The figure in each photo looked like a different man.

"What if I told you I liked my job?" Dowland asked.

"Is that why your drinking has become increasingly problematic? Especially after a job is finished?"

Dowland didn't react to the comment. "I'd ask if you're spying on me, but I know the answer to that."

"And I know the answer to whether you like your work or not. Being the best at something doesn't necessarily mean you love it. Or even like it."

"For the right price I'd quit."

For a moment the elderly man studied him. Not sizing him up but rather seeming to observe him with both curiosity and respect.

"I know you didn't enter the Federal Bureau of Investigation in order to murder men and women," Bohmer said.

"I've never killed a woman," Dowland quickly replied.

"It's interesting that you didn't contest calling it murder."

"What final job are you proposing?"

Bohmer touched the virtual monitor lit up on their table and tried to move one of the images. For a second the screen turned off, then turned on again, but he couldn't get the photo to budge an inch. Bohmer cursed again. "I used to hate working on my laptops. Then they invented a microscopic strip to fit in your brain. Now all you have to do is speak or motion in a certain way and, voilà, you have virtual reality right in front of you. I had a hard enough time with so-called smartphones. Now screens have become air."

Dowland moved over and, using his index finger, dragged the photo of the man with ease.

"Yeah, okay, it's not rocket science, I know," Bohmer said. "This man. The one we're all looking for. You recognize the images, right?"

One photo simply showed a tall man with the physique and haircut of someone in the military, but it seemed to be a low-resolution picture. Dowland had studied this blurry picture just like all the rest of the photos.

"Of course," he told Bohmer.

"Yes, yes. Of course you know who you've been chasing for the past year. Supposedly it's the same man in each picture. In one shot he looks like a marine. In another he appears to be the nutty professor. What we're beginning to suspect after our men scoured all the material you acquired on your last job—your little outing in the middle of Indiana—is that there's not only one person calling himself the Reckoner, but there are multiple ones. Including the man you found in the motel room."

"He was not the Reckoner."

"He was part of a group that's been using aliases and code names," Bohmer said. "We discovered another name amid the data we retrieved. A man named Keith Burne. Businessman gone insane."

The name was new to Dowland. "You guys think he could be the one?"

"He is part of a group. And as you know, they're distributing propaganda and lies and misinformation and the usual. Circumventing security online. Managing to use old data and methods of communicating. They've discovered some ways that haven't been figured out even by the so-called experts."

"Example?"

"The biggest and most serious is the rumor they can infiltrate a stranger's SYNAPSYS."

Dowland shook his head. "That's impossible. I've seen several presentations by the experts that are irrefutable. There's no method of breaking into someone's SYNAPSYS. It's like being able to read someone else's mind."

The old man leaned toward him, his eyebrows moving up like two exclamation points.

"Exactly. And that's why this information is so startling. So interesting. It seems this group is planning to use that technology to their advantage."

"Planning what?"

Bohmer's face became grim as his dark eyes cut into Dowland.

"They seem to have a surprising amount of information in their possession. More than we could have ever imagined."

Dowland didn't have to ask what this information might be. He was probably talking to Bohmer in person because the man feared others might discover his identity. His and a small group of others.

"So this isn't a new job you're giving me, correct?" Dowland asked.

"No. But as I said before, this one will be your last. Whether or not you complete it."

Dowland cursed. "I'm completing it. After all this time I'm finding the fool who calls himself the Reckoner."

"This man here," Bohmer said, pointing a skeletal finger at the image on the table. "He could be anybody. He could be working for me as far as I know. What I do know is you are not this man, because of what you just did, because of those you've already killed to get this info. And because of when and where this photo was taken."

"Please tell me Hawaii," Dowland said. "You're putting me on a plane and bidding me a big fat *Mele Kalikimaka*. Right?"

"This was taken in Chicago."

Dowland winced and then had to laugh. "Have you ever been to Chicago in February?"

Bohmer swatted his palm over the image of the man.

"For finding and killing this man, you will be able to buy your own island in the Pacific. But, Jon, even though you have done good work, if any information manages to slip out into the open—*anything*—you are among those who will be the first to go. You know that, right?"

Dowland nodded.

I've known my place for a long time.

Bohmer rubbed his hands together and took a deep breath, staring out at the ocean in the distance. The smell of salt and sand seemed to drift around them.

"I know you don't have a pretty wife and four children, but there are others in your life. The others I deal with have the same sort of savagery you possess. So if this is not dealt with immediately, you will be. And it will be fast, and it will be monstrous. And as always, I will be the one to order it to happen."

Nothing about any of this surprised Dowland. He had an idea what to expect once he heard he would be having this meeting.

"I'll do my job before you have to do yours," Dowland said. "And as I said, I still think there's only one ringleader out there. And he's not going to be out there for long."

"Killing him isn't the hard part. It's finding him in the first place. It's like trying to hunt down a ghost."

"I have some experience at that sort of thing," Dowland said.

"I know. That's why you're the man for this job. You have to send a demon to catch a ghost. Now let me ask you again. Can I get you something real to drink? Something that will quench the thirst that's written all over you?"

Dowland couldn't help liking this old man's style.

The drink finally came, and as Dowland listened to the old guy ramble on about the "good old days," he thought about the Reckoner again. Whoever this guy was, he was truly deluded. If he could fathom what was approaching, the man would go into hiding and never come out again.

He's too stupid to realize the hurricane that's about to decimate his entire world.

2.

The stench surrounded the mountains of waste lining the buildings he passed. This was the part of Miami the city had abandoned, the section that housed the sort of men and women who were capable of anything. As Dowland studied the piles of debris he walked by, seeing food containers and socks and shampoo bottles and rotting fruit and the smear of leftover everything, he was reminded why the garbage business was so lucrative. The world was one giant waste heap, and nobody wanted to get up and do something about it.

Technology can't take out the trash.

The liquor store on the corner of the brick building had a broken sign above it and pale light inside revealing several patrons shopping. Dowland turned and headed down the alley as instructed, the dark enveloping him. The smell intensified, and the garbage wasn't as neatly piled in this dead-end strip between old buildings. As he reached the back wall, a flashlight made him stop and squint.

"Turn that off, Sergei."

"Dowland, is that you behind the scruff?"

He cursed and told his Russian friend to stop blinding him. The short, round figure came out of the night and gave him a huge bear hug.

"It's been so long, my friend," Sergei said, clapping two big hands on Dowland's shoulders. "So long that I didn't believe it was you."

"I've been busy."

"The world is busy. Unless you live in East Town and life slows to a halt."

"Why don't you leave this squalor?"

"Can't leave family," Sergei said. "Even the ones I'm restricted from seeing. Plus, Miami Beach is still as beautiful as the people walking on it."

"Miami Beach is a setting in the history books. A place that got washed away and submerged. That beach out there isn't Miami Beach. It's a beachfront along the eroding shores of a half-baked city that's quickly deteriorating as well."

Sergei laughed. "I see your outlook on life is just as cheery as it used to be."

"Did you pick the most foul-smelling place in the city to meet?" Dowland asked, rubbing his nose and shaking his head. He was getting light headed from the putrid air enclosing him.

"Pretty much," Sergei said. "Why did you reach out? It can't be to say hi. I've left more than a dozen messages the last few years. And yeah, yeah, I get it. You've been busy. So you must be looking for someone, and all your fancy contacts aren't looking so fancy after all."

"I happened to be close to Miami."

"Ah, so it was location. Convenience, correct?"

The sound of a siren blasted overhead as a police drone passed by, the bright spotlight momentarily lighting up a portion of the alley.

"Can we go somewhere—*anywhere*—to get out of this death trap?" Dowland asked.

"Are you still sober?" Sergei asked.

Dowland chuckled. "Are you still married?"

"Ah, well, there's a bar a couple of streets over," the stout Russian with no accent said.

"So how long has it been since I saw you last?"

"Five years, I believe," Sergei said as they walked out of the shadows. "I assume that you are no longer with Kamaria."

Sergei remembered.

"Yes, you assume correctly. Kam made me choose. Either her or living life my own way. She said it was the drinking, but for her it was control. In the big picture it was the right choice."

"At least you got to choose," Sergei said. "My ex-wife wasn't as cordial."

As they reached the street, a trio of police drones zipped past above them.

"I seem to recall you breaking one of your wife's ribs," Dowland said.

"I've dealt with my anger issues," he replied.

"We all have our vices. Some are just a little more noticeable and get us into trouble."

"No trouble tonight, my friend," Sergei said.

"Of course not."

3.

Maybe it was one of those tired stereotypes—a Russian and his vodka—but Sergei certainly lived up to it. The vodka was cheap stuff that his friend guzzled the way Dowland might drain a beer. The bar was packed even though it didn't seem to have a name outside. The haze of cigarette smoke and pot filled the pub, and blaring rock played as the two men sat at a table in the back, trying to keep their shouted conversation private.

"Marijuana is legal but cigarettes aren't," Dowland said as he glanced at the shadow of Sergei sitting in the smog. "Meanwhile, in East Town Miami, nobody can tell the difference between the two."

"Forget a little lung cancer," Sergei said. "Pique has decimated this place. The authorities have completely given up."

"You ever tried it?"

"Of course. Dangerous how *good* it makes you feel. Remember the days when people would use dirty syringes to pump heroin into their bloodstream? Forget the fear of heroin and using a needle. Then the opioid epidemic started when popping pills became all too easy. But Pique? It's easier to use than transferring funds from bank accounts."

"True," Dowland said. "The hard part is finding the code that keeps Pique alive in your system."

"We work harder to invent ways to kill ourselves than to improve our lives."

"That keeps me employed."

Sergei laughed. "You and me both. Cheers, old friend."

Dowland updated Sergei on everything he needed to know, telling him only the basics. An unnamed and unrecognizable man running a group. The photos, online correspondence, and any other known information was on a file Dowland had already sent to Sergei's SYNAPSYS. Dowland needed his friend to help determine whether the Reckoner was indeed one person or several.

"You have a strange way of knowing where people are even when they don't want to be found," Dowland said. "I know from firsthand experience."

What he liked about Sergei was that he never asked why. He didn't want Dowland to tell him details, like who wanted to know and why they were interested. It honestly didn't matter to Sergei. All that mattered was that he'd be paid for the job, and he needed income to provide for his family. Plus, Sergei was the best digital bounty hunter Dowland had ever known.

"What's the price for finding him? Or them?"

"Five times the amount I last paid you," Dowland said.

Sergei's whole demeanor changed, and he downed the remaining shot of vodka on the table as quickly as his smile flashed. He immediately flagged down the server and ordered another round for them.

"I will get you information, no question," Sergei said.

It was smart having people like him who weren't working for the government and weren't in the network. Guys who had been forgotten about, who weren't influential but who also weren't dangerous enough. Dowland knew those were the sort of people who could get things done. They had no choice to do anything but that. Men like Sergei had nobody to lean or rely on.

4.

By the time they had gone through several more rounds, with his Russian friend drinking several shots at a time, the crowd seemed thicker than the smoke, and the music sounded louder. Sergei's eyes were wide and glassy as he bragged about romantic adventures he had pursued in the last few years, but he simultaneously choked up about losing his wife and barely keeping relationships with his kids. Dowland felt loose and relaxed after half a dozen pints, but he wasn't flying as high as the vodka man.

They were having such a good time that they barely noticed when the seven-foot-tall man in a muscle shirt stepped next to their table. Shouts and laughter and shoulder-to-shoulder patrons filling this place at two in the morning made it easy to ignore some giant suddenly staring down at them. Led Zeppelin's second album played in full, and while most of the people in the bar probably had no clue who the band was, Dowland had to give the owner or bartender some props for setting the perfect backdrop for tonight's mood.

"Who is your friend, Sergei?" the stranger shouted.

Dowland snapped out of friendly mode and surveyed the man, knowing he meant business. He didn't let go of his lazy, having-a-good-time-blowing-off-steam composure, but he began to prepare for something.

"We're busy," Sergei told the man.

The shiny scalp glowed on the skinhead who peered at them, and the man didn't bother to hide that his eyes were lit with Pique.

"Have I seen you before?" he asked Dowland.

"Sorry. I don't think so."

"No, I think I've seen you. You're not from around here."

Dowland looked at his glass, then drained the rest of his beer before glancing back up at the freak of nature. "I'm having a drink with a friend, so you'll have to excuse us."

The stranger wouldn't budge. By the looks of his arms and shoulders busting out of the tank top, half of this man's life was probably spent in a gym.

"What sort of business does a guy like you have with my old buddy Sergei?"

I've been polite, and I've given him a chance.

Dowland knew several things about the men who employed him. Not the guys who had job titles, not bureaucratic officials or FBI agents, but the real men, the guys behind everybody else. The puppet masters like Bohmer. They wanted Dowland to get his job done, whether it was finding people or killing them. They also wanted him to take care of any trash and debris he might find on the side of the road he was on.

This guy was a very big, bulky piece of garbage.

For a second Dowland looked at Sergei and saw that his friend's eyes were on fire. He was drunk and inviting a whole lot of trouble. Dowland grinned, waiting for the second Sergei spotted his smile. Then Dowland propelled off his barstool with the pint glass in hand and bashed it across the skinhead's face, cracking the glass as the stranger's head barely moved.

With a shard of glass sticking out of his cheek, the man simply smiled down at Dowland, showing the power of Pique. "Oh man, you're gonna pay for that," he said.

Before he could do anything else, Sergei tackled the big guy, sending both of them into the crowd. They landed on several young women just as Dowland looked around to see if the skinhead had any friends.

Here they come.

There were three others, and all of them obviously worked out with their friend. For a second he thought of ending this right here with his Beretta, but then he shoved that thought aside. The beer was talking. So were the memories of former fun days with his friend. And of course, the music helped.

It's been a while since I was in a bar fight.

He laughed as "Ramble On" blasted in the background. Dowland didn't wait for the guys to come to him, but instead, he began to rush them like an old-school running back trying to burst through a defensive line.

For the next ten minutes, nothing but chaos ensued.

5.

"Here—you need this."

Sergei handed Dowland a big chunk of frozen steak wrapped in plastic. They were sitting on the steps outside Sergei's run-down apartment building.

"You keep this handy for bar fights?" Dowland asked, laughing as he took it and put it against his swollen and cut lip.

"I think I recall—and I may be wrong—but aren't you the one who slammed your glass in Fritz's face?"

"You know his name?"

"Oh yeah," Sergei said, holding a bloody rag against the gash on his temple. "He's one of the big smelly fish in this little rotten pond. Sells Pique and is an addict as well. I see him sometimes early in the morning on the street. I'll bet most of those guys won't even remember the fight come morning."

"If they do, let me know. You don't need people messing around with you or your kids."

"They won't. They need me. Occasionally I have to track down people who don't pay their bills. And don't judge me either. You have to work hard at earning a decent wage these days."

"No judgments here."

Dowland winced as he stretched out his mouth. They had managed to fend off and fight the four men, but half the bar had somehow gotten into the mix, creating a free-for-all that finally prompted him to grab his gun and fire into the ceiling, which sent everybody running to the doors. Right before everybody split, however, a lone woman had slugged him in the mouth. Perhaps for no reason other than he had disturbed her fun night out.

"You probably don't hang out much in seedy areas of the world like this, huh?" Sergei asked him.

Dowland chuckled. "I've been in the seediest. Wealth doesn't make something reputable. It only cleans it up and makes it pretty."

"I'm still surprised to see you here. Now. After all this time."

"The older I get, the more I realize that trust is very difficult to find. Probably harder than even love, and that's virtually a miracle. And I know I can trust you."

"So why do you do this?" Sergei asked as they both looked out to the abandoned and burned-down building across the street.

"Do what? Get in barroom brawls?"

"Your job," Sergei answered. "You've been doing this a long time."

"Why do you do your job?"

"I've already told you. Money. And I need that for the family. That's why I do the work I do and live where I live. But you. Do you have some kiddos on the side I don't know about?"

"Nope. Unless I don't know about them either."

"You're a shrewd man. I know you have savings. Why not retire?"

"Retire? Do I look like I'm seventy years old?"

"You look worn out."

"A bit beaten up, sure," Dowland said.

"You look like your soul's weary," Sergei said as he stared at him.

"Yeah, well, maybe it is. Maybe you get so lost in the work that you have no idea *what* you look like, right?"

"Do you ever hear from her? At all?"

Dowland paused for a moment. "Who?"

"You know who. Come on."

The beer Sergei had also brought out tasted like cold, flat syrup. He took a sip from the can simply because his mouth was so dry.

"I see her all the time," Dowland said.

"Yeah, me too. But I'm not talking about bikini ads. Have you had any contact with her?"

He shook his head, then told Sergei no. There was no reason to tell him about the last two encounters with Kamaria. Sure, he had seen her, and those two times had been bittersweet.

Mostly bitter.

"You two made a good couple," Sergei said.

"Thanks. Good to know years later."

"Shut up. You know you did. I thought she might get you out of your profession."

"To do what? Work for a corporation, wearing a suit and tapping at invisible keys all day long? Shuffling meaningless files from one place to another?" Dowland cursed.

"Normal work hours. A salary with benefits. Vacation days. Sounds like a normal, healthy way to live."

Dowland finished the beer and then chucked the can across the street, joining the dozen others. "Sounds like prison."

"This man you want me to find information on," Sergei said, then stopped for a moment before continuing. "He must be really important for you to pay me that much."

"Seems to be so," Dowland said.

"Any idea why?"

Dowland looked over to his friend in surprise, seeing more fear than curiosity on his face.

"You never ask me that," Dowland said.

"I know. This—what you've told me, the price, even you coming down here . . . It's different."

"Why's it different?"

"I know you won't tell me, and I don't want to know, but I'm pretty confident who you might have met with about this. And if you did, in fact, meet with this person, it means this is in a whole other league than either of us has ever been in. The kind that swallows people up. Not only individuals but families too."

"You don't have anything to worry about," Dowland said.

Sergei chuckled, looked at the rag in his hand, then put it back against his forehead. "I wouldn't worry, except I can see something in your eyes I can't remember ever seeing before."

"What's that?"

"Fear."

THREE

What We Do in Life
Echoes in Eternity

1.

When it was time to deplane, Cheyenne stood up and turned around to take one more glance. The man following her apparently didn't care if she saw him. At one point during the trip, he even gave Cheyenne a nice round grin. The company was monitoring her for any unusual activity, and her jumping on a plane definitely was unusual. She would have to escape his beady eyes before she left the Denver airport.

What am I doing here in the first place?

She knew why she had made this trip, and she knew where she was supposed to go. But what then? Would her father finally come out of hiding? Did he have a full-time job waiting for her to replace the one she'd just lost?

Being here in another city and state was foolish for multiple reasons. Of course Acatour was going to closely monitor her actions. Regardless of any random data that hadn't already been exorcised from her accounts at the corporation, the most important information she had resided in her head, and so far no one had invented a way of deleting the brain's information. Since so much was stored on a SYNAPSYS, memories had never been better.

She didn't rush once she was inside the terminal. Cheyenne knew she wasn't in any real danger, not yet. After grabbing a coffee, she looked down at the small carry-on bag next to her. It was the only piece of luggage they allowed on planes these days. Cheyenne didn't need much anyway. Her father had trained her to get ready quickly, to pack light, and to be frugal with her belongings. She always watched in fascination when people seemed to need to bring their entire bedroom with them on a trip. This bag contained only the important things. A handful of bigger items were safely stored in a rental unit called The Security Vault. Her stuff would be waiting when she went back.

If I go back to Chicago.

A communication table in the back of the coffee shop became unoccupied, so she sat down and typed out the private number for Dina. In seconds her former colleague's voice could be heard on a non-SYNAPSYS link.

"Can you talk?" Cheyenne asked.

"Yes. I'm outside on the sidewalk. I wasn't sure if this cell phone even worked anymore."

"I can hear you breathing."

"That's because I forgot my training shoes, so I'm walking in these uncomfortable boots."

"The new black ones with the heels?"

"Terrible," Dina said. "I never should've let you convince me to buy them. Did you arrive at your destination?"

"Yes. Denver."

"I thought you wanted to keep it a secret."

"I did, until little Mr. Spy decided to tag along with me."

"Are you sure?" Dina asked.

"Absolutely."

"Who's following you?"

"It's someone from corporate. Acatour is merely protecting its investment. Not me, of course, but what I know. It doesn't matter. I'll lose the guy. Were you able to find anything?"

"Nothing," Dina said. "I did what you wanted. Nothing in the company's main system, of course. I tried to log in to your account but couldn't. It's frozen or locked. I'm going to keep trying. I have a few friends checking into things too."

"I don't want you getting in trouble," Cheyenne said.

"We're just looking for your father. This has nothing to do with PASK."

"I just got fired from PASK because of my father. So, yeah, this sorta does have something to do with the company. I don't want you to be next."

"Maybe I wouldn't mind. The way this place erases you . . . It's scary. It's like deleting a file."

Or a coworker.

Perhaps while they were looking for information on her father, they could also try to find Malek. She could use his help, or at the very least she would enjoy his company while searching for her dad. She genuinely missed the guy.

"Do you really think you'll find this person your father told you about?"

"I'm not certain of anything anymore," Cheyenne said, "except that I have done nothing wrong. To anybody."

"Yet you can still be fired and followed and treated like a criminal."

Cheyenne could only nod. "I'm going to do my best to escape like one. I'll contact you later."

Cheyenne sat for a moment, scanning the coffee shop and seeing the man following her sitting on a bench near the entryway, and tried to think of a plan. Her mind drifted to her job and how she had figured out solutions to problems online. When others were distracted by lights or motion in one direction, Cheyenne investigated the shadows in the other direction. So that's what she began to do now.

It didn't always take a scientist to discover the best solution. Sometimes it just required stopping and considering options and applying a little common sense.

It was natural to think the coffee shop in the airport had one entrance and exit, the one that Beady Eyes waited by. The well-dressed employees in their uniforms came and went through the doors. This was what the public saw. The store wanted to remind the customers of their hard-working and gregarious employees. Nobody wanted to be reminded of bored young people strolling in to work an eight-hour shift in part-time jobs they couldn't wait to get out of.

Employees arrive and leave in another way. They probably change into their well-pressed shirts in the back. No big deal—just a simple thought. Now she needed to talk to someone to figure out a way to leave through the back door. The friendly kid with the cool hair and glasses who served her the coffee was the perfect person.

"I was wondering if you could help me out," Cheyenne said to him as she walked up to the counter.

He immediately stopped what he was doing and said "Sure" without hesitation. Cheyenne was reminded what Malek had once said to her. *"You don't realize the whole sexy vibe you can give off."* A comment like that between coworkers wasn't tolerated at Acatour. Since the gender and misogyny wars a couple of decades ago, the rules were strict about using even simple adjectives like *sexy* or *hot*. But Malek wasn't trying to hit on her, nor was there any hint of harassment. He claimed to be simply stating a fact, at least in his opinion. Since Malek liked to tease her as well, she took it as a joke.

I couldn't be sexy even if I tried.

The guy behind the counter was probably just being nice instead of being enthralled by her rapturous beauty. That's what she would have told Malek.

"There's a creepy guy who was on my flight from Chicago, and he's been following me ever since we got off the plane. Don't look but he's right outside."

"Want me to call security or something?" he asked.

"No, I don't want a commotion. I have a job interview to go to, and if some kind of situation happens—even something minor—I know I'll be stuck here for a while."

"So what can I do?"

"Is there any other way to leave the shop?" she asked.

"Yeah, sure. There's the employee entrance, and it links up to the workers' hallway that leads out to the parking lot. You can go out that way, but then you'll be out of the airport."

She continued to evaluate the situation.

"Okay, I have another question, then. What time do you get off work?"

2.

Ten minutes into the car ride with the young man from the coffee shop, he told Cheyenne he could drive her all the way to Colorado Springs.

"It's not far. I know some people there too. Are you staying long?"

Malek would have been really teasing her now. She could hear his voice: *"Oh, you've done it now. He's totally into you. Look at the poor guy. He's smitten."*

There had been only one way to leave the airport—exiting through the employee entrance. Since the coffee shop guy had only another hour on his shift, she asked if he could drive her to a nearby transit station where she could get an Autoveh to take her to Colorado Springs. He obliged and was eager to oblige a little more.

"That's very kind of you, but no, thanks," she said.

As he steered the small car, Cheyenne watched his every move, noting the digital monitor on the dash that showed all the angles outside.

"What? Am I driving funny?"

"No . . . I just realized I haven't been in an actual car in a very long time. City girl."

"I live in the foothills, so there aren't any trains," he said. "Lots of winding roads. And I don't trust Autovehs."

Looking through the sunroof, she studied the sky, a bright blue stretching for miles in every direction.

"It's stunning how beautiful it is here."

"Chicago, huh," the guy said. "Guess you don't see scenery like this around there. But you do have that ridiculously big supertower, right? Have you ever been inside that?"

She nodded and said with a slight grin, "Once or twice."

"That's my dream. To one day take one of those glass elevators to the scenic level. I've seen pics and videos, but nothing beats actually being somewhere."

"Reminds me of something my father once told me," Cheyenne said, looking out her passenger-side window at the white-capped Rocky Mountains in the background, guardians of the distant horizon with their grandeur.

"What?"

"He said people like to build monuments to themselves, but nothing can compare to God's masterpieces."

"Your dad a religious man?" the driver asked her.

Trick question. And tricky too.

"No," she said. "But observant."

When they reached the busy transit station, Cheyenne thanked the young man for his generosity.

"No problem—my pleasure," he said. "You ever been to the Springs before?"

"No. But like you and the Incen Tower, I always dreamed of visiting. I told my father once if I could live anywhere, it would be Colorado Springs."

"Drink lots of water, as they say."

"Tell me something," she asked as he pulled up to the curb next to the facility. "What's a great place in town to grab a beer?"

"Oh man," the driver said with a chuckle. "There's like twenty amazing places. Hard to say which one is the best. Lagger's Pub. The Drift. Taylor Street Bar. Those are a few off the top of my head."

"Thanks."

"Oh yeah, there's Stouts. It's a place the locals love. Usually find some shady people there, but the beer is outstanding."

"Stouts?" Cheyenne asked, making sure that was the name.

"Yeah. Obviously known for their stout beer, though it's an acquired taste since they make it so strong. A pint of that could get you lost and wandering in town."

"I'll be careful."

"You have my contact info in case you need something. A shuttle. Or a drinking companion."

"Thank you for your kindness," Cheyenne said, climbing out of the car. With her travel bag in hand, she headed into the main building, where she could get her Autoveh. Dina had reserved a vehicle for her, so Cheyenne's name wouldn't pop up on the network once the car arrived.

She knew it was only a matter of time before someone caught up with her again. Vanishing from the network and the ever-watchful eyes out there took hard work and talent. That was why her father's disappearance had been so shocking. Even a handful of the most ingenious hackers who she contacted, most of them through Malek, couldn't find anything on Keith Burne. That meant her father must have had help erasing himself.

But why? What was he disappearing from?

As she found a kiosk and typed in the code Dina had given her, Cheyenne looked through the outer glass walls to see if anybody nearby was paying attention to her. She could see travelers—an elderly woman talking into the monitor at another kiosk and a couple who were waiting by the doors for their vehicle. But there were no workers at the transit station. Nobody sat behind a desk or a steering wheel. Everything was automated and interconnected. A few taps on a screen and she'd be the next in line for her transportation. Then a few taps on the window of a car, one that didn't have a door handle but opened and shut on its own, and she'd soon be on her way. That was why she had watched the guy from the coffee shop in fascination. He wasn't just sitting and being driven around. He was driving himself.

Simple things like that were taken care of by others. Her apartment, for example. Indy, her LC, would wake her up and help pick out her outfit, reminding her what she had worn the last month and making suggestions based on the latest trends. In the past how did people find the time to make those decisions themselves? Her bed automatically remade itself the moment she left to go to work. Her coming and going and even her going back to get something she had forgotten were all recorded and monitored, not out of suspicion, but simply because that was the way things were. Technology had replaced so many things. So many that now people didn't even bother to learn how to do simple, basic functions.

"Why learn to fly a kite when you can have a machine do it for you?" Malek had once said while they discussed the pros and cons of AI and technologies. "And since you don't know how to fly a kite, then you're not going to show your child how to do it, because you can't. Because you don't *need* to. And so the dominoes go, falling down. We become more stupid, and the machines become more powerful."

"Since when did I suddenly have a child?" Cheyenne had replied, loving to give her coworker a hard time.

"But you see what I'm getting at, right?" he had asked, not taking the bait.

"These things improve our ways of life. We don't have to worry about learning to drive or watching the road. Instead, we can engage in conversation or read books or—"

"Wait, wait, wait. Hold on. 'Engage in conversation'? First, why do you sound like a college professor? And really? People don't talk in moving vehicles. And read? Yeah, they read the world reports and the news from strangers, and they check their accounts, but actually read? Come on, Cheyenne."

"We work in the technology field, yet you always make it seem like it's a bad thing."

"You know it yourself. Fallible and very flawed people built that technology, some of it set in place decades ago. Algorithms can take on lives of their own, but ultimately there's always one of us giving birth to the code. And who are we to suddenly play god in others' lives?"

As the door to the red Autoveh closed and the car began to coast out of the parking lot, Cheyenne couldn't help missing Malek. It was those types of conversations and thoughts that ultimately led to his dismissal.

"Well, hello, miss," an older gentleman's voice said in speakers all around her. "Name's Bennie. Where are we headed today?"

He sounded like a grandfather, and she could picture him already. A beard and a big belly, the sort of man who loved to sit in a rocking chair and watch the sun fall behind the mountains, then later cook his family their favorite meal and read his grandchildren a bedtime story before they were tucked in. This whole mental picture arrived in her mind after hearing his voice.

The reason there wasn't anything visual representing the driver like the mechanical baristas at Incen Tower was simple: the mind was far more effective in conjuring a picture that could create an impression. No algorithm or advanced bit of technology could ever replace the vitality of imagination.

Not yet.

"Colorado Springs," Cheyenne said.

"Lovely place," Bennie said as the small and sleek electric car made several smooth turns and soon found itself on a one-lane highway built specifically for Autovehs. "And whereabouts in Colorado Springs?"

That was a very good question. She hadn't gotten that far yet.

"I haven't made any reservations." She knew that's all she needed to say for her "driver" to list several hotel suggestions that best fit her. It didn't take long for her to book a room at a boutique hotel.

"What would you like to listen to?" Bennie asked.

Normally an Autoveh would have instantly known what sort of music she wanted since it would be connecting to her SYNAPSYS, but since she had turned it off, it needed to ask.

"Surprise me," she said, watching the countryside spread out as the vehicle drove at 120 miles an hour, passing the black security boxes every ten minutes.

For a moment she closed her eyes. Just a single second.

"Remember why you're here," the voice said.

Cheyenne's eyes shot open, and she bolted up in the seat.

"What was that?" she asked the voice.

Grandpa Bennie was the one who answered. "I asked what you would like to listen to, and you said 'Surprise me,' so I was sorting through—"

"Yes, but the other voice. What was that?"

"I'm sorry, missus, but I didn't hear anything else."

Bennie wasn't lying, unless someone specifically had programmed him to lie.

"I'm sorting through my collection up here," the driver said as if he were going through a case of compact discs or, better yet, picking through a bag of cassette tapes. Ridiculous, of course, since the choice had been made in a fraction of a second, but that was all part of the mirage. It also gave someone like Bennie his charm.

"You didn't hear that voice?" Cheyenne asked.

"No, but my hearing is getting a little iffy these days."

Normally she would have smiled and engaged in a playful conversation with her imaginary AI driver. But the voice . . . She knew she had heard it.

It was Dad.

Four words. That was all. But it was enough.

In the same way the other voice had spoken to her through her SYNAPSYS, her father had somehow gotten through to her.

But how? How could he? Especially since my SYNAPSYS is off? Is that really him?

"Here's a nice nine-minute melody you will like," Bennie said.

A low bass and piano began to play, soon joined by the trumpet and delicate drums. A wave of goose bumps and chills, or whatever they could rightly be called, folded over her. She smiled as she looked at the selection scrolling on the front windshield glass.

"So What" by Miles Davis. From *Kind of Blue,* released in 1959.

"Perfect selection," Cheyenne told Bennie.

This wasn't a funny coincidence, since there was no way the song could have been randomly picked. Bennie's choice had been made for him by someone else.

It was confirmation that she was in the right place. And a reminder of the person she was looking for.

3.

The first person she asked was a busy bartender, who was completely uninterested in both serving some stranger and chatting with her about anything. He only shrugged as if he didn't even hear her inquiry. The second person she set her eyes on appeared to be a manager of sorts in this bar, so as Cheyenne carried her beer to a table, she casually stopped to ask her.

"Hi, I'm wondering if you could help me?"

"Of course," the focused blond thirtysomething said.

"I'm looking for someone named Jazz. Does that name sound familiar?"

"No," the woman said, the quickness in her response and her split-second blink giving her away.

"You sure? I heard that he comes around here a lot."

"Sorry. A lot of people come around here. It's hard to keep track of everyone."

Now the blonde sounded as unfriendly as the bartender. Cheyenne thanked her and walked to the back of the long, rectangular establishment full of old western and Coloradan artifacts hanging on the wall and from the ceiling. As she sat at a table next to a rusty wagon wheel, she noticed the manager she'd spoken with was whispering in the ear of a man at the end of the bar. The man stood and looked at her.

Seems like they might know someone named Jazz. Someone who probably doesn't want to be found.

Her father had tried to convince her over the years to listen to jazz music, telling her how fascinating it was, how its beauty came from its unpredictability. How no computer system or AI could ever produce anything close to a jazz masterpiece. Creativity was something that still couldn't be artificially or mathematically generated, though Cheyenne had often argued with her father about that, showing him the magnificence of some of the algorithms she had created, ones that took on a life of their own.

"That's not creativity," her father had told her with a bit of alarm. "That's more like a virus that can grow out of control."

As with so many things, this was an area where they disagreed. She knew her father would have been very intrigued to see how far she had progressed with her work as an algorithm architect. He also would have certainly been against the ethics behind putting algorithms into SYNAPSYSes. She remembered his warning to her when he asked what would happen when the algorithms knew you better than you knew yourself.

"Excuse me," a voice behind her said.

A man walked up to her and grinned. It wasn't the same guy the blond manager had been talking with.

"Rosie said you were looking for someone," he said.

Could it be this easy?

"Yeah. I was wanting to talk with Jazz."

"Jazz, huh?" he asked, rubbing his face. Stubble from perhaps a week of not shaving could be seen with the orange glow of the lights above them. "That's someone's name?"

"Yes."

"Like his real name?"

"I was told he went by it."

"Yeah? Strange. Maybe I can help you."

"Are you Jazz?"

The guy laughed. "No. Do I *look* like a Jazz? I'm more of an ambient man myself. Can I ask why you're looking for him?"

"Well, you just did. It's personal business."

The big guy gave her a laid-back nod. He seemed amiable enough.

"You have a slight accent. You visiting?"

"I don't have any accent," Cheyenne said. "But, yes, I'm visiting."

"Where are you from?"

"Lots of questions."

"Sorry. Don't worry. I'm not trying to pick you up. I'm the brewer here at Stouts." He patted his stomach and smiled, showing crooked teeth. "I know . . . it's hard to tell, right? Rosie said maybe I could help you."

"This Jazz is supposed to be a regular."

"Yeah? Well, the thing about regulars is we want to keep them regulars, right? What if you were a regular and someone came in here asking about you? Would you want me blabbing to a stranger about you?"

She still believed this man could be Jazz.

"A man named Keith Burne sent me," she said.

He waited for her to say more, but she didn't.

"Okay. So you're looking for a Jazz, and someone named Keith Burne sent you. Sorry. I got nothing for you."

"Thanks," she said.

"Are you sure I can't help with anything?"

"Yeah, I'm sure."

He gave her a nod and picked up her cue of being finished. The brewer started to leave, then paused and turned around.

"If I do run into someone named Jazz, where could he find you?"

"I'm staying at the Ridge Hotel," she said.

"Okay, great. And a bit of advice. Take it or leave it. But you might not want to be publicly asking around about this Jazz character. I mean, what if he was some bad dude or something like that? You know?"

"I don't think he is," Cheyenne said.

"Yeah. But just saying."

The big guy disappeared into the crowd. Cheyenne waited around for an hour, sipping her beer but only managing to drink half of it before she left the bar. There had to be something more about the man she had spoken with, whether he was Jazz himself or knew him. It had to be one of the two. She hoped there would be another sign or clue or even a voice in her head, but none had come.

Once she was on the sidewalk, she scanned for anybody who appeared to be trailing her, but she didn't see anyone suspicious, including Mr. Beady Eyes. The Ridge Hotel was close by and could be seen with its floors angling like the curves on a woman. She wondered if part of the reason the hotel had been a top choice was that it towered above the rest of Colorado Springs just as her former home, Incen Tower, rose high above Chicago. She always evaluated algorithms and why they made a certain choice or suggestion.

I would have preferred a two-story building.

Yet again the suggestion had picked up on pieces of her life but not the information in her heart. That was the great mystery she had been working hard to uncover—the magical components of people that computers couldn't detect. Perhaps there were more ways of figuring out someone's true wants and needs, the wants and needs of a soul? To find not only logical and smart choices for them but also to fill in the holes they had inside. And all people carried those holes, no matter who they were.

Automated security guards stood on the corners of several intersections she walked by, uniformed police officers that one could have thought were men and women in the shadows of the night. They all looked different and had dozens of expressions based on their experiences, but in the light of day, they still looked like robots. Lifelike robots were too expensive to reproduce in any number, so these still resembled moving and talking mannequins. What was frightening about them was their strength and speed.

Crime and accidents are down, but fear has never been more rampant.

Cheyenne was used to the intense security guards at Incen Tower, but most of them were actual human beings. She had watched machines like this only on the network but remembered hearing about the Atlanta incident where an early police-officer model malfunctioned and killed twenty-two people on a city street in the middle of the day. Not because it had been programmed to do that or suddenly decided humans were evil, but because the intelligence had a virus, and its confusion led to it unleashing all its ammunition on civilians. After lawsuits and trials and government mandates, law-enforcement robots were forbidden to carry weapons. They were still dangerous, however. They could simply pick people up or ram into them.

The hotel doors opened after recognizing her SYNAPSYS, and so did the elevator doors. Like most hotels, it had no counter and no attendant. A lounge was on an upper floor as were the two restaurants. It was rare to see anybody after entering or exiting a place like the Ridge.

The news of the day played on the steel doors of the elevator as she headed up to the 34th floor. There had been looting and fires set overnight in downtown Chicago, a result of the continued rioting over politics. Another terrorist act of vandalism had taken place, this one painting Michigan Avenue with quotes of the Bible that told people they were going to hell. Just another ordinary day in her former city.

As the elevator doors opened, Cheyenne wondered if this was all a big waste of time, if she had gotten the information wrong or if this Jazz person would pop up. At least she knew she wouldn't be late for work tomorrow morning.

4.

"Miss Burne?"

The voice awoke Cheyenne, stirring her out of a groggy half sleep. Daisy, her hotel concierge, spoke to her through the control box next to her bed. It showed the time: 2:35 a.m.

"Yes?"

"I have a guest waiting for you in a vehicle outside the front of the hotel," the voice said. "He said you had called for a vehicle."

"What?"

"The man also said that he will be taking you to a jazz concert and that you need to leave as soon as possible."

Cheyenne turned on the light next to her bed. "Please tell him I'm running late. Give me ten minutes."

"Of course," Daisy said. "Can I help you with anything?"

"No, thanks."

Cheyenne took five minutes to dress, pull her long hair back into a pony-tail, shove her toiletries bag and purse into her travel case, and then use the bottle of mouthwash the hotel provided.

So much for sleeping in that comfy bed.

After the glass doors of the hotel slid open, Cheyenne stepped onto the sidewalk and felt the sting of early-morning air. She couldn't find any Autoveh waiting for her; the only thing around was a beat-up Jeep parked down the road a bit. She wondered if her ride had left, so she started back inside to get warm until something made her pause.

The taillights.

The black and boxy off-road vehicle blended into the night except for the red flashes of its taillights going off and on, several times in succession. A faint fog of exhaust could be seen, telling her the Jeep was running and someone was behind its wheel. Someone telling her to get inside.

The only time she had seen a Jeep Wrangler like this was in older movies, so she wasn't sure how to open its door until it popped open for her.

"Get in." The voice sounded indifferent and not very friendly.

This is a bad idea.

The doors to the hotel were closed and almost twenty yards away. She wondered how quickly they would open if she sprinted back and whether the driver would be able to get to her before she got in.

"Come on. It's cold outside. Let's go."

The twentysomething driver waited for her to climb in and sit in the passenger seat next to him. She noticed a diamond earring peeking out from underneath the dreadlocks that fell to his shoulders. He had a casual, let's-get-on-with-it sort of look about him, as if he were only running an errand.

"Where are we going?" she asked, still unsure about taking a ride.

"You wanna talk to Jazz?" he asked in a laid-back tone.

"Yes."

He waved her to get in, so Cheyenne finally relented. For a moment she waited for the door to shut itself.

"You gotta do it yourself," the young man said with a laugh. "Doors used to have to be pushed and pulled to open and shut."

After closing the door, the locks clicked. Cheyenne thought about jerking it back open and getting out of there, but she remained calm.

"Anybody following you?" he asked.

"No. Not anymore."

He reached into the side compartment and produced a miniature cylinder that looked like a shiny tube of lip balm.

"I need to reset your SYNAPSYS," he said, putting the flat edge of the device against her temple until Cheyenne swiped it away with her palm.

"Why do you have to reset it? I already have it turned off."

"We don't want you tracked."

"I won't be connecting. All I'll be doing—"

"Listen, this isn't an option. This device helps put you off the grid a bit more. It's an on-and-off switch, to put it in layman's terms."

"I don't need layman's terms, nor am I a man," she said. "I know exactly what this does. This shuts down the Siphatic sensor, the kind the authorities use when trying to search for someone, the reason idiots who are clueless are found by the cops less than twenty-four hours after going on the run."

"We're going somewhere that the powers that be can't know about. The address cannot be given out in any sort of way."

"That's all you had to say," she responded, allowing him to place it next to her head again.

Soon the engine roared to life, and they were racing down the street. The low throb of bass from the speakers around her could be felt more than heard. The driver said nothing as he ignored the stop sign.

"So where're we going?" she asked.

"We have about an hour's drive. You can go back to sleep if you want. I turned down the music."

"What'd you say? I can't hear you over the pounding in the background."

The driver had a wide and friendly grin, and as he gave a short laugh, his eyes looked as if they could belong to a mischievous fifth grader.

"That was funny," he told her, not bothering to adjust the volume but instead accelerating.

The bright headlights cut through thick snow flurries. Cheyenne decided she would wait to ask more questions. This guy probably wouldn't bother to give her answers, and maybe he didn't really have any to give. She still expected to see the stout brewer she'd met last night.

As the road began to weave upward through the mountains, the sound of drums grumbling and reggae singers rapping put her in a drowsy state. Several times her eyelids drooped shut and stayed that way for a few moments until she jerked herself awake. She was tired from the last few days, but she wasn't about to pass out sitting next to a stranger.

The farther they drove, the thicker the flakes became, and the more snow covered the road. Soon they were moving at a sluggish pace of twenty-five miles an hour. She could tell by her ears popping that they were continuing to reach higher elevations.

"Can you tell me where we're heading?" Cheyenne asked one more time after they had been in the car for forty minutes.

"We're about to drive through a town that used to be called Divide. I guess it still is, but nobody lives there. The buildings are abandoned. The 2024 blizzard killed half the hundred or so residents. The other half who got away never moved back."

"I remember seeing the footage of the snow in Colorado and Utah," Cheyenne said. "I was thirteen."

The pothole-ridden and torn-up road they drove down took them past shells of buildings with broken windows and scattered rubble. They appeared to have been destroyed not by snow but by bombs.

"So is there a nice bed-and-breakfast around these parts?" she joked.

"You're quite witty for three thirty in the morning," he said.

"This is an ideal place to kill someone and leave their body behind."

"Ah, don't let my skin color and dreadlocks scare you."

"I think having someone driving me is more unnerving than anything. Especially in an old car like this."

"Hey, this Jeep Wrangler's in great condition considering it's twenty years old. I hate being driven around. Even if it's in the big cities where they don't allow you to drive yourself."

"Well, you're driving me somewhere in the wilderness. How far away is this place we're going to?"

"Not far," he said.

"And will I be seeing Jazz when I arrive?"

"Not sure about that. You'll have to see."

The roads they were driving on now had as much as half a foot of snow on them, yet they made steady progress.

"Four-wheel drive," the man said. "Can't beat it."

The pine trees on each side of them were clustered for fifty yards. After that nothing but dark countryside could be seen. Soon they were traveling in a thick forest, the road weaving around like a maze, with some snowdrifts a foot tall.

"Are we going to be stranded here?"

"We're all stranded in this world," he said. "The key is how prepared you happen to be."

The road seemed to fade away, yet the Jeep continued to drive into the woods and down the side of a mountain. Soon the forest thinned out, and she could see a small shack in the middle of a field.

"We're here," the driver said.

She couldn't see anything else in the glow of the headlights.

" 'Here'? What's that? Looks like an outpost from the eighteen hundreds or something."

"Yeah," he said as he stopped in front of the nondescript wood cabin. "Or something. Come on."

5.

The cold early-morning air woke her up fully, and it didn't get much warmer as they walked into the building. Inside it appeared to be a garage of sorts, containing a riding mower and a tractor, neither of which had apparently been used in years. A wooden table contained some tools, and there were empty boxes and pallets stored against one wall.

The tall stranger went to the center of the room and pulled back the gray floor mat, revealing the door to a hatch. He lifted the heavy door up.

"Follow me," he told her as he began to walk down the stairs into the white light.

Instead of asking one more time where they were going, she simply continued to trail him. The steps were sturdy metal, and they were on them for quite a while before reaching a shut door. He touched the scanner on the side of the wall, then turned the knob. A large room opened up that made Cheyenne think of pictures of her father at his old company.

"Here we are."

Cheyenne watched as the door shut behind them. The young man with the dreadlocks gave her another charming smile.

"In case you haven't already surmised, I'm Jazz," he said, offering his hand. "I'll properly introduce myself now."

She shook it while still taking in everything around her. "I'm Cheyenne."

"Of course you are," he said.

Ten monitors surrounded them, all connected to various computers, each screen on and displaying either a data page or an old-school screen saver like her father used to have on his ancient physical computer.

"Yeah, I know," Jazz said. "Like seeing an old movie with someone using a cell phone the size of a shoe. Don't let the hardware fool you. There are advanced things going on. It's just that we gotta stay off the network. Some of the technology we're using is very outdated, but it works."

Cheyenne walked up to a nearby silver computer and touched the screen. "My father had one of these. I remember sitting on his lap taking pictures with him using it."

She looked back at Jazz, who was checking another monitor and using a mouse to do so. "Is my father alive?" she asked without waiting any longer.

He paused what he was doing and looked up at her. "I don't know. I swear. He's gone silent, which is the reason you're here now. The reason you were contacted. He set everything up in case something happened."

"In case *what* happened?" she asked.

"We've been regularly in touch, and if he missed two different contacts, we were basically to set off the alarm. The letter you got. His instructions."

"What about the voice in my head?" she asked.

Jazz looked at her without any indication of knowing what she was talking about.

"Someone was talking to me. Through my SYNAPSYS."

"That's impossible."

"That wasn't you?"

"No," he said. "I don't know a thing about it. Were they speaking crazy to you?"

"They were helping me. Guiding me."

He only nodded, continuing to proceed with whatever he was doing on his computer. "I've seen crazier things happen, so I'm not ever gonna say that someone's making something up."

"What is all of this? This place?"

"I'll explain everything in a minute," he said. "Well, not everything, but enough. I'm checking to make sure we're all good."

A large print on the wall above a set of monitors showed the image of a brick building with red handwriting saying, "What we do in life echoes in eternity," except the final word was being wiped away by a ghostly apparition of a street cleaner complete with a cloth and bucket.

"Like it?" Jazz asked her, noticing what she was examining.

"Sure. Something you did?"

"Yeah, right. It's from a graffiti artist named Banksy."

"Sure. I've heard about him."

"Love his work. Jealous of it, to be honest. Computer code's not as sexy as street graffiti."

There were no personal belongings that she could spot, not a photo or an opened bag of potato chips. Other than the computers alive with activity, the room looked abandoned.

"Is anybody else here?" she asked.

"No. Only me. It looks like everything's cool. Nothing negative. No word from anybody and no chatter, which is a good thing."

He began to head to another door at the back of the room. "Want some coffee? Something else to drink or eat?"

"Coffee would be wonderful," she said.

"Come on. I'll give you a tour of my humble abode. I don't ever get a chance to show it off. In fact, the last person who visited was your father."

6.

As sparse and bare-bones as the computer room had appeared, the rest of this underground hideaway was the opposite. Jazz had made it very much his own space, and he showed the surprisingly large space off after getting her a mug of hot coffee.

"Was this a government bunker or something that you had remodeled?" she asked as they stood in the kitchen with white cabinets and stainless steel appliances and a long bar with stools in its center.

"No way. No, it was one of the many survival complexes that people started setting up like crazy after 9/11. After having presidents that scared everybody, and *especially* after President Garrison was shot, the billionaire techies went crazy with these. This particular one belonged to a guy from San Francisco. I guess this was his Colorado getaway, but he had them stashed away all over the world. So if things went to hell, he'd be close to one."

"So he still owns it?" Cheyenne asked.

"Oh no. He swallowed a bullet when the market crashed. So this had been virtually abandoned. I guess you can't escape the end of the world when it's your bank account that's blowing up."

The coffee warmed her and tasted good. All of this was fascinating and made absolutely no sense since it had nothing to do with her father.

"I know you have a million questions," Jazz said. "Let me show you the rest of the place while I try to explain some things."

The shelter was four times as large as her apartment in Incen Tower. There was a main living area, complete with two long couches and a wall that substituted for a television and movie screen. A wet bar in the corner of the room had enough liquor in it for him to survive a couple of apocalypses.

"Good to know you're prepared," she said, pointing at the stash.

"Yeah, and the irony is I'm three years sober."

"Seems as if it would be too tempting to have it around."

"Or I can go to bed every day feeling victorious that I didn't need to open any of those bottles."

Along with more framed prints of artwork from Banksy, movie posters and album covers and family photos covered the walls.

"I've been down here for a couple of years now. Living and working here, that is."

"Doing what?" she asked.

"Preparing for the end," Jazz said. "Like all the preppers. Only our preparation is a bit different. But you'll see. Here's one guest bedroom, as I call it, and then there's another. Each has a bathroom. Running water. Hot water."

"It's as big as my bedroom—my old bedroom. They even have queen mattresses. I don't have one of those."

"This is a fun room for all those times I have my buddies over, which is never," Jazz said, showing her a space with a pool table and another loaded wet bar.

They reached the main bedroom, and above the doorway handwritten words were scrawled in black paint. She paused to look and read them out loud. " 'That terrible day of the LORD is near. Swiftly it comes—a day of bitter tears, a day when even strong men will cry out. Zephaniah 1:14.' Wow. That's a motivating verse."

"It's pronounced *Zef*, not *Zep*," he said with a smile.

"I don't think I could find that in a Bible."

She glanced into his bedroom, which looked not only messy but also a bit alarming.

"Sorry. I didn't have a chance to clean it," he said as he picked up a pair of boxers near the entrance.

"Those sorta resemble a horror movie," she said as she pointed at the walls beside and behind the bed.

"Yeah. I know. It makes me look a bit whacked out. I get it. Just hear me out. Okay?"

Cheyenne stepped closer to the painting, another print, but this one covered half the wall above his bed. The image looked like a mouth of fire and hell opening to consume a city in ancient times while a few terrified people in robes were running away. Looking closely, Cheyenne could see another figure nearer to the burning buildings, a woman staring back at them.

"This poster is a replica of a painting called *The Destruction of Sodom and Gomorrah* by John Martin," Jazz said, "a painter who lived in what used to be England during the mid–eighteen hundreds. He liked painting end-of-the-world stuff like this."

"Doesn't this give you nightmares?" she said, staring at the flames spewing from the sky.

"I don't sleep," he said with a smile. "Do you know the story of Lot in the Bible?"

"No."

Jazz shook his head. "You know a million different ways to sway people using your computer, but you don't know one of the most common stories from the Old Testament?"

"My father used to take me to movies on Sundays, not church."

"Lot was the nephew of Abraham. You've heard of him, right?"

"Yes," she said, but she wouldn't have been able to say exactly who he was.

"Abraham, the father of all Jews? Come on, girl. His nephew, Lot, was living in this really bad city of Sodom, and God decided to wipe it, along with Gomorrah, off the face of the earth using fire and brimstone. And this lady right here? The one down the hill from Lot and his daughters? It's Lot's wife. She disobeyed God and looked back and—boom—turned into a pillar of salt."

"Were these the sort of bedtime stories you were told as a child?"

He turned to her, the smile no longer there, a look of urgency on his face.

"If it's a fairy tale, then it's a rather spooky one," he said. "But if it really happened, then it's terrifying."

"That God can kill thousands of people just like that?" Cheyenne asked.

"No. It's scary to wonder why He doesn't do it more often."

The steady and calm manner in which Jazz said this alarmed her. "And you believe this really happened?"

Jazz nodded as he picked up a backpack and stuffed a few items from his desk in it.

"I expected to see lots of things related to jazz here," she said.

"That's the irony of my nickname. I don't even particularly like that type of music, though it's grown on me. The name was given to me by Acrobat."

"By who?"

For a moment he stopped and looked at her, and then he nodded to himself. "That's right. You really don't know anything, do you?"

"Obviously not."

"He calls me Jazz. I call him Acrobat. He's the reason I'm here in the first place. The guy who connected me with your father. He's the one who's about to make everything happen, to expose the head of the monster."

No smile, no hint of humor, no sign of being even remotely sarcastic. Jazz opened and shut desk drawers as if he was checking to make sure he had everything.

"And what is this Acrobat going to do?" she asked.

"You'll see soon enough."

Jazz moved over to the painting and tapped on the red-and-orange flames pouring out from the heavens. "This. This is what's going to happen. And, yeah, I believe it, and, yeah, I assume you're gonna think I'm insane for thinking this. But there are signs. Numbers and figures and dates. All leading back to the hydra."

"The what?"

"The leaders, the cabal, the heads of it all. The ones Acrobat and your father are going to expose. That's why your father suddenly disappeared."

"To hide?"

"No," Jazz said, starting to walk out of the room. "To prepare. And to help warn others. Come on."

7.

They went back to the first room they had entered, the one with all the computers. Jazz moved a chair and put it beside another chair in front of the largest monitor in the room, telling her to have a seat next to him. He maneuvered the mouse and typed out numbers and passwords to get through a variety of screens. Soon he had several browsers open from different websites.

"I'm not even sure how to start here, whether it's with Acrobat or how I connected with your father or why he—and all of us, frankly—are in danger. All I know is that I had specific instructions that if a woman looking and sounding like you came asking for me, I was supposed to bring you to this bunker and get you up to speed. And to wait."

"Wait for what?" she asked.

"Orders for what to do next," he said as he continued looking at photos and files open on the computer screen. "Okay, look at this. It's half a dozen, just to give you a tiny sample."

The first image he pointed to was of a handsome businessman in a suit, perhaps in his thirties, standing on the sidewalk and holding out his hand as if to tell the photographer "No pictures, please."

"This is Armand van Namen. A top guy at Hope Trust."

"If he's a top guy there, he's very high," she said.

"Yeah, especially when you're the only health care provider out there. He disappeared four years ago. Vanished without a single trace. Didn't have a wife or kids, and there were absolutely no leads. No hints at foul play, no personal issues. Nothing."

Jazz went through several short reports on him.

"This was all the coverage he got, which as you can see was nothing," he said. "That alone was interesting enough to make one wonder. A head of one of the biggest corporations on this planet—someone people said could maybe even be the CEO one day—suddenly vanished. So I started to investigate in my own way, through the networks and the webs."

"Were you already here?"

"No, not yet. I was living in Park City in the basement of a run-down hotel. Long story for another day. Anyway, I'd already been collecting lots and lots of data. For what or for who, another long story. But this fit into my many files and findings. It turns out that Armand van Namen—this brilliant and talented young leader dedicated to his job who also was charismatic and so Aryan-looking that he would have made Hitler proud—just so happened to find God only months before disappearing."

She felt her skin buzz as she continued looking at the face on the screen.

Finding God just before disappearing. Just like Daddy.

"Yeah, I can read your mind. I know exactly what you're thinking," Jazz said. "And yes."

"So did this guy quit his job? Did he tell people about what happened?"

"I don't know exactly what happened at Hope Trust. He didn't come right out and say, 'Yeah, I believe in Jesus Christ now.' That would be publicly saying you believe in racism and hatred of nonbelievers. Armand wasn't public, not in a big way, but there were some who knew. A few people shared things in various interviews or online. I even tracked down one woman who said she had seen a visible change in him. Then suddenly he was gone."

"What do you think happened?" Cheyenne asked.

"I think he was killed. Without a doubt. And I have—I don't know—maybe forty or fifty other examples of people like this. Important people, some influential and others outspoken, who disappeared during the last twenty years. Some have had their corpses pop up. Let me find one."

Jazz showed her reports on a woman named Rosalina Garza, who worked as a professor at Harvard University. She had been an outspoken atheist and proponent of expelling Christian bigotry in the country until a dramatic conversion caused her to recant everything.

"This was a public thing like five or six years ago," Jazz said.

"I remember hearing about it in the news."

"Yeah, she got fired, fined, even arrested. Then when the smoke finally cleared, she was judged by the public as a racist. She couldn't be lumped with white supremacy since she wasn't white or male, but having the public imprison you is worse than being sent to a penitentiary. It wasn't until a year ago that I discovered—buried and not reported, of course—that her body had been found on the shores of a lake in Louisiana. A place she had no connection to."

"So you think she was killed?"

"Absolutely. I have lots more examples, and these are only the disappearances. These are not random things I've found but a careful and systematic extinction of our country's Christians. That's it in a nutshell, pure and simple."

Or maybe more like nutjob.

"My sources and info mentioned Keith Burne—your father—after he was missing for a couple of days. Same modus operandi. Influential power player becomes a Christian, often in dramatic fashion, and then suddenly goes missing."

"But you said you didn't know if he had been killed," Cheyenne said.

"I don't know. I can't tell you with certainty that most of these missing people were killed. It's just that we know they're gone. I've had the fortune—and the misfortune too—to learn network secrets and tricks. I also have a lot of contacts, most of whom I don't trust but still sometimes use. This sort of info is better than the kind the FBI might gather. Everything I know, every single piece of data I've collected and uncovered, leads to one single person."

Jazz pulled out a large photograph of Jackson Heyford. "Acatour's CEO. The great founder of PASK. The most profound revolutionary in technology and business since Steve Jobs."

Cheyenne could detect the mockery in his tone. "You believe Heyford is secretly killing Christians?"

Jazz put the photograph back. "That's only one of many things he's doing."

Lot and his wife and Heyford . . . This guy's spent too much time down in the bunker by himself.

All she wanted to know was the answer to the question that had brought her here in the first place, the one she'd carried like a battle wound every day for the past year.

Where is he?

"The note my father wrote me . . . When did he write it?"

"Months ago when he and Acrobat set this up."

"Set what up?"

"You reading that letter and you being right here right now."

But why? For what reason?

Jazz shifted in his chair, staring down at the floor for a moment, visibly searching for what to say to her next.

"Look, I know this is all a bit *much*. Acrobat—I tell the truth on the grave of my grandmother, who believed in the blood of Jesus Christ and who I think looks down on me every day with smiles—is the real deal. He is a bona fide prophet of God. Like the kind the Old Testament had. He's been told to expose the heart of the evil in this world to everybody."

"And you're going to help him do this?"

Jazz nodded. "But this is what I know. What I believe. The reason I'm in Acrobat's life. Look, these preppers have been preparing for the end for decades, and a lot of them think it's gonna come from some crazy ruler. But no. It's gonna be God, and it's been a long time comin'. He's angry. And look at Sodom and Gomorrah. You don't want to anger God."

"People have been saying we're living in the end times for the last hundred years," Cheyenne said.

"I'm not talking about Revelation. We're still in the book of Jonah, except I'm not going to run the opposite way and get swallowed by some whale."

"Where's Acrobat now? Can you reach him?"

Jazz shook his head. "I don't know. Nobody knows, really. Even those working with him. Let me show you something. This is how scared they are about the work we're doing."

Jazz typed on the actual keyboard to bring up some videos on the computer. The footage showed firemen putting out a blazing building while police and EMTs were swarming around them.

"The massive bomb blast a few years ago that almost leveled what used to be the historic Chicago Theatre," Jazz said, then cued other videos showing smoke and the aftermath of what appeared to be some terrorist act.

"More than two hundred people died," Cheyenne said. "We thought it was 9/11 all over again."

Pictures showed the splendor of the former seven-story building that opened in 1921. Filling half of an entire block, with a marquee that glowed and showcased the word *Chicago* above it, the theater once included a grand lobby, mezzanine, and balconies, all resembling something built at Versailles, France, in the sixteen hundreds.

"This is what it looked like thirty years ago," Jazz said.

The pictures after the carnage showed the front of the building obliterated, as if some giant had taken a large bite out of it.

"I still have nightmares about that day," she said.

Cheyenne thought of the tragedy three years ago. Her father desperately trying to get in touch with her but unable to with the network cutting off Illinois for fear of a cyberattack. When she finally spoke to him, he was in tears and wanted her to leave the city, fearing that the Incen Tower would be targeted, especially since that would be the most notable building in the state and in the entire country, not to mention the headquarters of Acatour.

"The blame went to the GG," Jazz said and showed her more articles and pieces on the network. "The white supremacists calling themselves the Goebbels Group. A bunch of Nazi freaks that make former white supremacists look sane. And Acrobat was listed as the mastermind behind it."

"Was he involved in any way?"

Jazz shook his head as he clicked on new images, including several pictures of Jackson Heyford talking with other men.

"The Acrobat wasn't involved, and neither was the GG. But your leader—your *former* leader—was."

"Do you have some vendetta against Acatour or something?" Cheyenne asked, only half joking.

Jazz gave her an animated and serious look. "Do you believe in any of the 9/11 conspiracies?"

"What? That the Twin Towers were blown up by our own government or something crazy like that?"

"Something crazy like that," he said, mimicking the mockery in her voice. "I've spent a good chunk of six months researching everything from US government securities, to Building Seven's collapse, to the Pentagon being hit by a missile. Do you know that half the country used to actually believe some of the truth behind these 9/11 conspiracies?"

"A journalist put all of those conspiracies to rest ten years ago."

"Oh, the whole Kurt West circus? Did you ever think he was purposefully chosen because of his charm and wit? There's no way he could have uncovered all that information. He's an actor, one of the many puppets they bring out to spin their evil lies."

I've flown halfway across the country to talk to some guy who's going to put on his tinfoil hat any second. "So I bet you believe there was more than one gunman who shot JFK," Cheyenne said.

"Yes, I believe shots were fired from the grassy knoll," Jazz said as he stood up. "And, yes, I believe in the 9/11 cover-up. But I'm not a lunatic, and I don't believe Elvis is alive, nor do I think Lizard People are running the world. We know *exactly* who's running this world. And we're going to expose them."

"So the Chicago Theatre—"

"They did that specifically to try to shut down the Acrobat. To force him to go away. But all that did was ignite the fuse inside him. Before this, he'd only been sending anonymous messages, asking questions, confronting people online. All under different monikers, such as Acrobat and Reckoner. He already had a good portion of this list."

Jazz handed her a page full of pictures of men and women with information next to them. "There are forty-two people listed here," he said. "These are all key people who've suddenly died or gone missing. Every single one of them was a believer. And only one of them has been found alive and well."

"My father," she said, seeing his face and information among the other names.

"Exactly."

Cheyenne sighed and handed the sheet back to him. As she looked at him, trying to sort through the thoughts and emotions rising inside her, she felt as though Jazz was a familiar face she had known for years. For the moment she tossed this sentiment aside.

"Even before I began working for Acatour, there were plenty of psychos who claimed everything under the sun about Jackson Heyford. He's a target because he's running the biggest corporation in the world. So, yeah, I do believe in one sense he's running the world. He's certainly one of the most influential business leaders out there."

"Are you calling me a psycho?" Jazz asked as he opened his eyes as wide as they could go, along with his wide grin.

"No. I'm referring to people who pull stunts. Like the one a couple of years ago where twenty cows were let loose all over Michigan Avenue. Ever hear about that? A message to the city of Chicago to wake up and smell the coffee."

Jazz laughed. "Of course. That was Acrobat's work."

"How do you— Are you serious?"

"Sure. He was inspired by an Old Testament prophet, a passage about Israel being stubborn as a heifer."

"A what?" she asked, confused to hear *Israel* and *heifer* in the same sentence.

"A female cow."

She let out an exasperated sigh and then a wry chuckle. "I'm talking to a man using ancient computers in an underground bunker about a conspiracy junkie who releases heifers as a warning about God's judgment?" Cheyenne let out a louder and more ridiculous laugh. "This is absolute bonkers."

"I would have said the same thing two years ago. But I've seen things with my own eyes, Cheyenne. Not shooters on grassy knolls or explosives under the

Twin Towers or even the secret plans behind the Chicago Theatre bombing. The things I've seen, the dark things, are the same twisted stuff but on a personal level."

"I don't understand."

"You don't have to. Look, I wouldn't have trusted Acrobat if I hadn't met him. I'm suspicious of everyone. Even you being here. I don't like it. But when I met him and spoke to him, I knew. The Holy Spirit moved in my heart."

"Did he give you any Kool-Aid to drink at this meeting?"

Jazz turned away from the computer, nodding at her dismissal.

"I met him in a bar, and the first thing he tells me is that the people who are crazy enough to think they can change the world are the ones who do. Instantly he's got my attention, and I'm like, 'That's such a brilliant quote.' He laughs and says he stole it from Steve Jobs. Then he starts to explain everything he knows about The Thirteen."

"The Thirteen? What's that?"

Before Jazz could answer, a heavy pounding echoed in the room.

"What was that?" she asked, looking at the ceiling.

Jazz tightened his lips and then inhaled deeply. "Someone's knocking at the door."

"Someone's *what*?" she asked. "Don't you have any sort of security system?"

He shook his head. Cheyenne couldn't believe it.

"So you have all this down here, and you're doing this sort of hacking and spy stuff, and you don't have any sort of device that a third grader could set up showing you have people on your property?"

"Nobody knows this place exists," he said. "At least they didn't until I brought you here."

"Don't blame me for not having common sense."

He moved close to her, his expression suddenly cold and threatening. "I'll only ask you once, okay? Did you lead anybody here with you?"

"How could I? I don't know who I would lead to what since I have no clue why I'm here and ultimately what's going on."

"Good answer," Jazz said. "At least you know a little more. Okay, grab your bag."

"We're not going upstairs, are we?"

"No," Jazz said, then pressed a button on the side of each computer in the room. "I might not have set up a security system, but there was an escape route already built into this place."

"Can we use it?"

"We'd better pray we can," he said.

8.

Cheyenne followed Jazz, this stranger who looked so familiar, this young man spouting strange conspiracy nonsense but somehow making it seem real. Cheyenne kept hearing in her head the hip-hop song from the superstar of the day, License: *"Hell-bent to attack, full a hate. Time to repent, react, and relocate."*

"Come on. This way," Jazz said after stuffing his backpack with a few more things.

A door that appeared to be a closet in the game room turned out to be a secret passage or really just a cement hallway since the entire structure was a secret. Every few yards, long strands of yellow lights were set on each side of the floor, resembling lit-up dashed lines in passing lanes. They walked for about five minutes before reaching another door. It creaked as Jazz opened it.

"It's been a while since I've come here," he said.

It took him a minute to find the light switch. As a pale white glow filled the bare space, the first thing Cheyenne noticed was a tire almost as tall as she was. A shiny black Hummer was the only thing in this space, facing down what appeared to be the longest garage she had ever seen.

"Climb aboard," Jazz said, opening the passenger door that looked like a fence gate.

Once he was behind the wheel, he scanned the dashboard to take in everything. Then he peered down the passageway that was plenty wide for the Hummer.

"This driveway goes for a mile or so until we reach the far side of the property," Jazz said. "There's another road we can take over there. If, of course, this beast starts."

"You don't know if it will start?" she asked.

Jazz smiled. "You know in the movies when people are on the run, and they get into a car, and they try to start it, and it won't?"

"Way to jinx us."

"I'm just saying. Otherwise we'll be sprinting down this. Did you bring your running shoes?"

He closed his eyes for a moment, then pressed the button to start the Hummer. It roared to life, and Jazz let out a big sigh. "Okay, let's go."

"Are you going to tell me where we're headed this time?"

"I honestly don't know," he said. "We'll be told the safest place to go."

"What about your place? All the computers?"

"Those little buttons I was pushing will wipe them clean in seconds. Completely destroys anything on the machines."

"Yeah, but all your personal belongings?" Cheyenne asked.

"I have everything I need in my bag. Probably like you."

The passage was dark, so the Hummer's lights guided the way. After a few minutes they could see daylight. Once they exited, the bright morning snow surrounding them caused Cheyenne to squint and shield her eyes, and Jazz stopped the car and scanned the area. They had emerged on the side of a mountain, with the faint clearing of a road winding downward through the white forest below.

"Nobody's around. Good." He looked at her with a grin, brushing back a few thick locks from his face. "So are you ready?"

"Ready for what?" Cheyenne asked.

"Ready to try to save the world."

FOUR

Consider This

1.

The empty space in the brick building on Water Street looked exactly as Will Stewart remembered from when he first fell in love with it. The bookstore had always been a dream. Who in the world would buy a book in a store? He had always known that this outcome was a possibility or, if he was honest with himself, that this was the probability. Yet it had been almost ten years since he opened Ink. The name had changed over the years from The Ink on the Page Bookstore to The Inkstore to now simply Ink. Everybody called it that. Will had always stressed the uniqueness of a brick-and-mortar store in today's age that slighted the richness of a space dedicated to books made of paper and filled with ink. Those titles would be handpicked with care and love instead of fed to consumers based on manipulative algorithms and machines designed only to make money. His goal wasn't only to earn a profit but to connect with a community of people.

Now Will stood in the center of the space all alone. The bare walls, the clean floors, the emptiness of it all . . . The only thing remaining was an open box by his feet. One of those square white storage boxes, the kind you could mark with a pen to remind yourself what you put inside. The sort that was usually accompanied by similar boxes, perhaps a dozen that contained similar *things*. But out of everything that had been here, this was all he was taking with him. Favorite books, the rare ones, along with the ones he got in trouble for selling, the kind that were supposedly hateful and promoted venom in an already venomous society.

It was only a matter of time.

He gently kicked the box and then looked at the top of his boot, the worn leather with the hole getting bigger. These were his favorite boots, and he always went back to the things he loved the most. Loyal to a fault, as the cliché went.

The cover for *Precipice* stood out, a lightning rod of a book that made people take sides and draw lines in the sand and continue to think in the conversation of clichés. The book had been a bestseller from a controversial pastor, speaker, and radio host who lost all those titles shortly before being imprisoned for supposed fraud—charges that most said were phony and were designed simply to get the man behind bars. Thad Riley. Not Pastor Riley or Dr. Riley but Thad, of all names. All the guy was doing in *Precipice* was saying the country was literally on the edge of falling into hell itself, and using the Bible as his resource, Thad Riley took shots at everything and everybody: the government, corporations, celebrities, the entire culture. And the book had started making an impression. That's when it became dangerous, and it wasn't merely banned, which would have made it even more popular. It was taken out of circulation, and like anything deemed an offense under the hate act, it was against the law to own a copy, much less sell it.

Will wondered what it would have been like to live in the era of so-called free speech instead of in the shadow of censorship and silence. Perhaps there was a legitimate reason this country was taking God out of everything—the real God, not the feel-good, higher power, Zen, pop-a-pill, lowercase *god* that united everybody these days.

Not because He's hateful, but because He doesn't listen.

Or worse, Will thought, *it's because in the end He's not really there.*

Don't go there you know that's a lie.

Next to the book was the photo of Will and his wife, Amy. Like the books he had sold, the kind you could hold in your hand, this was a photograph that didn't float and couldn't be turned on and off. You could feel it with your fingers.

Paper, like everything else in this world, would eventually dry up and disintegrate. New releases had a limited shelf life, not because of the lack of sales but due to the elimination of bookshelves. Everything in the world—every single thing—was being downloaded and converted into ghosts and shadows, tucked away in clouds, and brought to life in the blink of an eye.

Our spiritual world has been replaced by a cyberspace we access every second of every day as if our very souls depend on it.

It used to be that people ran away from or ignored matters of faith. Now their belief systems revolved around the machinery of now, the technology inside each person.

The scratching on the glass door outside Ink—outside what used to be a bookstore called Ink—made Will turn around. The mutt was back again, the third time this week. He was small and mostly dirty white with a black face and ears right above his white nose, making him look as if he were wearing a mask. The dog had a limp and smelled and had weird eyes, like a shell-shocked soldier experiencing PTSD. Will had asked around and put a photo of the dog with his number along his building's windows. He had even asked a few places if they took in strays, but the animal laws were very strict, and this little guy had a one-way ticket to the afterlife if Will took him to them. No tags, not great health, no owner or history . . . It didn't look good for the pooch.

He opened the door, and the dog hurried inside, wagging its tail and then sniffing the box.

"What's your name, huh?" Will asked, scratching him behind his ears. "What's your story?"

Like every book he had ever read and each one he had sold or tried to sell, everyone had a story. Some kind of story. And it didn't have to fit into neat chapters or one particular genre.

The last thing I need now is a dog to take care of.

The dark eyes looked up at him, glassy eyes seeming to ask him to help. Will shook his head, sighed, then laughed as he picked up the dog and fit him in the remaining space of the box to take to the Autoveh station and get a ride home.

At least the girls will be happy tonight.

As he slipped out the door one last time, he didn't bother to lock it, knowing there was no point.

Everything of worth in the store had already been stolen.

2.

Before he got ten yards from the building that still had the sign Ink on it, Will was stopped and nearly trampled by a bearded stranger.

"Excuse me," said the man in a tweed overcoat that was as vintage as Will's boots.

Will gave a polite nod and kept walking until he heard the door behind him open. He stopped and turned around to see the man, seemingly in a hurry, walk into the bookstore and then just stand there.

For a moment Will wasn't sure whether to keep walking to the station or to stay and let the guy know what had happened. He waited, the box still in his arms, the unnamed stray dog still sitting on top of its contents. The guy was in the store for maybe two minutes. Then he walked back out.

"Store's closed," Will said to the man.

The stranger rubbed his thick, dark beard and gave him a grin. Almost as if he already knew that. "What a loss," he said. "What's his name?"

For a second Will wasn't sure what name he was referring to. Then he looked at the furry head staring up at him.

"Good question. He's a stray that's been coming around this week. Can't find its owner. Nobody wants him."

"Nobody except you, huh?"

The man had an accent, perhaps Brooklyn based. Definitely not Midwest.

"Well, I won't be here the next time he comes pawing at the door."

"Good man."

"You look desperate for a book," Will said.

"The world is desperately in need, my friend. I love buying books for others even if they use them for campfires afterward. There's still something about giving away a printed book, is there not? When you simply send it over to people's SYNAPSYS, they can delete it as quickly as blowing out a candle."

"So you were looking for a gift?"

"No, not this time," the man in the tweed coat said. His intense eyes didn't waver as they focused on Will. "I heard you actually had a collection of A. W. Tozer books."

This suddenly had become interesting, enough so that Will put down the box. The dog hopped over its side and went up to the stranger, sniffing and wagging its tail. "You've read Tozer?"

"Of course," the man said, taking something from his coat pocket and giving it to the dog to eat. "You say that as if he were some sixteenth-century poet."

"Did the sixteenth century have notable poets?"

"My point exactly."

The man fed the dog another treat from his pocket.

"Are those breath mints you're giving him?" Will joked.

"I have a dog myself. I love them."

"So what Tozer book were you looking for?"

"Are you keeping the rest of the inventory in storage?"

Will shook his head. "You missed the going-out-of-business sale. And the shutting-my-doors barn burner. Oh, and the here's-the-reason-they're-shutting-me-down private giveaway. I only have my library."

"I bet it's considerable," the man said.

"No. Now my father-in-law's is considerable. Big enough to one day be donated to a college. To actually make an entire library out of it. Mine is a hodgepodge assortment. I only keep books I know I'll reread."

"You can't take it with you. Not where you're going."

Take what? Will wondered. *And going where?*

"The Set of the Sail."

"Excuse me?" Will asked.

"That was the specific title I was looking for."

"I'm not familiar with that one, though it doesn't mean I didn't have it."

"It's a collection of essays Tozer wrote. The title refers to having our sails set to the will of God so we'll be headed in the right direction no matter what storms life brings."

"Interesting," Will said. "Seems like a book I need to check out."

The man smiled. "It all starts with the Holy Spirit stirring our conscience. But the great con of the last few decades is we've replaced that word with science. And, of course, ourselves."

Will stood there, not sure what to say.

"I hope you end up finding the right one," the stranger told him.

"The right what?"

He smiled and brushed his hand through his thick, curly hair. "The right name for your dog, of course. Here, take these for him. He seems to like them."

The man handed him several round dog treats. Then as quickly as he had stopped Will on the sidewalk, he said goodbye and walked away. The dog looked confused, starting to follow the man, then staring at the treats in Will's hand. He suddenly sat and propped his two front legs up.

"Wish I knew what brand these are," Will said as he gave the dog another one, "and how expensive they are."

Walking to the car station again, he wondered who the man was and what his story happened to be.

3.

The older their three girls got, the louder their small house became and the greater the chasm sometimes felt between Amy and Will. They had always been different and even joked with their pastor about those vast differences during premarital counseling. Parenting had produced a whole new level of viewpoints and varying perspectives. Lately, especially in the last couple of years, every single act and decision Will made seemed at odds with Amy.

So naturally, bringing the dog home hadn't exactly helped matters. The girls couldn't believe it was for them to keep, asking him continually who it belonged to. Amy, upon first seeing it, was speechless, something that seldom happened to her.

"It's a stray I've been seeing lately. I couldn't leave it. And I can't take it anywhere."

"He's so cute," Callie said, her hand rubbing his head as if she were washing a car.

"He looks strange," Bella said, giving the mutt a funny look.

"Can we keep him?" Shaye asked. "He can stay in my room. He can use my old comforter."

"Okay, just calm down," Will said.

The first word Amy eventually said when she approached him in the laundry room was "Really?" It was the sort of one-word response that carried an entire encyclopedia of past uses inside its pages. One of those *really*s came after he told Amy he had quit his corporate job to open the bookstore. Just like scooping up this dog and bringing him home, that hadn't been a joint decision either.

Lately they hadn't been doing anything that could remotely deserve the word *joint*.

"I lost a business but gained a dog," Will said, trying to inject a little humor.

Even lame attempts like this were thrown to the side and replaced with frustration and anger.

"Do you realize the cost of keeping that?" Amy said. "We'll have to take it to the vet to get shots and see if it has a SYNK chip, and that's just for starters."

"There you go, instantly getting out the checkbook."

"That's all you talk about, so how can I not bring it up?"

"We haven't made any decisions."

"I haven't even been asked anything," Amy said. "You know the girls aren't going to want to take it back. We've had those conversations about getting a puppy. I thought we *decided* we weren't going to get one."

"We didn't. I didn't. That's not a puppy."

"Yeah. That's— I'm not sure what that is," she said, regarding the animal in a clinical fashion.

"I haven't paid a cent for him. Not yet."

"Of all the days, you do this today." She sighed and shook her head, heading to their bedroom with a basket full of clean clothes.

He went back to the girls, who were playing with the dog. Their joy was good—as always—to see.

"We have to name him," he said without asking Amy.

She didn't want the dog, so she didn't have to worry about names.

4.

The night was cold, the clear sky glossed over by the glow from the streetlamps and neighborhood houses. Will waited outside for the dog to do his business in the backyard, and while he stood on the steps to their patio, he looked up as he often did. Sometimes praying, sometimes planning, and sometimes simply peering into the silent space as he did now.

When will all this junk inside ever go away?

The wind cut against his bare arms sticking out of his T-shirt. Sometimes he liked to step out in the frigid weather just to wake up, just to try to get a little of the fog out of his mind. But the haze wasn't in his head; it was in his heart. It had started to suffocate his soul.

Believing wasn't the issue, nor was knowing the truth. It was following and obeying and getting with the program and not having this awful uncertainty running through his system day and night. It was a dizzy and breathless feeling, like deathly cold air on a subzero morning blowing through his veins.

Will thought once again about spending an hour on the network trying to find *anything* mentioning a book by A. W. Tozer called *The Set of the Sail*. What was utterly bizarre was there was no mention of that particular title or *any* other Tozer books online, not even the briefest of summaries. He would have to get out of the system to find backup data for that sort of information. Will used to consider it a nuisance to see things like this happening, to realize that anything related to Christianity was suddenly vanishing online. Now it was simply the reality of the way things were. What used to be called the internet had belonged to everyone. Now the network was monitored by the government.

"Come on, little guy," he said, regretting that he'd decided to bring the dog home.

Like pretty much everything Will did, bringing home the newfound mutt had prompted an argument with Amy. A bouquet of flowers would bring on a debate about spending money. Staying late at work would stir up the never-ending who-does-more-work fight they always seemed to have. She had recently increased her hours as a senior food technologist at Nestle-Mars Co., working overtime as often as allowed. It was always the same two-headed monster: time and money, money and time, both chipping and cutting and cracking an already-brittle foundation. When the dust settled and the girls were asleep and the nighttime routine set in, Will would try to find some respite. Momentarily freezing only distracted him from his doom.

Why can't I be like the rest of them? Not worrying about God and not feeling guilty for not being strong enough? Not carrying this load of fear and brokenness around while also hurting for all those who are so deluded, so far gone?

He thought about the words Amy had said not long ago: *"I wish I'd never married you."*

They were spoken, of course, in anger and were so unlike her. The apology that came the following day seemed to make it all fine. These were simple words that said he was acting worse than a jerk or that she couldn't get what he was doing or why. But, in reality, this had been a statement of faith, a battle cry, a declaration of war. The words weren't the sort that a simple *sorry* could erase. They had been carved in the concrete of the step he stood on, and every time he slipped out of the house, he could feel their edges against the heels of his feet.

Will knew she was right to say them.

He had waited long enough. It didn't matter that he was wearing socks and a T-shirt. Will stepped out into the yard to try to find the dog. As he rounded the tall arborvitae trees on one side that blocked the view of the street, Will saw the outline of a commuter car, sitting as if it was broken down. He couldn't see any light or anybody inside it.

He paused. Then he began walking toward it, the frozen ground cracking underneath his feet. When he was twenty yards away from the vehicle, the engine roared to life, and the car began to drive away, still without any lights inside or out.

Someone had been watching him. Why, he had no idea. At the moment he didn't care either. He had bigger problems to figure out. Starting with trying to find the mutt he'd let out here ten minutes ago.

5.

In the dream Will sits on an old wooden bench in the woods, not connected to anything, no SYNAPSYS to use as an intellectual crutch, no means to communicate with people other than talking to them. Like all dreams, this one feels real and distorted at the same time, and in this case he can feel the person next to him but can't get the person's attention. He can't find the words to say, so he remains silent even though he can still hear her beside him, breathing, moving, waiting.

Her.

The moment his mind whispers that word, he knows he's dreaming, yet he doesn't want to wake up. He wants to remain there, and he wants to finally speak. He wants to talk, to try to connect, and then to listen if she'll do the same.

But the leaves underneath his feet and the sun peeking through the trees turn black as he opens his eyes. The bench and the moment are gone.

Yet Amy is still there, still breathing and moving.

Still waiting.

6.

The snow on the playground in the midday sun made Will squint and wish he'd brought his sunglasses for lunch duty. More than one hundred kids from kindergarten to third grade played throughout the field, most of them having fun packing the snow now that temperatures had risen. As he walked down the sidewalk, making sure to scan all the kids, Callie and Bella remained close by, talking to him about their days and wanting him to watch and asking him to help roll the snowman. Spending time with the twins over lunch was an advantage of being his own boss.

Until, of course, I ended up firing myself.

He had signed up for this duty at their elementary school, something parents were encouraged to be a part of. Will would go a few times a month. Today he was glad to be busy, even if this wasn't exactly what he should be doing. Figuring out what was next was on the top of his to-do list, and it was the only item on it as well.

After being outside for ten minutes, he spotted a familiar figure walking from the parking lot and through the doors near the playground. Because he wasn't wearing his glasses and it was so bright, Will couldn't see the man's face clearly, and he didn't want to squint and appear to be closely examining him. The man began walking in his direction.

"Bookkeeper, do your kids go here?"

It was the guy with the dog treats, the one with the dark hair and beard, the one wanting to be his last customer.

"Yes," Will said. "Our three girls."

He didn't want to point out the twins to this stranger, but they did him the courtesy of suddenly making their presence known.

"Is this a special daddy-daughter thing today?" the man asked.

"Lunch duty. I think I'm the only father they have who does this."

"Good for you. Hey, at least you didn't have to take time off from work, right?"

The tone wasn't mocking, and the expression on the man's face made it appear that he was simply making a legitimate point.

"I guess you could say that."

"I'm friends with Donovan. Mr. Clark. The art teacher."

"Yeah, sure," Will said, never having heard about a Mr. Clark before.

"He's in upper middle school. Good guy. Used to work together." He paused for a moment and then gave Will a smile, extending his hand. "I'm Raylan. But I go by my last name. Hutchence."

Will shook his hand and introduced himself.

"How's the dog working out for you?"

"My wife was not happy."

That produced a loud chuckle. "Surely you weren't surprised by that. Bringing a living, breathing creature home to what's probably already a pretty loud and rambunctious household."

"Yeah."

"I need to get to my meeting and let you monitor these urchins. But I've thought about your bookstore closing down, about the book title I was looking for, about, really, the state of the book business."

"Is there a state?" Will asked. "I think it was overthrown years ago, and only a handful are in the rebellion, trying to fight a battle that can't be won. Amazon destroyed bookstores and publishing. Then Acatour helped destroy Amazon."

"That is the saddest thing I have heard in a very long time, my friend. Perhaps we need to stage a rebellion of our own. So . . . were you able to locate that book online?"

"No. I couldn't find a mention of any Tozer books. Every day more things are erased."

"Does that really surprise you not to find anything? You, the man forced to shut down his bookstore?"

The man reached into his jacket pocket, the same jacket he was wearing the other day, but this time he pulled out a business card instead of a dog treat. On it was his SYNAPSYS key—a set of words mixed together with numbers and colors. At the top it didn't have Hutchence's name but rather THE TRÉMAUX GROUP in big, bold letters.

"It's strange to hold a business card," Will said. "What's the Trémaux Group?"

"It's a French company I use to launder money and finance clandestine transactions," he said without blinking or the hint of a smile.

Will found himself thinking, *Wait. What?* until Hutchence laughed.

"No, just kidding. Sounds kinda like that, right? It's a business of mine."

"What kind of business?"

"The business of souls. Search that French name online. They haven't deleted him. Not yet. Look, contact me so we can keep talking. You can get out of the house. Just don't bring the dog."

The card in his hand suddenly felt heavier, more mysterious.

7.

Maybe he simply wanted to get out of the house, away from all the pink and purple and princesses, to hang with another guy.

Or maybe he could tell himself this was probing around for a possible job opportunity.

Perhaps something very curious about Hutchence made Will reach out and set a time to get together a few days later.

Then again, maybe Will just wanted to go to a bar to have some beer. Perhaps that's why he had arrived half an hour early.

Hutchence showed up as Will was on his second pint, and he ordered an iced tea, then asked about the dog.

"We came up with a name," Will told him. "Well, not 'we' but the girls. He's going to be Flip."

"Flip? As in I like to flip hamburgers on the grill?"

"Exactly. He shakes his thick hair, and his ears go back and forth in a funny way. They keep saying, 'Look, he's flipping his ears!' So, yeah, I'm now the proud owner of Flip."

Will shared for a few minutes about the girls driving him crazy but then dialed it down, realizing not everybody shared the love of stories about being a parent of young girls. "I start overtalking when it comes to books and our daughters," he said as an apology.

"That's fine. That's a world I certainly can't relate to. I've never had the patience to deal with kids."

"Not that into beer either, huh?"

"Ephesians puts it well. To not be drunk because it will ruin your life. Another version says it will lead to debauchery. To instead be full of the Holy Spirit. I realized one day that there was never anything *good* about drinking alcohol. It never led to anything remotely better for me. For a while in the life that was before true life, drinking only made me more angry and irritable, and I had a whole lot to be angry and irritable about."

"Yeah," Will said as he took a sip of his beer, not disagreeing with anything Hutchence had said. "Wish I had self-control like that."

The grin couldn't be hidden underneath Hutchence's beard. "In time. First things first. I hope that my words won't seem too intrusive. I know we've met in passing only twice. But with the things I want to talk about, the urgency of the now makes small talk not only seem tiny but also inane."

"No worries. Unless you tell me I can't order another beer."

"I won't judge any self-imposed debauchery. I will stay out of your way." He laughed, easing any tension. "So with your bookstore— I know the realities of owning any sort of retail shop you can walk into that isn't run by one of the giants. Mom and pop have passed away, and bricks and mortar have been torn down. Stores are no longer real. They're ghosts. And a bookstore to me feels like the yearly watching of *It's a Wonderful Life*. A nice fairy tale but good luck trying to sell it."

"If only you could have told me all this ten years ago," Will said.

"Yes, sarcasm, and I know you know all this. And yet I want to know the truth. What really happened?"

"With what?"

"What was the actual reason your store shut down? I don't believe it was revenue, correct?"

"Typically that's the reason a store shuts down," Will said.

Hutchence leaned over the table. "Yes, but yours wasn't a typical bookstore. You've gotten in trouble in the past for certain books you've sold. Right? For the sale of 'profane' works. For even publishing scurrilous books that are against the law."

How does he know all that? Will didn't want to take the bait, if that's what this was. "You said it yourself. Making money from a bookstore is a fantasy. No big mystery there."

"But it certainly seemed as if Ink might have had its best year yet," Hutchence said.

"Suddenly this is feeling a bit 'intrusive.'"

"That's why I started with that caveat. You see, Mr. Stewart, I've been paying attention to your store for some time."

"Really? I don't think I've ever seen you there, have I?"

The stranger shrugged, not answering, as if the question wasn't relevant. "I like paying attention to things of eternal value."

"But how'd you know about some of the pressures? What'd you say? How I've 'gotten in trouble.' That's not public. And I know Amy's not told anybody."

"Perhaps I know people on the other side."

"Tell me again what you do," Will said.

Once again Hutchence didn't answer but continued down the rabbit hole of his.

"The Sedition Act of 1918. Ever heard of that?"

He knows quite a bit of what's been happening. "Sure. Hasn't everybody?" Will joked.

"The first Sedition Act was enacted in 1918 when the United States was engaged in a little thing called World War I. It basically outlawed the use of abusive and disloyal language against our government or the armed forces. Speech that ended up producing 'contempt' for the American powers that be. Imagine that."

"Well, the government did manage to shut down things like Twitter and Facebook after they turned into hate machines," Will said.

"There's another act—the Matthew Shepard Hate Crimes Prevention Act. Passed in 2009."

Will shook his head, not knowing about that one either.

"This one protected people from hate crimes. Four years ago they modified it to include language and speech," Hutchence said. "The Hate Propagation Law. Restricting free speech and the freedom of ideas. A quiet little thing President Valdez ended up doing, and the very thing President Blackwood has used to systematically *outlaw* Christianity. So something the government created during a world war and that soon after the war ended was deemed inoperable has resurfaced in a very ugly and sinister way. Something meant to eradicate extremism from our language has become an extreme interpretation of a law passed almost thirty years ago."

"Yeah, and it didn't even take a third world war to create it."

"Oh, it's here," Hutchence said. "I see us in the worst war ever, one that's been ongoing since the dawn of time, since Adam and Eve left Eden. You don't view that as a fairy tale like most, do you?"

"Of course not."

"Then you'll understand when I say the spiritual war that's been happening on this planet has never been bloodier, and the rebellion against the dark forces has never been more depleted."

"A spiritual war?" Will questioned.

"Strange expression when nobody says it anymore. The notion of angels and demons seeming real instead of a movie by comic-book makers. You have been involved in a struggle for some time, and it might seem as if the Enemy has won, but the battleground has shifted for you."

"My biggest enemy is Visa," Will said with another cynical chuckle.

"No, it's the one who controls your debt."

"The bankers?"

"The serpent that tricked Adam and Eve, the great liar, the angel guilty of pride, the one who knows the end yet wants to take as many with him as he can."

Will finished his beer and needed another one fast. "So you're saying ultimately the devil closed my doors."

"Do you believe he's real? Not a notion or an idea but real and true, a leader of an army of demons?"

"Sure."

" 'Sure.' Your blasé tone is startling. Do you think when someone asked Winston Churchill if Hitler was real and controlling a deadly army ready to smother this whole world, he gave an apathetic 'Sure'?"

"I'm not trying to sound blasé or apathetic." *But I didn't think I'd be coming here to talk about heavy spiritual matters.*

"Our souls are assaulted daily, and yet we are all so passive, acting as if the bombs didn't just destroy the home around us and refusing to arm ourselves and go into battle. We are pacifists, not because of some strong belief to be so but because we don't have strong beliefs in the first place."

The cute server with the animated eyes momentarily stopped the conversation to check in with them, so Will ordered another beer, a stronger one.

"As I said, I'm not big into small talk," Hutchence continued.

"I guess I'm not used to big talk, then."

As he had done several times before, Hutchence scanned the bar, casually and without any suspicion on his face, yet Will knew he was watching for others.

"Perhaps conversations like this aren't a natural part of your life. What makes me curious is this: When you first began to be pressured by the city, when you first got into trouble, why didn't you stop?"

"Stop what?"

"Selling unlawful material. Instead, you, my friend, seemed to double down, going ahead and *publishing* a book, of all things."

Will didn't reply. Again he didn't want to take the bait, still having no idea where this guy had come from and what he ultimately wanted.

"It's nothing you have to deny," Hutchence said. "Six years ago the book was written. The author met you five years ago, and you reluctantly agreed to publish it. Correct?"

Will couldn't help smiling.

"*Consider This* by Pastor Brian Wallace," Hutchence continued. "Published by Water Street Books. Ring a bell?"

"Quite the bestseller."

"Why, Will? Surely some spark was lit that fueled the creation of that book."

"I was a means to an end. That was all."

"'An end'?" Hutchence pounded on the table, jarring Will from the melancholy coming over him. "This is just the beginning for you. Do you know what your sad little 'means to an end' ended up doing?"

"No clue."

"Pastor Brian said 1 Peter 3:15 was the inspiration to write it. That we must worship Christ as the Lord of our lives, as holy. And if someone asks about our hope as believers, we should always be ready to explain it. Always. So he wrote the book as a way for him to articulate that hope and for others to as well. When I asked a close friend of mine four years ago during a real time of debauchery for me—when I asked how he could have such hope in the midst of this ruinous world, he answered by giving me *Consider This*. In it were simple and straightforward truths. I had reached my end, Will, and this book helped open a door I didn't realize I was standing beside. And eventually, as faith became real and tangible in my life, as I started my new life, I always told myself one thing."

"What's that?"

"I promised I would meet the man who wrote this book that changed my life, and I would also meet the person responsible for it. I would meet them and thank them for their courage. So finally I've been able to thank you the same way I thanked Pastor Brian."

"Uh . . . sure." Will didn't want to say, "You're welcome," since he didn't feel he needed to be thanked.

"Did you receive any resistance in publishing that book?"

Will thought about the stress and anxiety that seemed to follow every single step of the process involved with putting *Consider This* together and finally printing it. Even he grew to realize something supernatural was happening, that some type of spiritual animosity had been stirred up by him and Pastor Brian. But Will didn't want to go back there and dwell on the unseen things of this life, especially not with this man. So he shrugged and shook his head.

"Didn't FBI agents talk to you on three different occasions about *Consider This* and search your bookstore and house?"

"How do you know this?" Will demanded as he sat up and leaned over the table so the stranger could see how serious he was.

"It was public knowledge," Hutchence said.

"They didn't prove anything. Being searched and investigated doesn't mean you're guilty."

"I'm sure all this hasn't affected your life. Loans you've tried to get. High school and college friends. Perhaps your social status. Or how the neighbors feel. Or even more personal, like the relationship with your wife—"

"What do you want?" Will asked, his tone saying he was one second away from getting up and walking back to his car or punching the man in the face.

Hutchence's mood suddenly changed and not because of Will's words but because of something he saw or realized. Was there someone in the pub he recognized? Or did he suddenly see the time?

"I can't tell you everything, because I can't stay, though I do know we'll talk again," Hutchence said. "Just one more thing. What if I told you that your store closing is a tiny window into the bigger conspiracy happening out there? And that it goes to the very top of those who control this world?"

"I've heard about conspiracies my whole life. No big surprise there."

"But you can't search them online and read what sort of things people are thinking. The World Wide Web used to have so many theories that it made them all sound the same, like some ludicrous punk rock record with the same track sounding like angry noise. Now they're all gone. Once again, forbidden because of things like the Hate Propagation Law and those monitoring it."

"What's this have to do with me?" Will asked.

Hutchence grinned and watched him for a minute as if they were playing the final hand in a poker game. "We both know what this has to do with you," Hutchence said.

Will didn't reply but looked across the table, trying to figure out exactly what Hutchence was suggesting. *He knows a lot, but he doesn't know that. There's no way he can.*

"That's not a threat, Will. That's not a gotcha! I know that you don't know me, and I know that the last year—the last few years—have surely been rough. Just answer one question: Have you ever thought about getting back at them, the forces that put you out of business?"

"I've seen it as a lost cause," Will said. "Especially when there are too many to fight. And when a lot of them can never be touched."

"My point *exactly*. Some can't be touched. Except—*except*—by a very, very select few."

Hutchence gave him that knowing look and that leading grin. "You are about to embark on something beautiful, Will Stewart."

8.

The couple in front of Will couldn't get enough of each other, pulling each other closer, her whispering in his ear, him kissing her neck, laughing and watching each other, and being oblivious to the man twenty years older waiting behind them for an Autoveh. They had been at the same bar and were now heading home. Perhaps this was a first date, or perhaps they were a steady thing. They could belong in any number of stories, but Will knew without a doubt their genre was romance. "Windswept and passionate and burning and forever after" sort of stuff.

For a while those passions can blow the sails of love deep into an ocean. But eventually they'll fade like all dreams. Reality—getting older, some might call it, or gaining wisdom, as others might say—would come, and people would learn that love and passion and desire can't survive during the storms. So instead of remaining out in the wild tides of a restless sea, most people returned to the safety and security of dry land, casting out their anchors and rolling up their sails.

I'm thinking of sails and storms. Maybe I need to get that Tozer book.

The couple climbed into the car and fell into each other's arms, laughing that Will was watching their antics. As the door shut and the Autoveh drove away, he looked at the wall of the station that lit up specifically for him. The ads and the video were tailored for him, not by a person but by countless well-tuned machines. The wonderful algorithms of life.

"The search for meaning doesn't have to take place inside your mind and in the pages of a deep book," a voice said as it showed a university library and a college student looking overwhelmed. "It can be found in a place full of adventure, in the promise of a grand journey." Soon the same college student was walking up what appeared to be a mountain somewhere far away, like New Zealand. "Sometimes we don't need to journey to find what we believe," the voice said as music began to play in the background. "Sometimes we journey to finally believe in ourselves again." The classic song "Still Haven't Found What I'm Looking For" played.

The machines literally can see what I'm feeling in my soul. At least that's how Will sometimes felt.

He could picture Amy's reaction if he signed up for this "adventure of a lifetime" the ad showed. *"Hey, honey, I need to find myself, so I'm heading to New Zealand for a month."* Amy would definitely make him take Flip.

When his Autoveh came, Will entered the car without thought, the destination already known. He had decided to make things easy tonight and take this instead of driving himself. As soon as the voice inside introduced itself, this time in the form of a woman, he interrupted with a curt "I'd like silence, please." Then he checked his messages on the front dash to see if Amy had replied to his last note. But so far she hadn't typed a word.

The problem wasn't that he needed to figure out what he believed. He knew that years ago and had dared to pursue exactly that, believing in himself as he set off for the promise of a grand journey. And for more than ten years, he'd been climbing a steep mountain, and each year the sights appeared a little less beautiful, and breathing became more difficult. For a while it seemed there was no summit in sight. He now wondered if he had not only been hiking up the wrong mountain but had also started in the wrong country.

He thought about the last words Hutchence had said to him: *"This is a starting point for you. If you're interested in continuing to talk and in pursuing something bigger, contact me. I'm not on the network and don't have a SYNAP-SYS, but the info you have will get to me via a third party. Let's keep talking."*

Perhaps Hutchence was right. Perhaps this wasn't the end but rather a beginning. Maybe the spark was still lit, just flickering in the dark where it had been stored away.

Maybe there was more work to do and a bigger adventure to come.

FIVE

Bird of Prey

1.

What a ridiculous spectacle.

Stuck and suffocating, Dowland stood beside the glass of the penthouse suite overlooking the dizzying grandeur of Nashville, the center point of celebrities and media that Los Angeles used to be before the earthquake of '28 hit, which was only four years after the 2024 winter wreaked havoc on the middle of the country and the already-struggling economy. Even though the city had been rebuilding for years, the devastation and decline of LA meant everybody and everything moved to Tennessee. Whenever he came back, he marveled at how alive the metropolis appeared, especially at nighttime. Cities and towns across the United States were cutting back on electricity costs but not Nashville. This city was only getting bigger and brighter.

Dowland thought about the first time he heard about the earthquake a decade ago. He had gotten a call from Kamaria, before they were married, before everybody's skulls got implanted with chips, before she stopped loving him. Even now, he looked back on that moment not as a foreshadowing but more as a black hole.

"My building just shook for a few minutes. I have to get out of here."

That's what Kamaria had said, but at the time he didn't really hear it because he was in a blackout, living large and blowing off steam as he tried to deal with his new profession, a James Bond kind of life.

"Jon, you need to get here. You need to help me."

She had been fine, of course, but that wasn't the point. Later that day, actually in the evening, he woke up in a stranger's apartment and replayed their conversation. Then Dowland had realized that he had laughed and dismissed Kamaria's terror. He was too busy, and she would be fine, and he really needed to go, and everything was going to be okay.

Ten years later Los Angeles was a ghost town. Southern California hadn't been obliterated by a tsunami or by falling into the ocean but rather by a series of natural disasters that had been predicted. The fires came first, worse than anybody could have imagined, propelled by another drought. Emergency crews dealt with people being trapped and carnage everywhere, so when the earthquake came, they were overwhelmed. It was impossible to get out of the city, yet the great exodus occurred. Electricity and water were gone, but since communication was better than ever, the rest of the world watched Los Angeles set ablaze, as if the city were filming the burning of Rome on the largest scale imaginable.

"You need to help me."

But no. Dowland hadn't been there for her. Even though he couldn't physically get to her—that would have been impossible—he could have been there emotionally. He could have lived up to what he told her about how much he loved her. But his drunken antics had taken over, and later on when he was halfway sober again, he retreated in shame. Yet Kamaria let it go, holding up her end of their relationship and their love.

She should have never married me in the first place. She should've stayed far, far away.

Los Angeles resembled their relationship in many ways. Along with the aftershocks that continued to shake the city for days, fires seemed to rage for months. So many buildings couldn't be saved and were left empty afterward. No water was left, so it wasn't a question of whether people would leave the city but how quickly. The cost to repair everything was too huge, and even though efforts had been made locally and globally with all the political rhetoric and celebrity nonsense, Los Angeles was left on life support after the earthquake.

He heard the heels walking from the bedroom and through the kitchen. Stella had dressed and looked as beautiful as ever.

"Want me to stick around?" she asked.

Dowland shook his head and then leaned over and kissed her on the cheek. He knew she didn't want to stick around. She liked him enough to drop everything whenever he contacted her to say he was in town. Stella even joked that she was his Nashville girlfriend, which in some ways was true. *"Yeah, but you don't have to pay girlfriends an hourly rate,"* he had told her. *"Oh yes you do,"* she had said. *"Only you pay them a lot more, and you don't always know exactly what you're going to get."*

That's why he liked Stella: she was smart. And with him she was honest and always had been. She hadn't minded when Dowland had talked about Kamaria, both when they were married and after they got divorced. He didn't like talking about Kam to other women, but sometimes the drinking loosened his tongue.

"You seem more tense than usual," Stella said as she slipped on her long overcoat.

"Yeah."

"I don't have to leave." Blue eyes lingered on him, still young enough not to have let the world erase the tenderness inside them.

"You need to find a good man to take you away from guys like me."

"Then I'd need to move to another city," she said, flipping her blond hair over her shoulder. "I don't think there are any left in Nashville. At least any that aren't taken."

"Are you busy tomorrow?" Dowland asked.

"I don't have to be."

He wasn't even sure what day tomorrow would be.

"Maybe I'll call."

She grinned and traced the scar on his right jaw with her finger. "Maybe I'll answer."

She left without saying anything else. They never said *hello* or *goodbye*. Rather, it was like this. Every time. And Dowland always knew what to expect.

With the door shut he knew he would be alone again, feeling this restlessness inside, wishing he could take some of the energy from the city below and plug it into his soul. He wanted some of the life out there, some of the bright lights to illuminate the darkness inside him.

Dowland had flown from Miami to Nashville to pursue the most promising lead Sergei had found on Reckoner. Lots of the leads he had uncovered had gone nowhere, and some in fact had been deliberate decoys and dead ends.

Fortunately, Sergei knew how to tease out the wandering leads going nowhere. Tomorrow Dowland would pay a nice little surprise visit to whoever was using Reckoner's name off the network grid.

After finishing the bottle of ridiculously overpriced vodka, he found himself scrolling through all the photos of Kamaria and him. Thousands he hadn't dumped off his SYNAPSYS. Each picture stung a bit, and each minute of the night somehow turned into smoke. His memories of her weren't chronological—or logical, for that matter. They were random bursts of information. He saw a picture of their trip to Greece and then a picture of the time he decided to tell her what he really did and shared it with her by joking about it. There was the quote from the Bond movie with Daniel Craig—he couldn't remember which one—where he was asked about his occupation, and his reply was classic.

"That's not the sort of thing that looks good on a form," Bond said.
"And why is that?"
"I kill people."

Kamaria, naturally, hadn't taken this revelation very well. She had been scared at first, but eventually she learned to accept it. Like overlooking his selfish response to the earthquake, she had also chosen to accept his job, even though Dowland knew she was actually in denial.

The more photos he looked at and the more he drank, the closer he drew to the inevitable. He was in her city, so how could he not? The teeny, tiny voice of reason that still was somewhere inside him was lost at sea and couldn't be heard over the waves. He decided to contact Kamaria. To at least let her know he wasn't far away.

"Kam," he said. Then he heard the ding for his message to start. "It's me. I know I shouldn't . . . but I am. I'm in Nashville. For work."

He paused for a minute, looking out the glass again, wondering where she might be. "I have a job. One of those 'one more job is all I need and that's it' sort of jobs. Financially I'll be set."

Do I sound drunk? Is my voice slurring?

Of course she could tell. He didn't even have to say anything, and she would have known.

"There's still a chance, Kam. I can change. We can change. We were a good thing—I know that. The way I felt around you. Nothing's ever made me feel more alive. And right now this world's oppressive. It's everything and any-thing, and right now it's ultimately nothing."

He wasn't making sense, and he wasn't quite sure what his point was other than telling her he wanted to see her. That he wanted her.

"Come find me. I'm at the Spire. I'm just . . . It'd be good to talk. Just come up here. Top floor as always. Just like James Bond."

That was an attempt at a joke, but she had stopped laughing at those a long time ago. Maybe one day he'd make her laugh again. The very thought of it made him laugh too, even though he had no idea why.

2.

Half-conscious, Dowland didn't feel the two hands yank him out of bed, but he did feel the carpeted floor when he fell face-first. Without thinking, only reacting, he turned over and reached to his side for his Beretta but instead felt his boxer shorts. Opening his eyes, he saw the body standing over him, the face looking down. A hand gripped his throat, the grip so strong it both choked him and lifted him up, forcing him against the wall.

As Dowland curled his fist and tried to gain his balance, sharp metal jutted into the right side of his throat.

"This twelve-inch blade is sharp enough to cut both your jugular veins and your carotid arteries. So do not move."

The voice, husky and controlled, didn't sound familiar. That didn't mean anything, not to Dowland. He knew he had plenty of enemies out there, a lot he had never met or heard in person.

"Turn on the light so you can see me," the man said, keeping the knife against Dowland as he stepped over to the nearest light.

The assailant was several inches taller than Dowland, who was six foot one, and he looked like solid muscle. Not overblown to look impressive but the kind who could really hurt another man. The square face and expressionless eyes looked at him. He was in a custom-fitted two-piece suit, with the barrel of a gun sticking out above his belt.

"I'm going to tell you this once, okay?" the man said. "And I don't care who you are and who you work for and what you do. You got that? You might work for someone powerful, but so do I. The kind you don't want to mess with."

Dowland refrained from laughing as he normally might, his head still swimming in alcohol. *You have no clue, buddy.*

"These late-night calls to Kamaria, the messages for her to call you back, for her to see you, for her to pay attention—these are officially stopping tonight."

So that's what this is about. Examining the man with this new bit of information in mind, Dowland assessed what relationship the attacker might have to Kam. Hired hand? Bodyguard? *No. He's the boyfriend.*

Kamaria always had a thing for strong, dangerous men. The more alpha, the better. That was one reason she had been with him and why she had stayed as long as she did. He didn't look like a wrestling champion as this buzz-cut machine did. But he wasn't exactly the cuddly type either.

"How'd you get in here?" Dowland asked.

"I wouldn't worry about that. I'd worry more about whether you'll see the sun come up over our wonderful city."

Dowland had regained his clarity. With the man a few feet away, holding the knife out but no longer against his skin, he surveyed whether he could act. *No way I can without being cut, even just a little.*

"You do anything to me, and you're a dead man," Dowland said.

"Don't threaten me. She told me not to believe any of your drunken lies."

"I'm not the threat here."

The man pressed the blade against him, this time slicing the skin above his abdomen. Square-Jaw leaned over to share his hot, peppermint breath up close. "You're weak, and you prey on helpless people. Like Kamaria. But I'm not like them."

Dowland could feel the blade inches into his gut. He gritted his teeth, not backing away from the man. "The next time I see her, I'll tell her you feel this way."

The guy cursed, then whipped the knife toward his ear, the blade burning through it.

Dowland shouted and cupped it, feeling blood on his palm.

"You leave this city and never set foot in it again," the man said. "You never contact Kamaria again. If you do either of them, I'll be back with my blade. And the next time I'll cut off more than your earlobe."

As the assailant walked away, Dowland first scanned the room, then realized his handgun was tucked away where he always hid it in a hotel room: underneath his bed. For a moment he thought about getting it, but he knew Kam's boyfriend had one too. The last thing he needed was a shoot-out in the penthouse suite. Publicity like that was frowned upon, even if he had jurisdiction with the local cops and could get them to go away.

Feeling dizzy and still holding his cut ear, he heard the sound of alarm from Alfred: "Sir, you are experiencing dramatic blood loss due to the removal of your lobule on your left auricle." His SYNAPSYS spoke in an English accent like an elderly butler, like the kind Batman had.

"My lobule on my what?" Dowland asked, taking a look at his right hand and seeing it drenched in blood.

Then he looked on the floor and saw what Alfred was talking about. His cleanly cut earlobe lay on the carpet right by his feet. Dowland cursed, shaking his head, and reconsidered grabbing his Beretta.

Not now. Just wait.

Square-Jaw had just signed his death certificate. He had no idea. For the moment Dowland needed to find a towel to stop the bleeding. Then he needed to find someone who could stitch his earlobe back in place.

3.

After the doctor who couldn't speak English left with her medic android, who translated for her, Dowland sat on the couch with a cup of coffee mixed with rum from the room's wet bar. The bottom half of his ear was secure in its black bandage that protected the work the robot had done. The wound wasn't deadly, of course, but he needed some instant plastic surgery. The doctor told him in Vietnamese that they couldn't simply sew the earlobe back on, but they would recreate one with on-the-spot plastic surgery, the sort they did for the wealthy and famous who didn't want to leave their homes and possibly be seen having the work done. Dowland just needed to keep the bandage on for a few days to make sure half his ear wouldn't fall off.

The news he watched on the digital wall in his room showed off the daily circus of hell, as he liked to call it. Even though world hunger had been solved and they had nearly cured cancer, people still wanted to hurt and kill one another. Not only over gorgeous supermodels like Kamaria, and not only over issues of religion and politics, but because of drug deals and gang violence and white males becoming unhinged with females. Every single week.

So much for the drug and gun and gender policies that are enforced.

The report that made him sit up and turn up the volume came out of Chicago.

"Half a dozen offices in Incen Tower in Chicago were vandalized overnight as someone broke in to deliver handwritten notes that all said the same thing. There were more than one thousand of these notes, each in the same handwriting, which authorities are trying to identify."

The news shared only a little portion of the note, choosing to be careful not to offend viewers with something as brazen as a Bible verse. Dowland was curious, however, so he asked to hear the whole note, which had, of course, been shared by many on the network. One woman who received the note at her desk read the whole thing in a video:

> *Wake up. Do you find desires inside you that nothing in this world can satisfy? The most probable explanation, as C. S. Lewis wrote, is that you are made for another world.*
>
> *There is a heaven, friend. But there is a caveat.*
>
> *Jesus. Not the historical figure that's put in the same category as Gandhi and Martin Luther King Jr. and Mother Teresa. No.*
>
> *Jesus, the Son of God, who said, "I am the way, the truth, and the life. No one can come to the Father except through me."*
>
> *There is a hell too, fellow traveler.*
>
> *The ones who control this world, who control YOU, know this. They serve the god of this world.*
>
> *"Satan, who is the god of this world, has blinded the minds of those who don't believe. They are unable to see the glorious light of the Good News. They don't understand this message about the glory of Christ, who is the exact likeness of God."*
>
> *It is time to know who is controlling you. It is time to open your eyes.*

It is time for the world to understand the message of Christ,
which a few have decided to forever silence.
  Sincerely,
  Reckoner

Dowland was surprised not by the rhetoric of the message but by the way the notes were delivered.

More than a thousand notes, each with the same handwriting . . .

Surely these were artificially generated. No way one person could have written that many. What would the point of that have been?

Before he could utter Mel Bohmer's name, the incoming message arrived, signaled by the slight pinching alert around his forearm.

"Open," he called out, revealing Mel sitting right in front of him, still by the pool, still under an umbrella in the sun. "I was about to call."

"Glad you're awake to see it," the old man said with a mocking grin. "Is that a new fashion piece on your ear?"

"It's a story not worth mentioning. Any idea how the Reckoner got into Incen Tower?"

"I was going to ask you, Mr. Dowland, since this is exactly what you're being paid for."

"There's a reason he hasn't been found. Yet."

"I just got off a rather dreadful conference call. They used to be so awful, being on a phone with four others, interrupting each other and talking over people and then having awkward silences. They were brutal. Technology has made it so that you feel as if you're in the same space as others, like the way we're talking now. This conversation was brutal for a whole other reason. These people do not have conference calls. That's how—*frustrated* is the word I'll use, which is so tame compared to the reality—but that's how frustrated they were to have to be talking about this nuisance. *Again.*"

"I understand," Dowland said.

"Do you?"

"Yes. *Sir.*"

Mel chuckled. "Just look at that fire inside you," he said. "I miss it, you know. Sometimes I do. It's what made me. It's the thing that makes people like you and me. But the difference is you still need to contain it sometimes. The men and women I had a nice impromptu meeting with this morning wouldn't like that fire. Someone would put it out immediately. Just because they can."

"I don't like being questioned about my job," Dowland said.

"Then do it."

Before he could reply, Mel was gone. Dowland cursed and headed for the shower, filling his cup along the way.

4.

The black condor stood on a cement statue, from head to tail more than five feet long. It had an ugly face spotted with yellow, and a sloping, ivory-colored beak that resembled a dagger. The beast didn't move but watched him as he passed by, as if it was guarding the entrance to the jungle inside the large building.

The humidity and temperature and overhanging trees made it feel like the Amazon, but in fact this was the tenth through fifteenth stories in the National Zoo of the Americas, which had finally been finished five years ago. Dowland had never been inside since he didn't have children and didn't really have the time or the desire to check out a hundred different types of animals from all over the world. The zoo was open for guests 24-7, 365 days a year. Being built inside a skyscraper, the first of its kind, the state-of-the-art zoo allowed control over the environment and permitted people to visit anytime they wanted. It had been very costly, of course, but not too expensive for Jackson Heyford, the man behind this monstrosity.

A small path had been cut through the trees, winding around bushes and underneath branches that held singing and sitting winged birds. He didn't stop to study them, but he could spot a variety of unusual species. One had bright red feathers and a sleek golden crest and was sitting next to a large metallic-blue macaw. Another bird wandered out of the small pond, its wide rainbow beak looking two sizes too big on an otherwise stumpy body. Dozens of other birds flew overhead and past him. A hummingbird seemed to like him and stayed nearby.

Dowland followed the trail to the back of the echoing chamber, toward a hallway marked Exit. The door he was looking for was tucked away in the semidark of a hall resembling a cave and housing owls. He ignored the Do Not Enter: Staff Only sign and opened the door.

"Show overview," he said, wanting to see one more time the image that Sergei had sent him. The photo of the woman appeared again. Thirty-three years old. Pale skin afraid of the sun, and hair that went months without getting cut. It made sense that she worked at the zoo, hiding away from society, surrounded by birds as her coworkers. What didn't make sense about Regina Daigle was how she could have gotten involved with the group behind the recent national disturbances.

A place like this is as good as any to be out of the public eye.

The office smelled like burned coffee and was littered with bird feathers. Several cages contained more exotic birds that spoke and called out and chirped and wailed. A number of screens were open on the wall, showing half a dozen spots in the space known simply as Birdland. Dowland scanned the visuals, knowing he had easily been seen walking into the building.

There she is.

Dressed in a khaki uniform of a button-down shirt, pants, and a cap, Regina hurried over another path in the building. It was impossible not to notice the anxiety on her face.

Dowland turned around and sprinted out of the office, then retraced his steps, nearly stepping on a peacock and striking a bird in flight with his forehead. He raced up a small hill, then down, as he scanned the area to figure out where she was heading. Stopping for a moment, sucking in air, he listened. A soft, mumbling voice spoke nearby, and he rushed toward it.

Regina was twenty-five yards from the entrance when she looked back and saw him. Panic covered her face, and she began to race to the doorway.

"Stop!" he called, taking out his handgun and aiming it at her.

She didn't stop, so he raised the Beretta and fired off a round. The very loud shot pulsed through the space and sent what seemed like a thousand birds bursting into the domed ceiling.

The woman froze, looking back at him, her arms and hands pointed at him as if she were trying to shove him away.

"Don't move," Dowland said. "I don't want to waste another bullet in here."

He didn't have to ask for her name, nor did he have to follow any ridiculous protocol the way police and FBI agents had to. Instead, he simply walked over to her, his gun still aimed at her, his focus on the surrounding area to make sure nobody else was there.

"You need to come with me," he told her. "We need a private place to talk."

As she was about to say something, the doors opened, and a family of five with young kids burst into Birdland. Dowland put down the gun right away, expecting Regina to stay put and smile and act as if they were having a nice chat about birds. Instead, she took off again, actually knocking into him as she ran in the opposite direction of the family. They didn't pay her any attention, their focus being on all the flying animals above them. Dowland shook his head and sighed and then started to follow the woman.

The very stupid woman.

Why do they always have to run?

He paused for a minute, then walked back to the parents who had just walked in. "You guys might want to go look at the monkeys or the dolphins," he said, holding out his Beretta in plain sight.

Without saying another word and with looks of terror on their faces, the couple promptly grabbed their kids by the arms and led them out.

5.

There was no other way to exit this room, so he didn't have to worry about Regina escaping. But before he could walk back into the office to see if she was hiding there, a group of birds swooped down and began to attack him.

At first it was just a few small birds. Colorful birds about six inches long, pretty except for the large eyes and the pointed black beaks. They came in a swarm, perhaps half a dozen, and they launched themselves at him. The beaks struck him and punctured the skin on his neck and forehead and arms. At first Dowland thought they were a nuisance, but then he realized they were indeed attacking him. He tried to shoo them away with his arms and then attempted to swat or bat them away with the Beretta. He was successful a few times, but more birds began to come. All different types in all different colors, all of them dropping down and slamming against his arms and legs and head.

A white medium-sized bird about ten inches long seemed the angriest. It had black tips on its wings and tail and a tiny yellow tip on its bill. Dowland saw the yellow tip since the bird was trying to peck the skin off his cheek. He cursed as he flailed and cowered and tried to shoo it away.

The number of birds kept increasing. One of them pecked and tore some of the bandage on his ear.

These aren't regular birds. You couldn't train all these birds to attack like this.

They had to be artificial. But their lifelike beauty was incredible.

Then he remembered who had built this place. *Jackson Heyford could create these.*

Dowland ran to one side of the building, noticing the colored-glass window with the round glow of the sun behind it. After his first two shots merely cracked the glass, he touched the button on his Beretta next to the safety. Then he shot one more carefully aimed round, this one coming from the second barrel underneath the primary one. The caliber was the same as the other .40-caliber bullets he was using, but this one packed the power of a rocket launcher. It was very expensive and illegal, and he carried only one in the Beretta's magazine. Sure enough, the explosive punctured the glass, opening up a hole the size of a picnic table and revealing the blue sky beyond it.

Suddenly all the birds seemed to notice the gaping hole in the room and swarmed to it, flying out as if they were sucked by a cosmic vacuum cleaner. Dowland watched them dispersing into the heavens, finally free.

He heard Regina's footsteps before he saw her. When she appeared before him, she seemed oblivious to Dowland as she gaped at the escaping birds.

"No!" she cried out, tears coming to her eyes. "What did you do?"

"What did I do?" he said as he winced and looked at all the bloody marks on his arms. "I'm not the one sending a pack of birds to attack people."

"Do you know how much those are worth?"

"Do you know how much I care? Those are artificial, right?"

She didn't answer but continued looking at the cracked glass as if the birds might come back.

"We need to get out of here right now," Dowland said to her.

Regina still seemed more concerned about the birds leaving than the gun he was holding.

"The change of environment . . . ," she began to say. "They got confused and didn't know what to do. The whole change of temperature and the sky above them caused them to act like real birds."

"Doesn't the public think they're real birds?"

She looked at him with a defiant stare. "What do you want?"

He pointed the gun at her forehead. "I want you to come with me. Right now."

6.

The woman seemed less anxious about sharing information than she had been about initially talking to Dowland. He had escorted her out of the building, and they had walked several blocks to a fast-food restaurant, where they sat in a booth to talk. He showed her the images of the Reckoner that he had been given, and then he asked about her connections with him.

"I've never had contact with this person you call Reckoner. I haven't done anything except provide shelter for someone who knows him."

Dowland pointed to one of the pictures where Regina could barely be recognized. "This is you, right?"

"Yes."

He pointed to the guy in the suit. "So who's this?"

"That's Keith Burne. A longtime family friend. He came to visit last year."

He thought she was lying but then enlarged the grainy image. *She could be right. This could be Burne.*

"So these other pictures. Is this Burne too?"

"I can't tell. Maybe."

"Is Burne the one going by these aliases?"

She shook her head. "I don't know. All I know is he contacted me and asked for help. A place to stay. I was a childhood friend of his wife. His ex-wife."

"Are you still friends?"

"No. We lost touch years ago. But I remained in contact with Keith and his daughter."

"When was the last time you saw him?" Dowland asked.

"A few months ago. He contacted me and needed a place to stay. I have a spare bedroom. He was around for about a week or so."

"Any contact since then?"

She shook her head, and for some reason Dowland believed her.

"You're also part of a group that meets twice a week, correct?"

Her eyes gave her away easily, yet Regina didn't seem to have a reason to stay quiet. "Yes. But how do you know these things?"

"That's not your concern," he said, looking at the frayed cap she still wore.

"Surveillance on a private citizen is illegal."

"So is propagating hate."

She shook her head. "'Propagating hate.' That's what you call a group meeting for worship?"

"I didn't come up with the definition, miss. The lawmakers did."

"Carrying concealed weapons is against the law too. Or did you forget that one?"

"I didn't conceal it from you," he told her, opening his jacket and showing it tucked to his side in a holster. "It's easier to carry this way. Plus, I have the authority to carry it."

"I assumed as much. Keith warned me about men like you."

"There are women like me too. Don't forget those."

Regina looked around the restaurant full of families and people taking their lunch break. Nobody paid them any attention.

"I can easily have you arrested," Dowland said.

"'The Devil is about to throw you in jail for a time of testing.' That's a passage from Revelation. Are you the devil this verse is talking about?"

"Lady . . . I've been the devil for quite a few people."

He knew that she had told him everything she could and that she didn't worry about being thrown into jail. *She probably thinks she'll get some big reward in the afterlife if she gets jail time.*

"You're going to be watched very carefully, Regina. You're a simple phone call away from your life being utterly destroyed. Not by going to jail but by being put into a personal prison. Losing your job and your friends and any part of your life that you love. So if you're contacted by Keith Burne or anybody associated with him, you need to call this person to get hold of me."

Instead of a digital card, Dowland gave her a sheet of paper with a name and a network ID number. As her long, bony fingers took the sheet, he was surprised to see they weren't shaking. "If I were you, I might be a little more scared about the current situation you're in," he told her.

She smiled. "I can say the same about you."

7.

Of course his name is Zander. And of course she's dating him.

The information on Kamaria's boyfriend filled the entire glass windshield in his rented Audi. Dowland studied it as the car remained running and parked at the curb next to the gate for the high-end neighborhood southwest of Nashville. The details he had been given reported that on most Friday mornings Zander's nondescript Autoveh left this community between nine and a quarter after nine. Dowland read the details on the man he was about to meet again.

> Zander Stock. Twenty-seven years old. CEO for Zander
> Entertainment. Primary shareholder for Zander Entertainment:
> Jackson Heyford. Worth: $34.5 billion.

More details filled the screen, but Dowland toggled through it with his finger to find what he wanted: the personal stuff only people like him had the ability to access.

> Addictions: Functioning alcoholic. Steroid abuser. Occasional
> Pique user. Police record: Public drunkenness, theft, assault,
> battery.

The assault and battery charges looked interesting, so he tapped for more information. Several dates and charges were listed, but he saw a charge of battery one year ago and another charge of assault only two months ago. Both charges had the name Kamaria Dareigo by them.

She never learns.

Now there was no question about his plans for this cold but clear morning. Sure enough, the square, gray-colored vehicle cleared the guard and was allowed to exit and start its usual morning commute to work. A guy like Zander used an Autoveh for publicity reasons, to look like a noble and upstanding citizen in compliance with environmental protection. He also wanted to travel discreetly.

Dowland followed him for ten minutes before speeding up next to the Autoveh as they wound around on a two-lane country road through rolling hills and by large lawns. The rental car quickly overtook Zander's car. Dowland jerked the steering wheel, slamming into the front of the Autoveh and sending it directly into the ditch next to the road.

The Autoveh balanced itself as it hit the side of the hill, and Dowland jammed on the brakes of his Audi, sent it into reverse, and then shifted quickly into Drive again. He plowed into the side of the Autoveh, denting and cracking its steel frame. The air cushion in the Audi went off, but it took him only a few seconds to rip it apart with his pocketknife. Dowland got out of his car and ran to the other side of the Autoveh, shooting the side window instead of bothering to wait until it opened itself.

If the bullet struck Zander, that was fine, but he hoped to have one more little discussion before the inevitable happened.

The big guy with the shaved head was screaming inside his Autoveh, not because he had been shot but because he was terrified. Glass littered the floor and the seat as Zander held up his hands, his suit jacket ripped and his tie hanging to one side.

Dowland didn't bother to wait. He struck Zander across the cheekbone with the barrel of his Beretta, hard enough to break bone and tear skin and hear the wailing of this weak man now that he wasn't sneaking up on him in the darkness.

"Get out," Dowland told him. The large knife he had brought was folded in his pocket, but part of him wanted to use it. Especially for what Zander had done to his ear.

"I said get out. There. Go over there and kneel."

Zander did as he was told. Sweat covered his forehead as the gash against his cheek gushed blood. He knelt as he was told, holding his arms above his head.

Dowland looked around to see if there were any houses within sight but saw none. He walked over to Zander and shoved the top barrel of his gun into his ear.

"I'm going to ask you this one question," Dowland said as he jammed the Beretta forward so Zander would be forced to lift his big head up. "Who sent you?"

"Why does it matter?"

"Because men like you never take the initiative themselves."

Zander spit out curse words along with blood. Dowland only dug the barrel deeper into his ear, seeing some of the skin tear.

"Look at me. Look at me! You've met death today, and you're staring him in the face, and the only last words I want you to utter are the first and last name of who sent you. Tell me now."

Dowland needed to know. Just to make sure.

Laughter. First barely audible coming from Zander, then trembling aloud, then suddenly convulsing into a shivering tornado. The laughter was soon joined with more mocking curses. "Here's a parting gift to you," Zander said. "One you'll love. One you already know. Kam sent me. She told me to kill you. Not just warn you but kill you. She hates you *that* much to plead with someone to execute you."

For a moment Dowland froze, expecting this information but still aching inside. *No, it can't be true. How could she? He's lying. She would never do something like this.* The moron crawling around in the ditch beneath him coughed up more blood and continued to laugh.

Dowland pressed the trigger. Then pressed it again. Then again. And again. As he stared at the mess on the ground at his feet, he could feel the emotion pulsing through him. His right arm shook, and he had to take deep breaths to get control of his anger.

Looking into the sky, he sucked in air and let it out again. *She really did do it.* The love of his life and the woman he would take back today without any question hated him so much she had gotten someone to do the very thing he did for a living.

Zander's laugh had shown him that Kamaria had told him enough. He knew that Dowland would never hurt her, would never touch her. His fury would have to be bottled and thrown into the sea and set adrift.

The same love so ripe with passion can become so raw with hate.

Dowland couldn't—wouldn't—hurt her. But he knew how to answer this wonderfully sweet valentine from her. He was going to make the rest of her life a living nightmare. The worst kind of hurt doesn't break your skin but crushes your soul.

I still know you, and you think you know me, but you have no clue.

Nobody knew him, and that was a good thing.

Nobody needed to see all the darkness residing in his shattered soul.

8.

"You still seek the soul you think you miss."

Dowland wished the man speaking through the Autoveh was present so he could reach over and punch him in the mouth.

"Stop talking like Yoda with a German accent," Dowland said.

Mel Bohmer's laughter echoed in Dowland's head, somehow louder than any song he might be playing.

"See, *this* is why you're the man for this."

"The man for what?"

"The man to do the necessary dirty work," Mel said to him.

"And why is that?"

"Because you can't help but be yourself, Mr. Dowland. And you can't help but be honest, even to men like me."

"We're all going to die one day. Nobody's immortal. Not even powerful men like you."

"I agree, though at times I feel some of my associates actually consider themselves immortal."

"Immoral, yes, but you can't add a *t* to it."

"Your passion is your wound, Dowland. You temper it with your vices and use it with your profession."

"Is this a counseling session?"

"No, this is an intervention, and I'm the only one here who cares one bit about you. There's something fascinating about your savagery, Dowland. About the absolute out-of-hand way you approach life."

"That's why you employ me," he said.

"We could find any sort of lowlife who can show instability and absolute chaos. But you— It's different with you. And this isn't the first time I've vouched for you."

Dowland wanted to tell him to stop being so wonderfully charitable, but he had enough common sense not to say this.

"I'm fine with your habits, with how you need to cope," Mel continued. "I've never killed a man with my own hands, so I can't imagine what it would feel like. I've imagined this too. Many times. But I know I'd be afraid when it came time. I couldn't. So the weight of what you carry with you— I'm sure I can't imagine that. But the reason we pay you and not some insane thug is because you *can* carry that. And look and act normal."

It was two hours after Dowland had officially ended Zander's pathetic life on the side of a road. He had done the necessary job of cleaning up the situation, getting rid of both the body and the car. He didn't have to worry about the authorities; Dowland had to worry about men like Mel.

"These little messes you continue to make on the way, like this morning—they have to stop. You can blow off steam and get into barroom fights or go off on benders. That's fine. But this morning is a no-no. These are the things that can leave breadcrumbs for those who might be so bold as to follow them. You cannot risk the vitality of what's at stake here. I'm stepping out *again* and vouching for you. I won't do it again if you do something else stupid like that."

"I understand," Dowland said.

"Wow."

"What?"

"No witty retort. I think, perhaps, you do get it."

"I've always gotten it. It's just that sometimes the better parts of me—or I should say the lesser parts of me—drown out reason and rationale. This won't happen again."

There was a pause from Mel, and then he eventually spoke. "I, too, would fight to get her back. A woman like her is a miracle. She is a diamond in this charcoal world."

"I agree."

"Yes, but you decided long ago to light the charcoal around her with gasoline, torching everything. Sometimes you have to accept what nature gives you. The fire and the ice."

"I understand," Dowland lied.

"Tomorrow a plane will take you to your next destination."

He didn't ask where, nor did he ask what he was supposed to do once he arrived. All he did was utter two very familiar words. "Sounds good."

He tapped the surface of the Autoveh's console as the robot driver pretended to navigate the car. For a moment he opened his palms and looked at them.

These are the hands that have done nothing right. The limbs that have done far too much wrong.

They weren't finished either. They still had a great deal to do.

SIX

The Beginning of the End

1.

For the first time since meeting him, Cheyenne saw Jazz looking worried. That casual and carefree attitude he first carried was gone.

"There's no question. We're being followed."

They hadn't spoken much since getting in the Hummer and driving, first around snow-covered roads that snaked and sneaked through the endless Rocky Mountains, then as they arrived on a long stretch of highway that made her eyes droop and her mind drift off for a while in the morning light. Since waking up, Cheyenne hadn't bothered asking Jazz more questions. She couldn't help thinking of the painting in his bedroom titled *The Destruction of Sodom and Gomorrah*.

As Cheyenne looked out her window at the side-view mirror, she spotted the nondescript gray vehicle that resembled many of the other commuters on the highway. She recalled seeing it half an hour ago.

"Are they following you or me?" Cheyenne asked.

"Right now there's only a 'you' they know about. But that might change soon after they scour every inch of space back at the bunker. Somehow they're tracking you."

"How?"

Jazz shook his head. "We solve that after we figure out how to get rid of our tail."

"How do we do that?" she asked.

After thinking for a few moments, Jazz began to look at the dashboard of the Hummer. Then he turned a few times to peek at the back. His eyes moved back and forth, and then his demeanor changed as he appeared amused.

"What's so funny?" she asked.

"God has a funny sense of humor," Jazz said. "I'm thinking of the guys I got this vehicle from. Sketchy dudes. This Hummer isn't registered. It's off the market, off the grid, off everything. They used it to smuggle drugs and guns."

"Friends of yours?"

He shook his head and chuckled. "Just people I met along the way in my other world. Look, they can't see in here because of the tinted windows. Are you claustrophobic?"

"Umm . . . I'm a bit frightened to answer that."

"Seriously. Yes or no."

"No. Tight spaces don't frighten me."

"Okay, good." Jazz continued looking in his rearview mirror. "We're going to get off at the next rest area coming up in about ten miles. I want whoever is following us to come by and take a peek into the vehicle."

"Are you crazy? Why?"

"They're looking for you, not me," Jazz said. "So they're not going to find you."

"Where will I be?"

"A place claustrophobic people would really, really hate. But you gotta get inside it while I'm driving."

Cheyenne thought for a moment. "Would it be a place large enough for drugs and guns?"

"Yes. Lots of them."

2.

She barely fit into the space in the back cargo area of the vehicle. Cheyenne had to perform some magic to figure out how to get the floor panel off, climb inside, and then position the panel back over her. Inside the small space was a rubberized area three feet long and three feet wide but only twelve inches deep.

"Wish you weren't so tall," Jazz said as she shifted the seats in the back in order to move the floor panel.

"Blame it on my Comanche heritage. They were supposedly among the taller Native American tribes."

"Obviously that was on your mother's side. I've seen your father, and that boy don't look like no Comanche."

She could only laugh, having heard that before. Cheyenne did a trial run, slipping into the narrow enclosure, curling up in a ball sideways, and tightening her arms and legs to her sides.

"Good thing I'm so flexible," she said to Jazz.

"Can you stay like that for a while?"

"How long?"

"I don't know."

"I'll try," she said.

"Wait until I've stopped," he said. "I'll only have a few seconds to close the panel before they can see what's happening."

Right after parking in front of the building at the rest area and turning off the engine, Jazz scrambled over the seats and shoved the floor panel exactly in place. As he did, she suddenly couldn't breathe.

"Are you okay?" his muffled voice asked.

She calmed herself, taking slow and steady breaths. Soon it was fine. "Yeah," she said as loud as she could.

She wondered how thoroughly the person following her would search the vehicle.

Ten minutes into hiding she heard the tapping on the window, as Jazz predicted. The stereo was playing a rap song, and since the bass was right next to her, she felt as if she were one of the speakers throbbing in the back of the Hummer. At first the music continued, as if Jazz hadn't heard the knocking. Then the knocking became pounding. The music went off, and the door opened.

Soon she could hear him talking to two other voices. For a moment the conversation was muffled, but then the hatch opened. She could feel the cold breeze slipping into the interior of the Hummer.

"Where are you going?" a man asked Jazz. "Where's the woman with you?"

"I told you guys. It's just me."

A hand patted the top of the floor right above Cheyenne's head.

Surely they'll know. They'll figure out I'm in here.

Breathing became difficult again. She tried to move but couldn't and became a little more panicked with each passing second.

What if they take Jazz away and I'm stuck inside here? The thought seemed to suck out any remaining oxygen. She wanted to wipe the sweat off her face, but she couldn't move her arms. *Calm down, Cheyenne. Relax. Smooth and steady.*

"What's a guy like you doing driving something like this?" a woman asked Jazz.

"What are you saying? That a young black man can't afford a classic Hummer?"

"It's unregistered, just like you are," the woman said. "Want to tell us exactly what you're doing in New Mexico?"

We're in New Mexico? That was news to Cheyenne.

"Wanna tell me exactly why it's any of the FBI's business?" Jazz asked, imitating the stereotype of a scary gang member from the hood.

"The only business to worry about is the sort you're going to find when you're stuck in a prison cell," the male said to Jazz.

"Why do you look familiar?" the woman asked.

"I sound even more familiar," Jazz said.

When the beatbox sounds began, Cheyenne tried to understand what she was hearing since the music was so machinelike and artificial sounding. Then the voice started singing, or more like rapping, and Jazz's voice sounded lower and soulful.

"They take it away, you take it away, we take it away, that's just the way," Jazz sang out before his beatbox sounds began again. "Or how about this one? 'Show you black and you see the night, show you white and you see sacred light. I spent a life studying the mirror, but the picture's no clearer.'"

Both of the FBI agents suddenly began talking. The man was laughing, and the woman's tone changed to one of surprise.

Cheyenne had trouble believing it, but her sarcastic self told her it could certainly be the truth. *Of course Jazz is the hip-hop and rap star named License.* Perhaps she would have realized that if she listened to more music or knew more about pop culture, but then again, she hadn't heard much from the megastar for the last few years.

Because he's been hiding away in a bunker.

"So how'd you get involved with this?" the female agent asked him, her tone light and friendly now.

"I told you. I'm not involved with anything, and I'm not hanging out with some woman. I'm not traveling with any criminals. I used to, but those days are done."

"You've been off the scene for a while, haven't you?" she asked Jazz.

"You still go on tour?" the other agent asked.

After several more questions Jazz tried to shut them down.

"Guys, look. This ain't a meet and greet here. You searched me, and you questioned me. Is there anything you need from me?"

Suddenly there was silence that lasted a few minutes. Then the doors shut, and the music started again.

"Have a great day, guys!" Jazz shouted from the front seat.

Still taking calm, slow breaths, Cheyenne realized Jazz had simply been telling the FBI duo a lie. She couldn't believe they had bought the lie. Yeah, right, this was License, living in a hidden bunker and now carrying someone being investigated by the FBI around in a Hummer.

Why would the FBI want me anyway?

The big question: *Why would they believe he's some mega hip-hop star?*

The even bigger question: *When is he going to get me out of here?* For now that was the only question that mattered.

Five minutes later, when the engine roared to life, the floor panel above her popped open. She jerked upward and tried to suck in as much air as she could, which started her coughing for a few seconds. Finally she was able to sit up.

"You okay?" Jazz asked.

"What was that all about?"

"They're gone," he said.

"FBI? Were they really FBI?"

Jazz sighed, offering her a hand and pulling her up out of the space that now looked smaller than she first thought.

"Man, I hate having to do that," he said, looking out the tinted glass in the back of the Hummer.

"Do what?"

"I hate having to use my 'get out of jail free' card."

Cheyenne wiped the sweat off the back of her neck and stretched her shoulders and arms, digesting his comment.

"What do you mean . . . Are you seriously saying that you're License?"

"Do I look that old and out of shape?" he asked as he chuckled.

"I don't really know what License looks like, but you sound just like him."

He laughed. "Well, I should. I gave them my credentials. I carry my SYN-APSYS with me. My former life and soul, as I call it."

She studied his face more and saw the resemblance.

"Come on. Don't be a cliché like everybody else and get starstruck," he told her, his disappointment sounding genuine. "All that is an elaborate illusion anyway."

"It's just— Now I really and truly don't get what is happening here."

"Let's get back on the road, and I'll fill in a few more of the blanks," Jazz said.

"Wait. Hold on. You have to tell me the truth. You really are License? You had all those hit songs a few years back? Married and divorced Juniper Campbell?"

Jazz gave her a mocking, shocked look. "Wait . . . That marriage was *never* official. You've been listening to the paparazzi." He broke out into laughter.

She sat there, confused and nervous. Things had gone from surreal to absurd.

"Okay, fine," he said. "I'll answer the question you're dying to ask."

"What's that?"

"Jazz. Why I have that nickname. You probably don't even know my actual name, do you?"

"I'm having a hard time keeping up with your personas," Cheyenne said.

"Jamil C. Taylor. That's my name. *Jazz* comes from my middle name, which my father gave me."

"What's the *C* stand for?" she asked.

"Coltrane."

3.

As they drove through Texas on their way to Tulsa, the designated city Jazz had been given, he began to share his story with Cheyenne. She took it all in without saying too much or asking too many questions. She allowed him to paint a picture of the person he once was and the man he now happened to be. As she looked out at the vast, barren flatlands outside of Amarillo, the shapes and colors of his life's self-portrait started to form, and she conflated it with every-thing else that was happening.

"I'm seventeen years old, and people start using the word *wunderkind* when talking about me. Ten years ago. Wow. I make an album. Nobody even bothers these days, right? I make physical copies and sell them on street corners. People have to figure out how to even play the CDs. You got it right by calling it a persona. That's exactly what I created. I added a whole bunch of mystique to it. From my supposed background to the music I made."

"Did you make up your bio? Living on the streets and all that? Didn't you say you killed someone when you were thirteen?"

"Yeah. My father worked at Sillc Technologies."

Cheyenne knew them well. "Before or after Acatour bought them?"

"He was one of the founders."

"Money was never an issue in your house, right?"

"Exactly." His earnest eyes stared at the highway in front of them. "Every-thing was manufactured and manipulated."

"But that's your voice, right? You were the one singing."

"Sure. I made the music. I have that talent. But it became not just a com-modity. It became a religion for some. And by the time I was twenty-one and living in Nashville, I was a shell of a man, living without a soul. All the doors to the world opened up to me, and I found myself in some really twisted places. Wicked places, with stuff happening that should've revolted me. The more exclusive the scene, the more evil it seemed to be."

Cheyenne didn't want to know the details of those scenes. She was more curious how he finally got out of them.

"I remember reading a review of some of my music in which they used words like *moody* and *gloomy* and *grumpy* referring to me. They asked where the carefree License had gone. I was so resentful and lashed out at the critic, proving the point he had made. The reality was, yeah, I was miserable. And that started my journey of trying to learn *why* I was the way I was."

"You don't seem miserable now," Cheyenne said. *Deluded, yes, and maybe a bit delirious, but certainly not miserable.*

"I'm not. Life has a point and a purpose now, even though it doesn't *quite* align with the purposes of the rest of my family. Or my former fans." He chuckled. "There's a lot more joy."

"What changed?"

He shrugged, looking down the highway as if to choose his words. "If I say I found Jesus, I'm sure that'd sound pious or predictable, right?"

"Maybe," she said.

"Yeah, well, who cares how it sounds? It's the truth. I was broadsided. Especially since— Well, that's another long story. One involving a girl and love and tragedy and grief."

"Did someone die?" Cheyenne asked.

Jazz laughed and slapped the steering wheel in amusement. "No. Come on. She dumped me at a McDonald's. For real. The only thing that died was my heart. No, scratch that. It was my pride that died. But it was part of God's grand plan. It opened a door. All that to say, I was living a manufactured dream that paid me and others an insane amount of money. I eventually discovered it wasn't others' plans that I should choose to follow, but God's. So I got out of that scene. That world."

She couldn't remember ever hearing anything about this, though she hadn't exactly paid attention to lifestyles of musicians or other famous people. Unless, of course, they were in the tech world.

"So you became a hermit?" she asked.

"Hardly. The powers that be wanted me back. I was part of the club, and if I wanted out, they were going to make sure I would pay. First they threatened me. Then they began to cut me off. Relationships, career, everything. Family members came to me, wanting to have me committed and doing everything possible to stop this so-called insanity. That lasted, well, until I finally dropped off the face of the planet. I've basically been in hiding now for a couple of years."

This time she couldn't resist. "But how, then, did you—"

"Find myself living in an underground bunker?" he asked with a laugh. "Working on global conspiracies?"

"Well, the first question about the bunker came to mind. Not sure about conspiracies."

"My faith—it was real. And I knew I needed to tell others about the evil things that I'd seen, that I'd been a part of. I'd heard about people being 'called,' but this was different. My life suddenly had purpose and direction and meaning. To refer to it as a calling seems to dial it down too much. I was all in from the very beginning. And then I met someone I consider a modern-day prophet. I kid you not."

"Who?"

For a moment she wondered if he was going to say her father's name.

"A man calling himself different names like Reckoner and Acrobat. He came to me, knowing my change of heart, the change in my life. He told me about his big plan, which was already in place. A plan to expose the cabal controlling everyone and everything in our world. That's when all the preparations really began."

"The preparations for what?"

Jazz looked at her. "The beginning of the end."

SEVEN

Darkness Sleeps

1.

She's drowning inches away from him, but he can't grab her and pull her back up to the surface. Her mouth moves, but she can't speak, can't utter his name, can't make a sound. The seas close in all around them, but somehow he continues floating as he watches the waters swallow his wife.

Even knowing he's dreaming, Will can't breathe because of his terror. The nightmare feels so real. His clothes and skin feel soaked. He can even taste the salty ocean. The topsy-turvy of the endless tides have made him seasick even as he feels his body resting on his side, his head against two flat pillows, the soft blanket mostly covering him.

He takes her hand and tugs at her, but then she tugs back, waking him up even more. It's not her hand that he's holding but rather the cover, and Amy is yanking it back, even though she already has most of it wrapped around her.

In the darkness of their bedroom, Will opened his eyes, feeling as though his heart were exploding—like a strand of lit firecrackers. He breathed in and out slowly, trying to calm himself. It was early morning, around three. That was all his eyes would tell him without his glasses. He felt a brief moment of relief, but then he let the dark reality seep back into any spots where sunlight had leaked in.

He was starting over in his career from scratch. But he wasn't twenty-two; he was forty-six. And he wasn't shiny and pristine anymore. Like an item in a thrift store, he was scratched up and tarnished. Whatever price he had written on his tag, Will knew it would be very, very cheap.

2.

He hadn't been able to fall back asleep until after Amy woke up, so by the time he got out of bed to help the girls get ready for school, he felt as beat-up as he had felt in his nightmare. Coffee hadn't done anything for him, and he hadn't done much good in getting the girls dressed and out the door with their mother on time. He had failed to get their teeth brushed and had lost his patience.

Life's hard enough without having to worry about being a bad daddy.

The morning hadn't been any more successful with the variety of things he had worked on. Or *tried* to work on. Like the call to connect with Grant Borley, a friend from his Northwestern University days who had become a head guy at a waste-disposal company. He wasn't exactly sure what Grant's title was, but it didn't really matter since this wasn't an interview. Grant had graciously agreed to talk to him. Will appreciated the gesture, especially since his last dozen contacts hadn't resulted in anything.

"You still look like you're thirty years old," Grant said when he popped up in front of Will on the 3-D–image connect call.

Will sat at his desk staring at Grant behind his desk, not in the usual flat visual you got with regular calls but with the new technology that allowed the conversation to feel as if the two of you were really in front of each other. Not like the old hologram visuals that never appeared lifelike, but rather a very realistic and very expensive interface.

"Give me another couple of years," Will said. "With these girls of mine, I'll look like Lincoln after the war."

Grant did look his age, with thinning hair the color of a dull nickel and a face a lot thicker than it used to be.

"How's Amy doing?" he asked.

"Great," Will said, then talked up her talents and her food technologist position at Nestle-Mars Co. in a way he never did with her personally. Grant had always had a crush on Amy. He would have found it interesting or ironic to know Will had once brought up his name during a heated and heavy argument, telling his wife she should have married someone like Grant instead. Grant was divorced with several kids himself, so he wasn't exactly the model for a great husband.

"So you have to wear a suit every day?" Will asked him.

"Yeah. That whole business-casual thing that used to be so popular got yanked out from under us. You're lucky you get to wear jeans."

"Hey, I dressed up for you," Will joked about his button-down shirt. "Listen, man, thanks for taking the time this morning."

That was the lead-in to talking about his current job situation and any input his friend might have. Like perhaps telling him, "Hey, I have this sweet job that just opened, and I know you're perfect for it even though you don't have the first clue what the garbage business is like." Before Will could even get started, a dreadful sound came from the hallway outside his upstairs office.

"Excuse me for a quick second," Will said, then opened the door and saw the mangy mutt throwing up all over their cream carpet.

Will cursed and then stood there for a second, trying to figure out what to do. Let the dog keep messing up the carpet and go on with his call or . . .

"Grant . . . you're not gonna believe this. Our dog is sick and is throwing up in the house. And it looks like— Well, it doesn't look pretty."

Grant only laughed. "You got a dog?"

"Yeah. Big mistake. Amy wasn't happy."

"You didn't ask her?"

"Nope."

The high-pitched retching continued.

"I gotta go," Will said. "I'm so sorry."

"No sweat. Just contact Raini, and she'll get another call on the schedule. I'm heading to New York tomorrow for a few days, but once I'm back, we can talk."

"Sure. That'd be great. Thanks."

Grant disappeared as Will went back out to the hallway. The poor dog looked up at him as if to say *sorry*.

"You okay, buddy?" Will asked.

It looked as though the dog had found some of the girls' crayons since his mess had a rainbow of colored chunks in it.

"That is disgusting," Will said, picking up the mutt. "But you waited until Mommy was gone, so that's cool."

He took Flip downstairs to see if he needed to go outside. And to get a bucket and some cleaning materials.

Not the best way to start job hunting.

Several hours later he hadn't made much progress. He had filled out half a dozen job applications on the network and then had followed up with a few more friends about talking with them. Meanwhile, he had avoided looking at the fifty unopened messages with bills waiting for him. Two debt collectors called and left messages. He had made the mistake of picking up a third call, thinking it might be Grant again.

"Is this William Stewart at 745 Parkway Drive?" a woman asked.

Nobody called him William except people who wanted him to pay his bills.

"Yes," Will said.

"This is an attempt to collect a debt, and all communication will be recorded for—," she began to say.

It was a real human being. He knew that because they got a better response with actual humans calling. This woman was from Movement Apparel, asking him about the $21,413.58 he owed them for clothing he had bought twelve years ago when he worked at a corporation.

"Look, I plan to pay, but I have negative seven hundred bucks in my account," Will told her. "So it's gonna be a little while."

He let the woman go through the regular routine, asking why and talking about getting him on a payment plan and gently threatening to turn him over to collection.

My credit is already shot, so that doesn't exactly scare me.

After getting off the call with the woman, Will checked his bank account and realized they were almost two thousand dollars overdrawn.

Alone in his house, at his desk without any distractions or noise around him, Will knew it was a good time to pray. Not only was this a great opportunity, but it was a necessity. Yet he didn't. He couldn't.

Like talking to Amy, prayer felt impossible for him right now. Not because he didn't think he'd be heard, but because he had no clue what he would say.

3.

More riots broke out in the streets of Chicago, with dozens of arrests after three confirmed deaths. The news couldn't determine whether the shootings came from the protesters or from the police trying to break them up. As he picked at a sandwich for lunch, Will watched the melee of men and women yelling and fighting and throwing things and clashing with one another. It grew depressing because it was such a common occurrence. The country had never been more divided, and the division had never been more indecipherable. Will didn't know what they were fighting about anymore. Some kind of rights, yet there were too many disagreements and debates in this piping-hot stew that boiled over in the center of the city.

He grabbed a paperback that was held together by packing tape. The poem he found inside written by Siler Wright seemed fitting. It was called "Darkness Sleeps."

Does the darkness sleep
and shiver
next to the light?

Cloaked in covers
and smothered
and waking at dawn
only to tempt
the light to come over again.

The darkness remains
a shadow to her steps
who can't escape even if she runs.

He had never been a big fan of poetry simply because he had loved prose so much more, and he understood its confines. Poems were mysterious and sometimes unapproachable, yet Will had gradually learned to embrace them. The poet Wright wrote words like this that spoke to him. Especially on a day like today.

Darkness waits in the shadows until it strangles you from behind.

The darkness could apply to the world at large, to the violence and the anger that began in homes and offices and then took to the streets. Or it could describe his bookstore and how its flickering light had finally gone out, bringing shadows and fog to the world outside its walls.

More than anything else, Will knew the darkness slept in the heart. It lingered like a virus and could stay around, even when the light finally came back in. Bad karma, some might call it, or suppressed feelings, a counselor might say. But the darkness was an evil spirit, and Will believed those demons were real.

That belief was what got him into trouble in the first place. The powers that be, both physical and spiritual, had destroyed the hope he was trying to put out there.

"Ever thought about getting back at them?" He heard Hutchence's voice once again. Another thought came back around too, the one that nudged him to give the guy a call. *Go see what else he has to say. Even if he's completely crazy, at least he understands what happens. That's more than most people.*

After contemplating it for a while, Will decided to send the stranger another message. He was stuck and frustrated and definitely wanted to do something, especially lashing out at those who had shut down his dreams and his life.

4.

"Media outlets in the suburbs of Chicago were greeted this morning with an unusual wake-up call on their sites and in their inboxes. An anonymous video message was sent to them, and it was, to say the least, quite unusual."

Coffee in hand, Will turned to the family room wall where the morning news played, his curiosity piqued. He saw a fluffy cat standing on two legs, dancing to a Rolling Stones song blasting in the background. Then it showed a series of videos, from the landing on the moon to Steve Jobs with his first Apple computer to Albert Einstein to the shaky footage of atom bombs going off in Hiroshima and Nagasaki, all while Mick Jagger sang, "Oh, a storm is threat'ning my very life today . . ."

Then it changed to footage from the last decade, from the first human to carry a SYNAPSYS, to the Mars expeditions, to the much-hyped unveiling of the AI construct, Lydia. A voice began to talk over the music. "Mankind has created life and death, has pinpointed cancer cells and flown to the moon, has made the impossible possible time after time. But what if King Solomon was right? What if 'what was will be again, what happened will happen again'?

What if 'there's nothing new on this earth'? What if everything really is 'the same old story'?

" 'Nobody remembers what happened yesterday. And the things that will happen tomorrow? Nobody'll remember them either. Don't count on being remembered.' "

A series of images flashed by as the voice—male, flat, and most likely artificially created—continued talking. These showed scandals and violence and wars and evil that littered the news daily.

"Wake up, people. Listen to the words of the prophet Zephaniah: 'That terrible day of the LORD is near. Swiftly it comes—a day of bitter tears, a day when even strong men will cry out.' "

As he spoke, there were videos of the well-dressed masses walking the city streets in the machinery of the working day, a mother and father hopelessly looking on with their children crying, the president meeting with the Korean government, a survey of how many households in the country subscribe to adult entertainment.

The narrator continued, " 'It will be a day when the LORD's anger is poured out—a day of terrible distress and anguish, a day of ruin and desolation, a day of darkness and gloom, a day of clouds and blackness, a day of trumpet calls and battle cries. Down go the walled cities and the strongest battlements!' "

The skyline of Chicago was shown, first early in the morning, then late in the afternoon, and then at night with the great Incen Tower gleaming and pointing up to the heavens.

" 'Because you have sinned against the LORD, I will make you grope around like the blind. Your blood will be poured into the dust, and your bodies will lie rotting on the ground.' "

Now there were videos showing the destruction of cities, bomb blasts, and then fires raging. The voice continued its haunting words. " 'Your silver and gold will not save you on that day of the LORD's anger. For the whole land will be devoured by the fire of his jealousy. He will make a terrifying end of all the people on earth.' "

The screen then went black except for the large message written in white:

THERE IS HOPE . . . ZEPHANIAH 2 . . .

The voice ended the message with a closing comment. "This is the Reckoner, and you will be hearing from me again."

Will felt the electricity cover his skin, the way it often did when he read an incredible passage in a book or heard a glorious moment in a song.

What was that all about?

The pretty blond-haired news anchor came back on with an amused look. "Authorities have not yet determined how the video message was delivered to the media in the Chicagoland area, nor have they been able to identify the party responsible for the so-called warning. Members of the FBI division responsible for network regulation have been called in to oversee the investigation. We'll keep you posted on any developments in this strange and ominous online prank."

Will told the news to mute itself as he checked any messages he might have overlooked this morning.

"Check inboxes," he said, his kitchen counter displaying the four places he would get any incoming communication. Nobody had called, and the only message was from Amy, reminding him to take out the garbage. He had opened any important-looking emails, and the image bank had nothing new in it.

He said to repeat the morning news footage, wanting to see the message again. Will ended up watching it three more times. The voice changed at the end, from the automated robotic voice to a human.

"This is the Reckoner, and you will be hearing from me again."

5.

"Did you see that weird hacked video that was sent out to the news today?"

Amy never sent him messages when she was at work in the Nestle-Mars Co. headquarters in Libertyville, so this was unusual. It felt strange to hear her voice pop out of nowhere.

"Yeah," Will said in their conversation feed. "Saw it half an hour ago. Watched it a bunch of times."

"That was pretty eerie."

"Yeah," he said as he scrolled through the series of online job descriptions he had up on his screen in his office. "Did anyone at your company receive the message?"

"Lindsey did. She's one of the heads of our PR division."

"Yeah, I remember her. Maybe it was a warning to her to stop talking. She's a chatterbox."

"It's as if there's going to be another terrorist bombing somewhere," Amy said. "Like what happened at the Chicago Theatre."

"Don't worry. There won't be. Whoever this was sounds as though he at least reads the Bible."

He said it more to be witty and cheer her up than anything else, but he knew her silence meant she wasn't amused. Amy worried often, but the daily news could worry anybody. The volatility of the world. The violence all across the country. The number of child abductions and the rampant drug problems. All great stuff to keep the nightmares going.

"Come on," he said, unable to see her but at least communicating by voice. "What are we always telling the kids? God doesn't want us to worry, right?"

"I know."

"So I have to remind myself of that. That video was probably from some twelve-year-old tech genius who's learned how to get into people's heads."

"That's terrifying. What if he sent something far worse?"

"Amy, don't worry about anything. Okay?"

"Yeah, okay." She paused, then added, "Thanks."

He seldom gave her good counsel or set the sort of biblical and godly example like he knew he should. This felt—different. Nice, even. Not that what he said was profound. But he did mean it.

"How's work?"

"Someone on the team asked about you," Amy said. "Said he'd heard about the bookstore closing."

"Who? And did he know the reason?" he asked, more alarmed to hear this after watching the video warning earlier that morning.

"You don't know him. Hugh Daschton. I didn't ask what he knew. I just shut down the conversation very quickly."

"I'm sorry."

"Yeah," she said in a faraway voice. "I am too."

6.

After half an hour Will thought Hutchence wasn't going to show up. The only confirmation he had received after saying he wanted to continue their conversation was this Mexican restaurant's address and a photo of a clock showing 7:00 p.m. Now it was 7:33 p.m., and he was on his second basket of chips and salsa, and he hadn't gotten any sort of message that the meeting was still happening. He decided to go ahead and wave down the server to order, not wanting to waste a visit to what already seemed to be a great dining place. Before he could find his waitress, Raylan Hutchence walked toward him, taking his time before sliding into the booth across from Will.

"That was called sauntering," Hutchence said. "How'd I look?"

"How'd you look?"

"Yes. Sauntering. One of my New Year's resolutions was to saunter more since I have this horrible tendency to half jog like a crazy man every place I go."

Will shrugged, a bit confused. "I guess . . . the sauntering is going well."

Hutchence laughed. "I'm sorry I'm late. I could explain, but I would have to explain the bigger explanation, which would then force me to go into lots more things when ultimately all I can do is apologize and ask that you understand it wasn't because I'm a tardy person."

"It's okay," Will said. "I'm on my fourth margarita."

Scratching his thick beard, Hutchence let out another chuckle, knowing Will was joking as he looked at the Diet Coke.

"I'm glad you wanted to get together again," he told Will. "How's job hunting going?"

"Fine."

"Fine as in 'I've gotten nowhere, and please don't hound me about it'?"

"No. Honestly, just fine. I'm trying to connect with some friends to see if there's something temporary I can do. I'm putting out some feelers." *And I'm frankly feeling a bit screwed and freaked out, but that's okay 'cause I'll keep that to myself.*

"Do you mind people who like to use quotes?"

"No," Will said.

"Well, good, because I use quotes."

"What if I said they really annoy me?"

"Selfishly I would go ahead and use them anyway. They're my arsenal since my own thoughts often pale in comparison. I promise I don't use my fingers for air quotes, however. So here's some encouragement. 'Become a possibilitarian. No matter how dark things seem to be or actually are, raise your sights and see possibilities—always see them, for they're always there.' That's a favorite from Norman Vincent Peale."

"Thank you. Can I enroll in your motivational course soon?"

"Yes. I only take Bitcoin, however," Hutchence joked. "Here's another one. This is from King David, and I love it. 'GOD made my life complete when I placed all the pieces before him. When I got my act together, he gave me a fresh start. Now I'm alert to GOD's ways; I don't take God for granted. Every day I review the ways he works; I try not to miss a trick. I feel put back together, and I'm watching my step. GOD rewrote the text of my life when I opened the book of my heart to his eyes.'"

That's bizarre.

"What?" Hutchence asked. "You look puzzled."

"No, I'm not puzzled. I'm just— That's the second Bible passage I've heard today."

"Really? Are they that foreign to hear?"

"Well, from others, yeah. Except for Sunday mornings, and even those can be rare at times," Will said.

"You know, there's a reason the Scriptures are called living. It's a great mystery, but they are alive, and they can be instruments of change in your life. But you have to open the Bible's pages or read the text if pages are a thing of the past to you. Which I know for you they aren't."

"I grew up being told *not* to read the Bible. To stay away from it, like a German child being told never to discuss Hitler. Naturally, because I tended to do everything my father told me not to do, I ended up reading the Bible all the way through when I was eleven years old."

"Did your father find out you disobeyed him?"

Will nodded, looking down at the blood-red salsa that had spilled onto the table. *That was when I lost one father and gained another.*

"Did your father ever discover you were giving Bibles away at your book-store?" Hutchence asked.

Once again Will looked at the man across from him, trying to decipher how much he knew, trying to determine if the tone in his voice was changing.

"I never told you I was giving Bibles away," Will said.

"You never told me the name of your father either."

He knows.

Will breathed out and then forced a smile on his lips. "Maybe I don't need to tell you. Maybe you already know."

"That's not the important thing," Hutchence told him, rubbing the bottom of his beard like a mad professor. "What I'm curious to know is whether you reached out at any point in the last few years to ask your father for money."

"Of course not. I haven't spoken to him in years. And he wouldn't give me a cent even if I did."

"Ironic, huh? Jackson Heyford is one of the world's wealthiest and most powerful people, and his son is bankrupt."

"I haven't declared bankruptcy yet," Will said. "And that's not the ironic part. The irony is I followed my father's entrepreneurial passions and dreams with my bookstore, and he was the very one who ended up shutting it down."

As the server approached to take their order, Hutchence told her to bring them the bill.

"I appreciate your vulnerability to a stranger talking about strange things," he told Will after the waitress walked away. "So I'll repeat the question I asked you before, but I'll be more specific. Have you ever thought about getting back at your father? At the man who put you out of business?"

"The moment I first picked up a Bible was the moment I began getting back at him," Will said. "But I made my decision years ago, when I turned eighteen, that I didn't want to have anything to do with Jackson Heyford. I still don't."

"Changing a name doesn't mean you're no longer his son."

"In my eyes it does," Will stated. "Now why didn't you let me order a burrito?"

"I want to show you something. Something that might help paint a picture of the reality of this situation."

7.

They ended up heading out into the night in a nondescript Toyota car owned by the enigmatic stranger. First Hutchence showed him three different large buildings, one an old church and two structures on bigger campuses. At the third one, as they sat in an empty, sprawling parking lot that seemed capable of holding several thousand, Hutchence explained what he was showing Will.

"All three of the places I've showed you were churches at one time, the three biggest in the western suburbs of Chicago. These were like your bookstore, being run by men and women who didn't want to conform and bend and break. But since President Blackwood, it's been impossible to resist. Right?"

Will nodded.

"Do you guys publicly attend a church?" Hutchence asked him.

"Sorta. For the girls. But not consistently. It's a bit of keeping up with the Joneses. And I struggle with whether to go to a place that never utters the name of Jesus."

"Yeah," Hutchence said. "I'd break bread and drink wine if there was a church I could receive them in."

With multiple buildings attached to one another, this former church looked more like a college campus.

"Life Springs Church," Hutchence said as he started the car and began circling the building. "Ever heard of it?"

Will nodded. "We thought about trying it, but it was too far from our home. I don't recall hearing about it closing."

"We hear about white Christian skinheads bombing an abortion clinic," Hutchence said. "And about secret groups of believers being discovered and arrested and made out to be weird cults. But we don't hear about things like this, about ordinary churches being *forced* to close. They were growing. They had never been stronger. But Alden Blackwood put an end to that."

"You're not telling me anything I don't know," Will said.

"I know. But I'm showing these as a matter of contrast. Just wait. We're driving out to the farmlands that used to exist the further west you drove in Illinois."

After they had driven another fifteen or twenty minutes west, Will knew there was absolutely nothing but abandoned countryside here. The farms a hundred miles west of Chicago had been turned into waste-disposal sites, stretching out for thousands of acres of flat, dry country with hard soil capable of growing very little if anything on it. On a highway that was crumbling from neglect, no longer used in lieu of the federal byways occupied by Autovehs, they drove for an hour, the surrounding land as black as the cloudy night above them. They didn't talk much since Will didn't want to hear another blast of preaching. He was tired and wondered what Hutchence was going to show him.

The glowing lights on the immediate horizon seemed to appear all at once, as if someone had turned on a switch that lit ten thousand bulbs in the ground, all spaced out several feet from the others in straight lines. Will let out a curse in shock and amazement.

"What is this?" he asked, feeling as if he had suddenly stepped onto the set of Stanley Kubrick's *2001*.

They soon began passing lights on each side of the highway, warm and golden and covering everywhere he could see. Like strands of Christmas lights decorating the cold countryside. An endless land of illuminated speckles. For a moment Will wondered if they slightly trembled in place.

I feel like I'm in a dream.

"Amazing, isn't it?" Hutchence asked. "It's not something you can see during the day. Or on our wonderful mapview on the network where we can pinpoint anything we want in the world."

"What are these lights?"

Hutchence didn't answer but continued to drive, the occasional potholes jolting them in their seats. No other headlights could be seen either coming toward them or driving behind them. The brilliance painted the fields as far as Will could see facing the north or the south.

"Play 'Dollars and Cents,'" the driver said, filling the car with a tapping drumbeat and a hushed, warped guitar with haunting strings just before a screeching, high-pitched voice began to sing.

"Are you trying—"

"Sh," Hutchence said and told Will simply to listen.

Will had a hard time making out the lyrics and making sense of the song being played. It certainly wasn't uplifting or hopeful as it circled downward in despair.

The glimmering they were smothered in now seemed to set the landscape ablaze in every direction.

"It's spectacular, right?" Hutchence said above the music. "Seen for the first time, it's miraculous. But change the context—like set it to a different song, something more ominous like this—and it suddenly looks different, right?"

A mile passed, then another, and the lights still remained. Everywhere.

As the song faded away, Hutchence slowed the car down on the side of the road and turned it off. Then he got out, leaving Will for a moment until he did the same.

The shimmering dots began about fifty feet away from the edge of the road. Outside in the cold night air, they appeared even more crisp and vibrant. Will scanned the exact lines that resembled grapevines running along the side of the hills in Northern California. Hutchence stepped up beside him, his face lit bright enough to see bumps underneath his beard.

"These are the SYNAPSYSes that belong to everybody, including you and me. Look at them. Each light represents more than a thousand of them. So what you're seeing is perhaps a whole country's worth of SYNAPSYS data right here. In this wonderful little state of nowhere—glorious Illinois."

Will felt a wave of cold even though he was nice and warm underneath his coat. "Are you serious? I've never heard anything about this."

"Of course you haven't."

"But you could see these lights from Mars," Will said with an incredulous sigh. "How can these be hidden?"

"It's the first time you've ever driven out here, right? These highways are no longer used. Autovehs transport people working in the garbage dumps out here on their own highways. The supertrains now carry everything the truckers used to transport."

"But surely people have seen this and wondered—"

"Of course. Officially, they are a new type of solar power. They supposedly absorb the sun all day—even on the cloudy and rainy days—so they remain lit at night. People who have questioned and probed further . . . They've been quieted. A handful have even disappeared. It's amazing how many people have disappeared over the course of the last decade, and nobody is paying attention."

Will took a breath and ran his hand through his thick hair.

"Now you see why Illinois was able to suddenly stop being bankrupt and has become so financially viable. California collapsed, so the country needed a new Silicon Valley. With Incen Tower in Chicago, it makes sense these are here since the two are connected."

All these things Hutchence had been talking about . . .

"Look," Will said as he turned to the stranger who was enveloped in this warm glow surrounding them. "I don't want to be rude, but I don't get it. All these things you keep talking about. You keep telling me and showing me things, but I don't know *why*. It's like I'm waiting for a sales pitch that's never going to come."

Hutchence turned to him, nodding to say he understood Will's confusion.

"On March 29 of this year, a month from now, this area will be wiped out by God. His wrath and righteousness will come down hard on Chicago and its neighboring towns. All of this will be gone."

The tiny, illuminated stars all represented millions of lives, surrounding them, appearing to want to swallow the two men whole.

"God told the prophet Zephaniah, 'I have wiped out many nations, devastating their fortress walls and towers. Their streets are now deserted; their cities lie in silent ruin. There are no survivors—none at all. I thought, "Surely they will have reverence for me now! Surely they will listen to my warnings. Then I won't need to strike again, destroying their homes." But no, they get up early to continue their evil deeds. . . . Soon I will stand and accuse these evil nations. For I have decided to gather the kingdoms of the earth and pour out my fiercest anger and fury on them. All the earth will be devoured by the fire of my jealousy.'"

Everything inside Will wanted to simply accept that the man in front of him was a bona fide lunatic, but he couldn't. He wouldn't.

The words made sense to him.

Maybe I'm fed up and tired of this world. And tired of being fed up.

"What are you planning?"

"Will, listen to me. I was sent not only to deliver this message of God's coming wrath to the people of Chicago, but I was also meant to tell certain people. Like you."

"So God told you— He said, 'Go find Will Stewart'? Is it because of who my father is?"

"I understand your skepticism, your urge to consider this irrational and ridiculous."

"I didn't say that," Will said.

"I can see it on your face. In your eyes."

"Yeah, well, I'd be a lot more skeptical if I wasn't standing in the middle of a gazillion sleeping fireflies."

"God told Abraham about His plans for wiping out the cities of Sodom and Gomorrah. And after Abraham pleaded for mercy, bargaining with his own creator for the lives of the godless heathens in the cities, God told him He would spare His wrath if only ten righteous were found. But there weren't even that many in those cities."

"This is a Sodom and Gomorrah thing, then?" Will asked.

"God's judgment is the same in the Old Testament as it is in the New Testament. The difference is Jesus. I'm no Abraham, and I didn't think of bargaining with God. I was terrified and I'm still terrified. Like so many of the people God has called to do His work, I'm messed-up and broken and trying to do the right thing."

The wind picked up as if spurred into activity by their conversation.

"So what does this place have to do with all that?"

"This is why I showed up the day you closed the door on your former life," Hutchence said, his grin showing through his dark whiskers.

"My 'former' life?"

"Yes. The one before you heard the call of God in your life, urging you on to something bigger and better. To something far bolder than simply and quietly selling and giving away Christian books and Bibles."

"What is it I'm supposed to do, then?"

"Warn the world of God's judgment. And deliver a message of the hope of Christ."

"And how are we going to do that?" Will asked.

Hutchence pointed all around them to the glowing lights.

All these lights . . . "So you want to—"

"I don't want to," Hutchence said. "I will do this. There's a message that needs to be communicated clearly and precisely to every single person represented here."

"To people's SYNAPSYSes? How are you going to do that?"

Hutchence laughed, shaking his head, staring up at the sky and then back down at Will.

"*That* is why I need your help. Why you're the only one who can help me, Will Stewart Heyford."

8.

Late at night in the playroom/entertainment room in their basement, Will started to watch the movie Hutchence had told him to check out. It was an odd suggestion, but everything about the man had been odd. Or perhaps not odd. That felt like too simple a word, too safe. There was something dangerous about this man since he was talking about God and demons and an apocalypse on the horizon, all having to do with Will's father.

March 29 was only a month away.

Will all of this be gone?

Naturally he didn't tell Amy or anybody else about this prophet and fortune-teller he'd met. It would have been easy to simply write off Hutchence as another crazy political junkie. Someone who spent the entire day chasing conspiracy theories. Yet he was a fellow believer, a brother. Plus, he somehow had discovered that Jackson Heyford was Will's father. Very few knew that, not just because of efforts on Will's part but also because of his father and brothers. It was one thing to be cut off. In Will's case the knife had not only severed the family cords, but it had also dug deep into his own skin and bones. Hutchence was planning to expose some of his father's dirty laundry, and Will couldn't help wanting to be a part of this.

Before leaving, Hutchence had given him an assignment of sorts. "I know how this all sounds coming from someone like me," Hutchence said. "But do me a favor. Watch or rewatch Tarkovsky's *Stalker*. And consider what the stalker tells the writer and the professor when they reach the room."

He had watched the movie during a college course on foreign films, but all he could remember was something like three hours of trying to stay awake. It probably was a bad idea to start a movie like this at midnight, but Will knew he didn't have to be at work at seven in the morning as he used to do with the bookstore, arriving a couple of hours before opening time.

Rewatching the film was fascinating, revealing the difference between the twenty-year-old Will and his current self at more than twice that age. First, the artistry of the film felt otherworldly. Everything wasn't crystal clear as in every modern film, and it obviously wasn't perfected like the shimmery movies these days. But the long shots and the lack of plot and the long diatribes all made sense in this picture. They also felt somewhat relevant.

The story premise was so simple, involving a "Stalker" taking a writer and a professor into a sealed-off place guarded by armed security called "the Zone." Supposedly they had to get past all these dangers to reach a room in a building that could grant them their deepest wish. The story line sounded like the outline for an action film, and the 2030 remake had indeed taken so many liberties that its name had been changed to *Stalk,* because it was basically a scary, shoot-'em-up thriller.

This time he didn't drift off but found himself mesmerized by this whole other world he watched on the cinema wall in their basement. He had forgotten what happened when the men reached the room. So after they arrived and had endless conversations, Will finally heard what Hutchence wanted him to hear. The bald-headed and quite strange-appearing Stalker talked to both of the men, encouraging them to go inside the room since that's what he'd been paid by them to help them do. Yet he gave them a warning as well: "I know you will be angry . . . Anyway, I must say to you . . . Here we are . . . standing on the doorstep . . . It's the most important moment . . . in your life; you must know that."

The Stalker continued to talk. "And, above all," he said, pausing as he headed to the room. "The most important is . . . to believe! Okay, and now you can go. Who wants to go first? Maybe you?"

The Stalker looked at the writer, waiting for his response.

EIGHT

Nighthawks

1.

"I believe," Dowland said with all the conviction and soul he could muster.

The woman across from Dowland—young enough to remember what it was like to be wild and free and accepting in her twenties but old enough now to know better—looked down at the table once again, brushing her brown hair back behind her ear to continue to read the article on the screen. He had dropped in on Lucia Gonzales's lunch at the dining hall on the 56th floor of the Incen Tower, where she could be found every day around one o'clock. A loner, a studious type behind thin glasses, always reading or analyzing data.

"Yes, I've seen reports of some of these things," she told him. "But what does this have to do with me?"

Dowland looked around the cafeteria as if he were worried someone might be watching him. It was something he never ever did in real life.

"I know you're connected with these people. With whoever did this."

The tight lips and searching eyes and fingers twisting a gold band on her finger all revealed the truth. Sometimes Dowland came in and simply put a gun down someone's throat. Other times, like now, he acted out a part, telling a lie to get more information. He couldn't care less about this woman, but he knew she could lead him to someone up the food chain.

There's always a food chain. Always a pecking order. Always that chain of command. Always a pyramid rising to the heavens above.

"I don't know what you're talking about," she said. "Are you a cop or something?"

He shook his head and chuckled. "Do I look like a cop? What do you think this is?"

He pointed to the bandage on his earlobe. It was too obvious to miss, yet her choice to ignore it told him she didn't want to talk.

"What happened?" she asked.

"I was prying into some things, and it turned out someone didn't like it. They snipped off a chunk of my earlobe. Told me to stop snooping around where I didn't belong, that the next time it would be one of my eyes."

She made a grimace looking at his wound. "What sort of things were you prying into?"

"The Reckoner. He reached out to me, but when I tried to find him, he'd disappeared. Along with Regina Daigle."

"You know Regina?"

Dowland told her he did. "All she said was I could trust you."

This time it was Lucia who scanned the half-full set of tables in the hall.

"We can't talk here," she said.

"That's what we're doing right now."

She gave him a blank stare. "We can't talk here."

"Okay, then where?"

She took a matchbook out of her purse and gave it to him. It had two red circles on it.

"When the sun sets," she said, picking up her plate and other belongings before leaving him alone.

Dowland examined the matches, turning them over to see the name and address.

He had never been to the Art Institute of Chicago. Between hunting people down for a living and dating mentally unbalanced supermodels, things like hanging out in museums never really fit his agenda. He could experience some culture this afternoon.

Hopefully he wouldn't have to leave a dead body behind.

2.

The wind froze his face as Dowland waited on the sidewalk by one of the two bronze lions guarding the entrance steps to the Art Institute. Lucia arrived as daylight started to dim, making Michigan Avenue even colder.

"Interesting to see which of the lions you decided to stand beside," she told him, pausing to look up at the two-ton statue.

"Why's that?"

"The lion over there on the northern side of the steps was made to look like it's on the prowl. This one has the attitude of defiance."

"Yeah, that would be fitting." He rubbed his face, trying to feel his nose again.

"These have been around since 1894," Lucia said, still admiring the creation.

"Will you be giving me the guided tour?"

This got her attention. She looked at him with the same apprehension she had in the cafeteria earlier that day, her humorless eyes examining him behind the stylish spectacles.

"We can talk while inside," Lucia said. "I know the museum has strict regulations about recording and photographing. At least we know we can't be photographed or recorded."

You are always seen by someone. But the less she realized that, the better for him.

"I was told to trust you," she said to him as she began to walk up the long steps toward the towering portico. "It's hard to trust anyone these days."

Dowland scanned the impressive limestone blocks of the building, knowing they didn't make structures like this anymore. The Art Institute was truly a work of art itself. Once inside, Lucia held out her hand at the two pillars that scanned guests for paid tickets and also for any weapons on them. Dowland hadn't brought the Beretta. Instead, he carried the H-38 synthetic polymer handgun, the sort that went undetected by most of the machinery designed to find it. Like the government, Dowland had very special tools he used for very special assignments.

Heading up the grand staircase, Lucia seemed to know where she was going.

On the second floor of paintings, airy and opulent rooms fed into each other, grouped into categories like Impressionism and European Art.

"Have you ever been inside the museum?" she asked.

"No. But I have gone parasailing on Lake Michigan."

She looked perplexed by his comment, which was understandable but not worth explaining. With each new room, they passed a hovering metal block lit up on all six sides with blinking red lights. Dowland knew it was a security device that monitored all activity and could take action whenever necessary.

"I like seeing the American art from 1900 to 1950," she told him.

"I like getting answers," Dowland told her in a gentle and nonconfrontational tone.

"Yes, I know. Just . . . please indulge me for a moment."

Lucia Gonzales seemed pleasant enough, but Dowland knew she had a strong will. For her to be defying laws and working with the people she was working with, there had to be a fire inside her. She stopped at several pieces, sharing some thoughts on each that he didn't really pay attention to. The art was fine—something he could never do, something most people couldn't do— but it meant very little to him. It was flat and lifeless, unlike most modern art that enveloped you and took on a life of its own.

"Before algorithms took over painting and drawing and creating, there was a simplicity," Lucia said, studying a historic painting of people in a park. "It used to be only a canvas and colors of paint. Now it's tapping air and letting machines think and create and paint for you."

"Saves time," Dowland said with a smile.

Her brown eyes didn't seem to particularly like his sarcasm. She led him to a moody-looking painting of a diner at night with three people sitting at the counter, the server behind it bent over working on something. Standing in front of it, Dowland felt a strange sense of disorientation, like standing next to a cliff and staring down at the lagoon he was about to jump into. He had seen the image before, a piece interwoven in the fabric of pop culture, yet taking it in there in person was something else entirely. He looked to see the description of the painting on the wall: *Nighthawks* by Edward Hopper.

"Haunting, isn't it?" Lucia said, noticing Dowland's curiosity. "The artist was said to have been inspired by a Hemingway short story called 'The Killers.'"

He wondered if that was some kind of subtle or not-so-subtle message for him, but nothing on the petite woman said so. As the painting drew him in, everything about it felt bleak and hopeless. These characters—not talking, not smiling, not interacting, not even the couple sitting next to each other.

Lonely Souls—*that's what I would've called it.*

The two male customers wore dark suits and fedoras, but it was the one by himself that intrigued Dowland. He sat, his back facing the window you looked into, his arms on the counter and his head notched downward. For a few moments Dowland watched the man, waiting for him to get off his seat, to say or do something. But he just sat, waiting perhaps, or thinking or killing time.

Or planning to kill the couple.

"What are they thinking?" Lucia asked.

Dowland stepped closer to look at each character.

"The couple—they're at a crossroads. He's numb, reality hitting him. He's tried to figure things out, but he can't, and all he can do is numb the pain. She's enduring it, enduring him and their relationship, and waiting to move on."

"Interesting," Lucia said. "Keep going."

"Yes, professor. The guy behind the counter is tired from working ten hours, his legs and back sore, his spirit impatient for these people to leave. And then this guy here . . ."

The guy sitting by himself is me.

"He's from out of town. Sent there to find the woman, who's running from the police and who's a wanted criminal. The guy by himself is waiting for them to leave. He's been watching them, unafraid to look them in the eyes but not saying a word to them."

"Is he a private detective?" she asked.

"No," Dowland said. "He's a killer, just like the Hemingway story that I haven't read. Maybe the man next to the woman knows their lives are over. Maybe he knows they're both going to be killed, so he's having his last cigarette before dying."

"Not a lot of hope with your vision."

"No. We can't do a thing either since we're outside of the glass. We can't call out to warn them or protect them. All we can do is stand and watch as the horror unfolds in front of us in the bright lights of a late night."

Lucia looked at him, studying him carefully. He broke his reverie and grinned.

"Then again, maybe they just really, really love coffee," he said.

3.

Near a set of modern art pieces that Lucia had no interest in, she began to talk to him, telling Dowland what she knew.

"Reckoner contacted me out of the blue. Not personally but through a letter."

The same way Keith Burne liked to communicate. "Reckoner, Acrobat—what's his real name?" Dowland asked.

"I'm not sure. I like another one he used: the 'Man in Black' alias. I've never been able to find any information on him. Nor has anybody ever given me a name."

"What'd he want?"

"To talk about some of the people I'd been meeting with. And some of the things I was saying. He knew about my faith. He had actually been watching me."

"You know what they say about Big Brother."

"At first I thought he was someone official, someone from the government. Maybe the rumors were true. Maybe powerful people really were killing Christians. I finally realized that he was not only a leader but a prophet."

He wanted to make sure he acted as if this was information he had already heard.

"I want to meet Reckoner. In person."

"Nobody's done that. Nobody knows him—what he looks like, where he lives. At least that I know of. He's sort of like a ghost."

"Keith Burne told me all about him," Dowland said.

"But he never met him. We were both messengers. People helping to deliver messages. The news doesn't cover the people who have been individually contacted. Are you one of those? Is that how you came to know Reckoner?"

Dowland nodded, not having a clue what she was talking about.

"I need to meet with him in person," he told her. "I can deliver messages to powerful people. Those who control things. Those who are dangerous."

"But you don't just knock on a door and find him."

"How do you communicate with him, then?"

"He finds you," Lucia said. "He has been able to talk through my SYNAP-SYS. His voice sounds different each time."

"How? How is he able to do this?"

"I don't know. Honestly. I— I work at my information-processing job at Incen Tower and spend my weekends binge-watching shows from the golden era of digital content. Nothing is really different or special about me, but Reckoner thinks I'm different and special. He makes you feel that way. Of course, I see Christ in him. In his spirit. In his love."

She's as trapped as the four souls in the Hopper painting. Only she's crazy as well. "Who are the people in this city that you work with? People who know the man?"

"All these questions . . . They make me nervous."

There was a third thing Dowland sometimes used to help his job. Instead of pointing a gun or telling a lie, he simply looked at Lucia for a moment. Then he smiled.

When she finally smiled back, really smiled, he knew she was going to share as much as he needed to know.

4.

He waits. Patience is a key to this job. Along with letting go of the guilt after it pays off.

Dowland thinks of the painting again. Those silent figures, so alone even in the midst of one another.

It's a portrait of this world.

People pass, talking with someone through their SYNAPSYS, or listening to music with eardots to avoid the outside conversations, or watching the walls of visuals, from the daily news draped over the sides of buildings to vintage music videos and movies playing on the sidewalk. His eyes find a woman walking across the street, all business as she argues with someone somewhere else, and then his attention lingers on the intersection as he sees footage of the Spielberg classic *Jaws*.

We used to go into darkened rooms to escape reality and watch lit-up life on the big screen. Now we've become those darkened rooms since life is lit up all around us.

He waits to spot the man who is using an alias of Jim Johnson, perhaps the most common-sounding name to make it all the less memorable. Lucia told him this wasn't *the* Reckoner, the one behind everything, but Dowland suspects that's something everybody will believe. A man who has done the sort of things Reckoner is doing is not only dangerous but also smart enough to keep everybody at arm's length, even those who might be his most committed.

Committed . . . That's the right word to use.

He sits on the sidewalk table watching the evening activity and feels as if he might be drinking on a sidewalk in Phoenix or Florida or Mexico instead of Chicago. It's February, and the temperature is five degrees and getting colder, and snow will be coming tomorrow, but still he's warm and comfortable on the sidewalk table. It's not some tacky plastic-covered veranda, and he's not being blasted with heaters the size of semitrucks. It's new technology a kid probably in the eighth grade invented, allowing the stone on the sidewalk and building to make an invisible bubble of temperature set as warm as you'd like.

Dowland remembers being a kid and thinking heated cement sidewalks were cool. As he finishes his cocktail, he wonders what would happen if the temperature accidentally got set to 120 degrees. Would people start passing out or possibly burst into flames?

A man hurrying down the sidewalk across the street stops Dowland's wandering nonsense.

He's wearing the Cubs beanie and thick winter coat, just as she said he would.

It's hard to make out the man's face since his mouth is covered by a goatee and he's wearing a hat. Dowland opens up a screen on his table and looks at the scan on the man's SYNAPSYS. Sure enough, it's an alias, with the name registered as James Joseph Johnson. As if he's actually trying to be ridiculous with this cover-up. There's a fake Chicago address, fake work name, fake spouse, fake everything. But at least he knows this is Lucia's contact.

The man is tall and lean, maybe in his late forties or early fifties. The patch of beard makes it tough to really examine him, but there's no gray in it. Then again, he could easily color it, or the goatee could be fake. These days it's hard to know what's real and what's fake with someone.

Dowland has already paid for his drinks, so he stands and then leaves, jogging down the sidewalk and soon feeling the temperature drop by about seventy degrees. He stops at the intersection, watching mostly similar-looking Autovehs passing by. A security robot waits at the corner, giving him one of those creepy android smiles as if it knows it could crush him in two seconds, and as if it is angry it has to be standing there watching, as though it has something better to do.

Crossing the street at the green light with twenty others, Dowland weaves through the city folk going about their normal lives without a clue. A pair of young girls carrying shopping bags. A couple locked in each other's arms at perhaps the start of a date. An older couple, reeking of money, walking as if they owned not only this boulevard but the entire neighborhood.

Not a clue. Not one bit.

The wind cuts, and he's reminded his thin coat isn't suitable for this weather. He passes an Irish pub and then another fancy restaurant. The man he's following stops in the middle of the block, with people passing in both directions slightly knocking into him, one even cursing at him to keep going. Dowland halts too, in such an obvious way that it draws attention to him.

The man ahead of him turns, the Cubs beanie facing him.

Dowland sees a pair of eyes staring at him, then scanning the rest of the sidewalks around them.

As Dowland starts walking toward the man, casually without an obvious care, Mr. James Joseph Johnson tears down the sidewalk, hitting and plowing through the evening shoppers and strollers who are braving the cold night.

Dowland curses and takes off as well, reaching for his Beretta for a second, then changing his mind. He's not going to give himself away. Not yet. He can still be who he claims to be while chasing JJJ. Taking out the handgun changes everything.

Something about the way Johnson is running, though . . . There's something about it he doesn't like.

Johnson gets to the corner and slows down, walking by the security robot, then runs once again in the middle of the street while crossing. The light turns red as Dowland steps to the curb. Valuable seconds tick off slowly as he waits, cursing and moving his body back and forth, trying to force himself to be patient.

With a steady line of vehicles coming both ways, Dowland darts into the street, holding out both hands while the cars screech to a stop. One even slightly hits him as he tries his best to roll over its hood like some cool seventies cop, but instead, he jams his hip while the artificial driver doesn't say a word.

I kinda miss the days of the jerk taxi drivers with their disregard for everything other than their cabs and customers.

He continues running down the sidewalk, telling others to move but never apologizing. He keeps wondering whether to get the gun out. At the next intersection he can't see Johnson. Then he turns to see the man heading east toward Lake Michigan. Dowland continues his pursuit even as the lights dim where they're headed. He grabs the short, round grip of his Beretta and pulls it out of his side holster. Fewer people can be seen on this side street between office buildings. Johnson's dark figure is the only thing moving ahead of him.

It takes a minute to run down the block, the echoes of his boots on the cold cement seeming to bounce off the buildings. Johnson is at another intersection but keeps going down this side street. The man knows he's being chased and has no desire to stop and see who it is.

Dowland knows this is his man. *It's gotta be Reckoner. There's no way some ordinary, regular person would have any clue who I am.*

Lucia believed Dowland was who he said he was.

With his breathing rapid and sweat on his forehead, Dowland stops in the middle of the block. The lights on this section of the street are off for some reason. It's dark, and he's lost sight of his man. Pausing for a moment, he holds his breath to listen as carefully as possible to his surroundings, but only a passenger vehicle can be heard as it races past him to the next stoplight.

The barrel of his gun tracks where his eyes scan, to the five-story government building next to him, to the tracks of the Mag-Train in front of him.

He opens his left hand and looks at his palm to see the digital map displaying the streets around him. One of the millions of tools the SYNAPSYS gives you when it's turned on like now. He sees that Lake Michigan is only six blocks away. The building next to him is unoccupied, thus the look of abandonment everywhere.

As he starts to walk again heading east, a black shape emerges from the shadows of the brick building.

There's a door there—

And before he can move his gun forward, a flashing, hot streak of white flame blinds him and causes him to jerk backward. He falls on his side and feels a searing pain tear through his arm as all his weight jams it—all while the pyrotechnics in front of him continue spewing dazzling sparks.

Then they stop, and the flares turn into thick smoke that rushes over him, causing him to choke.

A Phantom Tear.

As he gags and spits while getting on his feet to sprint away from the toxic fumes, Dowland realizes exactly what type of instrument is being used on him. It's a combination of heavy-duty fireworks and tear gas, used only by the military and the National Guard. The initial flames are meant both to dazzle and to distract the targets, right before an explosion of black gas swarms over them, causing temporary blindness and the inability to breathe. And if they inhale too much of the fumes, they end up spending the night in the ER.

Dowland emerges from the smog but continues gagging. His eyes feel as though they're on fire as he blinks and tries to see his surroundings. As he squints and begins to regain some focus, the passenger vehicle that just passed has its blinking red lights on, meaning it's picking up somebody.

He races down the sidewalk, coughing again, one hand wiping the tears from his eyes. He calls out for the vehicle to stop, and then he aims and fires three loud rounds, the shots seeming to go off into nowhere. Soon the car is one block farther away. Then it turns and is gone.

Dowland curses and bends over and retches. Everything tastes and smells like burning flesh, something he's smelled before. Of course, it's the toxins of the Phantom Tear used on him.

There's no way that James Johnny JimJam is anybody other than the Reckoner.

He's made contact, which is good. He's close, which is even better.

In another day or two, the Reckoner is going to be found. And then I'm going to make him pay for this Fourth of July display tonight.

NINE

Death Is Inevitable

Do Not Trespass signs appeared around the cracked pavement of the parking lot in front of the block-long warehouse. The building looked abandoned and not even worthy of the money spent to bulldoze it. As they drove up to it, Jazz made sure it was the correct address, not via his SYNAPSYS but from the scrawled directions on a note.

"This is it," he told Cheyenne.

"The place we're staying?" she asked.

"No. Well, at least not tonight."

He grinned but he sounded serious. They passed the building and continued driving down the road on the outskirts of Tulsa. Cheyenne hadn't seen any other vehicles in the last ten minutes.

"Good luck trying to hide the Hummer," she said.

"Nobody's going to bother us around here. Everything has moved to the center of the city, and the industrial section is on the other side of town. These buildings used to have actual men and women working inside them instead of machines."

The sinking sun hovered behind a three-story brick apartment building that looked as if it hadn't been lived in for twenty years. They parked on the side of the road, a couple of blocks away from the warehouse, then walked over the chunks of cracked sidewalk toward the building.

"What are we going to do here?" Cheyenne asked.

"How about you just wait and see?" Jazz suggested.

"I've been doing that for the last few days."

"Then you're already used to it."

"Do you think anybody knows where I am? That we're being followed?"

Jazz stopped for a moment and turned to her. "You'd be in a little room being interrogated if they knew where you were."

"And what about you?"

"A saved-by-grace rapper isn't on their priority list for the moment. I haven't stirred up any commotion. I haven't gone public by exposing the blood rituals and human sacrifices."

No sign of sarcasm or banter could be detected.

"Are you talking about the Old Testament again or the current day?" Cheyenne asked.

"Never mind. Just listen up. Forget about me. I want you to be open about what you see and hear inside. Okay? I haven't met these people, but I have word that they're good folk."

"I think I've been pretty open about everything, especially hiding in claustrophobic places."

"Good point."

2.

The normal Cheyenne would have felt too restless and incredulous to sit on a folding metal chair surrounded by twenty-five strangers as they sang worship songs and then prayed as a group until finally an older man gave an informal talk about Jesus and His disciples. But then again, the old Cheyenne would have never ended up in the back of an abandoned warehouse hiding out in a gathering that someone might have passed off as a recovery meeting.

If only Malek could see me now.

The old Cheyenne, the person she used to be, was gone. She hadn't gone out and found religion or some cause to follow. It was more like she had been thrown into that volatile concoction, and she was desperate to find her way out of it. So in order to do that, she had to do one thing: find her father.

With the reality of what was happening, with someone like Jazz leading her to this place, Cheyenne could tolerate coming to this makeshift church service. She didn't feel any kind of surprising, Zen-like peace, but she did feel accepted in this group of people. Whatever they believed and however they felt they needed to express that was fine with her, especially since they weren't threatening or judging. She had a problem not with Christianity as a religion but with the few radical zealots who had made the government impose such strong regulations in the last few years.

As the preacher or pastor or whatever he was called addressed all of them, not behind a pulpit or on a stage but rather standing in front of them, he spoke about "doubting Thomas." A quote he said caught Cheyenne's attention.

"Oswald Chambers said this about faith: 'Seeing is never believing: we interpret what we see in the light of what we believe. Faith is confidence in God before you see God emerging; therefore the nature of faith is that it must be tried.'"

As the story went, Thomas *had* to see Jesus in order to believe. But faith was believing before one saw Jesus in the first place.

"The nature of faith is that it must be tried." It was a good quote, at least the last part of it. Faith could come in many ways and could focus on many things. For now, Cheyenne needed to have faith in herself, along with needing to keep going and keep believing there was some light at the end of this tunnel.

3.

"There are only ten of us left from our former church," Susan Parschauer told Cheyenne and Jazz. The service had ended an hour ago, but most of the people had stayed around to talk and drink coffee. Just like a regular church service.

Or recovery group.

Tom and Susan Parschauer were a sweet couple, probably in their late sixties, who had been leaders at a large Baptist church in Tulsa before it was officially shut down. They shared how government regulations over the years had crippled its finances, making it impossible to keep their facility and scaring off much of the congregation. President Valdez had been secretive about putting the Hate Propagation Law into place, but after Alden Blackwood's campaign of "We Are One" got him elected as president, the government began acting on "hate crimes" committed by law-abiding Christians.

"They modified US Code Section 249 to include language and speech," Susan told Cheyenne. "Nobody realized the new law basically made it a crime to share one's faith publicly if it's deemed 'offensive' in any manner."

Cheyenne didn't know much about politics and law, so all of this was news to her. "Were you involved in politics?" she asked.

Susan laughed as she shook her head and looked at her husband. "I've always been a pastor's wife. Still am. But that doesn't mean I can't understand what's happened, even if most Americans don't know it."

Tom shared how he had continued to preach the same gospel message he'd been giving his church for the last two decades. Because of that, he ended up actually going to jail. Demonstrations around this time turned violent, scandals emerged, and the entire church body seemed to implode.

"Just as the Enemy wanted it to," Susan said.

Cheyenne wasn't sure which enemy Susan was referring to—the government or the locals who wanted to shut them down. Or maybe it was the devil.

They sat around a plastic picnic table sipping instant coffee from paper cups. Surprisingly, the coffee wasn't as bad as she had imagined. Jazz let the couple share their story with them, asking them questions but never sharing any details about himself or Cheyenne. The only thing the Parschauers knew was they were friends of Reckoner and were "sympathetic to the cause," as Jazz put it. They also knew Jazz and Cheyenne needed a temporary place to hide from the authorities, something the Parschauers were increasingly helping with.

"So you've been meeting here since they closed your church doors?" Cheyenne asked.

"Well, we've always believed a church can be anywhere that believers are gathered," Tom said. "We've had to meet in several different locations, always in secret, always trusting God will protect us."

"Sometimes he fancies himself one of the early disciples, like the ones he spoke about today," Susan said, her wrinkles surrounding the smile she gave her husband.

Now there was something truly unusual: wrinkles. Most of the older men and women Cheyenne knew had them digitally removed, an expensive procedure but way more natural looking and effective than the surgery or laser jobs in the past. Still, something always looked *off* whenever Cheyenne saw those wrinkle-free grandfathers and grandmothers. Susan's appearance was refreshing. *Maybe because it looks real.*

"I never thought things would get so bad—not in Tulsa of all places. I could understand what happened in Chicago and New York. But to see all those people leave—to disappear when the reality came knocking on their door—was sad. But it's a wake-up call too."

"How long after that did you meet Acrobat?" Jazz asked the couple.

Tom looked confused for a moment and then gave a knowing smile. "Acrobat? Is that what you're calling him?"

"He hasn't given me his real name yet," Jazz said. "And I haven't been able to find one either. That's an early name he used."

"He already has enough aliases and code names, but we call him Scout," Tom said.

"For Boy Scout," Susan chimed in.

They both chuckled, an image that was cute to see. It reminded Cheyenne of one of those holiday movies where an elderly couple, still madly in love with each other, were living on a farm and were always dispensing advice to the younger and more idiotic generation. She hadn't grown up with a set of parents caring or even being around each other. So to see that it really existed outside someone's imagination inspired the same feeling as Susan's wrinkles.

"We called him Scout because he knocked on our door one evening like a Boy Scout selling popcorn. The way they used to do it, when they were Boy Scouts and Girl Scouts instead of just the all-purpose Scouts. He showed up and asked to talk about our church, and one thing led to another."

Tom paused, not saying anything more.

What led to what? She wanted to ask and almost did before Jazz spoke.

"When was the last time you saw Scout?"

Tom and Susan looked at each other.

"A month ago?" he ventured.

"No, longer than that," she said.

They volleyed back and forth, finally settling on last month.

"He only stayed for a night," Tom said. "He looked tired, and he was worried he was being followed. But he still managed to talk with us late into the night about everything that was happening. About the good news he had to report."

"Then he left? Where'd he go?"

"I don't know," Tom told Jazz. "He didn't even tell us he was leaving. We didn't ask either."

"So how long have you two been a part of this?" Susan asked, looking at Cheyenne first.

"A part of what?" Cheyenne asked, looking at Jazz for assistance.

"She's new," Jazz said. "And I've been on the fringes for several years. Hoping to stay there too."

"We have some families and friends in the Chicago area." Susan rubbed her discolored and bony hands together, trying to warm them. "We don't know much, so all we've been able to do is warn them that something bad is coming. We've told them to prepare for something cataclysmic. Of course, they all think we're crazy."

"I'd rather have someone believe I'm insane than pity me," Tom said.

For someone so unassuming, he sounded fearless. It was obvious he wasn't full of pride, yet he was proud of what they stood for and what they were doing.

"I've grown used to people thinking I'm insane and pitying me," Jazz said with a glance at Cheyenne. "And, yeah, sometimes I think I really get those disciples. Those brothers had the whole world standing against them. I imagined their isolation when I'd be alone for weeks at a time back in Colorado."

"Do you know how long you'll be here in Tulsa?" Susan asked. She quickly added, "Please stay as long as you need to, of course. No pressure at all. Nobody knows about the safe house."

Cheyenne studied the look on Susan's face. Was it a look of alarm?

"I'm not sure how long," Jazz said. "We need to wait and lay low. And, like you talked about, we gotta have faith."

4.

As the flashing red traffic light outside lit up the room every other second—the narrow window blinds failing at their only job—Cheyenne replayed the night with the Parschauers.

She felt welcomed. And she felt safe. There wasn't one specific thing that happened to make her feel this way, not a statement or line of thought. The couple had something about them. An attitude and an air that could truly be summed up by the word *grace*.

They weren't rushed and weren't cynical and weren't overly worried about anything.

Cheyenne couldn't remember the last time she met someone who wasn't carrying a ticking clock and who didn't think he—or she—was being watched. Technology both enabled and eradicated things in one's life. In the name of convenience, people sacrificed anonymity. In the name of communication and connection, people sacrificed peace of mind. Yet the Parschauers seemed to have that very thing: peace.

Was it all an act? Are they that deluded?

They didn't talk down to her, nor did they speak as if they were trying to prove something, as if they needed her to believe as they did. They spoke as if they were talking about their family or some other important reality in their lives.

Over a home-cooked meal of lasagna, salad, and bread, Tom shared about his wilder days growing up and how his life was completely shaken up when "God got hold" of him, as he called it. Now, hours later, Cheyenne thought again about what he had said: *"I've always told people the same thing. Remember the story of the* Titanic *and its survivors? Don't you think they spent the rest of their lives talking about being rescued? And that every single day they could still see that massive ship slowly sinking into the dark ocean? I bet they could still feel those cold waters surrounding them. Some had to swim, and others rowed away. But I'm sure every single one of those survivors was not only grateful but spent his or her remaining days speaking about it. That's how I've always viewed coming to faith. This life here on earth is shorter in the grand scheme of eternity than a trip on an ocean cruiser. To know we've been spared . . ."* Tom had wiped the tears in his eyes and then smiled at Susan.

Cheyenne knew that even if every single belief they held was for nothing, they were a hundred percent committed. Just like Jazz.

The most amazing thing she witnessed that night was far more simple and subtle. She could still picture it vividly. A simple and brief moment, hidden from view, in the kitchen while the Parschauers cleaned up.

It was truly something remarkable.

Susan walked over and put some plates on the counter next to Tom. Then she put her hand in his as he leaned over and kissed her on the cheek and told her dinner was great.

In all her time growing up and in every relationship she had ever known, both her own and others, she had never witnessed a moment like that. It hadn't been a husband kissing his wife in hopes of getting some action later in the night, nor was it the passion of a young couple or the common courtesy one might see in public. It was so simple yet profound. The hand held, the peck on the cheek, the affirmation. All without strings, without expectations or baggage, without anything other than one beautiful thing. *Love.*

They weren't newlyweds. They were grandparents, a couple who had been married for decades.

There had been a time not long ago when she had believed something like that might be possible. A friendship that seemed to be slowly turning into something deeper. Then suddenly he was gone. Malek had been missing ever since.

She thought about her father, then found herself starting to stumble down an emotional mountain when she thought about her mother. Cheyenne regained her footing like always. That was a place she couldn't go.

Perhaps she wouldn't have been so guarded and careful in her life if her parents had stayed together. If she had a mother.

She could think of a thousand *ifs*.

Forget AI. We all set up our own unconscious algorithms based on history and hurt, and they can take us down dangerous rabbit holes if we're not careful.

Cheyenne knew this all too well. At least she thought she knew. But this faith thing seemed to disrupt the algorithms in life. She had, after all, seen this firsthand and knew it from research. That's what Acatour wanted ultimately— to overcome one's personal faith by using the machinery of deduction and deception.

The Parschauers showed all of that could be tossed aside when there was something bigger in its place. Cheyenne couldn't fathom that it was real.

5.

"We need to disappear into thin air for a while," Jazz said the moment she walked out of the apartment building where they had spent the night.

"So that's our plan? To remain in hiding?"

"Until I hear more," he said, looking refreshed and almost giddy. "We're going to have breakfast with the Parschauers."

"You obviously slept better than I did," she said after they climbed into the Hummer.

"Not really. I don't sleep much. Look. Check this out."

The screen on the dashboard lit up with news images from a city street.

"Is that Chicago?" Cheyenne asked.

"Yeah. Right along Michigan Avenue. Near the Incen Tower."

She could see cars that looked as if they had sayings painted on them in bright colors.

"Those are all Autovehs," she noticed. "Is that the work of—"

"Yeah. Acrobat's been busy."

The volume was turned down, so she couldn't hear what the reporter was saying, but she read words and phrases on the tops and sides of the Autovehs. "'I want everything.' 'Death is inevitable.' 'Hype hope.' What is all this?"

Jazz shook his head, laughing as he began to drive down the street to find a coffee shop. "I provided a little help in this. Not in the actual decorating but in coordinating it."

"'Ambition bites the nails of success'?" she read.

"You know the Acrobat is a big fan of music. No? Well, I guess, how could you? He explained this all to me and showed me old video clips. He got inspired by the band U2."

"My father loves them."

"Yeah. They made an album in East Berlin. No, I think they made it in West Berlin when there was an East and a West Berlin, when there was a wall. And the wall went down during this time. He told me that lots of East Berliners drove around in little, poorly made cars called Trabants, so U2 used them in marketing their album and their shows. They painted them. Just like those Autovehs."

"What are the sayings?"

"All different slogans and phrases the band used for their album. 'Acrobat' is a song on that album, by the way. He went into detail about what he's trying to communicate, but the gist is the Trabants symbolized the fall of East Berlin."

"He's going for symbolism with the Autovehs?" Cheyenne asked.

Jazz parked on the curb close to a place where he could get coffee. "Mostly he's trying to get people's attention in a world where attention is the most precious commodity of all. This is like the cows in Chicago wandering around. Remember that?"

"That was him?"

Jazz laughed. "Yeah. That was him having fun and also trying to make different statements."

"Sounds like a thirteen-year-old boy."

"I know. But it's all part of the plan. Shaking things up."

"It's spray-painting cars," Cheyenne said as Jazz climbed out of the vehicle and closed the door.

"There were messages around the necks of those cows, just like there are messages attached to the steering wheels of those cars. The media won't always reveal what those messages say, especially when they're talking about Acatour and Jackson Heyford."

"Still," she said, unable to contain her bafflement, "we're talking about cars and cows. *Cars* and *cows*."

6.

After picking up four cups of coffee along with some assorted pastries, Jazz drove them to the house where they had enjoyed dinner last night. Moments before they arrived, Jazz's demeanor changed from upbeat to uneasy.

"Stay in here," Jazz said as he slowed the vehicle and then stopped fifty yards away from the Parschauers'.

"What do you mean? Why?"

"Something's not right."

"How do you know?"

Jazz's eyes shifted back and forth. He looked in the rearview mirror and on both sides of the Hummer.

"Look, there's supposed to be a signal at the base of the stop sign where we just turned." He pulled closer and looked at the front steps leading into the house. "And there's supposed to be one on the front door too."

"What kind of signal?"

"A welcome sign on the door. Says 'Home Sweet Home—The Parschauers.' If it's up, then it means things are fine to meet. But it's not."

"Maybe they forgot."

"No." Jazz looked all around them again. "You have to stay in here. If I'm not back in ten minutes, take off."

"And go where?"

He shook his head. "I don't know. Just get out of here. Hopefully you'll hear from someone. I've got a bad feeling about this."

Jazz jogged down the sidewalk, continuing to look all around him. He climbed the steps to their porch and then knocked on the door. After a moment he disappeared inside.

A minute passed. Then another.

"Come on," Cheyenne said, getting out of the car. She hated waiting when she had no clue what was happening.

As she arrived at the base of the steps, Jazz darted out of the house, his head moving back and forth, his eyes wide as they scanned the neighborhood all around them.

"Come on," he told her, grabbing her arm and guiding her away from the house.

"What happened?"

"Nothing. We have to go."

She jerked her arm away from him and then could see it on his face. He didn't look just concerned; Jazz appeared to be scared.

Without waiting for more of an answer, she bolted up the steps to the house, opened the door, and rushed in.

"Hello? Susan? Tom?"

She smelled a combination of bacon and something like burned toast. She called out their names again, and when she reached the kitchen, she jolted to a stop.

Cheyenne could hear her weak, airless scream come out like a suffocating whimper. Her hand cupped her mouth, her eyes squinting at the blood. Oh, the blood. So much of it. On the walls and the tile floor and the counters, splattered in horrific bursts. Susan Parschauer was crumpled in the corner on her side while Tom lay facedown near the kitchen's entrance. Cheyenne almost tripped on him.

Hearing steps behind her, she grabbed the large cleaver on the floor and held it up, ready to wield the bloody instrument.

"Cheyenne, come on," Jazz said as he reached her. She dropped it and could hear herself crying, wailing, as he put his arm around her. "Come on. We need to leave."

She had no words and could barely breathe. All she could hear was the pounding of her heart. Jazz led her to the Hummer and helped her in. Quickly he was behind the wheel and peeling away and rushing down the street.

"What . . . How could . . . I can't . . ." She still couldn't breathe, couldn't think.

"You're gonna be okay," Jazz said, putting his hand on hers.

She thought about Susan doing the same thing, reaching out to hold her husband's hand.

Cheyenne screamed.

TEN

The Charmed Watchman

1.

The seconds tapped at his forehead, the pendulum of a grandfather clock swinging back and forth in his head. Will knew he shouldn't worry. He knew that worry, in fact, was a sin. Right? Or maybe those were words from some pious person who didn't have to be concerned about finding a job or paying three months of mortgage payments or buying groceries or getting a call from an estranged father.

Worry means that you don't trust in God. That you aren't believing the very words He's spoken to us.

He sat in his office with midnight closing in, the soft-leather illustrated Bible open on his desk. As he skimmed through its pages trying to find some hope and light, he eventually came to Matthew 6 and read Jesus's words. Not just words, but commands.

That is why I tell you not to worry about everyday life—whether you have enough food and drink, or enough clothes to wear. Isn't life more than food, and your body more than clothing? Look at the birds. They don't plant or harvest or store food in barns, for your heavenly Father feeds them. And aren't you far more valuable to him than they are? Can all your worries add a single moment to your life?

His girls, especially Shaye, were growing so fast. He got stressed about not being able to buy her new shoes. Or new outfits that actually fit. He worried about the girls not eating the right types of food. They were so picky, and he couldn't afford to invest in the healthier options of food designed specifically for finicky eaters.

Look at the birds, Will.

Jesus's admonition to His followers answered Will's wandering thoughts.

> So don't worry about these things, saying, "What will we eat? What will we drink? What will we wear?" These things dominate the thoughts of unbelievers, but your heavenly Father already knows all your needs. Seek the Kingdom of God above all else, and live righteously, and he will give you everything you need.

He looked at the list he had written down next to him. A list of options, of hopes, of things to do in his job search. Next to it was a big to-do list, things he needed to do and things he wanted to do. Underneath those lists was another one. This list was a compilation of all the bills he had to pay. Two pages' worth. Credit cards and utility bills and payments owed and debts from the store. They were all filed online, but having them written out in blue ink gave them greater meaning. It made them feel more urgent. The gravity of all he needed to do and pay and discover and get out of could be felt more strongly after seeing these notes to himself.

Are you not paying attention? It's time to wake up, Will.

All these doubts and worries felt foolish in light of the bigger and more troublesome fears. The kind involving his father and Hutchence and the supposed storm of judgment coming to Chicago. He took a breath and read the final verse in Matthew 6.

> So don't worry about tomorrow, for tomorrow will bring its own worries. Today's trouble is enough for today.

Of course Jesus was right. His words were perfect. Will couldn't do anything about tomorrow, not in his office at almost midnight. Tomorrow would arrive, and he would try to handle it the best way he could, tackling his to-do list and working on these items and trying not to panic and trying really hard to lay it all at God's feet, knowing He was in control.

Sometimes faith was so hard.

2.

Midway through the following morning, Will checked his network mailboxes and noticed a familiar name attached to a note.

> Hi, Will. Hope you and the family are doing well. Sorry for the short message, but I'm wondering if you can call me on the same number you've always used. It's important. Thanks.
>   Brian Wallace

The message had been sent on the network to his general inbox, one not connected to his SYNAPSYS. General incoming mail like this didn't generate notifications, especially since most were simply spam. Will knew why Pastor Brian was contacting him this way. He specifically didn't want their connection to be tracked or noticed in any way.

He found the old smartphone in a desk drawer and had to charge it for half an hour before he could call the pastor. The phone rang only once.

"Hey, Will. Thanks for calling." Pastor Brian sounded as friendly and thoughtful as always.

"Is everything okay?"

There was a pause for a moment. "I'm doing well. So's the family. I wanted to talk to you about some important matters, stuff that can't be mentioned on the phone."

"We always used this for our discussions about your book," Will said.

"This is different. This concerns your recent new friend."

"Have you spoken to him lately?" Will asked.

"Yes. I've seen him, actually. And I'd like to do the same with you."

"You'd like to get together?"

"Yes. But because of the position I'm in, I need you to come up and see me."

Will was about to ask what sort of position the pastor was talking about, but he doubted he would get much of an explanation. "The person you're talking about," he began, "is he in any way threatening you or your family?"

"No, no, no. That's why I want to talk to you. In person. Immediately. He asked me to give him a personal endorsement."

"He's completely legitimate?" Will asked.

"He's more than that."

"I don't need to drive up to see you in order to believe that. If you say it's the case, that's all I need to believe it."

"I appreciate that, Will. But there's more to talk about. He informed me of your situation."

Will forced a chuckle. "So you know I have time on my hands."

"Hardly. Life for you is probably more urgent now than it ever has been. I understand. I've been there. But once I can share more, you'll see why the timing of everything is providential."

Without needing to hear more, Will told Brian he would leave shortly. He needed to tell Amy why he was leaving, something he couldn't completely explain even to himself.

3.

Amy looked surprised to get a connect call from Will, but she'd accepted it since this was technically her lunch break.

She was sitting in her cubicle, a half-eaten salad in the plastic container on her desk next to a dozen notes. Even though there were a hundred more productive ways to put together a talk or a paper, Will knew she had always preferred writing out by hand important quotes and thoughts and then putting them into an electronic document. The physical act of moving a pen and writing in cursive made her remember the information more clearly.

"You look busy," he said.

"If only you could see the ten documents I'm working on with all this."

"I would ask what your presentation is on, but I know it's over my C-student head."

"It's not difficult to understand," Amy said in her matter-of-fact manner. "I've been concentrating on a study related to the percentage of food demand being met within East Asia as compared to the population and productivity growth in the region. The fact that it's only forty-five percent is quite alarming."

As he thought about her answer, Amy said, "Why do you suddenly look perplexed?"

"I thought you worked on ways to keep food fresh and tasty," Will said. "East Asia? I don't get it."

"This is work on my master's," she said. "I've decided to speed up the process. That bump in my pay grade would certainly help us."

He had virtually forgotten about the three years she'd been working on her master's degree in food science. Strange how everyday things faded from memory. "I wanted to let you know I'm driving up to Grand Rapids today to meet with Pastor Brian."

She looked busy and distracted as she took a bite of her salad and simply nodded. "Why?"

"To talk about job stuff, among other things," Will said, not exactly lying but not necessarily telling her the whole truth either.

Maybe the pastor knows about an opportunity.

"Job stuff? Is there a job opening with his church?"

"He doesn't exactly have a church."

"Well, I know that," Amy said as she sipped from her water bottle. "So what 'job stuff' would you be talking about?"

Amy was a black-and-white sort of person who liked specifics, so whenever Will used words like *stuff,* she seemed to get back at him by repeating the vague word over and over until she got clarification.

"I'm looking at everything," he said.

"Are you going to see my parents?"

"Are you trying to be funny?"

This got her attention, and she shook her head, looking at him with a serious expression. "No. But I could let them know you're coming if you wanted to stop by."

"Uh, no. I don't want your father asking me to come work for him again."

Amy was silent as an incoming message on the screen next to her caught her attention for a moment. As she turned, he noticed how pretty she looked. The way her hair bounced and the blue in her eyes stood out. He rarely got to spend time with the professional Amy Stewart. At home she was always Mommy.

"But I don't get it," she said. "Why drive up to see Pastor Brian? Can't you just talk to him like this?"

"No," Will said. "It needs to be more private."

She understood his answer, knowing the sensitivity of the work they had already done together. Amy had continually warned Will about this and about the bookstore, telling him he had a family he needed to worry about. Getting thrown in jail for producing Christian books was the last thing they needed at this time.

He wanted to tell her more, but he couldn't. Not just because their conversation might be overheard, but also because he wasn't sure how even to start telling her about Hutchence.

I think I might be losing my mind, because I'm talking to this stranger, and he's telling me all these things about God and being a Christian and how the time is now and warnings and stuff.

Amy would be even more worried, wondering who this stranger was and what he wanted her husband to do.

"I'll be driving back late tonight," Will said to her. "Tell the girls Daddy says hi when you pick them up from school."

"Can you really see yourself getting a job in Grand Rapids?" she asked. "All of us moving?"

"I don't know. Maybe."

"Didn't you once say—"

"I've said a lot of things in my life," Will interrupted.

He knew what she was referring to. One of those edicts he used to make all the time. Like he would never buy a minivan, never borrow money from his in-laws, and never have to shut his store's doors. And he would never, positively never, contact his father again. Will had also once openly declared that they would never move to Grand Rapids, even doubling down on it and adding the wonderful phrase "over my dead body."

My soul's feeling pretty dead these days.

At this point he didn't care about having to eat his words. Or having to swallow his pride. Maybe he would have to grovel in front of his father-in-law. It didn't matter. It wasn't about him anymore. It hadn't been for a long time.

"I'll do whatever's best for this family," Will said. "And I'm not trying to sound noble or anything. I'm trying to figure things out."

She looked at him with searching eyes. He could tell she was afraid of saying the wrong thing but wanted to say something.

"You don't have to say anything," he told her.

Amy didn't look relieved. Instead, she looked hurt.

The two of them could have an entire conversation simply through looks and expressions and body language. That's what a long marriage built, for better or for worse.

"I think God is trying to tell me something," he admitted. "And not that owning a bookstore in this world is a dumb thing. That was clear about five years ago."

"Owning a bookstore is a good thing," Amy said.

Will almost believed her, but he still couldn't accept those words from her. "You can't use the present tense anymore. It's not anything right now. Maybe it *was* a good thing. But I'm talking about something else. Something . . . bigger."

She waited for more, but he couldn't figure out the more to sum up the conversation.

"I'm meeting Pastor Brian for dinner and then coming back."

"Will it be worth it?"

He shrugged. "I don't know."

He quickly told her goodbye and said he'd connect later. In the car heading down the street in their subdivision, he thought of the departure as he watched snow starting to fall on his windshield. He never used to leave Amy without telling her he loved her. Sometimes over and over again, as if uttering the word made it more real.

Maybe it does.

4.

The lake-effect snow made for slow driving on I-94 as it curved north so close to the shores of Lake Michigan. When he saw the sign for I-196, Tolkien, his artificial friend, warned him in his thick English accent about taking the exit.

"You should stay on I-94 heading east to avoid the heavier snow," Tolkien said in his articulate and flowing manner. "You can then take US 131 north to Grand Rapids."

Will ignored him and instead thought how incredible it was to have a personal digital assistant who could not only sound like a real human being from history but whose voice actually came directly from the source. The figures had to be famous historical individuals, so one person might have President Barack Obama giving instructions, while others could have Eddie Murphy ranting at them. Will once met a patron at his store whose artificial assistant, Marilyn, sounded like Marilyn Monroe at her most sultry and seductive. In picking specific voices like these, people received their personalities as well.

"You are driving far above the speed these weatherworn and bare tires can handle," Tolkien told him, sounding exactly like the linguist and professor. "Tire treads are meant to help whisk the water away—"

"I know what treads are for, thank you very much. New tires are expensive."

"So are funerals."

Will laughed. "That's a good one," he had to admit.

"This whiteout will remain for the next ten minutes at this current speed."

"You know, I wonder if Hemingway would be lecturing me on tires. I was going to pick him as a digital comrade."

"Why did you choose the term *comrade*?" Tolkien asked. "Most use words like *assistant, aide, guide,* or *partner* to describe their artificial helper."

"I hate how they were all originally called Life Companions, LCs. Especially since the CEO of the company that makes you guys has been very public with his thoughts on why marriages are ridiculous."

"In the *Oxford English Dictionary* one of the definitions of *comrade* is 'a fellow socialist or communist.' So am I a socialist or a communist?"

Will shook his head, keeping his eyes on the road. "Right now I'd say you're a communist, and I'm very much feeling the Cold War coming. Just let me drive for a while in silence."

Half an hour later as Tolkien guided Will on 196 to the restaurant where he would meet Pastor Brian, he also provided an overview of the job market in the Grand Rapids area. "There are two bookstores in the great Grand Rapids area, which includes the southwest towns of Grandville, Wyoming, and—"

"I don't need a list of all the communities," Will interrupted, something he never felt guilty for doing with any kind of AI. "And, please, I'm not looking to start another bookstore."

"There would be an above-average opportunity in this market, considering the numbers for Ink the last few years and comparing them to the numbers with—"

"Tolkien! Even if they had a free building space and were going to pay my rent for a year, I would not open another bookstore!"

Interrupting was one of Will's bad habits with the AI, but persisting with an idea Will didn't like was Tolkien's.

"This area still has the highest percentage of churches in the country," Tolkien said. "That means there would be more patrons receptive to the nature of your products."

"Receptive to the nature." Will laughed. "And what 'nature' is that?"

It was fascinating to hear what an AI said about faith. Will had asked questions like this before, always curious what the answer would be.

"The dangerous nature of some of your literature. For instance, the work of Dietrich Bonhoeffer."

The wipers were going at full speed but still couldn't keep up with the thick flakes coming down.

"Oh yeah. Good old Bonhoeffer. He sure got me into trouble, didn't he?"

"For you the books were dangerous to keep since the FBI fined you and threatened to prosecute you on grounds of promoting prejudices against others. On the other hand, the books are dangerous to the powers that be because of the message inside them."

Interesting, Tolkien. "So what message is that?" Will asked.

"'Christianity preaches the infinite worth of that which is seemingly worthless and the infinite worthlessness of that which is seemingly so valued.' A quote from *The Bonhoeffer Reader*."

The wealth of all information was always on the tip of Tolkien's artificial tongue. The interesting question was not only how the information was selected but also how it was processed.

"Before you start quoting more of Bonhoeffer, tell me about the jobs you've found," Will said, simply curious after having told his wife he was looking into them.

Tolkien spent the next ten minutes going through a variety of jobs that were currently listed in the area—ones that might be a good fit or at least a decent fit for Will. As always, Tolkien did get the wrong information on a few of the listings, like the managing editor position.

"Do you know the magazines that company produces?" Will asked with a big grin.

Whenever Tolkien paused, it wasn't because he needed the time to look up something, nor was the time needed for him to process the information. It was the human quality he had built within him, one his algorithms had developed, where he paused out of slight embarrassment.

"Yes, I guess you would not want to edit journals such as *Ladies of the Night* and *Escort Tales*," Tolkien admitted, sounding as if he was chagrined.

"Yeah, Amy might not like that." Will laughed.

There they were again, those so-called "genetic algorithms" put to use, the kind that the big and mighty Acatour had developed in one of their brainchild divisions.

None of the job listings sounded even remotely promising.

"We will arrive at Midpointe Restaurant in six minutes," Tolkien said. "Do you want me to repeat any of the job postings?"

"No. I'm not talking to Pastor Brian about them, anyway."

"What will your primary topic of conversation be with him?"

"You're kinda nosy," Will joked. "He knows a lot, especially about his faith. He's a strong believer and really an overall good guy. I need to get some advice. Not smart advice, but the kind that comes from the soul." *A kind that you, my AI friend, won't ever truly have, no matter how many brilliant algorithms some genius gives you.* "I hope Pastor Brian will help me see some meaning in what's been happening lately," Will said.

"As Bonhoeffer said, 'There is meaning in every journey that is unknown to the traveler.'"

Will felt a wave of goose bumps over his skin.

Even though Tolkien was a machine, it didn't mean God couldn't speak through him. It seemed more and more that God was doing exactly that.

5.

Brian Wallace looked the same as he had when Will had last seen him, except with perhaps a little more gray edging out his dark hair. Even though he was more than sixty years old, he was more fit than Will. It probably came with the territory of not only being an athlete himself but also having three sons who were heavily into sports. Six years ago Pastor Wallace had stepped away from his leadership role at the small church he had led, one that was more of a home church than the kind he used to have twenty years ago that filled several thousand seats every Sunday morning.

Will greeted Pastor Brian at the entrance to the breakfast place, and things felt as natural as they had four years ago when they had worked together on Brian's book, *Consider This*.

"How's the book business?" Pastor Brian asked after they had sat down in the booth and caught up on how the families were doing.

Like so many others Will knew, Will hadn't told him about the bookstore.

"I closed shop," Will said, tightening his lips and giving a whatcha-gonna-do sort of look.

"Really? That's surprising."

"Yeah."

Although it wasn't, not to Will.

"Last time we spoke, you said things were going well."

"They had been, for a bookstore. But it's a little like asking a kid how sales are going with a lemonade stand. 'Going well' is always a relative term, especially when you're getting flak for some of the literature you're promoting."

"Did they shut you down?" Brian asked in a voice just above a whisper.

"Yeah. Now I know a little more of how you must've felt when the church closed its doors."

"So what are your plans?" Brian asked.

"Good question. I'm still trying to figure that out."

Brian took a sip of his water. "I'm sure our mutual friend has only managed to make things a little more confusing."

"You could say that."

"I appreciate your coming up here without any reservations."

"What do you mean?" Will asked with a grin. "I have a ton of reservations. I just brought them along for the ride."

"We needed to talk like this, in person. It's better this way."

Will nodded, knowing what the pastor meant. Realizing that Big Brother was indeed watching in some capacity, especially with any network communication, made them cautious.

"I couldn't drive to see you for a variety of reasons," Brian said. "The same reasons that I can't explain everything to you right now in this restaurant."

Will couldn't remember a time he had ever seen the man look so grave.

"But I'll say this right up front: the work our friend is doing is important. It's necessary." He sighed, looked around the restaurant, and then looked back at Will. "It's God inspired too."

"Okay."

Their omelets arrived, and the discussion about Hutchence was temporarily paused. All Pastor Brian told him was they would pick it up again somewhere else.

"I want to show you a new business venture after we eat," Brian said. "It's a lot quieter. It's a great place to talk about books."

Is someone listening to this conversation right now?

"Sure," Will said. "Always love talking about books."

6.

Will followed Pastor Brian's car to a large warehouse near the middle of a suburb, close to an old set of abandoned railroad tracks. They parked in the shadows, and Brian unlocked a back door leading to a narrow hallway that they walked down. Will didn't question where they were going or what they were doing; he knew he could trust the man in front of him.

The door at the end of the hallway led to an open and airy space with rows of older furniture.

"The owner of this building sells high-end midcentury modern furniture. Used to operate from Chicago until he got burned out by city regulations and taxes, so he came here."

All the items they passed—chairs and tables and sofas—looked minimalistic and featured bright colors.

"Is this stuff worth a lot of money?" Will asked.

Pastor Brian slowed down and nodded. "Of course. I don't know much except what Nadal tells me. But it's crazy. Like that piece right there. It's an Eames lounge chair and ottoman. I think he told me it's priced around thirty thousand dollars."

The stylish leather chair looked sleek but not enough to be so expensive.

"You're in the furniture business, then?" Will asked.

Brian laughed. "Hardly."

They reached a space where there were dozens of chairs of all sorts lined up in the shape of a half moon. Brian stopped in front of them, right next to a dining table with no chairs.

"This is my church, where I preach, if that's what it could be called. Though I prefer to say I'm sharing with others."

The hard white light above them was cold and distant, and the furniture looked abandoned and lifeless, regardless of its value. Nothing about this space resembled any church Will had ever gone to.

"You have meetings here?"

"Yes. For one reason the owner of this building designed it so that SYNAP-SYSes don't work inside it. They're blocked from doing anything like recording or communicating with the outside."

"Why'd he do that?"

"He's part of the privacy movement. You know, those who are speaking up for their privacy."

"I hope he's not one of the more violent protesters," Will said.

"He's not. He just wants to live his life without anybody intruding or looking over his shoulder. Like most of us."

"So that's why you meet in here?"

"Yes," Pastor Brian said. "And that's why I wanted to bring you here. So we can talk. In privacy."

"You think someone might have been listening in on us back at the restaurant?"

Brian nodded and then sat down in an office chair and sighed.

"People have been spying on me for a long time, long before they shut down my church. I know we used to talk about this, but I realize it now more than ever before. There's a war going on out there. You know it now from experience—how they forced you to close after selling some Christian materials. It's gone that far in this country. First you couldn't speak out about issues like homosexuality or abortion or refugees or a better understanding of racial equality, with everybody on social media slamming those they deemed on the *wrong* side. The condemnation became so extreme, and now our culture is attacking everything—churches, gatherings, literature, and the arts. *Everything.*

Christianity has been eradicated, and most of the country has sat back and done nothing to stop it."

Will listened and nodded but finally asked the question that had caused him to drive three hours to this Michigan city. "What is Hutchence planning to do?"

"He wants to reveal the truth to this country."

"By listing the bad guys who are supposedly in control? The secret society ruling all?"

"That's part of it," Pastor Brian said. "But he's going to show what they've been doing. He's sending out a warning. But most important, he's also going to share the gospel of Christ."

Will moved over to sit across from Brian on the edge of the sofa. "But how is he supposed to do this? And how are you involved?"

"There are specifics I don't know that center on the science and technology related to SYNAPSYSes. They are foreign to me and even in some ways to Hutchence. But he's been recruiting a group of people throughout the country to help him. To be a faction that is going to fight back against Christian persecution. He wants pastors like me. He says he needs pastors for leadership and wisdom."

"You're sorta a life coach for an underground fanatic," Will said, partially joking.

Brian laughed with him, nodding and saying, "I guess in some ways that is my role."

"Do you believe the things Hutchence is saying?"

"Yes," Brian said without hesitation. "I believe everything."

"You believe that God is going to *wipe out* Chicago? Really?"

Once again the pastor nodded. "I've prayed earnestly and sought to hear from the Lord about this. About this man. Like many others I assumed the days of the prophets were in the past. The true prophets, the ones God raised up to proclaim something, came to tell the Israelites about their sin and what was about to befall them. I believe that's exactly what Hutchence is doing."

Will rubbed the side of his neck that ached. Pastor Brian had never looked more earnest than he did now. Will stood up again and paced the floor for a moment, trying to decide if all this was actually happening.

"How is he going to expose my father? How is he even going to reach him?"

"You're going to, Will. You're the only one who can."

7.

They spoke for another couple of hours, with Pastor Brian encouraging Will more than giving him advice or preaching to him. This was what Will wanted and needed. He had spent a lifetime without the proper guidance or support from his own father, so he had always desperately craved it from others. The pastor encouraged Will first to pray and ask for God's guidance, along with asking the big questions. It was what Will needed to hear.

The main question that had caused him to drive to Grand Rapids was answered.

Not only did Pastor Brian know Hutchence, but he also believed the man was a prophet. He believed that God was going to judge Chicago and the surrounding area, sending a sign to the rest of the country that they had turned their backs on their Creator and Master. The judgment wasn't to get their attention but rather to pour out His wrath against the sin and rebellion God so hated. Exactly what this judgment was going to look like was unknown to the pastor, but he believed it was coming.

After figuring out a way to keep in touch with Pastor Brian off the network and then bidding him goodbye, Will drove back home, wondering how in the world he would even begin to explain this to Amy.

I still can't really explain this to myself.

How could he tell his wife about Hutchence and his plan? About God's coming wrath on Chicago? She often told him the world was so full of hate and all it really needed was love. Like that Beatles song said.

The drive felt long and lonely tonight. He thought about what the pastor had told him to do, the thing he often neglected to do: pray. Thinking about prayer made him feel guilty since he seldom had conversations with God anymore. Too many times the guilt made him stay away, knowing he would first have to explain to God why he'd been so busy.

I know You hear me talking to You throughout the day, sometimes asking

You questions, sometimes yelling at You, sometimes telling You to make things right.

Will never had a problem questioning why God allowed terrible things to happen, like earthquakes and tsunamis and blizzards killing thousands. He thought of a writer typing out his story only to find it turning against him, so the writer simply deletes the story and starts a new one.

God refused to delete His story. Instead, He ended up writing the most beautiful story one could ever imagine, giving His one and only Son to save the very story that had been deformed and distorted by the Enemy.

It was easy to think about God in big terms like that, yet when it came to himself and his family, he expected and assumed more. He didn't ask God outright why certain things were happening. Instead, Will assumed God was judging him too. For not witnessing enough or being good enough or strong enough.

Enough of that nonsense.

He knew better, but his flesh would overrule him too often. Will waded in guilt too often, while Amy simply wanted everybody to love a little more.

"'Love is of God, little children, so love everybody and all will be well,'" a voice spoke over the speakers in his car. "'Thus speaks the devil, using Holy Scripture falsely for his evil purpose; and it is nothing short of tragic how many of God's people are taken in by his sweet talk.'"

It was Hutchence talking to him over the car's speakers through his SYNAPSYS.

"Hutchence?" Will asked, but the voice kept talking.

"'The shepherd becomes afraid to use his club and the wolf gets the sheep. The watchman is charmed into believing that there is no danger, and the city falls to the enemy without a shot. So Satan destroys us by appealing to our virtues.' Some words from A. W. Tozer."

"Hey! How are you able to speak to me?" Will shouted.

"One question, Will. Just one. Are you going to help us?"

"I need answers."

"They'll come in time. There's only one answer that's necessary right now. Will you join us?"

Will let out a big sigh in the darkness of his car. "Yes."

"I'm ready, Will. Ready for the push."

There was silence, and Will called out Hutchence's name several times, but he was gone. Soon there was nothing but the sound of the car engine and the tires on the road.

Will tried once more to pray in the grip of a quiet dread as he drove, but he couldn't. He waited for Hutchence's voice to speak again. Instead, all he could hear was Pastor Brian's words from their discussion earlier.

"The Christian faith is either something that's going to give you life, or it's completely ludicrous. I choose life."

ELEVEN

John the Baptist

1.

For five hours from Tulsa to Missouri, Cheyenne was trying to keep her body from shaking. Trying to keep from seeing the Parschauers' bodies. Trying to keep from screaming or cursing. Trying to keep from forcing Jazz to pull the car over so she could throw up.

They drove in silence for half the trip. Jazz knew how shaken she was, and he was letting her calm down. He looked shaken himself, but he showed it by an intense focus on the road, plus constant conversation with his LC for information. He asked about any news on the murders, and then he wanted to find out if he or Cheyenne was listed anywhere. But nothing came up for any of them.

In those first couple of hours of processing everything, Cheyenne came to one definitive conclusion: she didn't believe in the God her father had given his life to. She thought Jazz was a bit crazy, but then again, weren't all artists? She still had questions, but she knew people were behind the deaths of the Parschauers, and she knew they had been killed specifically because of their faith. They weren't religious extremists, nor were they part of the rioters protesting privacy intrusion. Tom and Susan were authentic folks, as the colloquialism went, and their faith was authentic as well. And they had been slaughtered because of this.

Killed by the same corporation I used to work for. That Malek worked for.

Her methodical mind replayed the words from those who had crossed her path.

"Be careful," Hoon, the man who gave her the note from her father, had said.

Vice President Nakajima had warned her about her place in the company and about everything she knew: *"The problem is that you have participated in many more campaigns and have been presented with much more sensitive material."*

Then there was that mysterious voice talking to her through her SYNAP-SYS, which was an impossibility, so perhaps she had imagined it. Yet the man's words made more sense now than before: *"This is your wake-up call, Cheyenne. You've been sleeping your whole life, dreaming those dreams."*

All the work Malek and she had done on emotional algorithms was meant for good, meant for a better and more peaceful world. She had created a new set that saw beyond one's physical actions and impressions, that looked deeper than what people bought and how they spent their time and whom they were with. These were simply part of the innovative technology inside an individual's SYNAPSYS, algorithms the public didn't know about, ones hidden behind the machinery and the user agreements Acatour and PASK had in place.

Now she understood the truth behind what she had spent so much time working on. The very thing she was so proud to have been an architect for.

"I've just been a tool they were using," Cheyenne said, breaking the silence in the car.

"Most people are."

"Yeah, but they haven't helped Acatour invade people's lives the way I have."

Jazz looked at her, surprised by her words. "What are you talking about?"

"The work I've been doing at PASK. The creation of specific algorithms for SYNAPSYSes. That was called a miracle in our division by the select few who knew about it, of course. All I ever wanted—all I ever imagined—was helping people to become who they were supposed to be. Somehow they're using these algorithms not only to monitor everybody but to control them. Not in an oppressive, totalitarian way, but rather in a hidden, manipulative way."

"All the technology and advancement since I've been alive has only been to further the power and corruption of the evil rulers of this world," Jazz said. "Yet Jackson Heyford not only made history with his invention of the SYNAPSYS—science he *stole* from others, mind you—but he's behind reaching Mars and finding a possible cure for cancer. He acts as if he simply wants to make this planet a better place."

"That's what I believed," Cheyenne said.

"This stuff—what we just saw back there . . . This is real, and it's been happening for a long time," Jazz said. "Heyford's a part of something that's been around for decades. The world government. The New World Order. The Freemasons. The Illuminati. The deep state. The cabal. Names for secret societies that have become cartoons and comic books. Words that are punch lines. The figures change, and so do their names and networks. Yet the evil remains the same."

"I want to get back at them," Cheyenne said, a surge of anger filling her. "Those men—the ones ultimately responsible for killing the Parschauers. I want to hurt them. To expose them. To take them down."

"Yeah, I hear you. I get it. And I like the sound in your voice."

"What sound?"

"Fury," Jazz said. "But it's gotta be handled correctly. We have to be smart, because these people—as you know—are smarter. They find brilliant and talented people like you, and they suck them dry. They use them for whatever they want, to further their plans and goals. It's always about more and more. Because ultimately Satan wants everything. Every living soul. Every bit of this earth and every second of time."

"I've never seen such evil in my life. At least not so close, not so in my face."

Jazz nodded, reaching over and clutching her hand briefly. "The Enemy may win a lot of battles down here, but he knows he can't and won't win the war. In the end every knee will bow and every tongue *will* confess that Jesus is Lord. That's no conspiracy, Cheyenne. That's my hope. That's where I put my fury."

Cheyenne looked out the window at the grassy fields of Missouri, at the trees on the hills in the background, at the patches of clouds pieced together like an unfinished crossword puzzle and showing the blue sky behind it. The fury began to subside, floating away like the ashes of a dwindling fire.

"You make it sound so easy," she said.

"What?"

"Believing in something you can't see."

"Nah," he said to her. "That's not the hard part. It's having to live in this world with faith while you see everybody else around you living without it."

2.

So far, so good. Even after having his underground bunker discovered, Jazz was still anonymous to those following them. He was still able to use his SYNAP-SYS to receive instructions. The destination they were told to go to was a sub-urb of St. Louis.

"Who's telling us to go there?" Cheyenne asked after Jazz informed her of their new destination.

"A fellow musician I knew from back in the day. Someone no one's paying any attention to. He's in contact with Acrobat and is able to relay messages. A guy in a rock band communicating to a rapper and agreeing to meet in St. Louis isn't worth getting suspicious about."

"Is every conversation and communication through a SYNAPSYS being monitored? I know those clashing with the government and with Acatour claim that, but I haven't seen any proof of it while working at the PASK division."

"They have machines listening the same way they have machines driving cars and protecting streets and talking to us like spouses. And since they're machines, they can still be predicted and manipulated. As long as nobody discovers my identity, communication through SYNAPSYS is okay."

The neighborhood they drove through was affluent with mansions sitting on huge lots. "Old money" was how Jazz described it. To see how much land some people owned was unbelievable. Thousands of people were crammed into tidy little apartments in the Incen Tower, yet out here a family of four or even a couple might own a ten-thousand-square-foot house on ten acres of land. That was exactly the sort of house they were driving up to.

A side road led to another side road that led to a large metal gate that opened once it saw their Hummer coming. Then a winding road led to a white house on a hill, and only then did Cheyenne realize the road was, in fact, a driveway.

"Who lives here?" Cheyenne asked, looking through the windshield at the two-story mansion that seemed to consist of several different additions.

"This is my house," Jazz said without any expression.

"Are you serious?"

He laughed. "No. Are you serious? I made good money but not this kind of money. Years ago this place was owned by a senator who eventually got run out of Congress for what they called corruption. But that's another way to say they didn't like his outspoken and 'old school' faith. And guess who led the charge to get him out?"

"I imagine someone important," Cheyenne said.

"President Ozias Garrison, who was a pawn himself. They couldn't kill the senator outright—not back then. That would have been too obvious. He no longer lives in this house, but he kept it in his family. His son owns it, and as it turns out, his son has been a valuable resource for us."

As the Hummer ascended the small hill the house sat on, they passed a ranch tucked away in the woods.

"That's where the housekeeper used to live," Jazz said. "Now it's empty."

An ornately designed one-story structure could be seen next to the mansion.

"What's that?" Cheyenne asked.

"The pool house. Some place, huh? I've only been here once myself."

"What are we doing here?"

"This is our safe house. There's just one thing."

"What's that?"

"We won't actually be going into the house. We'll be staying in their bunker."

3.

To call this a bunker was like calling the Incen Tower tall. They parked in a garage and then proceeded to a doorway that didn't go up to the house but revealed a set of steps descending into darkness. Cheyenne followed Jazz into the black space, holding his arm as he took the steps slowly. Finally, at the bottom they opened another door that led to warm, glowing colors and the feel of an exotic hotel getaway.

Normally she would have marveled at the small fountain with running water they passed in the entryway or the black-and-white photography hanging in select places on the walls. The main room they entered had an entire digital wall broadcasting a live shot from some Caribbean beach, making it seem as if they could step right onto the sand and drift into the ocean. A table in front of the two plush couches contained a variety of food: fruit in bowls, cheese and meats on one dish, pastries on another.

"The senator's son is a big fan of mine. Sometimes that still comes in handy," Jazz said with his big grin as he grabbed an apple.

She didn't smile back. "Where's the restroom?"

"I think it's the first door down the hallway."

Once inside, she locked the door and then moved to the sink to turn on the faucet. The cold water felt good on her hands and even better on her face. She sipped it even though there was bottled water outside in the living room. For a moment she looked at herself in the mirror, realizing it had been days since she took a shower or bothered with makeup. Not that she ever wore much of it anyway.

Not only did the eyes looking back at her appear tired and anxious; they also carried grief. And the longer she looked, the more the grief began to swell and fall down her cheeks. She closed her eyes and thought of the Parschauers and then began to weep. A slight cry came out of her throat, surprising her, and she cupped her mouth to avoid Jazz hearing her. She didn't worry about him thinking she wasn't tough. Cheyenne knew she was tough and could deal with emotions. But she didn't want to hear any more talk about God and hope and joy. Not now.

You show up, and my father disappears. You show up again with Jazz, and soon we're being hunted down. And once again You show up with the couple, only to see them sacrificed for some reason.

This didn't make sense.

Wiping the tears away, she could hear her father talking about those thoughts. *"That's called a prayer, Cheyenne. You're talking to God. We all do that, even those of us who don't believe in Him."*

She remembered her father telling her this shortly before he disappeared. The memory made her cry even more.

Stop, Chy. Stop feeling sorry for yourself.

Life hadn't given her much room for self-pity, and she wasn't going to let it slip in now. With her mother leaving for whatever reason when Cheyenne was in kindergarten and her father working so many hours when she was in grade school, Cheyenne grew up fast and figured things out for herself.

So figure things out now. What's the next step? Leave faith out of this, and get rid of those Daddy issues.

She swallowed, ran warm water from the faucet this time, and splashed it on her face. Her mind tried to drift to the calculating machine she used to be at Incen, the one that kept working on perfecting algorithms to operate as individuals. To function as perfect individuals and not weak ones. Yet she couldn't get herself to grasp the facts. Instead, the emotion continued to drown her.

It wasn't every day she saw a couple of dead bodies. Grisly too. The memories of stumbling upon them would never leave her.

Taking a breath, she wiped around the edges of her eyes and widened them, then went back to find Jazz and figure out what was next. Nothing could make her heart stop hurting.

As she entered the big room again, Cheyenne realized she was mistaken.

"Hey, sweetie."

She stopped, her mouth opening and letting out a very loud gasp. If Jazz weren't standing beside him with a giant smile, she would have known she was dreaming.

"Daddy?" The word surprised her, and she said it more as a question than a comment.

Her father rushed to her without another word and embraced her as she heard herself start to cry again.

"Everything's going to be okay."

She knew this wasn't a dream, because she would never imagine those words herself. They definitely came from her father. He was alive and breathing and holding his baby girl in his arms.

4.

It took her a while to compose herself, to stop crying and to sit down next to her father on the couch. Jazz brought her some coffee, then excused himself, saying they surely had lots to talk about.

One of her father's best attributes was his smile. It was the reassuring and gentle spark that a parent should have, and Keith Burne had seemed to have it his whole life, from the snapshots of him giggling as a baby to the wedding pictures with her mother. Even now with the serious expression he wore, she could still see her dad's warmth behind his glance.

"I'm sorry about everything that's happened," he said. "Especially back in Tulsa."

"That was terrible."

"I know. Chy, at least you can understand now the true gravity of the situation."

She took a deep breath. "I do, but I don't understand the situation. Not fully."

"I know. There are certain things I've wanted—I've *needed*—to tell you. But as I said in my note to you, I went about things the wrong way the last time we talked. I've regretted it and have prayed that God would give me another chance to talk to you. I was passionate, but I was also stubborn, and I didn't take into account how you might feel and all the things you might be questioning. The things you're surely still questioning."

"You said the apostle Peter was impatient and didn't understand the bigger picture," Cheyenne said, remembering the note she had read multiple times by now. "Do you understand the bigger picture?"

Her dad nodded, holding her hands in his. "I don't know everything Jazz has said to you, but I know he's told you a lot. We're going to warn people about what Acatour is doing. Telling them that Christians are being singled out and executed isn't going to upset or concern lots of people. But showing them that they're not only being monitored but also manipulated? The country will be up in arms. America is no longer the 'In God We Trust' country, but people still believe we're the land of the free and the home of the brave. We're about to expose that citizens aren't free. Not one bit."

"And we're warning them about the judgment to come," he added. "Chicago is going to be destroyed. I know it sounds ludicrous. I get it."

"I understand exposing everything that Acatour is doing. But do you really believe this stuff about an evil society being behind everything? I know something bad is happening, especially if a couple like the Parschauers could be—" The reality was so awful, she didn't even want to say it out loud.

"There is a great spiritual war that's never been so bloody as it is now," her father said. "This country has turned its back on God, not in just subtle ways but now very publicly. And to some degree the heart of the depravity is in Chicago, in the building you lived and worked in."

"So now you're saying God's angry at PASK? At Acatour?"

"The leaders at Acatour are the ones who for decades have been systematically rooting out Christianity in this country. You've told me about the work you have done for them. You are setting up belief systems for people to digest daily without their even realizing it."

"I realize it now," she said as she moved to sit on the edge of the couch. "All this time I've bought the lie that Acatour has helped make this world a better place. All the things they've done for science and the medical world. The money they've given away. The programs they've launched."

"They certainly didn't hesitate to end your time with them after realizing who your father happens to be."

She shook her head. "It was a PR nightmare. I get that."

"Do you really believe that Christianity is promoting hate?" her father asked.

"Some of it, yeah. But that's beside the point. We're not talking simply about faith in some religion."

"Christianity and religion are two different things," he said.

"If you want to believe that. But you also believe in some mysterious prophet—and I use that term loosely—who says God is literally going to take out Chicago. How? Fire from heaven or some virus? A terrorist plot? And why? Doesn't that sound like hate to you? Isn't that what Christians would say if an extremist from another faith threatened the same thing?"

Keith Burne sighed. "I don't want to get you angry."

"I woke up, and my whole world blew up. My company is evil, and the work I've been doing has been for the wrong reasons. I thought my father might be dead, and now when I finally see you, it sounds as if you've lost your mind."

"What about Jazz? What about the Parschauers? Have they lost their minds too?"

"*What* is supposed to happen to Chicago?" she asked again.

"I don't know. We just know the date."

"How can you trust this man called Reckoner? Someone whose real name you don't even know?"

He seemed to understand her indignation and her need for answers. This was how she always operated. "There was a man who came before Jesus called John the Baptist, and he preached to all the people and told them that Jesus was coming. He was wild—someone who lived in the desert and lived off the land. He baptized people, hence the name, and he called himself a nobody, a 'mere stagehand' in one version of the Bible."

"And what does that have to do with anything?"

Her father smiled. "Always impatient. Always."

"Yeah. So?"

"John the Baptist told the people that Jesus was coming and would ignite a fire within the people. That He was bringing the Holy Spirit, who would change people from the inside out. He also said Jesus would eventually put things in their proper place, leaving out the trash to be burned."

"Where does the Bible say that?" she said, annoyed with this ludicrous line of thought.

"Matthew 3:10. Let me think. It's something like, 'The ax of God's judgment is ready to sever the roots of the trees. Every tree that doesn't produce good fruit will be chopped down and thrown into the fire.'"

"So, then, Chicago is the trash? That's very kind for God to feel that way."

"Chy, we're all sinners who need to be saved. You're asking how I can believe all these things, and I'm trying to explain it to you. My soul's been awakened—ignited—and I can hear God speaking through the Holy Spirit."

"You hear actual voices?"

"No."

"Yet this prophet . . . You think he can?"

"Yes."

"So, then, what's his grand plan? Besides letting cows run loose around Chicago or spray-painting cars?"

"We're going to deliver one final message to the people in the Chicagoland area," he told her.

"And how are you going to do that?"

"We're going to deliver it to every single person's SYNAPSYS. We're going to speak *directly* to them."

She shook her head and laughed mockingly. "That's impossible."

"Is it?" He paused so she could see the obvious. "We spoke directly to you, right?"

Cheyenne felt a wave of goose bumps cover her like a bucket of cold water. She put her coffee cup on the table next to the platter of pastries. "How are you going to do this?"

Her father once again took her hands and gently clenched them.

"We need your help to do it."

TWELVE

It Is Well with My Soul

1.

The day dawned with the weather seeming like a wet towel crumpled in a closet and starting to reek. Dowland stood on the sidewalk in front of the house, the street blocked off on both sides by police cars and officers, the EMT team and the coroner talking together.

Steady rain fell, but he ignored the drops running down his face. The cool water felt good, especially since he felt the rage inside him searing and waiting to get out.

"Where is he?" Dowland asked one of the detectives.

"He's in the back of my car," the police officer told him, pointing to the unmarked four-door SUV a few houses down.

FBI Special Agent Vallery Herrera glared at him, apparently not appreciating his interrupting her conversation with the detective. She was one of the few who knew Dowland other than by name and probably the only one who would openly show her disdain of him. Those who knew him carried that disgust inside, but Herrera had the guts to make sure he and everybody else around noticed it.

"I like your jacket," Dowland said, nodding at her FBI apparel that glistened with the morning rain as he walked past.

Herrera caught up with him and then blocked his way to the vehicle. "You're not going to talk to him," she ordered.

He grinned, even though he really didn't want to be dealing with any of this, not now and not here. "You're feisty as ever," he said. "But I gotta admit: you are still absolutely hot."

She sighed but didn't take the bait. "What I ever saw in such a chauvinist pig, I'll never know. I would've gotten any other guy kicked out of the agency for such misconduct and treatment of women."

Dowland raised his eyebrows, aware that she was trying to reverse roles and provoke him. "You have to know the right people. Then you're okay to act whatever way you want."

"Obviously," Herrera said. The dark eyes bored into him. "Why are you here?"

Reminiscing time was over. "There's a sweet grandma and grandpa inside that house who were not only killed but pretty much butchered for no reason."

"And that's why we're dealing with this," Herrera said.

He flicked the badge dangling over her chest on the necklace. "Sometimes these things mean nothing. When I show up, it means you can stand back and watch."

"Why's Costa a concern to you? How do you even know him?"

Dowland looked at the tinted windows of the SUV where Lorenzo Costa sat. The twentysomething hotheaded Italian had been an agent for the last five years, and Dowland didn't really know the guy. He just knew that Costa would do anything for the right people at the right time. "You need to stay here and wait for me and make sure nobody bothers me. You got that?"

For a second Herrera looked as if she was going to say something, but then she hesitated. She gave him that look again, the look she used to give him, the one he loathed. It was when he let his guard down while they were together, when she had him wrapped around her finger and he finally let someone inside the fortress. She would study him, wanting to know why he carried the weight he did, wanting to help him. Wanting to understand the hurt, as she once said during an intimate moment.

"Listen to me. This level of business . . ." Dowland shook his head, this time speaking in a hushed tone to be certain no one else could hear. "Stay away, Val. I mean it."

Her hard, protective shell softened for a moment. Just as she had been able to see the baggage he carried, Dowland knew about her deep-rooted wounds. For a second he saw the little girl having to survive in the big, bad world and the steel she protected her heart with, steel forged by the savagery of a painful youth.

He leaned into her, so close to the lips he had kissed too many times to count. "You once said I'd never change. But I have, and it's because of this world, because of the things I know. Every single time I try to believe it's not as dark and hideous as I think, *that* happens." Dowland pointed back to the house where the bodies of the elderly couple still lay.

"I've changed, Val. But not for the good. And it's because this world's changing in the exact same way."

2.

The back door was unlocked, so Dowland opened it and nodded to Costa to move over so he could slide in beside him.

There was no chance Lorenzo Costa was going to run. The FBI agent had willingly come back to the scene of the crime and explained what had happened. Initially it appeared as if he was going to take off. Or perhaps he had left to clean himself up and intended to come back to the house to do the same. But somehow the situation had gotten out of his control, and Dowland knew it.

Right now Dowland was the only one who knew everything. Even Herrera didn't realize the truth.

Costa's eyes looked wired, as if he was on something. He twitched, breathing rapidly, and moved around on the leather back seat of the vehicle.

"Look, man, things escalated and got out of hand, but we're good. They don't know, and I gave them some false leads. They don't like how I handled the initial call, and Detective Dobbs could see the Pique racing through me, so he told me to stay away, and then when you called—"

Dowland's hand sprang up and clutched Costa's sinewy neck, digging his nails deep into the skin. Then with his other hand, he blocked Costa's arm from grabbing his handgun, as he continued to squeeze the larynx. Costa couldn't even get out a cough as Dowland suffocated him.

"I wanna watch your head turn as purple as a beet as you die," Dowland said, cursing at the young moron next to him gagging and convulsing. He blinked and saw the images back there in the house as the man's muffled moans became weaker.

Finally Dowland let go. He had to. This was already public enough and already put him in a not-so-favorable light. He didn't want to suddenly turn it into a spotlight.

"You stupid animal," Dowland said as Costa coughed and regained his breath. "You make a rabid dog look good."

Gasping and sweating, Costa pleaded with Dowland and cursed as he told him that things were fine, that he had important information. Dowland didn't want to hear it.

"All I gave you were names. Just a couple I had information on and wanted you to go by and check out. And what happens? You think it's Thanksgiving and you're carving a turkey?"

"They were hiding something," Costa said, spitting and rubbing his neck.

"How do you know?"

"I just knew. And they proved it too."

Dowland knew now there was no question that Costa's mind was racing with Pique. He'd force Costa to shut off his SYNAPSYS, but suddenly disconnecting the digital drug and going from two hundred miles an hour to zero could possibly give the guy a heart attack. Which wouldn't be a bad idea.

"So what, then? What were they hiding?"

"When I got back, I spotted a vehicle in front of the house. I got the info on the car, but the people coming out of the house . . . That's why the old couple were so dodgy, why they didn't want to talk. Guess who suddenly popped back up on the radar?"

Dowland waited, not wanting to play any games or waste any more time.

"Jamil C. Taylor," Costa said.

"Doesn't sound familiar."

"Known officially as License. The rapper."

This came out of nowhere. "Are you certain?" Dowland asked.

"Absolutely. Took a pic to confirm, and it matched. First sighting of him in a while. No details as far as why he was connected to the couple."

"And that justifies your complete lack of judgment?" Dowland retorted.

"The woman we've been looking for—Cheyenne Burne, the daughter of Keith Burne. She was with the rapper."

How in the world are those two connected?

Dowland knew Costa was reading his surprised reaction and relishing that he had uncovered something even Dowland didn't know.

"What do you want me to do?" Costa asked.

"Did the two see you? Did they have any idea you spotted them?"

"No."

"Okay." At least the idiot had actually done something right.

"So what are the chances that those two suddenly show up together out of nowhere?" Costa asked. "That they're going to see that couple?"

"That is a question you're not going to get answered. You don't wanna answer it. Do you understand? It will take five seconds to get you two life sentences for what you did to that couple back there. And there's nothing I'd like more than to make that call."

"You were the one who got me to—"

"Shut up. My mistake was failing to know the character of the man I was dealing with. But listen to me. If you think you're holding some kind of card because of what you know, you're wrong. You, my friend, just torched your entire deck of cards. You are a very big liability, one that only I know about—at least for now. You get it?"

Costa cleared his throat, nodded, then looked straight ahead at the windshield of the car. Dowland watched him for another moment, his mind cluttered with scenarios and questions and tasks. Then he opened the door and climbed out.

It was becoming clear that the people Dowland worked for weren't the only ones with a secret network full of vastly different individuals.

3.

He doesn't say goodbye to Costa and doesn't worry about cleaning up the mess in Tulsa. Dowland gets in the Autoveh and tells it where to go. His SYNAPSYS is off and he's untraceable. It takes him ten minutes to arrive back at the airport and another ten minutes before he's in a lounge drinking vodka, though it's not noon yet. The rush is coming over him and telling him he's drowning. He might as well keep suffocating his soul. In order to try to think. In order to remain focused on his next step.

So this anonymous character is out there threatening to expose the evil running the world, and those in power will do anything to shut him up.

After Dowland's leads have gone nowhere, suddenly this has-been rapper enters the picture. How is he affiliated with the Reckoner, Acrobat . . . the man of many nicknames? And Cheyenne Burne? What does she have to do with this, especially considering her father and how he disappeared? He was put on the list of those to monitor, those who might be disrupters.

Dowland doesn't merely drink but drains the vodka, ordering one after another to feel a little something more in order to feel less. He can understand a person like Costa in some ways—resorting to a weakness like Pique that brings instant ecstasy, then long-term pain. Dowland knows enough to stay away from something like that, yet his vices aren't that different. He knows they're not manageable, not when he's hiding away like this, downing glasses as if they were shots.

I need to think. I need to get a plan before someone comes asking for one.

License. Burne and his daughter.

Dowland curses.

He thinks of the first time the group he called "The Thirteen" came to him. Two men, not very important, one now dead and the other sent into hiding of sorts. Two men setting up a meeting and presenting the facts. How people like his style. How they like his attitude and beliefs or, as they note, his lack of beliefs and his anger at those who have them. These two men know his past, all of it, every little bad thing that ever happened to him and the reasons behind his hate. They give him an opportunity of a lifetime where money will never be a problem again. Where he can play James Bond. And where he can take that hatred and do something with it. Of course, they don't define it as hate. And, of course, Dowland doesn't consider it as such. Instead, all parties agree it's patriotic and noble.

Dowland downs another drink.

"What if you can help end some of the hate that has so divided this country, that continues to erode the underbelly of our democracy?" Those were the words they used.

"And how can I do that?"

They show him a report on a man, a prominent businessman, who is leading a double life. Running an underground Christian ministry for men that's popped up in more than thirty states. Then they tell him why the men are meeting.

"We want him gone. Without a trace."

Just like that. And before he can say a word, they remind him. "The world doesn't need another Brock Hardy, does it?"

His father. The man of devout faith. The pillar of the community. The advocate and helper and philanthropist.

The fraud. The man who sang "It Is Well with My Soul" as loud as he could in the pew next to him, but Dowland knew the truth. His father had no soul.

"I'll do it." That's what he said. Years ago. Without needing anything more. And when it happened, when he strangled the man and disposed of his body, he didn't feel guilt. Not then. So why now?

Dowland looks at the old clock on the wall and knows his flight is taking off soon. He's not sure if what he's been feeling lately is guilt. Perhaps it's that everything is escalating. The price tag, the players, the predicament of finding the Reckoner . . . Everything.

He has to believe what Costa said—that no one else knows about Burne's daughter and the guy she's traveling with. So for now he can use their ignorance to his advantage.

"Russo-Baltique 2027," he says, turning on his SYNAPSYS.

The password to turn it on was taken from some ridiculously expensive vodka he was given by a billionaire who was enraptured by Kamaria and invited them to stay at his resort in Dubai. Whether something happened with the wealthy Arab, Dowland doesn't know and didn't care at the time. That night in Dubai in 2027 enjoying that Russo-Baltique bottle could never be topped.

With the SYNAPSYS on, he checks all the incoming messages and notifications. Nothing as earthshaking as what he found in Tulsa this morning.

"Call Margaux," Dowland says.

As expected, he doesn't hear a voice answer at the other end. He has to leave a message. "It's Dowland. I need your help. You know me . . . I don't like asking for it. But right now I need a colleague who does what I do. I'm flying back to Chicago. Call me."

There's time for one more drink as the names roll around in his head. The main target, the Reckoner. Now Jamil C. Taylor, aka License. Cheyenne Burne. And Keith Burne.

He looks at the clear glass, empty once again. Perhaps the answer has been staring him in the face all this time. Perhaps it's been crystal clear.

Maybe Keith Burne is the Reckoner.

THIRTEEN

Our Daily Bread

1.

"You have to pick up Shaye from school and take her to the doctor. Her readings dropped, and an ear infection was detected."

Will watched the message from Amy. He had been searching for job listings in the Grand Rapids area. He had actually looked at a position at a library in the town of Grandville, Michigan, a job more suited for someone retired who wanted to fill time and didn't really care about the pay. It wasn't full time, so there was no need even to look at it, but it involved books, one of his loves. After seeing no leads, Will began looking at houses for sale, which was foolish since there was no way they would be able to buy another house. Not with their dismal credit rating.

"I'm going now," Will said in a message that would be sent to Amy. He grabbed his coat and keys and quickly left the house. Once again the familiar sting of anger began to pollute his spirit. He never handled it well when anybody, including himself, got sick. The older he had become, Will found himself growing more and more impatient. With everything. It used to be the stress of work and lack of time he had, but now it was his lack of work making him stressed. So when someone in the family got sick, he was the opposite of a caretaker. He became cantankerous. And this past week after all of them had caught the nasty flu bug going around, Will found himself downright miserable to be around.

As he drove to the girls' school, he realized he was gritting his teeth, a bad habit he'd gotten into.

"You are driving twenty miles over the speed limit," Tolkien told him.

"Shut up. I know."

This time Tolkien remained quiet, perhaps able to monitor Will's levels and to assess that he would only be more incensed by further discussion.

Everything lately had felt so out of control. It hadn't started with closing the shop; the problems had come long before that. Years ago, in fact, when life became a chore, when the worries began to mount every day, and when all he could do was work and try a little harder. Try to get out of debt. Try to be a better father. Try to be more than a terrible husband. Try to be better.

All while trying to forget the family I came from.

Will cursed. He had worked so hard to remove himself from any ties to his father and brothers, and he had been successful, even though he'd paid a price. But was God now telling him to reach out to his father? For what reason? If Hutchence had been the only one suggesting this, Will would have said "Absolutely not." But after seeing Pastor Brian, he found himself considering the unthinkable.

What if Jackson Heyford's minions simply keep me out? What then?

Maybe he was losing his mind. Maybe the world had worn him down and there was nothing left. He'd let his SYNAPSYS take over. Maybe in the future people would be able to program patience and love and goodness into their systems. "For just a few more bucks, you can have the Ultracare package, which makes you a sensitive husband, a devoted father, and a devout believer! All for the cost of twenty thousand dollars!"

Maybe money did indeed buy happiness. Or maybe it just made happiness a little easier to reach. Perhaps money helped keep out the misery.

You know that's a big fat turd of a lie, you idiot.

"You're going thirty miles over the speed limit," Tolkien said. "A scanner is going to fine you, and currently you have only fifteen dollars—"

"Shut up!" he yelled. "Please stop. I don't want to hear your voice."

The voice wasn't the thing bothering him. As Will slowed down, knowing they couldn't afford a three-hundred-dollar speeding ticket, he realized he'd been speeding because he was freaking out inside. He couldn't control anything in his life, but at least he could control the speed of his car. There were bills he couldn't pay and illnesses he couldn't heal and arguments he couldn't win. And then there was this whole matter of Chicago as they knew it coming to an end soon.

Perhaps when he took Shaye to the doctor, he would ask to see a shrink for himself.

2.

"You still sick, huh?"

She nodded, looking out the car window.

"I thought you were feeling better."

"I felt terrible this morning," Shaye said.

"Why didn't you say something?"

"Because I didn't want you and Mom arguing."

Will looked at Shaye. He tried to think of a proper response, but a fog hovered over him, making it impossible to find the right words. Sometimes the only right response was an honest one.

"I know things have been stressful," Will said. "I think that's why all of us have gotten sick. Our immune systems are down."

Shaye nodded, still looking out the window, still not herself.

He didn't want to wake up one day and realize the silence and the space between them had grown from simply a crack to a hole and then to a canyon. But Will also knew he couldn't force things, nor could he simply repair the pothole between them right now.

"It's been hard to figure out things with the bookstore closing," Will said. "I know I haven't been the nicest person lately. I'm sorry."

She glanced at him, giving a sweet and sympathetic smile, the kind a mother would give to her son.

"It's okay, Daddy," she said.

Shaye was too young to be so smart and so responsive. Her age did allow for grace and forgiveness, however. The kind the world drained out of you daily until it finally sucked you dry, turning you into a bitter and angry person. If you allowed it to.

Please, God . . . I don't want to be that sort of person.

That's where everything started and where Will should have started. With God. Asking God to help him. But that meant giving God the keys not only to his car but also to his life. To every single aspect of his life.

God, help me figure out how I can do that.

3.

It didn't take much to find out what his father was up to. For Will all it took was a simple click on the news. Jackson Heyford was in the headlines nearly every day in some form. Even though it had been more than eleven years since they last talked in person, Will still heard his father's hollow voice and saw his father's soulless eyes through various forms of media even when he didn't want to. His father was a living ghost, haunting him day and night.

On the night after picking Shaye up from school, Will decided to do something he never did in the sanctuary of his office. He had spent the last hour trying to make sense of the family's financial status, and all it had done was motivate him to polish off a bottle of cheap red wine. This wasn't the rare occurrence, however. It was finally succumbing to the occasional curiosity he had but never acted on.

"Hey, Tolkien. Show me the latest news on my father."

"Is this a genuine request, or are you being sardonic?" the voice immediately asked him.

"Sardonic? I'm not trying to be a word I never use."

"According to the *Oxford English Dictionary*, *sardonic* is an alteration of *sardanios*, which was used by Homer to describe bitter or scornful laughter."

"Did you hear me laughing?" Will said.

"Deep down you were."

This prompted Will to genuinely laugh out loud. "That is freaky, Tolkien."

"That time I was using an expression of yours," the proper British accent stated.

"I know, but still. Can you look up the latest news on him? And I'm not trying to be sardonic."

One large virtual screen popped up on the wall in front of him while all the other screens he had open disappeared. Just like that, Jackson Heyford was in front of him, smiling and talking and looking like a trillionaire at a press event. He was at a hospital doing some noble, benevolent act guaranteed to make the world love him a little more.

"Jackson, Mississippi, has always been one of my favorite places to visit, and it's not because we share the same name," Jackson joked with authority and clarity behind the podium while surrounded on both sides by a group of men and women. "I remember how moved I was by the Civil Rights Museum when I was only eight years old. Of course, the Blues Extravaganza's annual growth makes me proud to have started it."

To his right stood a statuesque blonde thirty-three years his junior, grinning and looking on like a proud daughter might. Tiffany Shaw was a former Miss Mississippi, and her current occupation was being Jackson Heyford's second trophy wife and the third woman he'd married. This particular tie to the Magnolia State was perhaps the biggest reason he was there right now.

The only reason.

"On behalf of the Acatour Foundation, Tiffany and I are proud to announce the opening of the Jackson Children's Hospital and Research Center. As the largest and most technologically advanced children's hospital in the world, the $2.4 billion that have been spent still seems like a drop in the bucket in efforts to eradicate cancer and other diseases affecting our precious sons and daughters."

The old feelings and emotions enveloped him like the smell of a dumpster full of spoiled meat. He told Tolkien to shut off the video, then gave a cutting laugh that almost hurt.

"Such a philanthropist," Will said as the footage disappeared. "'Precious sons and daughters.' If people only knew what he was like as a father."

"Never laugh at live dragons."

"What?"

"A quote from *The Hobbit.* 'Never laugh at live dragons, Bilbo you fool!'"

"Ah, a quote *you* wrote. Very clever. So are you calling me a fool, Tolkien?"

"I would never say that out loud. Would you like to see other recent news?" Tolkien asked.

"Yes. But can you just read them to me?"

"Of course. 'The revenue growth at Acatour continues to be impressive, with shares valued at $3,549.82. Heyford recently said he doesn't see splitting the stock anytime soon, though he says he wants to avoid the Amazon financial earthquake that happened after shares grew too big back in the 2020s. The growth of the SYNAPSYS line has more than tripled in the last year, producing another new wave of models coming in the fall of 2038. The Acatour-owned Magellan Space Station will have $40 billion worth of renovations in the coming year, most coming from the corporation—'"

"Okay, got it!" Will called out in a loud voice he hoped didn't wake everybody else in the house. "Do you have any news that isn't related to money?"

"Some minor news buried but noteworthy for you is that the PASK division lost its top architect after she resigned, reportedly due to the controversy over her father being labeled a religious fanatic and being investigated by the FBI. One recent headline read 'Former Fortune 500 Exec Turns Rogue.'"

"Seriously? Do you have any pictures?"

Several photographs popped up of a businessman who might as well have been one of his father's coworkers.

"This is Keith Burne, the supposed 'religious fanatic' who was a VP for Corpus Investments Group. There are no pictures of his daughter, Cheyenne."

Will rubbed his eyes, the glow of the photos straining his eyes.

"Enough news," he said. "Can you put back up all the screens I had showing?"

"Can I give you a bit of advice?" Tolkien asked.

"Can I say no?"

"I suggest you don't continue to evaluate the state of your finances after checking on Jackson Heyford's status."

"Just put them back up," Will said.

Images surrounded him on all sides again, as if he were stuck in the middle of a meteor shower. Thirty-seven bills appeared from a variety of sources, such as websites, messages, a few phone calls, and a handful of digital assistants leaving messages.

There was his Comcast bill for $1,348.37. The latest monthly bill and last month's overdue balance. The typical monthly charges were around $600, and the late charges equaled almost $150. He could remember twenty years ago—during their double-income, no-kids days—when the monthly bill started to reach $200 simply for cable and internet. Inflation had almost tripled since then, but money no longer held any value to him. Not anymore. The numbers and the figures meant nothing. None of them felt real.

The Comcast bill was critical to pay because the company would turn off their link to the network, eliminating everything—from connecting with others to watching shows and movies to using their SYNAPSYSes. But there was also the water bill. And electricity. And gas.

And, oh yeah, how about the mortgage that's three months past due. He needed $18,470.09 to pay for that.

The credit cards, all five of them, were maxed out to the last cent. They were all over their credit lines, of course, and each missing payment meant a hefty late charge.

One by one Will tapped off the screens. He had only wanted to survey the plane crash, to see the carnage spilling out over everything. There would be no paying bills tonight or tomorrow night. They would have to wait until Amy got paid next, and then that little pebble would be thrown into the giant lake.

Paying off every single cent of our debt would be an even tinier pebble to my father. That wasn't an option. That would never be an option. Not anymore.

The latest bill from today hovered directly in front of him. It was $845 for the simple walk-in to the medical clinic to make sure Shaye was okay. This made Will think of the grandfather Shaye and the girls had never known, the man they wouldn't ever know. At least not as long as Will was alive. The last time he had seen his father had been for that very reason. Jackson Heyford had wanted to meet his first grandchild, but Will had refused. Jackson now had plenty of grandchildren, so his legacy and pride were fine without having Will's girls in his life.

Will took some pride in knowing that he still had something worth more than all of Jackson Heyford's trillions. Something Heyford could never have.

4.

Heavenly Father, I know I've been silent. Forgive me, God. And I know I've been trying to do it on my own and I can't. But I keep trying.

You control everything. I know this. And yet I keep trying and doing and failing. I worry so much. Lord, please forgive my doubt.

Whatever You have planned tomorrow when the sun comes up, help me to see it. To know it.

And whatever is supposed to happen with Hutchence and with my father, let me know what Your will is. I don't understand any of this. I don't understand my life now.

Take my fears from me. Take away all this bad, evil junk inside me, and let me feel Your Spirit.

Give me this day our daily bread, as we should pray. Help me forgive others as You forgive me. Even my father. Somehow. Lead all of us away from temptation. And please, please, please, God—deliver us from evil.

Everything is Yours, Lord. Everything. Thank You.

Thank You, Jesus, for letting Your heavenly Father hear these words and act on them.

Amen.

5.

The pounding on the glass behind him jolted Will for a second. In the empty retail space, which looked exactly the same as he had left it, he turned and saw Hutchence walking into his former bookstore, where they had agreed to meet.

"Yeah, I'm looking for a book by Tozer and heard you have a collection by him."

Will chuckled. "Sorry, but I just shipped those books to a special place since the apocalypse is approaching. But I do have an extra copy of *Consider This.*"

"Good for you. How did your meeting with the pastor go?"

"I'm not sure if it was good or bad since he convinced me to contact you again," Will said. "You shaved your beard."

Hutchence nodded, rubbing his smooth and angular face. "I like to change things up. So Brian influenced you to believe some of the things I've been telling you?"

"Yeah. But I made the mistake of looking up what my father's been doing lately."

"He's a very busy man," Hutchence said.

"He's got plenty of money to keep people busy."

"I can imagine how unsettling that might be since you're on the opposite end of the money spectrum."

"I don't want any of his money," Will said quickly.

Hutchence nodded. "I would suggest you don't buy any Acatour stock either. Because in a little more than a month, I imagine it's going to fall. *Plummet* is the more accurate way to put it."

"How's that going to happen?"

"The heart wants to know the plan before the soul has even prepared." Turning around as he scanned the room, Hutchence let out a loud groan. "It's sad, isn't it? Such a place of life is now so empty."

"Yeah," Will said.

"Why did you open this bookstore in the first place? And don't give me a pat answer. What was the real reason?"

Will thought about his answer for a moment, staring down at the familiar carpet he had walked on and looked at many times before.

"I think it's because of how much I've loved books. Because of the feelings I had when I was growing up reading them. The thrill of using my imagination. I miss those days. And I'd like to say I wanted to help others find ways to have those thrills themselves, but really, if I'm being honest, I probably just opened the store for myself. To surround myself with things I love."

"Quite a thoughtful answer," Hutchence said. "Do you believe the bookstore was blessed by God?"

Will sighed. "I don't know. Sometimes I think that it was the opposite, that it was cursed."

"Closing doors don't necessarily mean a place is cursed. It's only when we come to the absolute end of ourselves that we're finally able to receive the Holy Spirit. I'm paraphrasing Oswald Chambers. Come on. Let's go. I can give you the overview of what I'm planning."

6.

The bar in downtown Aurora looked abandoned rather than open, yet the scuffed-up, faded red door squeaked open when Hutchence pushed it. It was at the end of a block near the train tracks. They had parked several blocks away by the Fox River and had walked along cracked sidewalks and crumbling gravel roads until reaching the one-story rectangular building with an aged sign on the roof that said Jack's Brew. Will didn't expect to see lights actually glimmering inside the musty joint, nor did he think he would see anybody behind its oversized oak bar.

"What's up, Hutch?" the woman asked in a raspy voice that matched the place.

"Good afternoon, Cee," Hutchence said as he led Will past her to the back.

A door led to narrow and uneven cement steps that went down to a room that should have been used for a storage closet but actually had a small cot and a desk in it.

"Don't tell me this is where you're staying," Will said, seeing a duffel bag on the floor and an old iMac on the desk.

"Cee up there owns this place. This is her office, which used to double as the room where she went when she was too soused to drive home. She's sober now. I can't convince her to sell this place, not that she could get anything for it anyway. It doesn't do anything except serve cheap drinks to alcoholics. She lets me stay here, and I trust her more than ninety-nine percent of those I know. She's a good soul."

A handful of framed photos sat on the desk, all revealing a much younger Cee. A wall calendar from four years ago hung behind the computer. Hutchence grabbed a folding chair beside the bed and then sat down, turning on the computer and waiting for it to boot up.

"To answer your question, yes, this is where I sometimes stay," he told Will. "There's also a billionaire's mansion in the north suburbs. And numerous other places."

Will stood to the side of the desk, looking at Hutchence and noticing how much younger he appeared without the beard. He looked more like a movie actor than the rumpled professor. Even his clothes appeared different, with a modern shirt-pants combo and a trendy jacket.

"Are you hungry for lunch?" Hutchence asked him. "I could ask Cee to make you something."

"No, thanks."

"Yeah, probably a good decision all around. I have a bunch of materials saved on this computer. I'm scanning to find some things to show you."

Underneath the cot was a spiral-bound notebook. Will then noticed the handgun right next to it.

"Yeah, that's mine," Hutchence said without taking his eyes off the computer screen.

"You have eyes on the side of your head?"

"No. But I can tell you're staring right at it, and your body suddenly tensed, and you actually stepped back."

"That obvious, huh?"

"Yeah," Hutchence said. "Don't worry. That's only a precaution. I've never actually fired a gun at someone, but there are some pretty sick people out there who are looking for me."

"You're trapped in here if they find you."

"They'd have to get through Cee first. And her biker friends. Come over and look at all this."

For the next hour Hutchence led Will down a rabbit hole full of lies, greed, control, and hate—all pertaining to his father. Business properties overseas with inhumane working conditions. Foreign dictators and terrorists affiliated with Jackson Heyford and Acatour. Several foundations in Germany, the Cayman Islands, and India with empty buildings that served simply to launder money. From corrupt business associates to noted partners now imprisoned, this was a list of corruption after corruption.

"All of this—I'm skimming here—is public knowledge. Now these files here are all the really dirty stuff. Yeah, here, this one." A document opened on the screen. "This is a list of seven former business associates—close associates— who have all died. These were just Acatour employees. This was an early investor in PASK who died in a car accident. He was thirty-two years old. An accountant working solely with Heyford was shot in a 'mugging.' A woman had a heart attack, and she was only forty-four."

"Are you saying—"

"Absolutely," Hutchence said in a come-on-and-get-with-the-program tone a coach might use. "Jackson Heyford had something to do with each of these deaths. No doubt."

"Is there any proof?"

"Do you need proof? I don't. For most there are details that aren't mere coincidences. Several were in the process of leaving Acatour. Others had disagreements and disputes with Heyford. And this list is only the obvious ones who worked for him."

For a second Will thought of his mother, but he quickly wiped away the ghastly thought. He watched as Hutchence pulled up more grisly details about Acatour.

"Jeremiah 17:9," Will said, thinking out loud. "'The human heart is the most deceitful of all things, and desperately wicked. Who really knows how bad it is?'"

"We're seeing just how bad it can get," Hutchence said.

"I've always wondered if I was left to my own devices, how messed up would I be? Because I'm already a mess, and that's with the faith I have."

"You're lucky, you know that?" Hutchence said, turning from the computer for the first time since coming down to this tiny room.

"Why's that?"

"Because you can say that about yourself. Do you know the problem of today? Nobody believes we're totally depraved. Oh sure, the guys caught with human slaves chained in their basements or vicious gang members. The obvious ones, of course. But you and me and the 'regular' people of this world. We're not 'bad.' Right? Each generation has ushered in a new era of finding meaning. Of going after their passions. Of battling with the inequalities out there. I remember when I was a teenager, when everybody was on social media with their selfies and likes and opinions and demands for change. Before social media collapsed on itself."

"Yep," Will said. "Before the government and businesses out there forced the regulations."

"Sin was an afterthought twenty years ago. Now? The Christian faith is the offensive thing. Christians are the ones in the wrong, the ones sinning." Hutchence turned back around and began feverishly moving and clicking the mouse as he searched his computer. "Tell me, Will. You never answered whether you believe in secret societies, in governmental conspiracies, and men and women hidden behind masks orchestrating the fate of the rest of humanity."

Leaning against the wall with one foot, Will spoke in a quiet tone. "I believe in spiritual warfare and Satan using people for his purposes. And, yeah, I think there are certain powers at work. Powerful people like my father. But we can't do anything about them. They'll never be convicted."

"'The man who believes that the secrets of the world are forever hidden lives in mystery and fear. Superstition will drag him down.'"

"Is that a quote?" Will asked.

"Cormac McCarthy. From *Blood Meridian*. Writers have been writing about the apocalypse since they began to tell stories. And whether it's in a Western or outer space, it's the same thing. The darkness of this world. So bleak."

"It's always so cheery talking to you. You're not exactly the life coach someone needs after he's just lost his job, after he's lost his whole career and needs to start over again. As my luck has it, I get to meet the one man on the face of the planet who can make me detest my father more than I already did."

Hutchence looked up, whispering and slowly articulating his words. "Starting again doesn't mean the slate is clean. No, Will, your slate is very dirty indeed. It's a canvas that's been covered in graffiti, left outside in the rain, then trampled over with muddy tread marks. It's not a fresh slate, nor is it blank, but it's one you can do *anything* with. You can paint anything you want on it. Do you know why? Every mark you see resides only in this world. When God looks at it, the canvas is clean and white and perfect. Christ isn't a filter or gloss of bright paint. Christ *is* the canvas."

Hutchence clicked the mouse, bringing up a set of photos, all featuring Will. There was Will at two years old standing between his parents. There was Will with his older and younger brothers when he was probably ten. Another shot showed him as a teenager with his father. Half a dozen photos appeared, ones he hadn't seen for decades.

"Where'd you get those?" he asked.

"Don't worry about that. I'm giving them to you for a specific reason. You're going to use them as bait. They're going to be the brochures you hand to your father after knocking on his door for the first time in a very long time."

"And what am I supposed to tell him?" Will asked.

"You need to reconnect with him. And in doing so, you're going to help me."

Before Will could say or ask anything more, Hutchence turned off the computer, picked up the duffel bag, and began to fill it with items in the room, including the semiautomatic. When he was finished, Hutchence asked him a question. "What if you saw your life as a great epic battle, a bloody battlefield like the fields of Gettysburg or the beaches of Normandy? What if you felt death whizzing by your ears? John Eldredge says men don't worry about having regular "quiet time" with God because they feel it's not crucial. They're not tasting death. Yet there is a spiritual war occurring, a war far worse than those being fought by mere mortals. And the time has come. It's our D-Day."

"Are we going to break into Jackson Heyford's mansion?" Will half joked, still not able to make sense of everything Hutchence was saying.

"I can see that look on your face again," Hutchence said. "The look of distrust and fear of the unknown."

"You're wrong about that. I don't fear the unknown. I fear my father. I always have, and I think I always will."

7.

The river flowed despite the frigid temperatures. Walking back to his car from Jack's Brew by himself, Will took a detour down a path to the river walk. He sat on a bench in the cold, his breath visible as he stared out at the Fox River.

Doubt filled him, like a heavy stomach after a big meal. *I can't do this. Not me. I can't get sucked back into that world.*

Hutchence had said goodbye to him and that they would be in touch. That was as much detail about the plan as Will would get. He needed to digest all the information he had just heard back there. All the incriminating facts and the charges related to his father.

Can they all be true?

If only half of the accusations Hutchence had made about Heyford were accurate, it would be even more ludicrous to connect with him again. Will wanted to keep Amy and the girls as far away from his father as possible.

He thought of the "great epic battle" comment by Hutchence. Will wondered how he could ever stand up and put on any sort of armor and fight.

I'm no hero of the faith. I'm a pedestrian.

His life felt like a flicker of a star a million miles away, yet God had created that with so much more power and enormity. The only thing he had in common with the star was the ability to fall. Yet he remained, with a dull light flickering the days away.

Is this my chance to be brighter, Lord?

He didn't want to be a hanging glimmer. He wanted to burn bright. For once in his life, he wanted to take the knowledge he had and believed in and run with it.

Yet accepting this—all of it—felt like too much. He admired Hutchence's passion for promoting the good news of Jesus Christ, but striking out at Heyford and his empire? "God, I don't know," he said out loud. "That sounds so crazy."

He needed something else, someone else, to help him understand. To talk some sense into him. Perhaps he was so confused and so far into a downward spiral of worry that he wasn't thinking and seeing straight.

"Give me wisdom, God. Please."

As he felt his body shiver from the blast of cold wind, Will realized the someone else who could help him. The one God had placed in his life for that very reason, just as he was placed in her life for the same reason.

He needed to talk to Amy.

FOURTEEN

Where Did You Come From?
Where Did You Go?

1.

"I've been listening to a lot of U2 lately."

Cheyenne hadn't really noticed the music in her father's car, a Ford rental he'd been driving for only a few days. They'd been in the car for half an hour, making small talk and trying to find their way to something bigger, but it wasn't happening. Not yet. The euphoria of finding her father alive had subsided, while the reality of the mess he'd gotten her into felt even bigger.

"Wasn't that Grandpa's favorite group?" Cheyenne asked, looking out at the barren Illinois countryside passing by.

"Play 'One Tree Hill.' Yeah, he grew up listening to them. He told me I was born in the same month as their biggest album, *The Joshua Tree,* released. Mom and Dad were such fans that the following year they took a trip to the Mojave Desert to visit the actual tree photographed on the album cover."

"That's the framed picture you gave me on my sixteenth birthday, right?"

"Yeah," he said. "It was the fortieth anniversary of the album."

"I still have that. It's in my bag. One of the few things I brought with me from Incen Tower. I've been thinking about Grandma and Grandpa a lot."

Keith Burne nodded, looking down the highway as if he were waiting for an exit to show up. "They wouldn't believe how much has changed in this country. Their faith was strong. I just— I paid little attention to it, and then when I left to make my own life, I left that faith on a shelf like some old CD I never played."

Cheyenne wondered if her father was going to start talking about religion again or about Jesus, since he said there was a difference. She was tired of it.

"Remember going to the U2 concert five years ago?" she asked.

Her father laughed. "That was so much fun. 'The Geriatric Tour' as Bono called it. They still rocked. And they have continued to make albums even when younger kids don't know who they are."

"You pretty much forced me to understand the concept of an album," she said with a tinge of amusement. "Because you used to play entire albums to me."

"Your mother would have loved that show."

"Did she like them?"

"No. She wasn't that much into music. She was into the experience of everything. She would've loved the energy. Like some big celebration of life."

She could still picture one moment very clearly, when the lights of the arena were suddenly turned on and the band played as the audience seemed to all sway in unison. And during that moment, seeing the sea of people around them as they stood on the general admission floor, her father slipped his arm around her. She was twenty-two and an official adult, but for a moment she felt like a little girl again. Her father wasn't a man of a lot of emotion—at least he didn't used to be—yet as he smiled at her during that song, tears filled his eyes.

"Play 'Get Out of Your Own Way,'" her father said.

As the steady beat began, Cheyenne remembered they had sung this song also at the show. It built and built until it reached a crescendo, and then confetti rained down on a jubilant crowd.

"I think I understand your mother a little more these days."

She shifted, facing him, startled. "What do you mean?"

"I know I've never talked a lot about her."

"There's been no reason to talk about her."

The gray in his hair seemed to have spread, along with the wrinkles under his eyes. He gave her a sad glance. "You have so much of her in you. We were kids who were crazy in love. I was only twenty-four years old when we had you. Your mother was twenty-two."

"And yet somehow you managed to deal with it, didn't you?" She could hear the bitterness discoloring her words. The only time it ever surfaced was when the subject of her mother came up.

Maybe that's why we've never really talked much about her.

"She always felt like an outsider," Dad said. "Even though she was so beautiful, just like you, she'd always felt the prejudices of others. The narrow-minded views of people, not only about her but about her relatives. Certain minority groups have made progress, but Native Americans have been forgotten. At least, that's how your mother felt."

"We weren't the prejudiced ones," Cheyenne said, looking back out to the empty fields on the edge of the highway. "We didn't do anything to her."

"Some demons chased her. I knew that back then, but now I know they were literal demons. Ones that knew her vulnerabilities and her insecurities. Nova let her vices take over. She believed she couldn't ever be a fit mother or wife. So she took off."

It was strange to hear him say her mother's name. Most of the time he said "your mother." She wondered what Nova meant, if it had a deeper meaning.

"Do you know what happened to her? Really? I know if you did, you probably wouldn't tell me."

"I don't. I promise, Cheyenne. I tried to find her. I even hired people to look. But there was nothing. Play 'Iris' by U2."

The song started to play and sounded sad despite its urgency.

"I listened to this a lot after she left. You were in kindergarten, and I'd been promoted to a director at the company, and suddenly I'm there freaking out. Thank God for your grandparents. I don't know what I would've done without them."

For a moment Cheyenne didn't see him as her father but rather as a man who carried the scars of trying to make it in this world, who had tried to have the dream and then watched as it all blew up way too soon.

She let the music fill the space as she searched for something to say. Instead, the singer filled in the words for her. "I've got your light inside of me."

2.

Ten or twenty years ago the farm might have been pretty with its red barn and towering silo resting in front of a field of corn or soybeans. There was only a field of tall grass now, waving back and forth in the strong March winds. As the dirt road they had been driving on for several bumpy minutes finally came to an end, Cheyenne studied the abandoned property, wondering if anybody other than Jazz was planning to meet them.

"Can you fill me in on the plan now?" she asked her father.

"The plan was to drive here," he said, pulling into the circle that went around the house, the barn, and the silo. "Other than that I don't know anything."

"You know more than I do. Are we going to be farmers now? Live off the land. Eat grass."

"Very funny. Come on. Get your backpack."

"Have you ever been here?" she asked before climbing out of the car.

"No. But I know it's not going to be like the St. Louis hideout. Or the bunker in Colorado."

"Can we go back, then?" she joked, grabbing her bag that felt heavier than she remembered.

Her father carried a sports duffel bag. It matched his outfit, with the Nike logo on his workout pants and hooded sweatshirt. She had joked with her father and asked if he was suddenly trying to get into shape since she'd never seen him dressed like an athlete before. He told her that to prevent being spotted in public, he was trying to look younger and wear things that helped cover his face in as natural a way as possible.

As her father closed the trunk of the car, Cheyenne looked at his bag. "Do you have any dress pants or shirts in that bag?"

He laughed. "Nope. Nothing that has the word *dress* in front of it."

"What'd you do with all your suits? All those ties and shoes?"

"Goodwill was happy to take several boxes of stuff from me. All I know is that it's easier running away from someone when you're wearing tennis shoes."

Cheyenne felt sad hearing this and knowing he wasn't trying to be funny, not in the slightest. *He's been on the run for some time. And he left everything behind.* Everything, Cheyenne realized, except for her.

The front door to the red farmhouse squeaked open as she turned the doorknob. She figured nobody was here, unless their vehicle was hidden in the barn. The only light filling the entryway and room came from the windows, and as they walked, a haze of dust suddenly awakened and began to rise.

"Is anyone here?" she asked.

Her father stopped and pulled a calendar off the wall.

"It's from 2027," he said, coughing as more dust swirled around him. "I don't think the owners have been here for a long time."

"Is anyone else coming out here besides Jazz?"

He tossed the calendar featuring photos of cows onto a square wooden table with room for only four people. "They didn't say."

Cheyenne noticed a thin silver MacBook on the desk in the main living room area. She walked over and opened it. Instantly a video began playing, with a country singer crooning to a corny electronic disco beat as middle-aged men from all over the nation danced to the song.

This isn't a coincidence.

The song called "Cotton Eye Joe" was from the nineties, but the video had been a recent sensation since it was some worldwide contest for the best "Daddy Dancer" out there. Why they picked this song other than its humor, Cheyenne didn't know, but she did know it made Malek laugh. A lot. And he played it for her in the office. For about two weeks straight, the video began to play every time Cheyenne walked into the office.

She looked around the room again, quickly trying to see if anybody else was there. A part of her was hoping, just as she had with her father. As the fiddles and the sweeping techno music bounced along, she saw her dad giving her an amused and baffled look. Then a door at the back of the living room opened, and sure enough, the culprit walked out with a big grin on his face.

"Malek!" she shouted as she rushed over to give him a hug.

"Whoa, whoa," Malek said as he was smothered by Cheyenne. "Easy there."

She stepped back to make sure she was really seeing him. He looked the same, from his spiky hair to his casual clothes that he never bothered to update.

"Miss me?" he asked with his mischievous smile.

She couldn't help but give him another hug. This time he gave one back.

"Okay, let me turn that off," he said as he walked over and shut off the video. "Like my new computer?"

"What are you doing here?" she asked.

"Hello, Mr. Burne," Malek said.

Cheyenne had forgotten for a moment that her father was in the room with them. Malek and her father knew each other from the few times her father had visited her, either at the offices themselves or while staying in Chicago.

"Hello, Malek," her father said, appearing hesitant enough to indicate he didn't know her friend would be showing up.

"What are you doing here?" Cheyenne repeated. "Are you part of everything that's happening? Dad, have you been in touch with—"

"I saw your father the last time you did—right before he disappeared," Malek answered quickly. "But I've known about your father's involvement with the mission."

"Where have you been?"

Malek seemed to marvel at her for a moment. "You're crying."

Cheyenne shook her head, laughing and then wiping her eyes to see that he was right.

"I guess you really did miss me," he said.

"I haven't heard from you since you left. *Jerk.*" But she couldn't get the smile off her face.

"You didn't try very hard to track me down," Malek said.

"Really? How would you know? I tried."

He nodded. "I know. I wanted to be invisible. PASK does a good job of making you obsolete if they want to."

"Do you know Jazz?"

"Yeah. Mostly through CC—clandestine communication. So very spyriffic. I met him once."

"Why didn't you say goodbye before disappearing?"

"Thought you got rid of me, didn't you?" Malek asked.

"A little heads-up would have been nice."

Her father stood beside her now as they spoke in the deepening shadows in the room.

"Do you see everything that's happening? How could I possibly begin to tell you? You and that analytical brain of yours. I see it spinning like a top even now."

Cheyenne didn't respond.

"The only reason you're here is your father."

She shook her head and turned to her dad. "No."

"No? Then why else?"

"Tom and Susan Parschauer." She could picture the faces of the couple. "Did you meet them?"

Any joviality from Malek ended. "No."

"Whoever did that to them . . . Look, all I know is some very bad things are happening. And because of them, my world suddenly got uprooted. Just like yours."

"But I chose, Cheyenne," Malek said. "I believe the same way your father did."

"So belief means you're getting revenge against the company that fired you?"

"You don't understand," he said.

Keith Burne walked over to the door and opened it. "I'll let you guys talk."

As her father left them in the house, Cheyenne stood, waiting for more from Malek. He moved toward her, smiling and looking sincere.

"I can't believe you're actually here," Malek said.

"I could say the same."

"PASK fired me for the same reasons your father was fired. And they told me—they threatened—that if I contacted you for any reason, I would be killed. Or something would happen to you."

"So you went and found God and *didn't* even tell me?"

"It wasn't that simple, Chy."

"And I get it now about shaking things up. I'm okay with it. I see PASK and Acatour in a whole other light. After what happened to that poor couple—"

"You don't know a fraction of the truth," Malek said, picking up the laptop.

"But the things Jazz is talking about, like Chicago being destroyed by God. Do you actually buy into that?"

"Chy, you know me," he said as he briefly glanced out the window. "You know how I question everything. *Everything.* Right? You know that. You know that I challenge authority, but I swear, this isn't that. I'm not being rebellious for rebellion's sake. I'm not getting revenge over my job. And the things the Reckoner has said? Yeah, I believe them. I really believe something big is going to happen. And we're going to help make it happen."

For a few moments Malek searched the room. "I'm double-checking to make sure there aren't signs of someone having been here."

Before he could pass her, she gently held on to his arm and forced him to stop.

"Faith is different for everybody," she said.

"No, it's not. Faith isn't subjective, like staring at a piece of art and thinking how you feel about it. There's something that's truly incomprehensible about true faith, because it *does not compute.* There's no analysis you can make of it. You just give your heart blindly, and you know. And the most brilliant sort of algorithm isn't going to make someone believe. Only God can stir the heart."

"I guess He hasn't done that with mine."

Malek smiled at her. "Not yet."

Cheyenne shivered. This time it was Malek who initiated a hug.

"I've really missed you," he told her. "You never thought you'd hear me preaching to you, did you? Come on. Let's go to the barn."

3.

From the outside the barn appeared as if it might collapse at any moment, especially as Malek opened its wide, squeaking doors, yet inside a makeshift workspace had been created. A large oak table resembling one that could be found in a boardroom rested in the center of the barn, with business chairs on wheels surrounding it. Malek flipped a switch, and warm light spilled over them. As the outside dirt switched to soft rubber underneath her shoes, Cheyenne walked inside and heard Malek shutting the doors behind them.

"What is this place?" she asked, looking at the two sets of desks lining the conference table on each side. More chairs were set up with computers in front of them.

"Looks like the bunker in Colorado, right? At least a little?"

She looked at several black metal boxes the size of a shoebox resting on the table just as her father stepped inside the barn.

"What do you guys do here? Play video games?"

"Yeah," Malek said. "A game called *Preparing for the Unveiling.* It's quite fun to know that America is going to be in chaos in less than a month."

"I see you're cynical as ever."

"No. This isn't cynicism. It's sadness. I always wanted to get back at the powers that be, at the corporations, and even at the company that fired me, but this isn't any of that."

"What is it, then?"

Malek looked at her father for a moment, perhaps to see if he wanted to answer. But her dad seemed content to let him continue.

"I want to help wake people up. To show them the lies they're being fed. To show how every single person out there is being manipulated. And I want them to hear the truth. To at least hear God's truth."

She wondered what had happened to Malek to get him to this place. How had he been convinced to suddenly embrace this thing he used to mock? How had Christianity suddenly become so important to him?

I'll ask him that at another time.

"So how are you going to wake everybody up?" she asked.

He picked up one of the boxes and held it in his hands. "We, Chy. How are *we* going to wake everybody up?"

She sighed as she sat on the conference table, swinging her legs and staring at Malek. "This past week I've been to an underground bunker, a secret church in an old warehouse, a secret getaway in a mansion, and now I'm at an abandoned farm. I still have no idea what all this is leading to. What 'we' are supposed to do."

"After the Reckoner contacted me, I asked him the same thing, and his message was this: to be silent before God, for the day of the Lord is near. The Lord's prepared a sacrifice, and he's blessed those he's inviting in."

"Are you telling me to be silent?" she asked, a friendly smile on her lips.

He mirrored it. "Nope. I'm telling you you're blessed. You just don't know it. Not yet. You've been chosen, Chy. By something much stronger than fate."

FIFTEEN

The Great Escape

1.

Midway through the song, Will knows.

He's known it all along, to be honest. It's been so obvious, yet he's never really uttered it out loud. Some truths are harder to admit to yourself. That's why silencing them is so easy.

I've been silent for too long. Not only about this. But about everything that matters in my life.

The truth terrifies him. It's scary because it's so reckless, so unbridled and mysterious. Yet at the same time, it's amusing. Like a boyhood prank that's turned political on a worldwide platform.

All morning he's been watching and looking up images and video footage of the wave of graffiti spread over Chicago. Ten major acts of vandalism have taken place throughout the city at important places like Millennium Park, where the reflective "bean" art structure has been painted with the words "The Revolution Will Not Be Televised." At Navy Pier a colorful "A Change Is Gonna Come" covers the sidewalks. "Fight the Power" can be found in Buckingham Fountain, while "Get Up, Stand Up" is spray-painted at the front of the Shedd Aquarium. It doesn't take a music lover to know all the messages are song titles.

Will has a hunch, so he tells Tolkien to play a song called "Reckoner" if there is one, and sure enough, a Radiohead tune begins to play. Will thinks back to that trip into the country that suddenly felt like being in a spacecraft shooting into warp drive with a million stars passing by them. Hutchence had played a Radiohead tune then as well, so obviously he likes the band.

"You can't take it with you." The lyric pops out at him, because Hutchence has said it numerous times, often out of the blue, making Will wonder exactly what he was saying. Coming from the song "Reckoner."

Hutchence *is* the Reckoner. And, of course, it makes sense. All the ways of getting people's attention. All as a way of warning them what's coming. But realizing this gives Will a sense of dread.

Am I being suckered and hoodwinked? All for some false prophet who likes to quote Tozer and Radiohead?

He wonders if he's sipped the Kool-Aid simply because of his anger and hatred toward his father. What if all this comes back to haunt Will? What if Hutchence, aka the Reckoner, turns out to be just another wacko wanting to get back at the head of Acatour?

Lord, help me, please. Help me now.

2.

If Will didn't know Hutchence, he might have assumed Hutchence was the head of a tech company in the Incen Tower, based on his look and demeanor. He wore trim khaki trousers and a tucked-in, button-down shirt underneath a stylish overcoat. His brown boots made the outfit. His handsome, square mug was now evident with the unruly beard gone. Will waited for him at a stone bridge crossing the Fox River. Bike trails wove through the trees in a nearby park.

"Your message sounded rather angry," Hutchence said when he reached Will.

All Will could do was curse at the man.

"Wow. Having a bad morning with Flip?"

The sun hid behind thick clouds, trying to decide between snow and icy rain. Right now a slight mix of both could barely be seen whipping around them in the strong winds of midday.

"I know who you are, *Reckoner*," Will said. "I know all the things you've done."

Hutchence didn't look even slightly surprised.

"I know you're him—Reckoner and Acrobat and probably several other ridiculous names."

"Ridiculous? I rather liked them. I thought they were clever. Didn't you?"

"What are you doing? Are you crazy? Seriously. I mean that in all sincerity."

"I assumed you knew this much earlier, Will. And, no, I'm not crazy, not in the least, but as I told you already, many people will think I am. They thought Noah was crazy too, until people began to drown next to the big boat he'd built. Isaiah lived naked for a while. Did you know that? They also thought Jesus was crazy, not to mention sacrilegious. I'm not daring to compare myself with Jesus, not even Noah, but I'm telling you—"

"So why didn't you tell me, then?"

"Because I thought you might get a little hostile. I thought you might worry if I wanted to extort money from your father or something."

Will shook his head and began to walk down the paved bike trail to the wooded area. It was cold, and he was wearing only a sweater, having forgotten his coat. The wind cut through him, but there was enough fire inside him to make him forget about being numb.

"All these things you've done—graffiti and destruction of property—"

"I was getting people's attention. Nobody was harmed. No one. But many, many will be harmed when this chapter is done. And, Will, I'm afraid it is indeed just a chapter. I don't know how the story will play out, but I do know the day of reckoning for Chicago and for Acatour and for your father is fast approaching."

"And you want me to contact my father so his people can see that I've been hanging out with the very guy vandalizing the city? Making veiled threats against my father's company?"

"Do you still doubt the things your father and his company are doing?" Hutchence asked.

"No, but I don't like being lied to."

"I never lied to you, Will. I didn't tell you the obvious. Sometimes we don't want to hear the truth, and other times we can't discern it."

"I've done nothing wrong here," Will said, looking around the park to see if anybody was nearby.

"We're not being watched," Hutchence said with confidence. "And nobody ever said you've done anything wrong."

Will couldn't stop moving, pacing and shaking his head. "You know, for a while I took all the 'Christian' material out of my store. Then I began to ask what books fall under that definition. Books by Christian artists? Only those that are nonfiction? Those that specifically deliver the gospel? I saw dozens of books I couldn't decide on. And the whole thing made me sick. Ultimately I couldn't make up my mind. But I was scared. And I'm still scared."

"Angry too," Hutchence said.

"Yeah. Pretty much."

Hutchence rubbed his bare hands together as the wind cut through them. "I want to see that heavy weight of worry taken off you, Will. I can't do it, and you can't do it by yourself. You need God to do that, but first you gotta believe He can do it."

"Worry is what happens when you become estranged from your father who happens to be one of the world's most powerful men."

"Remember David asking how a pagan Philistine could be allowed to defy the armies of the living God?"

"Oh, come on. Don't give me a David and Goliath sermon." The wind blew his hair and made Will shiver. "You know, after I committed my life to Christ, I thought I would do something really big one day, the way all college students think. Dream big and believe you can and all those things. For a while I thought maybe I could be a writer but found out I don't have the gift. And when I didn't become something big, I realized that I could've done so much more with my life. I've had this lukewarm sort of life. First I thought of it in terms of my career, but I've never really done anything with my faith either. Selling a few Christian books and helping Pastor Brian publish one were good things, but they weren't particularly remarkable."

"Want to know what God wants from you?" Hutchence asked. "God doesn't want you to write the next great American novel or to cure cancer. What He wants is for you to love Him and to make Him the main priority of your life. To make Him known. Look, I understand the whole thing about regrets. I get that. But you can't let your past define your future, especially since we have work to do."

"Every time you say that . . . Every time you use the word *we* . . ."

"I can't force you to do anything, Will. It's up to you if you choose to be a part of this. But, please, for the sake of all those believers and nonbelievers being victimized by Acatour, you need to do what's right. And you have to decide today."

Will nodded and looked up to the sky.

"I will contact you tomorrow to hear your decision," Hutchence said.

With that, the man walked away. The Reckoner slipping away, the Acrobat going back to his work, whatever work he was doing.

For Will, there was an excitement in the things Hutchence was doing, yet there was also a terror. Knowing which category they ultimately fell into was the big question.

A question he needed to answer in twenty-four hours.

3.

The anger swelled, dominating the fear within him. The two emotions were similar to his fraternal twins taking turns acting out in disobedience.

Knowing he needed to get it out of his system somehow, he powered on his Envisage Bike, a Christmas gift from Amy half a decade ago. Will couldn't remember the last time he had used it. Two or three years ago? The workout bicycle transformed the augmented reality experience by interfacing with one's SYNAPSYS, meaning you could seamlessly program a ride through Nepal and have your wife and children show up at your side if you wanted to. He pedaled as sweat covered him, telling him how out of shape he was. His noise-canceling headphones weren't necessary since everybody was out of the house, but he still felt that he couldn't turn up the volume as loud as he wanted to.

Round and round and round the pedals went as he switched the scenery from the Himalayas to the city streets of Paris. After getting bored with that, Will decided to bike somewhere in the Sahara desert. Once again the sweeping beauty was straight out of some grand, epic film like *Lawrence of Arabia,* the endless sand all around him in a spectacular 360-degree view. Yet he wanted—he needed—something more.

"Random film!" Will shouted out between heavy breaths.

This had been a fun feature when he first bought it, and it reminded him that he needed to have Shaye try this out. Riders could use this setting and find themselves in any sort of film they wanted. All the films Will had called out could be used, even some obscure indie films or Russian flicks. Calling out the random setting meant his SYNAPSYS would pick it for him, the nature of the artificial intelligence and the algorithms setting the course for him.

Like every day for every person in every life.

All around him were rolling hills, glorious in summertime, with the sky blue above him and a packed gravel road underneath. It appeared that he might be somewhere in Europe. He heard the roar of an engine and saw a uniformed officer of some sort riding a vintage motorcycle. He began pedaling to follow as an orchestra played the soundtrack.

"You're inside *The Great Escape,* from 1963, starring Steve McQueen," Tolkien told him.

Will smiled, his anger easing a bit. He remembered the movie and knew that McQueen's character was wearing a Nazi uniform while finally making his big escape on a Triumph TR6 Trophy.

Ah, the glories of consolidated media. Everything incorporated into one big melting pot. With one license to rule them all, as the joke went. Nothing was off limits, nothing sacred. And while many opposed it initially, fewer did with each passing year, knowing how nice it felt not only to be the hero of your journey but also to insert yourself into any sort of journey you wanted. Not only in this biking experience but in everything else in this world.

"Change the tune," Will said, wanting to dispense with the classical music.

As he pedaled through the German countryside, African chants began around him. He wondered if Tolkien was trying to be funny as the bleak Brazilian drum played. But when the voice sang, Will recognized Peter Gabriel. The famous protest song "Biko" began to build, slowly and steadily like the drums.

Riding through a small, picturesque German town, Will could see McQueen being summoned by one of the many Nazis guarding the main road. The wild thing with this experience was that he was able to see the scene perfectly from where he was standing instead of seeing it play on a flat screen in front of him. Will waited for a moment before McQueen kicked the soldier and tore off once again down the road.

Pedaling harder, down a hill and over a little bridge leading to open fields, Will kept moving, knowing it was impossible to keep up with a motorcycle but having the system help him so he never fell too far behind. The Nazis pursued them in the background, firing shots that could be heard.

"I can only dream in red," Peter Gabriel sang. It felt like his voice drifted off into the Alps in the background.

Will moved past a barn and down more gravel roads that crisscrossed, with more Nazis showing up. McQueen remained defiant as he continued to weave his motorcycle around, and Will pumped the pedals to keep up in his imagination.

When they finally got cornered, with McQueen's character jumping over barbed wire, Will had an option to follow. He stopped the bike, sucking air and drenched, just as the singer sang, "And the eyes of the world are watching now."

Does Tolkien know everything that is happening? Is this another message from him or from Hutchence?

Maybe God was talking through his SYNAPSYS.

He stood up and began pedaling again with a fury, swooping down to the hill just above the barbed-wire fence. Soon he found himself soaring in the air, and he paused, waiting to see where he landed.

4.

"I've left a message for my father to call me this morning," Will told Amy on the Saturday after his conversation with Hutchence by the bridge.

"Are you serious? Why?"

So far Will hadn't told her anything about Hutchence and what was happening. He knew he should have, and he had planned to tell her, but so far he hadn't found the right moment. Even now he wasn't going to share everything with her. He couldn't, because he was still trying to decide how to handle things with Jackson Heyford.

"Is it to talk with him about financial issues? Because you know you can talk to my parents—"

"No," Will interrupted. "It has nothing to do with that."

"Then why? After all this time?"

"I know he's the one behind the store closing. I know he's the one who ultimately got it shut down."

"How do you know this?"

After everything Hutchence had shown him about Acatour, it was a foregone conclusion that his father had managed to do this, destroying one of Will's lifetime dreams probably with a simple click of his fingers. He had suspected it, of course, but now he wanted to know the truth.

"I'm going to get him to tell me in person," Will said.

"Why? Do you think he would even see you?"

Will knew how to get his father's attention. "Yeah. He'll see me. Or at least someone is going to contact me."

"Will, I wouldn't go there if I were you. What are you trying to prove?"

"I want to know the truth. And if it's true, I want him to hear what I think."

He had already told Hutchence this morning that he had contacted his father through a personal number to his SYNAPSYS. The number still worked, though he didn't hear his father's voice in the message. It just buzzed and expected him to talk.

The girls could suddenly be heard arguing downstairs in the playroom.

"I'll go," Amy said, starting toward the doorway that led to the basement. But then she stopped. "I spoke to my parents yesterday, and the offer is still there."

Will winced and shook his head. "Tell me you're teasing."

"Do I ever tease?"

She had a good point. "What'd you say to them?" he asked.

"I mentioned that you had a business trip to Grand Rapids, so this piqued their curiosity. You know my mom."

"Yeah, and I know your dad too."

He couldn't count the arguments they'd had over the in-laws. How her father expected more from him, making his case as soon as he and Amy started dating. Dick Van de Berg was smart enough to know his daughter, to know Will might be the one for Amy. To know she was rebellious enough to want someone unconventional, someone *not* like her controlling, alpha-male father. And indeed, Will had been that one. Mr. and Mrs. Van de Berg's disappointment only deepened when Will opened the bookstore, and it soon turned into dismay after Will and Amy started struggling financially.

"I told them my boss said I could work for their team in GR," Amy said.

"Were you going to tell me about that? Or maybe just move the girls in the middle of the night?"

"I'm telling you now. That doesn't mean it's going to happen. I know you don't want me to bring this up again, but you could just talk to Dad."

"No, I can't, and don't bring it up again," he told her. The anger began to clench its teeth and curl its fingers into a fist. *I can't believe she's even going there.*

Yes, there was *that*. Taking a job at Waste, Inc. The place Dick Van de Berg had worked all his life and made all his millions from. He wasn't insanely rich by any means, but compared to Will, he was the Bank of America.

Amy had reached the foot of the carpeted stairs descending to the playroom when Will called out her name. "Thanks for trying," he told her as she looked back at him, obviously disappointed.

"I just want to help."

"I know." He sighed, shaking his head, then rubbing his eyes for a moment. "There are worse things than my having to work for your father at Waste, Inc."

"Really?" she asked with a chuckle. "Like what?"

"One would be working for *my* father. That would be worse than going to jail."

"Who knows? Maybe your dad will make you an offer you can't refuse."

Amy disappeared downstairs, leaving Will with a bad feeling. She had no idea how right on her joke happened to be.

5.

The mix of ice and snow that came late on Saturday night right before the several inches of powder this morning had transformed their backyard into a glistening white replica of the fantastical world of Narnia. The tiny trees they had planted after first moving in—or, more accurately, that Amy had picked out and planted—had grown in fifteen years, with the river birch trees sprawling to twenty or thirty feet. The arborvitae were close to twenty feet as well, blocking out the traffic on the streets that lined their corner property. The limbs of the trees and edges of the shrubs were coated with thick snow, but the sky had cleared of clouds.

Will had shoveled a little path on their patio so Flip could do his business. The ten-yard clearing made him think of his bookstore in a weird, sad way. Flip didn't seem to understand what the path was about, hopping into the snow and then looking back at him as he got stuck in the packed powder that came up to his nose.

Will put on his boots and coat, then went went outside and picked up Flip. "You're a pain, you know that?" he said, holding the wet mutt and then seeing something bright near the river birch in the corner of their yard. Underneath the tree, someone appeared to be sitting on the bench. Will couldn't tell for sure, however, because he seemed to be looking into a powerful light, as if the bench had a mirror reflecting the sunlight.

Then the figure stood up, but Will didn't recognize him. At first he thought it might be Hutchence, but the closer the man got, the bigger he appeared. His black ski jacket looked brand-new and expensive, just like his boots and sunglasses, and his hair was slicked back in a modern haircut. He walked as if he owned the property. As Will watched him approach, he felt scared. And small. He suddenly had an urge to drop Flip and take off running the other direction. But he couldn't. He stood in place and felt his legs shaking.

"Good morning, Will."

He didn't have to ask who the man was and why he was here. As Will held Flip in a way that seemed to protect him, the stranger scanned the yard and then stared at him.

"What sort of business do you want with Jackson Heyford?"

As he suspected, the man had been sent by his father or his father's people. Will wasn't surprised.

"It's nothing to do with business," Will said. "And it's not your business either."

The man stood there, more motionless than the trees behind him. Flip wiggled in his arms, so Will put the dog down to wander by their feet.

"I assume Jackson Heyford's office received my message."

"Yes, but not the reason you want to meet."

"That's between me and him."

Jackson's well-dressed assistant or bodyguard or whatever he was just stood there, again seeming to wait. Or perhaps working extra hard to think of something to say.

"Tell Mr. Heyford that this has something to do with Jimmy," Will said. "You got that?"

Still nothing from Robot Man, or maybe Will should think of him as Frankenstein. Will picked Flip back up, but as he did, it appeared the stranger heard something.

"Ten o'clock tonight," Heyford's man said.

Ah. Dad was listening in. Will knew the very mention of his brother's name would get an immediate response.

"I'll pick you up," the man said.

"No. I'll drive myself. That way I have a tiny bit of control. I need every little bit I can get."

"Ten o'clock tonight at Mr. Heyford's residence." The big figure began to walk away in the mixture of snow and ice.

Will had done exactly what Hutchence had told him to do—make sure he wasn't taken to Heyford but rather would drive himself. That way Will could bring a guest.

SIXTEEN

Streaks of Red and Orange

1.

"Good morning."

The sound. Sudden, alive, surrounding, inside.

"This is your wake-up call, Mr. Dowland. One you will remember for quite some time."

He'd already grabbed the Beretta on the table by the master bed and crouched between the bed and the wall. The hovering red glow on the illuminated wall spilled out into the rest of the hotel suite, giving it the hazy look of a nightclub. No shape or shadow could be seen. Nothing was moving or out of place.

"Don't worry, Dowland. You don't have to get dressed for me. Instead of spying on you the way you like to do with others, I thought I'd introduce myself."

No way. "How are you able to talk to me?" Dowland yelled even though he knew he could have whispered and the man on the other end would hear him.

"Well, first, you left your SYNAPSYS on."

Since he was in Chicago, he had contacted a couple of guys he knew to look into any possible leads on the man he had been following earlier. Now he knew for sure it was Reckoner. The only way his contacts could reach him right away was through his SYNAPSYS.

How'd he get through mine?

"But the technology part? Frankly, I think guys like you and me aren't smart enough even to have that explained to us. Like you, I have colleagues. They just happen to be brilliant."

"Identify yourself," Dowland said as he walked through the two-room suite to make sure everything was clear.

"'Identify yourself'? You act like you're talking to HAL 9000. I think you know who this is."

"Why don't you tell me since you obviously have a lot more answers than I do."

Everything in the room appeared the way he remembered it before he fell asleep. Or the way it had been before his memory began to slip, before the alcohol finally set well into his bloodstream, before the familiar black took over. An empty bottle of gin sat on the bathroom counter, and another bottle was on the table in the sitting area.

"I'm not interested in playing cat-and-mouse games, Dowland. Nor am I trying to play head games, even though I am literally inside your head."

Dowland opened a screen on the desk and looked up the data on the caller. No image could be found, no information listed. It was blank and blocked. The voice continued to talk, undaunted by anything Dowland might be doing to learn his identity.

"I'm going to tell you the same thing I've been telling others, though I'll make it a lot more simple and straightforward for you. The people you're working for are no longer protected. The world is going to learn about the lies they're digesting daily, about the people controlling them. And about people like you hunting down and killing men and women for their faith. But as the Turkish proverb says, 'No matter how far you have gone on a wrong road, turn back.'"

Despite every sort of search and scan Dowland tried, his SYNAPSYS produced nothing. Not one bit of information. All Dowland could do was curse at the voice.

"I know you've seen plenty of the signs and warnings and proclamations I've given."

"Yeah. And it's going to be fun when I finally see you and give you a proclamation of my own."

There was a pause, and for a moment Dowland wondered if he had scared away the unseen intruder.

"God knows you. He sees you and loves you. And He has mentioned you by name, Jonathan Paul Hardy."

Dowland stood and looked around the room again, panic setting in. A sort he hadn't felt in a very long time. The gun still in his hand, he walked over to look at the glittering skyline of Chicago. In the distance the Incen Tower soared up to the heavens high above this miniscule building.

Nobody knows my real name. Nobody.

"Who are you working for?" Dowland asked. "Where are you getting your information?"

"Jesus told the people that unless they saw signs and wonders, they simply would not believe. Yet He also told them that they had indeed seen Him, and still they didn't believe. And you're one of those, Dowland. I tell you something as simple as a name you've kept carefully hidden your entire adult life, and you instantly assume I'm working with someone else, another small group controlling everybody else. But that is your world, not mine. I follow the person in control of everything, including you and me."

Dowland wanted to shut off his SYNAPSYS and easily could, yet every single second he spent listening to the man on the other end might help. If not to find his location, at least to figure out who he was and to possibly take him down.

"A man I know spent his life dreaming of being in those high circles, of knowing the people who knew the people who ultimately make every decision for this world. The secret societies, those above the governments, those with money and power. This man kept rising higher and higher in the spidery web of the financial market. But God never let go of him. God finally caught his attention and crushed his heart. He became a new man."

"And this is you, right?" Dowland asked.

"You should know by now that things in this world are never as they seem. And when it comes to the Holy Spirit, He truly does move in mysterious ways."

2.

She was crazy. That was for certain. But maybe Dowland was too. Maybe that's why they made a living doing what they did. He rarely called her, primarily because she scared him. But at this point he needed to stop the bleeding, so any way that could happen was worth it.

Margaux entered the doorway as if she had just completed a marathon. The logo on her athletic jacket matched the ones on her leggings, shoes, and headband. She swooped into the bar with long, quick strides, her raven hair pulled back in a ponytail. Margaux was a striking figure, and her allure was the very reason she was almost the best in this brutal business. Yet there was something undeniably cold about her.

"This had better be good," she said as she wiped a dot of sweat off her cheek.

No greeting, no "How's life treating you?" No casual comment whatsoever.

"I see you're really letting yourself go," he said with a grin.

"And I see you've never looked healthier."

This prompted a laugh. He always loved her bite.

"You were hard to reach."

"Some of us have lives," Margaux said.

"But you're here now, right?"

Her eyes glanced at the empty glass in front of him. "You're drunk."

"And you're judgmental."

Margaux slid onto the chair across from him and glanced around, apparently expecting someone to be there at that very second to serve her. "I always wonder why they put up with you."

"We're cut from the same cloth, and you know it. That's why you're here."

She flipped her hair, then drilled into him with her malicious stare. "'We' are two opposing universes here, always have been."

Dowland looked at the bartender and then shouted at him to get over here.

"I'm so sorry," the man said seconds after he bolted from behind the thick wood of the bar to run to their table. "What would you like, miss?"

"Give me a double," Dowland said.

For a second the short, bald bartender didn't know what to say. Margaux didn't appear surprised in the slightest by Dowland's rudeness.

"I'd like to order a muzzle," she joked.

The bartender really looked confused now, his wide eyes looking at Dowland and then at her again. "Is that some kind of drink?"

She sneaked an amused glance at Dowland, and for the moment they were on the same side. "Since he's picking up the tab, bring me the most expensive glass of wine you have. And if it only comes in a bottle, then let's uncork that sucker."

The man began to open his mouth, but Dowland told him to go, so he did. It was enough to make Dowland almost grin. Almost.

"You know why you don't like me, Margaux?" he asked her.

"It's a long list."

"It's because I don't run like that. I don't crumble under the Margaux factor."

Those long fingers spun her hair again in a way that looked like a habit, like someone who couldn't stay still, someone who couldn't help waving the world off.

"You don't need someone else to help you crumble," she said as the drinks were served.

Dowland didn't wait for her as he took a sip, closing his eyes for a moment, lost in the warm tug while the bartender opened the wine bottle and let her try a sip. He opened his eyes and took another sip of his double-barreled gin. The bartender was kind enough to bring two wine glasses, leaving his empty.

"I flew down to meet with Mel," he told her and saw the reaction in her eyes. "We met for a very specific job."

" 'Very specific,' huh? So you're saying there's no ambiguity here, right?"

He cursed at her sarcasm, which only made her laugh louder.

"I hope you looked a little more alive and awake in front of Mel than you do now."

Another curse was directed at her. "I don't want to trade insults like some married couple. There's a reason people like us aren't hitched."

Margaux raised her eyebrows as if surprised, then brushed her jaw with her index finger. She had mastered the art of seductive mannerisms when talking, a trick that helped her control most conversations.

"Relationships can be tough to navigate, right?" she said, looking at the bandage on his ear.

Ah yes. Well played.

He cursed again with a laugh, then finished the drink in front of him. "As the saying goes, 'Tis better to have loved and lost than never to have loved at all,'" Dowland told her.

"I believe our definitions of *love* might contradict each other," Margaux said.

The last thing in the world he wanted at this moment was to be talking to this woman about love. "I need your help," Dowland said.

Her head moved back. Then she feigned choking as she put a hand over her mouth. "Am I delirious? Did I just hear you say that?"

"I don't have the time or patience to try to be cocky." He sighed. "That's gotten me nowhere."

The gemstone green in her eyes appeared to brighten with his admission. "I've heard you haven't had much luck lately."

He leaned over the table. "What have you heard? Honestly, I need to know what's out there."

"I've heard it's urgent. Quite important, in fact. Acatour is anxious, something that doesn't happen. It involves the mystery man who keeps pulling pranks and predicting the end of the company."

"But have you heard any chatter—anything—in the last twenty-four hours?"

"No," Margaux said in a tone honest enough for him to believe her.

At this point he had to believe in someone. He needed at least one ally he could trust. Even if it was only temporary.

"The situation just got worse." He told her what happened with Lorenzo Costa and the old couple.

There was no reaction from Margaux, nothing that revealed she'd heard the story. Maybe Lorenzo was actually keeping his mouth shut.

"The problem isn't only the mess Lorenzo left back in Tulsa," Dowland said. "He spotted the first two people at the scene of the crime. One was the daughter of Keith Burne, the missing exec on our list. And—you're gonna love this—the other was the rapper named License."

"Odd combo," she said as she took a sip of her wine.

Dowland nodded and poured himself a glass, then tried it. "Wow, this is going to be expensive."

"Very." She looked amused. "You believe Lorenzo?"

"Yeah. He's scared. This was the only way he stayed out of trouble. Honestly, the only way he's not floating in a river."

"Has anybody ever connected either Burne or License with the Chicago vigilante?"

"No. If they do before I manage to find either of them, then I might be the one floating."

"You *do* need my help."

"Yes." He cursed to emphasize how much he hated asking for it. But like Dowland, she had her own contacts and connections, especially in a city like Chicago.

"There's something else," Dowland told her. "They're able to get through your SYNAPSYS, to talk on it."

"I thought you didn't use yours."

"Only at select times, only when I have to contact someone like you in an emergency. They knew. *He* knew. I heard him loud and clear."

"You're sure?"

"Positive," Dowland said. "This technology—it makes me wonder about the Burne girl. Cheyenne. The genius from PASK. Maybe she's been involved with this like her father."

"Their whereabouts . . ."

"Unknown. But I have a feeling. I'm pretty sure they're either in Chicago now or nearby. All the things the Reckoner is doing concern Acatour and Jackson Heyford."

Margaux rubbed her hands gently, then lightly touched the black tattoo band around her ring finger. "Have you spoken with Heyford about any of this?"

"No. It better not come to that."

"You think something big is going to happen in Chicago?"

Dowland looked across the room at the modern art painting on the wall as he pondered the question. The background was blurry gray with a round black cloud in the center coated with streaks of red and orange as if they were splattered rather than painted on the canvas. Staring into the six-foot painting, Dowland pictured his father's face the day he finally died.

"No," Dowland answered. "I think this guy and these people are putting on some big act. I don't think they know all that much. But it doesn't matter what I think. I'm just supposed to hunt them down."

"And what if I told you I can't help you?" she said with a devilish smile on her lips.

"Then tell me. Like I said, I don't have time for any games or bravado."

They both knew that the moment she became involved, her position of power in their universe rose a little higher.

"Okay," Margaux said. "And if I find any of them first?"

"Do what you do best."

SEVENTEEN

The Same Page

1.

The moment her father stepped foot in the barn that morning, Cheyenne couldn't help but let loose with an uproarious laugh.

"You have to be kidding me," she said, shaking her head.

Her father wore a black hoodie that said LICENSE on its front, the rapper's name and brand almost as well known as the Nike logo. Jazz stood next to him, looking professional in his sweater and black winter vest.

"What?" her father said, acting as if he had no clue what she was talking about.

"Big License fan, huh, Dad?"

"Oh sure." Keith Burne looked at Jazz. "At least the songs that don't have profanities in them."

"There aren't many," Jazz joked.

Soon all five of them sat around the conference table under the hard white light illuminating the barn. Looking at everyone, Cheyenne knew what an unlikely team they were. Her father sitting next to her in his very unconventional attire, and next to him was Jazz, studying the printed documents all of them had in front of them. On another side of the table, Malek sat typing on a Mac laptop, his fingers moving like a hamster running in its wheel. He had his get-up-and-go look today, as she used to call it when it appeared as if he had gotten out of bed and gone directly to work. He wore the same clothes as yesterday, and his hair was sharp and messy, as if he'd tried to style it with gel and only made it worse.

Jazz had arrived last night, and the four of them had spent the night at the farmhouse, waiting for the fifth member of this makeshift team. When she showed up, they were all surprised to see it wasn't the Reckoner but rather a woman named Lucia Gonzales. The woman wore a dark blue business suit and looked like a realtor or lawyer.

"I've seen you before," Lucia told Cheyenne as they shook hands.

"Really? When?"

"I work at the Incen building. I've seen you in passing. I'm sure you've never seen me."

"Seriously?" Cheyenne asked.

"You were pointed out to me. We knew you worked at PASK. One of the elites."

Cheyenne wasn't sure how to take this, if it was a compliment or a critique. Both Jazz and Malek appeared confused when she arrived, asking about the man putting the plan in place.

"I thought the Reckoner was supposed to meet with us," Malek said.

"I can't speak for him," Lucia said.

"It seems that nobody can," Cheyenne said.

Lucia had brought the handouts they were looking over, the "grand plan" as Malek called it. As Cheyenne started going through it, she couldn't help but laugh.

"He's given us our own code names," she said.

"I already have mine," Jazz said.

"We gave ours to him," Lucia said. "He told us to pick something to do with music. I picked a song my parents always played in our house."

"I'm glad you picked a short and easy name," Jazz joked.

"Guantanamera," Lucia said.

Cheyenne read Malek's name, "Vessel," which surely referred to an obscure song he liked, and then she saw her father's: "The Fly."

"Nice one," she said.

"I'm keeping a theme here," Keith told her. "I gave him yours too."

"It's perfect."

"Okay, Blackbird, pay attention," Malek told her. "Let's get on the same page. *Literally,* since we're holding actual pieces of paper."

"Clever," Cheyenne said with sarcasm.

"I know, right?"

She had missed Malek's sarcastic humor and couldn't-care-less attitude.

They went down a list of assignments Reckoner had for each of them. As she studied the document, she realized what they were about to do.

"This is crazy," she said, stopping the conversation just as it started.

"What part?" Jazz teased.

"Um, all of it? Starting with the Incen Tower. We can't get into those offices."

"You're reading ahead," her father said.

She had a flashback to fifth grade, with an impatient Cheyenne trying to rush through her homework while her methodical father wanted her to take things slowly.

Cheyenne kept reading, skimming through everything. Finally she saw the big picture. She tossed the pages back onto the table. "There's no way we can do this. Even if we were to actually break into the PASK offices and acquire the links necessary, even if we could break through the security codes, this is impossible. There is no system for SYNAPSYSes to retrieve the data sent to them. Whether it's to one person or to ten million."

"How do you think we spoke to you, Chy?" Malek asked.

"That was you?" she asked in complete surprise.

"I helped with the conversation."

"I don't know exactly how you did it, but I know one thing: that it's—"

"Impossible," Jazz interrupted. "I know. I thought so too. But they've figured out a way."

"How?"

"Why do you think I was fired?" Malek asked.

"I always chalked it up to your sunny disposition," she said. "But you said it was because of your faith."

"Yeah, those things were in their list of complaints. But they also didn't like my experimentations. They didn't like how much I knew about the nature of the work we were doing with algorithms and that I knew they've been using them on SYNAPSYSes."

"You've known that for some time," Cheyenne told him. "What concern is it to them?"

"They don't want the public to know the level and influence of those algorithms they're using. And it was through that very level that I was able to drill into data, to figure out a way to get into the elaborate SYNAPSYS."

"Yeah, I'd like to know how you did that," Jazz chimed in.

Malek scratched his spiky hair. "To use a simple analogy, I didn't have to scale some massive, impenetrable wall. All I had to do was swim in through their underground water system, so to speak."

"The underground water system being the algorithms that are fed to the SYNAPSYS?" Cheyenne asked.

Malek nodded. She looked at her father, who seemed confused but remained silent.

"But still . . . how are we going to deliver a message to the entire country?" she asked.

"Approximately three hundred and eighty million people," Malek said. "The Reckoner's got it covered. At least that's the grand plan."

"A man most of you haven't ever met is going to help us do this?"

All eyes were on her, seeing her complete lack of confidence in this.

Malek continued to explain things to her. "It used to be that everybody in the world could see the same thing just by going on the internet to view it. Until the government finally put regulations on that."

"And what message are we delivering?" Cheyenne asked. "Videos of pop stars from the eighties?"

Jazz laughed, and Malek pointed at her as if to say "Nice one."

"Again, it's covered," Malek said. "This time the Reckoner is pulling back the curtain and giving names and details. Up to now everything he's done has been to get people's attention. They've been movie trailers. Now he's letting people see the final film. Except in this case it's going to be documents and audio files and video clips."

Before Malek and Cheyenne could continue their conversation, Jazz suddenly broke in. "No, no, no, no."

Like Cheyenne, he had looked ahead in the pages.

"Wait a minute . . . I'm the what?" he asked.

"The driver," Cheyenne read.

Jazz shook his head and laughed. "Come on."

"What?"

"So someone's gotta pull out that stereotype, huh? The brother's gotta be behind the wheel."

"Well, you've certainly been driving me all around," Cheyenne said.

"Yeah, but that's all? After all the work I've been doing, I'm a cabdriver? Why not get a public transportation Autoveh in Chicago?"

"Look ahead at the timeline of events," Lucia said matter-of-factly. "Page five."

All of them turned to the hour-by-hour breakdown of the plan. Malek was the first to understand why Jazz was the driver. "We need a segue," he said. "That's how the information's gonna be transmitted. How all that data is going to be basically dumped into the stream."

Now Jazz understood too. "Okay. That's a little better. Now I feel a tad bit more important."

"So explain a 'segue,'" Keith said.

"Someone needs to be the center point that connects Cheyenne and me to the rest of us," Malek said. "We can't do it without a mainline server. So Jazz will be driving that process. His car will *literally* be a driver. It will serve as a transfer point for the data. That's where those little black boxes are going to come in handy."

Everybody paused for a moment and looked at each other with surprise. Jazz now nodded and then began grooving in his chair to a beat only he could hear.

"That's more like it," he said.

Lucia's job, as far as Cheyenne could see, was getting them through security at the tower. Nowhere did it say what her father was going to do, nor did it tell them if they would actually be meeting the Reckoner.

"When is this all supposed to happen?" Cheyenne asked.

Malek smiled. "In five days."

EIGHTEEN

State of Disrepair

1.

The shocks on his SUV seemed to be missing as Will's vehicle rumbled down a road being repaved. The last time he had been in the village of Winnetka, fifteen miles north of Chicago, he was visiting his father's property to attend the memorial service for his mother.

Twenty years ago.

The timing for Will felt cruel and anything but coincidental. As far as he was concerned, 2038 was turning into one hell of a year. It would be twenty years ago next month in April that his mother passed away from a sudden heart attack. *Sudden* being the key word since Melissa Stewart Heyford had been only forty-six years old at the time and in great health—except for the stress of having to deal with her ex-husband, who divorced her when Will was only ten.

Light snowflakes appeared out of the dark night as he headed to the Heyford residence. He didn't call it a house, because there wasn't only one structure on this property anymore. The primary home of the trillionaire sat on the edge of Lake Michigan with an immaculate view that grew bigger and better with each neighbor's lot he acquired. In many ways Will was glad that it was nighttime so he wouldn't have to see the monstrosity of the Heyford residence, something that had been discussed in the news for the last ten years.

Jackson and Melissa Heyford moved to their mansion off Sheridan Road back in 2001, three years after starting his company. By then the money was already starting to roll in, and he could afford the fifteen-thousand-square-foot house with eight bedrooms and ten baths on one and a half acres of land. Will had been eight when they moved to the lakefront home, and even back then it felt as cold and empty as his father's heart. His mother had the same sort of sentiment, with their marriage already crumbling at the time of the move and officially over two years later. His father had been the one wanting the divorce, and since he had a mistress along with numerous other strikes against him, he ended up paying a lot of alimony. Enough that it threatened not only his new home but also his company, PASK.

As he drove down Sheridan Road well below the speed limit, Will remained silent and tried to contain his nerves and the hostility building deep inside. He knew the house he visited with his brothers on select weekends from ages ten to eighteen was no longer there. Now there were five houses spread out over five acres, all connected and all designed by Frank Lloyd Wright. And all stolen, as he liked to say to Amy. Each famous house had been brought in its entirety from its original location to the Heyford property. The houses were virtually plucked out of the dirt and transported miles, with two being hauled all the way from California. There had been two documentaries on Heyford's obsession with Frank Lloyd Wright and how Heyford had managed to get the houses and transplant them to the Winnetka property.

Money can buy everything except eternal life and joy in this one.

Will knew several of the houses had been virtually stolen. Like Fallingwater, which was built in Fayette County, Pennsylvania, over a waterfall. This famous Frank Lloyd Wright house was one the Western Pennsylvania Conservancy refused to sell, yet after a yearlong campaign and a courting of the state, Heyford convinced them to allow him to buy it. There were many rumors about what had really happened, but speculation of this sort could no longer be shared and commented about online. Now such things could only be discussed in person.

Two well-known properties in Los Angeles, the Ennis House and the Hollyhock House, had been purchased, with large pieces of the homes transported more than two thousand miles. There were two other houses Jackson Heyford had been trying to buy but still couldn't, not even with all the money and power in the world. There was the Frank Lloyd Wright home and studio where the architect had lived in Oak Park, and then there was Robie House. His father's desire for the latter was the only thing of all this that didn't make sense. Will still couldn't figure out why his father would want this lesser-known and smaller Wright house.

The gatehouse up ahead was bright with both streetlights and spotlights. A stone wall stood on each side of it. There was a roundabout in front of the gatehouse, allowing sightseers to peek at the only entrance to the famous businessman's home. Heyford owned four other properties in the world, including a castle-like chalet in Park City and his own island. But since Acatour was in Chicago, this was where he spent most of his time.

Two security guards stepped out of the gatehouse, the first holding out his hand to tell Will to stop. Not that he could have crashed through the wrought-iron gate that looked strong enough to stop a tank.

"William Stewart," the guard said, staring at the black metal tablet in his hands that read Will's SYNAPSYS.

"That's me."

The other security guard searched the car with a flashlight. He first looked underneath and around the tires, then opened all the doors and examined the interior of the vehicle.

"Sorry. It's pretty messy," Will said, trying to act as nonchalant as possible. "We have three girls."

The first security guard held up his tablet and then moved it over the length of the SUV, the reader acting as a metal detector to check for any weapons.

"What's with the bookcases?" the second guard asked when he saw the two wooden bookshelves stacked on each other and resting on the lowered back seat.

"I own a bookstore. Actually, *owned* a bookstore. Just went out of business. Those are leftover shelves I need to sell or get rid of."

The man with the tablet looked back at the screen, surely verifying the information on Will.

"Yeah," he said to his colleague. "Bookstore is listed here."

The security guards shut his doors and then opened the gate to "heaven on earth."

"You'll drive for a few minutes, and then you'll see a road on your right," the uniformed man told Will. "Take that, and you'll get to the next security unit."

As Will drove down the wooded lane on his father's property, he turned back toward the bookcases and whispered, "Everything okay?"

"Everything's wonderful," Hutchence's muffled voice said.

Hutchence was curled up in the second, carved-out bookcase beneath the top bookcase. They'd put blankets down to provide a little comfort.

So far, so good.

"Midnight, right?" Will said in a low voice as he turned down what could be considered the main driveway for Heyford's home.

"Yeah," Hutchence said. He was silent for a few seconds, then added, "And if I'm not here, just leave. Okay?"

"I got it."

2.

After being checked at another guardhouse with one man on security, Will drove down a long stone road leading to a wide circular driveway in front of one of the Frank Lloyd Wright houses. This one had a Mayan look to it and had a pool with a fountain in its middle. A man in a suit waited as Will stopped the car. He left the engine running and squinted to see if he recognized the stranger. He knew it wouldn't be his father standing on the side of the driveway. Jackson Heyford would want a far more dramatic meeting place.

"Good evening, sir," the elderly man said as he opened the car door. "If you follow that lighted sidewalk alongside the Hollyhock House, someone will be there to take you to Mr. Heyford."

Will was going to say something about the car, but the man answered before he could get a word out.

"I'll park your car, sir. We have a parking lot for guests."

"Do you think it'll be safe?" Will asked.

The wrinkles in the man's face bunched together in the glow of the front drive. "I promise," he said.

Will had done his job of getting Hutchence onto his father's property. Now he was on his own. Whether or not he could get inside one of these houses was a whole other matter.

Maybe he's not even going to break into a house. Perhaps he's doing something else.

Hutchence hadn't been specific, asking Will to trust him and to be okay with knowing less. As Will walked down a twisting stone path past one house and then alongside another, he shivered and let out a sigh, his breath visible in the glow of the well-lit walkway. The walkway began to weave up a gradually rising hill, then turned into stone steps ascending a greater incline. At the top he found another house nestled in trees and could hear the faint sound of a waterfall. A tall, bald figure dressed in shirt and pants that flapped in the wind emerged from the warmly lit brick terraces at the front of the house. At closer glance Will was surprised to see it was a woman, probably in her mid-twenties, with a completely shaved scalp walking barefoot on the multicolored stone.

"Cold night to be missing your shoes," he told her.

Her chocolate-colored skin blended into the night, but the whites of her wide eyes stood out.

She grinned and then said in a British accent, "The stones are heated. Please follow me inside."

Her flowing pants and shirt had a detailed pattern on them as if they were a formal uniform from an African country. With too many things all around him to take in and the absence of daylight, Will had stopped bothering to look around. He didn't want to be impressed or awe inspired at any point during this meeting, yet it was impossible to ignore all the opulence surrounding him.

The last time Will had come to this property, none of these houses had been here. This obsession had begun in the last decade. The woman guided him through two pergolas at the entrance and into a small room and then into a large, open room with brown stone and long windows on all sides. The lights in this room looked like slow-burning embers. The woman stopped after entering the grand room, and Will looked at the fireplace and saw a dark silhouette in front of the flames.

"Thank you, Alika," Jackson Heyford told the woman.

Will nodded as she left the two men together. As his father moved closer to him, Will could see a face that hadn't changed much during the last two decades. Technology and wealth could help slow down the aging process without the use of surgery that made one look freakish.

"Welcome to Fallingwater." Heyford's eyes, shielded behind clear glasses, resembled the hard stone floor beneath him.

There was no attempt to shake hands or hug. His father knew better than to try.

"Do you know why I love this house so much?" his father continued without waiting to hear Will's greeting. "Frank Lloyd Wright was in his sixties. Forgotten and supposedly a has-been. Nobody wanted his creations, not after the arrival of the Great Depression. Oh, but he still had more to show the world. And that he did."

Jackson spoke slowly and deliberately like a man who never worried about being interrupted.

"I bet you agonize that he isn't alive to design a house personally for you," Will said.

"I do. But at least I get to wake up and go to sleep in the best he ever offered this world. His desire was to marry his architecture with people and nature in a perfect way."

Will walked toward the windows, peering out into the darkness. The furniture was all black and white and modern, nothing from the original house.

"You had to construct this hill in order to put the house on it, didn't you?" Will said.

"Yes. And in the daytime you have a remarkable view of the lake from where we're standing. I would give you a tour, but it's late, and it takes so long."

"That's okay," Will said. "I've developed an aversion to anything related to Frank Lloyd Wright." He turned away from the windows and faced Jackson. His father was more fit and trim than Will and wore jeans paired with a tailored but casual button-up shirt.

"Can I get you anything to drink?" his father asked.

Everything inside Will wanted a drink, a very strong drink that would make him relax a little and perhaps stop the sweat from coursing down his back.

"No, thanks," he said instead.

"Have you seen James?" Heyford asked.

"No."

"I knew you were lying about your brother, and I've been trying to figure out the real reason you wanted to meet. There is the obvious one, of course, and I really want to rule it out, but I can't think of anything else."

"I heard you had a job opening for a groundskeeper."

His father laughed at the unexpected joke. "You have your mother's sense of humor."

There were many things about this reunion that Will refused to endure, and talking about his mother was one of those. "I'm just here to talk about me," Will said. "And, no, I'm not here to ask you for anything."

"You refused to take gifts from me when you were sixteen. I doubt you've changed since then."

His father called out for a scotch, and a minute later a square, floating gray device the size of a thick hardcover book appeared next to him, balancing the drink on top of it.

"I've seen that in the news. What's it called again?"

"A Circumvent," Jackson said as he took the short glass. "I like calling it a magic tray."

The hovering gizmo silently retreated out of the room.

"Only five of those have been made, right?" Will asked.

"Yes, but only four have survived. I had an issue with my first one."

"An issue?"

"Yes. It no longer could fly after I swatted it with a baseball bat." Heyford smiled that dynamic smile the world knew and loved.

If only they knew the searing madness behind it.

"Are you by yourself tonight, or is Miss Mississippi somewhere polishing her crown?"

Jackson ignored his open contempt. "Tiffany is in Park City. My wife's younger and loves to play in the snow."

"Thirty-three years isn't merely younger. It's creepy."

"She would like to meet you."

Will grunted as he walked to the base of the fireplace and stared down at it. He needed to prolong his time here so Hutchence had plenty of his own. "So far all I've seen on your property is a bunch of houses a century old and a flying food tray," Will said, hoping he'd take the bait. It wasn't just anybody saying these words. No matter who Jackson Heyford was, this was his second-born child uttering the mocking statement.

"I didn't want to show off," Jackson said. "Mol, create a party."

All the lights shut off except for the flickering fireplace, swallowing everything in darkness until strobe lights began to pulse over the walls, ceilings, and floor. "Stayin' Alive" burst through the air and sounded as if the band were singing all around Will. He felt the deep bass and beat as each radiating blip seemed to dance in perfect timing.

"Congratulations!" Will's shout made his father stop the circus. "Seriously. Good job."

Jackson Heyford appeared to be waiting to see what Will would say next.

"Buying the Bee Gees catalog wasn't enough, was it? You had to turn a Frank Lloyd Wright house into a disco? Brilliant, Pops. Totally brilliant."

Jackson's curse wasn't subtle or even slightly amused. As the normal lights returned, Will could see the indignation on his father's face.

"Sometimes I wonder which of you boys is worse. The estranged son, the missing one, or the degenerate who's going to get my inheritance."

"Parenting's hard work," Will said. "I guess that's why you never bothered to try."

Will looked out the window and noticed another illuminated structure the size of a shack perched on what appeared to be a pyramid of pine beams.

"What is that?" he couldn't help asking Heyford.

"Ah yes. The cottage. A lot more impressive than the Bee Gees."

Will thought of Hutchence. "As much as I hate to say this, I'm curious what that one looks like."

"It's my newest piece." Heyford's eyes seemed to glow behind the spectacles. "How about I show it off before you say or do what you need to say or do and ruin this reunion."

3.

The Seth Peterson Cottage had been built near Mirror Lake in Wisconsin, Will's father told him as they moved up the pine stairs to the tiny house. Frank Lloyd Wright was ninety years old and broke, so when a passionate young fan, Seth Peterson, sent him a thousand-dollar retainer, he immediately spent the money and was forced to accept the commission. The eight-hundred-eighty-square-foot cottage contained a single bedroom and a sloping roof. When Will finally reached the top of several stories' worth of steps, he stood on the wide deck catching his breath while his father continued to share the story about this cottage.

"There's a haunting saga about this house," Jackson Heyford said. "During the building Frank Lloyd Wright passed away in 1959 at age 91. The young man building the house was struggling with money himself, and a year after Wright passed away, Seth Peterson committed suicide."

Wiping the sweat off his forehead while feeling the frigid air against his neck and cheeks, Will looked at the sandstone walls and then back at his father.

"The house was finished but sat abandoned, and after the Department of Natural Resources in Wisconsin took over ownership, they boarded it up and left it to ruin," his father said. "Nearly twenty-three years later a woman canoeing on the lake below saw the cottage, and soon the cabin was saved by local volunteers and underwent major renovations."

"And years later tech god and world philanthropist Jackson Heyford gobbles up the renovated cottage and sticks it on a set of wood blocks in the middle of his Frank Lloyd Wright museum."

"That's right, William."

"Please don't call me that. I haven't been called that for twenty years."

"We've spoken since your mother's death," Jackson said.

"I've tried to forget those instances."

Will looked across at the panorama of his father's estate, noticing all the Wright houses arranged in a creative way and connected to each other. He hadn't heard any alarms or gunshots or explosions, so he figured Hutchence hadn't been caught.

"Inside the cottage you will find my latest invention," Jackson told him as he opened the front door. "Please. Take a peek inside."

For the first time since arriving, Will felt scared. His body tensed, sensing danger beyond that doorway.

"Don't worry. There are no boogeymen in there."

His father had the gall to mock those constant nightmares he'd had as a child. Will smiled and walked into the cottage without another doubt.

4.

He waited for the lights to come on in this large room, but instead, all he found was darkness. The door behind him closed, yet he could see his father standing outside. Soon the glow of the night through the windows disappeared, as if all the glass had turned to black. Feeling a bit disoriented, Will reached out to find the handle to the door, but then he saw a face out of nowhere in the murkiness.

It was Bella looking up at him, angry and hurt. "You're mean, and you don't care about us. You told us that." She was there in front of him, lifelike, real. Younger than she was now, but as vivid as she would be in her own bedroom.

Without mouthing a word Will could hear his yell. "Don't you lie to try to convince Mommy! I never told you I don't care about you!"

As Bella disappeared, at his side appeared Callie. He could feel her tugging at him, pulling him, repeating "Daddy, Daddy" over and over again. She mostly did that in public when she was anxious and uncertain but also sometimes when she was bored and a few times when she simply wanted to be irritating. Then, once again, he could hear his voice, mean and threatening and terrible, yelling at her.

"Would you stop it and leave Daddy alone!"

When she slipped back into the dark, Will imagined what might be next. *What exactly is happening here? Did I lose consciousness?*

It felt colder inside this cottage than it did outside. Another voice came booming from all sides around him.

"Why are you being so mean? I didn't do anything!"

This time it was Shaye screaming at him. He watched her looking so distraught and confused and then saw her disappear and slam a door somewhere in this underground corridor of his imagination.

"You come back here right now! We're not done!"

He wasn't imagining a made-up scene. These exchanges had happened in the past and were reminders of why Will was never going to write a parenting book. He shook his head as if the thoughts were water that had collected in his ears.

Then Amy appeared across from him, a vision that stunned him because for a second he almost believed she was there. Yet she didn't look like herself. She looked empty and hostile at the same time.

"I wish I'd never married you," Amy told him.

This time Will didn't hear a response, but that's because he had never responded. The conversation had ended like that, with a lukewarm apology from Amy coming later. Not apologizing for the words but for her overall anger.

I'm just dreaming or remembering this. That's all. The really, really bad parts of the family journey.

These weren't just parts, however. They weren't simple dents in the car. They were the accidents on the road, the ones that had sent the vehicle into the shop for repairs.

Some things were never repaired.

He wanted to get out of here. Not only this cottage but this property and this space belonging to his father. As lights burst apart the darkness around him, Will found himself in an empty room with sandstone walls, wood floors, and a fireplace for a centerpiece. Without hesitating he rushed to the door and stepped back outside.

"What just happened in there?" Will asked, once again out of breath.

"Did you stroll down memory lane?" his father asked, his tone sounding more and more fiendish.

"Where'd that come from? What was that?"

Heyford walked closer to Will, stroking his chin as if he were a creative maestro. "There are many, many things a SYNAPSYS is capable of doing, things that people have no idea about," Heyford said. "It used to be that people were scared about Facebook keeping their data on the recipes and cat pictures they liked. They have no idea. In wanting life to be easier and faster and better all around, people have allowed themselves to be monitored. And even worse, manipulated."

"You have that information on file somewhere?" Will asked. "Are you serious? You just pulled up those little things?"

"I didn't have to pull up anything. My LC simply asked yours for a few memorable scenes."

"You're stockpiling people's *lives*? For what? Why?"

"I'm not collecting anything or monitoring anybody. It's your LC, your wonderfully creative Tolkien matched with your SYNAPSYS. Dangerous tools. When you know how to control and work them, they can be quite deadly."

Will knew it had to be close to midnight now. He had to get out of this place. But first he wanted his father to answer one question. "Tell me something. Did you in any way have something to do with my bookstore closing? Even some indirect way?"

Heyford laughed, a sound that made Will nauseous.

"There was nothing indirect about it. I specifically got involved. I made those calls and visits to the people in your town personally. I'm the sole—the only reason—your business shut down."

Will let out a long, seething sigh. "You have everything in the world. Does it anger you *that* much that I don't want to be in your world? Or are you just getting back at me?"

"I have no great sense of loss at what's become of you. Or James. With him I simply want to know what happened and where he disappeared to. But what angers me—what truly incenses me—is what you claim to believe in. Your God and your Jesus. This world has long forgotten them. There's no room and no place for Christ anymore."

"You're wrong."

"Am I?" his father asked. "So tell me, William or Will. Tell me, great man of faith. What kind of father acts that way toward his children? What kind of husband makes his wife detest him? Is that what a Christian union looks like?"

Will wanted to curse his father or, better yet, to reach out and clutch his neck and begin to squeeze and never stop. He stood still, however, and felt his body shudder from both fear and anger as snow began to fall on them.

His father walked closer to him, staring at him and emphasizing his words. "Soon there won't be any strong believers out there leading their flocks. There will only be followers like you, too weak and wounded to do anything. With a faith as fleeting as one of these flakes."

5.

Back in his car, waiting for it to warm up, Will sat and watched and listened. Wanting any sight of Hutchence. Any sign. Anything. But fifteen minutes after midnight Will drove back down the long driveway and began his trek off this property. Somewhere back there in the darkness was Hutchence. Will didn't know if he was safe or if he had accomplished his mission or even if he was alive.

NINETEEN

Emorithms

1.

Cheyenne could see four armed soldiers standing in the entrance hall to the Incen Tower, and that was just from where she stood. The wide and open lobby welcomed guests with its legendary 240-foot glass atrium that spiraled more than seventy-two stories above them, one of its many record-setting feats of architecture. In a wash of piercing sunlight on the Monday midmorning, the sprawling space crawled with all kinds of people, from businesspeople to tourists. She had never spent much time in the atrium simply because she always stayed in the sky, working and living and breathing away from all the curious. Away from all the commoners, as many residing in the building felt deep down, even if they never said it out loud.

The security guards in their official Incen Tower uniforms with handguns at their sides were visible, as were the stationary police monitors and the cameras set in various areas in this hallway. But seeing the military armed with assault rifles made her heart beat faster. Malek noticed it too.

"Appears people are trying to protect their important interests," he told her as they wove through the crowd to get to their designated meeting space.

As he led the way, Cheyenne wondered if she'd ever seen Malek in a suit before. They'd made a stop at a high-end outlet mall that morning, paying cash for brand-name clothes. For a few moments Cheyenne felt like someone out of a romantic movie, commenting on the clothes Malek picked out and then hearing him review hers. She liked the classic blue pin-striped suit with the blue-and-yellow tie, so he went with that. Seeing him wearing shiny dress shoes instead of the same faded Keds he liked to wear, Cheyenne had to admit that he looked handsome.

Like a typical guy, he had told her to buy a skirt and also suggested she go with the high heels even though that meant she towered over him. It felt nice for a moment in her imaginary world to pretend they were going out for a night on the town, heading up to a restaurant in Incen Tower all dressed up—until she almost fell over while trying on the four-inch heels. She told Malek she didn't want to be hobbling around, especially if they needed to leave quickly. She looked classy enough to have her outfit pass for business attire, with her skirt ending above her knees and modest pumps.

In addition to their dressy attire, Malek wore glasses, and Cheyenne had her hair in a new style with it tied to one side, making them look different enough for the cameras monitoring everything not to instantly pick up on them if people were, in fact, looking for them. When they reached the set of welcome kiosks for those visiting the tower, they looked for Lucia until she approached them out of the crowd.

"Looking very fashionable today," Lucia said as she handed each a gold card the size and shape of an eye. "Ready for your meeting today?"

Malek looked at the item in his hand. "I've always wanted one of these."

The gold card was security clearance for important guests who didn't want to be bothered with background checks and who wanted their visit and stay at Incen Tower to be discreet. It would be not only discreet but also unknown, since this card didn't connect with a SYNAPSYS.

"These will get you to the 118th floor atrium," Lucia said. "Look for the man who gave you your father's note."

"You're not coming up with us?" Cheyenne asked.

Lucia shook her head. "I have to act as if this is any ordinary Monday. Did you hear from the Reckoner yet?"

"No," Malek said. "But the plan only changes if we hear from him to stop everything."

"What if you don't hear from him at all?"

Malek shook his head. "We will."

Without a "Good luck" or "Farewell," the woman walked off and disappeared into the crowd. Malek and Cheyenne looked at each other for a second.

"Really charming woman," Malek joked.

"Think she's maybe a tad bit—oh, I don't know—freaked out?" Cheyenne asked, whispering the last two words.

"What's the worst that can happen?"

She thought of the Parschauers and wished Malek hadn't asked that question.

"Come on," she said, leading the way this time.

2.

The awesome grandeur of the Incen Tower once felt like the place of her dreams. Now it represented the enemy hovering over her. An epic, evil darkness right out of *The Lord of the Rings*. The first elevator took them up to the familiar 118th floor, where all the businessmen and businesswomen spilled out into the flooded space. For a moment Cheyenne thought about getting a coffee from Henry for old times' sake. Then she realized he wouldn't recognize her without her SYNAPSYS. Plus, if he did, that would even be worse.

My old life here is dead.

She wished she could talk to Dina one more time, not to tell her everything but to tell her enough. To simply say an official goodbye. Life doesn't often allow proper goodbyes or the chance to say the things you want to say to those you love the most.

As she was walking down one of the walkways, a businessman stepped in front of her much as he had done almost a month and a half ago.

"Good afternoon," Hoon said, smiling.

"Hello," Cheyenne responded, relieved to see a slightly familiar face.

They walked out of the flow of human traffic as Malek shook Hoon's hand.

"I trust all is going well," Hoon said.

"Thank you," Cheyenne told him.

"For what?"

"For my father's note. For letting me— For helping me find him."

Hoon grinned. "I believe *he* found you."

"You're right."

He reached into his suit and pulled out two more cards, similar in size to the gold oval. Except these were clear.

"These are for you," Hoon said as he handed them over.

"I thought you didn't have clearance for things like this," Cheyenne said.

"I don't. But there are always powerful people behind the scenes trying to maintain some control," Hoon said.

She wanted to know where he got these, but she didn't even know exactly who this man was. Did he work in the tower? Probably. And surely he lived here too. But how was he involved with the Reckoner and Jazz and especially her father? Perhaps—hopefully—she would find that out after this was over.

If this, in fact, will be over.

"Good luck," Hoon said.

"Thank you," she told him again.

3.

First they rode an escalator. Then they headed down a long hallway to another small atrium that housed an elevator made of glass. This wasn't a top-secret, VIP-only elevator like some of the others Cheyenne knew about in this building. Guests still could ride this, allowing them to go to one of the two exclusive restaurants near the top of the building or to visit the even more exclusive nightclub/lounge. It felt strange to ride this in order to go to a data room, but this building contained numerous mysteries and secrets.

There weren't suspicious security guards scanning their cards or bored workers at desks checking their data while they walked by. Having a card on you allowed you to pass freely and opened the doors to the elevator if you had sufficient access. Something somewhere, most certainly a machine, watched. But just like algorithms, artificial intelligence couldn't always detect what was right there in clear sight.

Cheyenne held her breath as she stepped onto the glass. The elevator was entirely transparent—the bottom, the sides, and the top. She didn't look down the 124 stories below her or out to the sprawling Lake Michigan they faced.

Malek swore. "Excuse my language, but . . . wow."

The doors shut, and they began to shoot upward in a steady, gentle manner. Not as if they were soaring, but as if they were calmly floating over the hundred stories below them.

"You look pale as a ghost," Malek said. "You don't like heights, huh?"

Cheyenne felt her body shake as she couldn't help staring straight ahead in the elevator. Malek stood at her side facing the other way, looking up and around in wonder.

"I don't like glass elevators."

"You know this is safer than riding in a regular one, right?" he asked.

"Sure. I took the tour and heard about it."

She wanted to close her eyes but also didn't want to seem so frightened. She looked at him and couldn't help letting out a slight chuckle. "You look like it's your birthday."

"I hope not. I never got presents."

"I'll admit I always wondered what it'd be like to ride one of these. Now I know. The grass isn't greener."

Even with her arms folded and her body tightened, her shaking was noticeable. Cheyenne could see Malek looking at her. He moved next to her, facing the doors himself, and put a solid arm around her.

"It's okay," he said.

"You're missing the view," Cheyenne said, looking into eyes that seemed to reflect the clear sky above them.

"No, I'm not."

4.

Other than the security guard looking bored outside the elevator doors, they hadn't seen anybody. Malek led the way through one long hallway along the wall of glass and then through a doorway leading into offices and away from the fancy restaurant and club.

"How do you know where you're going?" Cheyenne asked him.

"I know the plans to this building well. I got them off Acatour's network the first week I was here."

"Why isn't there more security up here?"

"There's nothing of value in these offices. This floor is for those splurging on dinners and drinks. Ninety-nine percent of the people who could get up here wouldn't be able to do a thing with the servers they have."

"And why were you looking up the plans to this building?" she asked.

"You know me. Curiosity."

A third door slid open as they approached and closed once they went through it. Malek looked at his palm where he'd written something down. Then he began to count the number of offices they passed.

"Seven. Okay. This should be it."

Malek opened the door, apparently not surprised that it was unlocked. In some ways this particular room reminded her of the PASK offices. Bare walls, average size, big enough for a desk and chair. She felt a chill in this space, as if the temperature had dropped ten degrees. On three of the four walls were black shelving units that went all the way to the ceiling. The dim fluorescent light above them made the room feel unusually bleak.

"All the data boxes are in these," Malek said, pulling one of the six-foot-wide drawers out to show racks of thin white metal boxes about the size of a compact disc. "People don't realize Jackson Heyford made most of his money on these microservers. He spent so much on technology when the SYNAPSYS was invented, and most of that money came from these."

Cheyenne knew what microservers were, but she had never seen so many of them. Several hundred were in this drawer alone.

"Acatour—well, before the big merge, when Apple existed—used to have massive data center servers all over the world. These massive warehouses were full of walls and walls of servers. This drawer contains the data that an entire Apple facility contained."

As always when talking about his favorite subject, Malek lit up with energy and excitement. Nobody would have ever guessed they were breaking the law in multiple ways, including getting ready to break into people's minds.

If that's what we're, in fact, doing.

They were trespassing, and that was enough. Especially for two people fired by the company they were hacking.

Malek sat down at the square table in the middle of the room and turned on the computer linked to the desk. Cheyenne sat next to him as a series of screens became visible in front of them. He worked for a few minutes to get into the main system they used in PASK and then began filling in password after password. All of this looked very familiar to Cheyenne.

"It looks like you're going into my emorithms files," she said, using her coined word only Malek had heard.

He looked at her and nodded. "I am."

She laughed. "That's great. Hacking my work."

"Remember when we used to argue about the algorithms we were creating, about their uses in people's SYNAPSYSes?"

"I've changed my mind on the work we were doing. Or at least who we were doing it for."

"Yeah. But the truth is worse than you might imagine. You believed we were building technology to improve the world. But those controlling the technology don't care about the world or its population. They're corrupting people's souls, not through a virus or spam but with subtle and secret messages."

"But how? I don't get it."

As pages began to load on the projected monitors in front of them, he turned in the swivel chair to face Cheyenne. "Remember my role at PASK? I was the one working on delivery systems for algorithms. You were tapping into their emotional capabilities. Both of these made us temporary rock stars when it came to cracking the almighty code of the SYNAPSYS. They don't realize I was keeping some of my work from them."

"You mean tapping into SYNAPSYSes?"

Malek nodded, looking like a teenager who had just sneaked out of his parents' house at midnight. He seemed to have a rebellious sort of glee about him.

"What exactly happened to you?" Cheyenne asked. "How'd you suddenly go from PASK genius to . . . this?"

"Good question. I guess I can blame it all on you."

"On me?" she asked. "Why?"

"Remember our last date?"

"That wasn't a date."

"Exactly. The time we went out on what I thought was a date and you didn't. My wake-up call."

"Malek, look, I wasn't sure—"

"It's fine. It happened. Just let me continue. After that one of my friends mentioned a girl to me, and then the next thing I knew, she called me. She was—nice, I guess. But once my SYNAPSYS connected with hers, it seemed like— I don't know. It was scary, Chy."

"Why?"

"It began to feel like fate was telling me I needed to be with this woman," Malek said. "Out of the blue a photo of her would pop up on my network connection. She was . . . quite attractive, and suddenly like the best photo ever taken of her would be right there to remind me. And she didn't send it. I didn't ask for it. It was little things like this all day long. Connecting when I didn't plan to connect. My SYNAPSYS would remind me and prompt me and encourage me, as if it was playing matchmaker or something."

Cheyenne began to see where this was headed.

"But none of that bothered me. We're used to that sort of stuff, right? I know the history of advertising. The background music that used to play in stores. The commercials that used to be on televisions. Pop-up ads on the internet. The feed people would see on their Facebook pages before the uproar over social media exploded. I get all that. But it was something else, something that really freaked me out."

Cheyenne looked at him carefully, holding her breath, waiting for him to say it.

"I started to— You're going to laugh at this, but this is what I felt at the time. I started to think I was falling in love with this woman."

"I thought you were incapable of such an emotion," Cheyenne joked.

"Me too. And I'm being serious. It was . . . these feelings inside me, not based on physical things. These were emotional. And I realized they were—"

"Algorithms," she answered. "They were coming from algorithms."

Malek nodded. "What are algorithms used for?"

"To influence people."

"I'd argue and use the word *control*," he said. "So who are the people behind them? The people influencing or controlling. What's their message? *That* is what I started to try to wrap my brain around."

The data on the screen in front of them went off for a second. Then it lit back up and resumed. Malek continued talking without seeming worried.

"I went a week without using my SYNAPSYS. Remember that? A few months before I got fired?"

"You told me you were doing a digital detox or something like that," Cheyenne said.

"I needed to know. And I was right. By day two I had no overwhelming feelings for this woman. It's not as if I didn't like her. She was nice and totally hot and a perfect match, but I just wasn't into her. You know. And that's when I felt a bit like the girl from the movie *The Exorcist*. Except this sort of demon . . . Chy, this demon was created by *us*. By people like you and me."

None of this completely surprised her, yet she had no way to respond to his statement. She'd always known the work they were doing wasn't perfect, but she hadn't believed it could be as harmful or as dire as he was putting it. Now she didn't know.

Something else suddenly dawned on her. "Do you think . . . Could the same thing have been happening with me?"

"What do you mean?" Malek asked.

"That maybe my algorithms were telling me *not* to be with you?"

A look of genuine surprise filled his face. His eyes searched hers, and then he nodded. "The last thing PASK would have wanted was for us to be a couple," Malek told her. "I wouldn't be surprised if somehow they were manipulating us. See what I'm talking about? There are so many public violations here. People's privacy being shredded big-time. And this is exactly why we're here. What we're going to tell people. Personally."

A progress bar on the screen was nearly full.

"How are you able to do it?" she asked. "Every test has said that SYNAP-SYSes can't be broken into."

"What nobody realizes is that *every* SYNAPSYS has receptors for these emotional algorithms, the ones you've been working on, the systems I've been manipulating and trying to get into. The public doesn't know about your emorithms, do they? They've been specifically designed for them to be received. That's how you can directly communicate to people."

"Our message isn't going to be subtle, right?" Cheyenne asked.

"No. That's the beauty. People are going to wonder how in the world they're getting this personal message delivered to their SYNAPSYS. Both spoken and written out. And even if they don't think another second about the Reckoner's message, they'll be trying to figure out how someone didn't just invade their privacy but pried into their very *soul*."

The screen went black for a second. Then a blinking orange word popped up.

READY

"Are you ready?" he asked.

"Ready to do what?"

"I can only get so far inside all these files. You're the one who knows what to do with everything."

"What do you mean? I have no idea what I'm supposed to do."

"Instead of putting in a complex algorithm for an emotion, you're going to substitute our message."

Cheyenne looked at him and shook her head. "I can't."

"Why not?"

"I still don't think . . ." She couldn't finish the sentence.

"What? You think everything the Reckoner has been saying is a lie?"

"I know what Acatour is doing is wrong. But God's judgment and people's salvation and all of that? I'm not there yet."

"Then consider this to be a great prank we're playing," Malek said with a smile.

Cheyenne tapped the desk for a keyboard and typed for a few seconds. She pointed to the file on the screen.

"Is it this?"

"Yep."

"Okay," she said.

"Okay what?"

"I sent it."

Malek looked at her with wide eyes and his mouth slightly open. "Are you serious? That quickly? What'd you do?"

She gave a knowing, calm, it's-my-secret-not-yours grin. They waited for a minute, then two. Then a bubble popped up.

Jazz received. Good to go.

Both of them remained silent, looking at the screens in front of them to see if anything was going to show a problem and sound an alarm. But nothing abnormal happened.

"So we just, like, sent out a message heading to three hundred and eighty million people," Malek said.

Cheyenne looked at him and nodded. Something about this was exhilarating.

"We should probably get out of here, right?" he asked.

Another calm nod.

Malek jumped up and then pulled her up off her chair. "Come on."

As they hurried down the narrow white hallway, Jazz's voice spoke to both of them. "We have a problem."

The only time they were to verbally talk was in an emergency.

"Tell me you got it, man," Malek said as he stopped.

"Yeah, I got it. I'm processing it to send to Reckoner. But I can't get in touch with Lucia."

"Why not? Didn't she leave the building?"

"Yeah. But I don't know *where* she is," Jazz said. "That's the problem."

"We'll find her," Cheyenne said.

"We can't go try—," Malek started to say.

"We'll find her."

5.

Only moments later Cheyenne was running as she followed Malek. Her confidence and calmness were gone. Any plans had been thrown out the window. Or, actually, they'd been confined to this floor, and it looked impossible to get off this floor and out of the building.

Jazz had alerted them about all the alarms going off and all the chatter in the Incen Tower communications system. They knew their security had been breached, a natural result of Malek and Cheyenne's getting into the company's network and then sending out the data to a secondary source. Not only did security know they'd been hacked, but they knew who did it. Now exiting the building the old-fashioned way was impossible. So was trying to find Lucia.

They had known this was a possibility, so Malek led the way to the first option for getting off this floor. He took a couple of wrong turns, but he generally knew where he was going—back to where they were and past the offices to reach a utility area with concrete floors and drab walls.

"The garbage chute is right this way," Malek said.

Immediately Cheyenne stopped and shouted at him to do the same. "The *what?*"

"Don't worry. The one on this side of the floor isn't used."

"We can't just slide down a garbage chute."

"It's large enough to—"

"Are you five years old?" she said, looking back to see if anybody was approaching.

"It's not like a waterslide," Malek said. "They're big units the size of a dumpster that move from floor to floor."

"I shouldn't have left the escape plans to you," Cheyenne said, starting to think about other options.

"I know you just don't want to get your fancy new clothes dirty," he said.

"And I know you just want to live out your childhood fantasy of being in *Star Wars*. But we can't just jump into the garbage disposal. This one really does crush everything before it moves from floor to floor."

"How do you know that?"

"Somebody committed suicide that way."

Malek looked at her, confused and disgusted. "Are you serious? When?"

"It was after you left. That's why you never heard about it. She wasn't merely crushed. More like pulverized. We're talking bones."

"Okay," Malek said, looking around, searching everywhere, including the ceiling.

"Why are you looking up there?" Cheyenne asked, marveling at how daft he could sometimes be.

"This is me panicking."

"Where is robot maintenance?"

Malek looked puzzled but pulled out the folded piece of paper from his pocket and examined it. "There are two of them. One is near the restaurant—back by the glass elevators. We don't want to go there. And one is . . . Let's see. I think it's down there. That corner door."

When she took off toward it, Malek followed, asking how the robot maintenance room would help them out. The doors weren't locked, maybe because this part of the floor was empty rooms that one day might be finished and made into a restaurant or very high-end condo. The robot maintenance room looked like someone's workshop or garage, with a variety of tools hanging on the walls and several tables with sophisticated tools attached to them.

"These were built when the tower was constructed," Cheyenne said, scanning the walls. "This one's never been used."

"Are you looking for a weapon?" Malek asked.

She stopped in front of the two black panels at the center of the back wall. A silver slit could be seen in the middle of them. As Malek walked up beside her, she examined all around the panels.

"You looking for this?" he asked, pointing at the black buttons that blended into the panels.

"Yes, I think so."

She pressed one, and it didn't do anything. But the second opened the doors.

As Malek looked in, he began to laugh. "Are you serious?"

Between the doors and the cement behind them was a clear tube, and at the bottom of it sat a silver cylinder, slightly more than two feet tall and wide.

"Yeah. But you have to go first."

"What is that?" Malek asked, bending down and peeking in.

"It's like a pneumatic tube, the kind that once was used by banks. But these are advanced and large enough to transport repair machines in the building. It's meant to carry only robots or other pieces. Obviously that's why it's this size."

"We can't fit in that."

"Sure we can."

Malek laughed as he crawled into the container and already filled up most of its space. "For once, being scrawny is going to be an asset," he said. "But you'll still have to push me in."

He found the touch screen where a floor number could be entered. "How'd you find out about these?" he asked her.

"Henry. My barista friend at the fourth counter in the 118th atrium."

"I knew it. You've been holding out on me."

"What do you mean?"

"I knew you had a secret boyfriend somewhere," he said.

"How about I help you in?" she said, placing her heel on his back and gently pushing.

It took him a few minutes to fit inside, curling up in a ball with his arms wrapped around his legs and his head tucked inside them.

"If Jazz isn't in the lower-level parking garage, we're going to be in a lot of trouble," he said.

"If another one of these cylinders doesn't show up, I'll be in even more trouble."

Before he could say anything more, she pressed 005 and backed up just as the doors to this unit closed. She could hear the suction of air as the container shot down two hundred stories.

6.

As soon as she pressed the same numbers for herself, she moved her arms and shoulders into a position like Malek had assumed in the cylinder. Only then did Cheyenne see her new black pumps sitting where she'd taken them off outside this repair transport elevator. She doubted she was going to need them anytime soon. The skirt she was wearing had already ripped as she squeezed inside the shaft, so she might have to retire this outfit after only one use.

The cylinder began to drop, and Cheyenne felt herself plummeting to the ground, knowing something was wrong, knowing that this wasn't working and that she was going to be flattened whenever and wherever she landed.

What was I thinking doing something this careless and stupid?

She felt the pressure of the speed, making her nauseous and dizzy. The cylinder shuddered and jangled, another indication it was broken. She could only close her eyes and wince and wait.

There was violent jerking as the cylinder began to slow. Soon after, all movement stopped, and the doors swished open.

"You okay?"

Hearing Jazz's voice made her feel a little better. She nodded as she grabbed his hand and let him pull her out.

"Where's Malek?" she asked.

Jazz nodded to a row of Autovehs in the parking lot full of Autovehs.

"I don't think he liked the ride," Jazz said. "He got a little sick."

Cheyenne had to fight throwing up herself. Jazz told her to take it easy, but she answered by telling him they needed to leave.

"Where's the Hummer?" she asked.

"It's up above on Michigan Avenue. It's all done. I sent out the data."

"Did you get any confirmation?"

Jazz nodded. "Reckoner confirmed they received it. I suspect there are about twenty cops surrounding the Hummer and searching inside it. We'll be taking one of these out of here."

When Malek finally appeared from between two vehicles, his eyes were watery, and he looked pale. But when he saw her, he still let out a loud laugh. "That was insane," he said. "I felt like I was going to die."

"Me too."

"Come on," Jazz urged them. "Let's get out of here."

TWENTY

Paint It Black

1.

No, no, no, no . . .

"Where are you?" Dowland stood on a Chicago sidewalk, leaning on a building, one arm against it, and staring at the sidewalk after getting the call on his SYNAPSYS from Margaux.

"It doesn't matter," she said. "You need to get over to the tower."

She had contacted him to say a woman named Lucia was dead. Margaux didn't need to specify that she had made it happen. Lucia was connected with the Reckoner and had been coming from the Incen Tower, where he needed to go now.

"They might still be there. They hacked into Acatour."

"Heading there now," Dowland said, walking swiftly. "Who's there?"

"The pair from Tulsa," Margaux said.

He started to jog. He hated talking on this stupid piece of technology in his head because he knew it allowed others to listen in. Dowland didn't understand anything about the technology, but he understood what they were doing with these things. It used to be people wanted to know where you lived and what you said online, but now people wanted to get inside your soul.

"Are you sure they're still in the building?" Dowland asked, racing down another sidewalk.

"Yes. How far away—"

"Ten—five minutes," he said as he gasped for air.

"You sound out of breath," she said.

He cursed at her. "Not helpful."

Dowland plowed into an older man walking down the sidewalk, but he kept going. So what if the geezer fell over?

"Anybody else with them?" he asked, his side aching.

"I hate running with a hangover," she said.

He launched another insult and told her to be quiet.

"Just speaking the truth," she said.

He took a breath and said, "Call off." Then Margaux was gone. *Thank God.*

Running and looking up, Dowland could see the spiraling, towering Incen building directly in front of him, looking like a spike aimed at the heaven above it. He slowed down and began to walk, taking deep breaths to overcome the dizziness. Then he stopped.

Last night was way out of hand. I overdid it even by my standards.

Dowland leaned over and vomited up everything inside his stomach, almost all liquid, but it didn't make him feel any better.

He cursed again as he felt his sides tighten like a knot. He wobbled. Then steadying himself, he regained his balance. He shook his head, fighting off the nuisance of the hangover as he began to walk again. Just like he always did.

This is what I do, what I always do, and I'm doing it.

"Call Margaux," he said.

He needed to find out if they were still in the building.

"What are you doing?" the voice yelled at him.

"I just needed to catch my breath," he said as Margaux yelled at him, and he looked up and saw a blurry, whirling shape holding something in its hand and flying toward him.

"You need to shut off your—"

2.

He looks up and sees only the sky. Dowland feels numb, as if he's been struck by an Autoveh and has passed out for a second. He feels his backside on the cement, and as his eyes focus, he sees a tall figure standing over him. The man has to be taller than six and a half feet, but he's not broad and muscular. At least he doesn't appear so under the suit and tie he's wearing.

Dowland tries to get up but then collapses, feeling dizzy. He tastes blood and touches the side of his mouth. Half of his face is wet and warm. He then feels a deep, throbbing gash above his right eye.

Again he moves his arms and tries to get away from the stranger by crawling on his elbows. He spots something in the tall man's hand—the grip of a handgun, probably what was used to bash his head. Still lying on his back and elbows, he starts to reach into his coat to grab his Beretta.

"Don't," the tall man says as he repositions his gun and points it at him.

The barrel is short and wide and stares him in the face. Dowland takes his hand back out and shows that he's unarmed.

Is this *Reckoner?*

"Look, hold off for a second until—"

A shot cracks through the air, then two more right after it. Dowland shuts his eyes and grimaces and expects to feel the blows. Yet he feels only the pain from the side of his temple. He's been shot before, so he knows he's not been hit now.

The next sound comes from the crumpling body in front of him—a sickening thud as the bones and the head land on the concrete. Dowland sits up now and looks all around him.

Margaux appears out of nowhere just like the stranger who hit him. "Come on. Get up." She grabs his arm and helps him to his feet.

Once again she looks like a runner in an advertisement for the hottest new leggings on the market. Somewhere inside her running jacket is the gun that took down the tall guy.

"You look worse than the dead guy," she says to him. "We have to clean up your face."

Dowland looks down at the man on the sidewalk. "Who is this?"

"I don't know. Come on."

With her hand still on his arm, helping him remain balanced, Dowland keeps pace with her as they rush down the block.

"You seriously don't know who that was?"

"No," she says. "We'll find out."

"Then how did you know to find me?"

"There are eyes watching you."

Dowland stops and looks at her. "What's that mean?"

"I don't want you taking off and leaving me with this mess you've made. That guy had been following you for about ten minutes."

"And you didn't want to tell me?" Dowland shouts, then spits out the blood in his mouth.

"Come on. Let's go before someone who thinks he has more authority than we do decides to show up."

3.

For a long time Dowland stood near the glass, looking out to the spiderweb of life below him. The working day in Chicago was coming to an end for many. For men like him the work never ended. He never punched in or out on any sort of clock. The ticking never stopped and couldn't ever be silenced.

"Excuse me, sir . . . Mr. Dowland. Would you like to interrogate any of the—"

"No," he said, still looking through the clear wall as he ignored one of the young FBI agents in the room.

He had heard enough. All that mattered was Cheyenne and her former coworker, a wiry nerd named Sef Malek, both managed to enter the building unnoticed and then casually took an elevator up to this floor, where they went into an office and hacked Acatour's network. Then somehow they managed to disappear. Nobody knew where they were.

"Hey, guys," a woman with a shrill voice called out to the group. "Any of you think of checking the robot maintenance room?"

This made even Dowland turn.

"Are they in there?" the head of the security department at the tower asked. He was one of a dozen people Dowland wanted to personally strangle.

"No," the woman called from the hallway. "They took the repair chute down."

Dowland shook his head and laughed. This was unbelievable. As the conversation continued with the police and FBI agents and security and all the other morons at the top of this building, he took the glass elevator back down to where Margaux was waiting. The ride felt symbolic of the state of his life and job.

4.

The woman the data files showed giving Cheyenne Burne and Sef Malek the keycard for the Incen Tower had been found, killed, and disposed of. Margaux had done her job.

But Cheyenne and Malek managed to elude an army of security and FBI agents in the building and leave completely undetected.

Dowland had not done his job.

The system had been broken into, and data had been manipulated. They explained to Dowland what had happened, but frankly, he didn't care if it had been erased or stolen or replaced by the latest version of virtual *Minecraft*. All that mattered was this job, one he was failing at. An assignment to find someone, a task he had not yet come close to completing.

The only thing that calmed him was drinking away the worries, and he knew the weakness inherent in that, but it didn't matter. He could figure out how to get sober after retiring. Of course, by then, all that would be left to do was to drink the days and nights away on a beach in Ibiza.

At this point in the afternoon, after several quick drinks even the detestable Margaux was looking charming to him. He wanted—no, Dowland needed—something to take his mind off everything. Even if it was very temporary.

"Everything boils down to this man," Margaux said as she pointed at the screen on their table in the bar. "To Keith Burne."

"You think he's capable of doing all this? There were acts by the Reckoner before Burne quit his job."

"Who knows when he lost his mind," she said. "But for his daughter to be involved? When there were no hints whatsoever she had any issues with the company?"

He went to the bar and ordered another drink, waited for a moment, and returned to the table. Margaux hadn't even touched her glass.

As he looked at her, he could tell something was wrong.

"Do you have your SYNAPSYS on?" she asked.

"Of course not. I never do."

"Turn it on. Now."

When he did, he began to hear the voice of the man who had startled him in his hotel not long ago by saying, *"This is your wake-up call, Mr. Dowland."* The man was speaking into his SYNAPSYS, talking as clearly and calmly as if it were a live call. After a couple of minutes, Dowland told the message to shut off.

"There's a document in your inbox as well with the same message."

"Open mail," he said, scanning the messages and quickly finding the one called "The Face of Evil." When he opened it, the stern look of Jackson Heyford could be seen.

Uh-oh.

As Margaux drifted out of the room, conducting a live conversation with someone, Dowland began to read the document. After the first few paragraphs, he stopped and cursed. Loud and furious for thirty seconds.

"You got the very same thing?" he asked Margaux when she walked back to the table.

"The exact same thing."

"Unbelievable. It's unbelievable. There's no way."

"I was talking to an agent. They got into the SYNAPSYS station."

"What? How?" Dowland asked.

"We don't know that."

It was unfathomable.

"Who got these messages? Every single person in the building?" He laughed at his exaggeration.

"At this point it looks like everybody in the country."

"What?"

"Every single person we've heard from nationwide. We don't know about other countries."

Dowland let out another burst of cursing while Margaux stood there and watched.

"Does your language become more graphic the angrier you get?" she asked him, sounding honestly curious.

"Hostility shows off my true colors."

"Colors? There's only one I see, Jon. It's black. Very, very black."

TWENTY-ONE

Flakes in a Snowstorm

1.

Seconds seemed to be stuck, refusing to move quickly, clawing over Cheyenne's skin as she waited for her father to show up. They were in the farmhouse, with Malek and Jazz standing over the laptop searching for reactions to their work while Cheyenne looked out the window again.

"Where are they?" she asked. "We've been here for two hours."

Jazz looked back at her. "It'll be okay."

"Listen to what one news outlet is saying," Malek said, looking at the monitor.

> Welcome to the dawn of a new era in technology. Twenty years ago we witnessed the abuse of algorithms in Facebook and search engines for Google, prompting mandates for government regulations and policies put in place for these privately held companies. Once claimed to be impossible to be hacked, the SYNAPSYS is no different than anything else, proving instead that good technology can always be manipulated and corrupted.

"Nothing about the *actual* message sent out there?" Jazz asked.

Malek shook his head. "Very little. Lots of words like *delusional* and *extremist* and *hate* are used when talking about the letter we sent. Here's another quote: 'This act constitutes a new era in the battle for individuals' rights and the regulations on new technologies.'"

No longer in the uncomfortable business attire but jeans and a sweatshirt, Cheyenne walked over and sat on the couch. Part of her wanted to pray, yet that was like walking up to a stranger and asking for money. Or maybe just knocking on a door with nobody behind it.

"Are we ever going to see the Reckoner?" Cheyenne asked them. "Is he ever going to be brave enough to show his face?"

Malek turned now, probably because he could hear the tone in her voice. Jazz moved and sat on the arm of a chair facing her.

"The fewer people see him, the fewer ways people can get to him," Jazz said.

"So he makes others do his work? People like the Parschauers?"

"It's not *his* work, Cheyenne. I'm not doing this because of a prophet. I'm doing it because that's what I'm supposed to do. Even before I knew about Jackson Heyford and others like him, I realized the great battle that we're facing. I saw it firsthand. The hate for Christianity. How leaders in all industries view it in a way Hitler viewed the Jews. Slowly and surely our country divided faith into two categories: one being light and fun, the other deemed fascist. And they've been getting rid of that so-called fascism."

She stood up, tired of listening to another round of this rhetoric. Cheyenne walked over and looked out the window again, but the dirt driveway looked exactly the same.

"Don't you guys think of the possibility that maybe, just maybe, you're all *wrong*? That you've taken an idea and whittled it down to something sharp, and now you're trying to gouge people with it?"

Again Malek turned back to look at her, but he didn't say anything.

"I've never once wondered if this is real," Jazz said. "I just wonder what God wants or why He does what He does. Or is about to do."

"But you don't even know if our message is going to do anything to Acatour and Heyford."

"Chy," Malek blurted out, "tell me something. If all the things inside our message—if all those things prove to be true, and if Jackson Heyford takes the fall and becomes incriminated, then what are you going to think?"

She breathed in, feeling her chest quiver. "I don't know."

"You don't know? Seriously? Are you still going to question if there's a God and if the Reckoner is actually a prophet?"

"I'm so tired of these stupid nicknames," she said. "And I didn't even read the entire message, not fully."

She walked to the edge of the table where Malek sat and looked at both of them.

"I'm sorry, guys. I just— All I've wanted from the beginning of this is to find my—"

The sound of the door opening interrupted her.

Once again her father had been found.

2.

"Someone—some woman—took Lucia before she could reach me," Keith Burne told them as he came up to Cheyenne and gave her a hug. "Good job back there."

"Do you know who?" Jazz asked.

"No. But I've seen her with the guy who's been following me."

"What do you mean?" Cheyenne asked. "Someone's been following you?"

Keith Burne nodded as he went to the kitchen and grabbed some water. "I've been making him think he's following me. Look, guys. We have to get out of this place, especially since Lucia didn't make it here."

"What do you mean, you're making him think he's following you?" she asked.

"You think she'll tell them something?" Jazz asked.

"Have you heard from the Reckoner?" Malek added.

Her father looked tired and anxious as he addressed Jazz first. "I'm less worried about her talking and more worried about their being able to get information from her. Her SYNAPSYS, her network, anything."

He sat down on the couch and drained the last half of the water bottle he'd just taken.

"It's too long a story to explain about the agent following me, Chy. And regarding the Reckoner, yes, I've heard from him. He was temporarily waylaid and out of touch. But he's safe." Keith looked over at Malek still tapping at the laptop. "What's the response been?"

"Everybody's talking about security and privacy issues and having conversations about being able to break into a SYNAPSYS."

"But what about the message itself?" Keith asked. "And the accusations about Heyford and Acatour?"

"It sounds like people don't want to hear it," Malek said.

"They're covering it up," Jazz said, "the media, the network, with what they're allowing to show and not allowing to show. They don't want people talking about our declaration. The very ones our announcement is about have the means to prevent it from making the news. They're going to distract and divert the public's attention to anything and everything other than the truth."

"Yeah, but that doesn't mean people aren't acting," Malek added. "Incen Tower is already flooded with protestors and people demanding answers. The National Guard is coming to assist Chicago police in dealing with the mob. Look at this picture." Every inch of space in front of the building they had just left was full of citizens standing shoulder to shoulder, yelling and chanting and demanding answers.

"This is three hours after getting the message," Malek said with a smile. "*Three* hours. Chicago's going to be in chaos by sunset."

Jazz watched the footage of the protesters, mesmerized for the moment. "So this is how it happens, then."

"What are we supposed to do now?" Cheyenne asked her father.

"It's time to get out of Dodge," he said.

"Get out of what?" a distracted Malek asked.

"It's an idiom old folks like me still use," Keith told them. "You need to leave tonight and head north. There's a pastor named Brian Wallace, who's been preparing for you guys to come. You'll have to hide for a while."

"I've gotten pretty used to that," Jazz said.

"Yeah, me too," Malek said.

"What do you mean 'you guys'?" Cheyenne asked.

"I'm not going with you."

She sat down next to him in complete disbelief. "What do you mean? Where are you going?"

He looked at Jazz and then at Malek.

"Dad? What?"

"I'm not going with you. I still have more to do."

"But why? What are you talking about? We did what we were supposed to do. Right? I've followed the plan. I might go to jail or even worse. What more is there for you to do?"

He sighed, giving her that look, the one she used to resent so much.

"Don't give me that," she said. "Don't give me your 'it's complicated' look. Maybe if I was ten years old, then, yeah, I wouldn't understand. But I'm not a kid. I've grown up. But it feels as if you forget that at selective times."

Before her dad could respond, she stood up and walked out of the house.

3.

The horizon battled with her mood, its glory overpowering her frustration. With the sun ablaze on the distant horizon, the clouds appeared to follow as they stretched out toward the west, their warm orange and yellow textures gently rubbing against the darkening blue canvas above them. Cheyenne stood next to the wood-rail fence on the farm and looked across the flat field of grass; she could feel the calm cover her.

"What if our life had been like this?" her father mused as he walked up beside her, staring at the same picture she did. "What if all we'd known was harvesting the fields? Planting and picking and storing and sending out the crops?"

Cheyenne smiled. "At this point it seems like a nice thought."

She turned and saw his eyes reflecting the shimmering light in the distance.

"What are you doing? Where are you going?"

"It's better that none of you know," he said. "It's to protect everybody. The same reason none of you have seen the Reckoner. The most valuable commodity in the world today is privacy. It's the biggest thing that's been stolen from people in the last thirty years."

"But what will you be doing?" she asked her father. "Is it dangerous?"

"I will be fine." Keith turned and put his hands on her shoulders. "I've been fine so far, right? Don't worry. God has a plan. He's always had a plan."

"Did that include becoming a single parent?" she asked, her tone not biting but sincere.

"That's a fair question."

"I don't think there's anything fair about it," Cheyenne stated.

"Do you know what first broke me? What God used to get my attention? It was when your mother told me she was leaving me. The first time she threatened it, years before she finally just left. You were only ten months old."

He turned again to the endless field in front of them and propped a foot on the fence. The glow of the fading sun lit his face. She noticed the wrinkles around his eyes and mouth and the way his eyes looked more weighted with sadness. He looked west as if he were still looking for her to finally come back.

"She got angry—she was a mess—and she told me that she was going to leave. That both of you would. She was going to take our ten-month-old baby and leave. We argued. She threatened me, and I threatened her. I remember she took off somewhere, and I tried to get you to take your afternoon nap. I rocked you back and forth, and while you slept, all I could do was cry and pray. I didn't know if anyone was listening to me, but I was hopeless and desperate. And you know what I prayed?"

He smiled at her, looking grateful and sad at the same time. "I asked God not to take you away. I said I would do anything—*anything*. I begged Him to keep me as your father. To protect you. To allow me to look after you. And you know, twenty-six years later I'm still praying that."

"I'm sorry she left," Cheyenne said, putting a hand on his shoulder.

"I am too. For both of us. She came back for a while but couldn't handle the responsibilities. But, Chy, God answered my prayer then. And I know He'll answer my prayer now too. I know He already has. You being here. You heading to Colorado Springs without knowing anything for certain. *That* was an answer to prayer, especially since I know you and your rational personality."

"If you prayed so hard for me, why aren't you coming with me?" she asked.

"It's not your heart I'm praying for," he said. "It's your soul. I don't want yours to have to be as broken as mine before you lift your eyes to heaven."

"I don't understand why you have to do this."

Looking at the horizon no longer seemed to interest her father as he faced her with a serious look. "We're not all here because of a random intervention. We've been called because God sees something in us. We're all part of God's greater plan. The famous rapper. Malek and you. The others helping out this prophet God sent. There was no way people could've learned the truth, not so many and not like this, without all of us."

"So your role was what? Convincing your daughter to come find you?"

Keith Burne could only chuckle. "Well, it's more like convincing everybody to come find me. I've been a decoy for a long time. But you—*you*—were the one, the only one, able to deliver that message to people."

"You have Malek."

"Yes, but he didn't do the specific work you did. And I knew the only way to get your full attention and your buy-in was to put you on a mission. That always worked better when you were a child. A lot better than my coming to you and telling you what to do. I had to disappear. But when I needed to reach you, I had to invite you to come find me."

The clouds above them didn't seem to move. Rather, it was as if an artist kept revising the painting, shading the hues and brushing the streaks of sunlight and allowing the horizon to tremble in its beauty.

"Why do you have to be a decoy?" she asked.

"Because God wants me to be. And I know you probably don't understand that, but I hope and pray one day you will. Not in a hopes-and-prayers sort of way, but in a knees-on-the-floor, can't-go-on-anymore, authentic Lord's Prayer sort of way."

"Daddy, please," she said, looking at him and trying to make him understand. She couldn't fathom losing him. Again.

"Chy, if today was your last day on earth, what would happen to you tomorrow? Where would you be?"

She shook her head. "I don't know."

"I understand that. But I do know. I have faith that I'll be entering eternity. I don't have to see the sun to know it's out there. When it finally turns to night, I don't have to wonder if it's going to rise again. My belief is like that. God doesn't have to show me heaven for me to know it's real."

4.

The white glow engulfed her as the screen sprawled out in front of her, the black text hovering like swarms of bees, ready to be scanned. Cheyenne couldn't sleep in this hotel room. Instead, she was thinking about what her father had said and wondering where he had gone.

Malek, Jazz, and Cheyenne had said goodbye to Keith Burne and then made the four-hour drive to Grand Rapids, Michigan. A couple of hotel rooms had been reserved for them, so they slipped into them shortly after midnight. Instead of resting, Cheyenne felt locked up and watched. She also couldn't stop thinking of everything her dad had said and the confidence he exhibited, even when he gave her a farewell hug and smile before departing.

They had watched the live scenes unfolding in downtown Chicago, the fires blazing and the rioters turning violent. The full details and documents of their message had been digested, and now it wasn't only citizens demanding action but politicians and leaders all across the country. Jackson Heyford and Acatour were now seen as predators and controlling invaders that had to be stopped.

She needed to read every last word, so she did what her father had suggested and began to read the message they had sent to the nation. She'd already read enough of it to get the gist. Like the rest of the country, she believed Heyford and his corporation were guilty of many despicable things.

I don't want to read this because I feel guilt too.

EVERYTHING YOU KNOW IS WRONG.

This is a wake-up call to this nation.

You are being monitored and manipulated by men like Jackson Heyford, CEO of Acatour and the PASK division.

The very same technology and tools we're using to break into your SYNAPSYS are the ones they're using to watch you. To control you. To lie to you.

Jackson Heyford is a leader of the elite, the men and women who rule the masses. They don't simply want to control. They want to corrupt.

Wake up, people.

This isn't a physical or mental war. It's a spiritual one.

Every human being must consider if there is a God and if He had a Son named Jesus Christ.

Our country hasn't forgotten the message of Jesus Christ. America has rejected it. The faith of our founders is now forbidden. The hope of God is now considered hostile as we strive for global harmony.

The churches have been shut down. The Bible outlawed. And Christians everywhere have been systematically removed from our society. The videos, photos, and reports included with this message will show you proof of that.

The world doesn't want to listen. George Orwell said, "If liberty means anything at all, it means the right to tell people what they do not want to hear."

Hear these words, America.

"For everyone has sinned; we all fall short of God's glorious standard. Yet God, in his grace, freely makes us right in his sight. He did this through Christ Jesus when he freed us from the penalty for our sins. For God presented Jesus as the sacrifice for sin. People are made right with God when they believe that Jesus sacrificed his life, shedding his blood."
—Romans 3:23–25

This is the truth from the Bible.

George Orwell also said, "In a time of universal deceit— telling the truth is a revolutionary act."

There is only one truth that matters.

The revolution must start now.
—RECKONER

After she finished reading, Cheyenne's eyes stayed open for a long time, the words floating like flakes in a snowstorm or ashes in a fire, uncertain where to land, content to remain in the air as long as they needed to be.

TWENTY-TWO

In Sight of Land

1.

Amy's call came ten minutes after the message about the evils of Heyford and Acatour had been sent out. Somehow and some way Hutchence had managed to break into every single SYNAPSYS in the country with a warning about the biggest corporation in the world. Yet Will still hadn't heard a single word from him since sneaking him onto his father's property the night before.

Needless to say, Amy had some questions and concerns, especially since the message was all about Will's father, the man he had visited less than twenty-four hours ago. She said one word to him, yet he knew it contained a dozen questions.

"Will?"

The afternoon sun spilled through the kitchen window as Amy called from her office in Chicago while the girls were still in school. Flip was nearby, chomping on one of Will's socks.

I have to tell her the truth.

"Lots to discuss," Will told her.

She waited, but he didn't proceed.

"All the things it said . . . I just started to watch some of the videos. I can't believe it."

"Believe it," Will said.

"Did you know? About any of this?"

"We need to talk," he repeated to her, obviously not wanting to do it via SYNAPSYS. "You should leave work now."

"Why?"

"I have a feeling things are gonna get pretty dangerous downtown."

"Okay."

"Amy," he said, thinking for a minute and realizing the obvious position he was in. That *they* were in. "Meet me somewhere before coming home."

"What do you mean? Why?"

"For privacy."

"Okay," she said.

"Remember the first place we met?"

"Sure. I forget the actual address, but I can look it up."

"Ask for directions," Will said. "Meet me there as soon as you can get on the train. I'll meet you by the station."

"Is everything okay? Are the girls all right?"

"Yeah. Everything's fine. I'll ask Julia's mom if Shaye and the twins can come over after school for a couple of hours."

"Will, are you sure—"

"Everything's fine. I'll explain. Just get there as soon as possible."

After calling Mrs. Schoppe to make sure the girls could come over after school, something Shaye frequently did with her best friend, Will checked on Flip. The mutt was still chewing and tearing apart the sock.

"Come on, buddy. Let's take you out before you do any more damage."

After throwing away the mangled sock and letting Flip sniff around and do nothing outside for a few minutes, Will changed into a button-down shirt and then left. He didn't need directions for their meeting place. Will knew it quite well.

2.

As Will backed out of his driveway, he heard a tapping at his window, causing him to jerk the SUV to a halt. All he could see was a figure in a black army jacket, and as the man bent down to look in the window, Will saw the buzz cut. He almost floored the pedal to get away from the stranger, but he held off when he heard his name.

"Will, can I hitch a ride?"

It was Hutchence. For a moment Will wasn't sure whether to let him in or to get as far away from the guy as possible. But he just nodded and motioned for Hutchence to get in the seat next to him.

"Did you miss me?" Hutchence asked after climbing in and then clamping his hand on Will's shoulder.

"I miss not getting spooked by strangers," Will said as he backed out into the street and closed the garage door. "Did you go off and join the marines?"

"Just trying to change my appearance," Hutchence said, rubbing the stubby fuzz on his head. "We did it."

"What do you mean 'we'? I didn't do anything."

"Of course you did. You were the key to the whole plan."

"The whole plan," Will said as he turned onto the avenue heading toward I-88, which would lead them east to Chicago. "I know the why part, but I don't know any of the hows."

"I'll tell you on your way to meet Amy."

Will looked at him, surprised and suspicious. "How do you know I'm meeting her? Were you listening through my SYNAPSYS?"

"Nope. It's far less technologically advanced. I put a bug on Flip."

Will slowed the car down in further disbelief. He remembered Hutchence coming out of the blue to meet him the first time only moments after Will had picked up the dog.

"Did you drop off Flip in front of my bookstore?" he asked Hutchence.

"Yes."

"To eavesdrop on me and my family?"

"I needed to keep tabs on you. To see if there would be any contact with your father or anybody else."

Will shook his head, trying to remember any embarrassing or personal conversations or actions with Flip nearby. "You know, you and my father have something in common with your invasions of privacy."

"The only way we were able to connect with the SYNAPSYS database field I showed you was to access it on Jackson's property. The tools are at PASK in the Incen Tower, but the addresses and information on the SYNAPSYSes are with Heyford."

"So what? You broke into his bedroom and hacked into his personal files?"

"Not quite," Hutchence said. "One of his wonderful Frank Lloyd Wright houses on the property serves as a set of offices housing lots of data. A man who used to work at Acatour named Malek was able to access the details on it. I simply needed to get inside."

"And you just picked a lock to get in?" Will asked.

"There are people watching the walls and grounds on the Heyford property. But once you get to the houses, there's only wonderful artificial intelligence guarding and securing the buildings. It's still a lot easier to get past machines than human beings."

At the red light Will scanned the cars around him. He couldn't help feeling watched and followed.

"So then what happened? Why didn't you get out?"

"There were too many people in the parking lot surrounding your car. I didn't want to take a risk. I stayed overnight in a closet, then had to use the lake to actually get off the property."

"You swam to freedom?" Will asked, laughing.

"It worked."

"Do they know what we did?"

"Not yet. And considering the chaos in Heyford's life right now, I think you're going to be merely an afterthought."

"Don't you think he'll find the coincidence of my being there the night before all this happened just too unlikely?"

Hutchence nodded. "That's why you need to do everything you can to get out of here."

"To get out of where?"

"To leave the house for a while. To get away from Chicago. I suggest you take a trip to see your in-laws. I wouldn't be surprised if your wife's office in the city shuts down for a while."

"Why?"

"Anger is going to be rampant in the streets," Hutchence said. "I don't have to be a prophet to know that. Just you wait."

"And that's what you wanted?"

"I wanted to wake the world up, Will. So tell me. Don't you feel fully alive?"

He didn't answer the Reckoner. Fully alive was far different from the storm settling inside him.

I feel fear and alarm. And I wish I could just go back to sleep.

3.

Will wasn't exactly sure even how to begin.

After they arrived at the train station, Hutchence told him goodbye and said he would be in touch. Will didn't ask when. He waited in the parking space watching the trains stop every fifteen minutes. After the fourth one arrived, he saw his wife walking down the steps looking out to the lot. He got out of the car and waved her over.

"Is everything okay?" she asked again.

As he leaned over and gave her a hug, Amy looked alarmed.

"Will . . ."

"The girls are at the Schoppes', and they're fine. And I'm fine."

"Have you heard about the rioting in Chicago?" she asked. "It's a good thing I got out of there."

"Yeah."

"Why did you want to meet here?"

Amy was logical and analytical, so he knew if he suddenly told her everything, from the first day of meeting Hutchence to helping with the message that had been sent out, it would probably feel like a tsunami hitting her.

Before saying another word, he told her to turn off her SYNAPSYS to be on the safe side. "I wanted to let you know about my meeting with my father," he said after she made sure the device was off. "When I explain, you'll know why."

Amy looked at him and was about to say something until he put a finger up to his lips.

"Just wait, okay?" he said.

"You're scaring me."

Just wait until you hear everything. "Don't be scared. It's only five minutes away. We can talk there."

Sure enough, they drove a few blocks down to Chicago Avenue, then they turned and pulled up to the house in the Oak Park neighborhood. Amy opened her window and looked out in disbelief.

"What happened to Wright Books? When did it close?"

"It's been a while," Will told her. "Come on. Let's get out."

The temperature had hurdled over fifty degrees today, so the air and sunshine felt inviting. Once they were outside and stepping onto the sidewalk, Will scanned the street and sidewalks around them.

"Why do you keep looking around?"

"Even in the broad daylight, I feel like someone's listening," Will said.

This made Amy look around, but when he didn't say anything else, her focus went back to the structure that was once called the Robert Parker House.

"Is every bookstore in the country going to close?" Amy asked.

"Probably," Will said. "I couldn't bring myself to tell you when it closed a couple of years ago."

"It's been two years?"

"Yeah. I thought knowing that might make you more nervous about my store." He stopped himself for a second, noting the use of "my." He used to say "our" until the bookstore became more of a burden than a blessing.

"When Wright Books closed, I saw the writing on the wall. And I was right. No pun intended."

The beautiful independent bookstore had been named after the famous man who designed this house, a modified Queen Anne style with two octagonal spires.

"I think the reason I fell in love with this years ago was because Frank Lloyd Wright built it under another name," Will said. "He couldn't work outside of the architecture firm where he was employed. So it's considered one of his bootleg homes."

Amy was looking at Will rather than the house. "Why'd you bring me to the place we met? To remind me?"

"Yeah, to let you remember that very dark day," Will said, actually making a rare joke around her.

"It wasn't a 'dark' day."

"I remember first seeing you in the side room with the spire roof. The one with all the windows. The sun lit up your hair in this dazzling sort of way."

"Oh yes," she said, rolling her eyes. "I was this glowing angel that captivated you."

"You were," Will said matter-of-factly.

"Please. So you began to stalk me in a bookstore, huh?"

"The irony is that you're not even a reader, though our whole lives have been under the shadows of books and fictional tales."

"Another way we're completely opposite," Amy said, finally beginning to stare at the house again.

"I didn't bring that up to be negative, even though it's hard for me *not* to be negative these days. I say that because . . . love happened. And love keeps us together. But it's not this you-and-me, romance-in-the-Frank-Lloyd-Wright-bookstore, the-sun-seeping-in-on-a-perfect-day kind of love I'm talking about. It's God loving me and knowing I needed you. Hopefully that we needed each other. And I say that because you have to trust me with everything I'm about to tell you. And I need to trust you to not tell anybody else."

Walking down a crumbling sidewalk, Will told Amy everything about Hutchence, about the first day they met and the subsequent meetings, trying to sum up a few of the things he'd said about the project he needed Will for and about how they'd been successful.

"*You* were a part of that? The greatest hack of all time?" Amy laughed and not in a cynical way but truly amused.

"You seem delighted," Will said.

"Have you lost your mind?"

"I lost it about five years ago trying to keep a bookstore afloat."

She wiped tears out of her eyes, tears prompted by her laughter.

"The fact that you helped do this to your father. *That* is priceless."

They continued to walk with Amy shaking her head, her ponytail swishing like a cheerleader's pom-pom.

"No wonder you've been walking around like someone half-possessed," she said. "I've been so worried about you."

But you don't seem worried now. I don't get it.

"I know I haven't been easy to live with. Not just since losing the bookstore but for the last few years. And the moment I finally closed the door for the very last time, a guy named Hutchence showed up and started talking about religious persecution and secret societies and God's judgment."

"But how did you get involved with breaking into people's SYNAPSYSes?"

"The only way to do it was to get onto my father's property," Will said.

"So that's why you contacted him."

"Yeah."

"And all those things that were in that message? The stuff about Acatour? I only began to read some of the documents that came with it."

"It's all true," Will said, "based on everything I saw and all the things Hutchence showed me. At first I didn't want to have anything to do with him, especially when I found out he knew who my father was."

"How'd he discover that?"

"I have no idea. I don't even know his background. Maybe he was in the FBI. Or worked for Acatour as a computer genius. But I got scared. I *am* scared. Amy, this shouldn't be happening. None of this. We should be taking our girls to soccer games and making popcorn as we watch the hundredth Pixar movie. Right? I didn't want to believe."

Will turned and motioned to start heading back down the sidewalk to where they'd started.

"So you think our house is bugged and we're being monitored?" Amy asked.

"I don't know about that. Hutchence hasn't been discovered yet. I do know my father has been keeping tabs on me with his wonderful SYNAPSYS. I'm officially done with mine. For good."

A giggle spilled from her lips, and Will stopped. "What is so funny?"

"I'm sorry," she said. "I know I shouldn't be laughing. It's just . . ."

"It's just what?"

"I'm proud of you. For being brave and standing up to that monster who didn't raise you. And for standing up for your faith. Something I'm not so good at, especially in my field."

They reached the Victorian house once again and could see its octagonal turret peeking through the trees in the front yard.

"I realized something about my father today," Will said, "something I think he doesn't even know. There's something about Wright Books I never told you, a reason I would shop there all the time. It's because my mother worked there before my parents had kids, when they were starting out and she had to help support him."

She looked at him in surprise. "Why didn't you tell me this?"

"You know I don't like talking about my parents. I hated thinking about her having this low-paying job to support that egomaniac. But it never dawned on me that he's been trying to buy back my mother in some twisted and sick way."

"With all the Frank Lloyd Wright houses he's purchased," Amy said, immediately understanding.

"Yeah, exactly. It's like in *Citizen Kane*. This place is his Rosebud. Well, the Rosebud was my mother."

"Did he apologize to you? Or try to make any amends?"

Will shook his head. "He's incapable of anything like that. But I do know something. Just like those houses he's digging up and transplanting to his property, he wants to own everything, including his three sons. Even me. He told me he personally put me out of business."

A slow-moving car made both of them look out to the street.

"We should go," Will said.

"What are we going to do now?"

"Something I should have done a long time ago. Something my pride prevented me from doing."

4.

"Hey, Callie? Bella? Can you guys come up to your room?"

It was the third time he had asked them this evening, and this time he was louder and more urgent. They eventually scampered up the steps and walked into the large bedroom.

"I want you guys to do something *very* important," he told the girls. "Okay?"

"What is it?" Callie asked.

"Does it have something to do with school?" Bella asked.

"No. It's just— Callie, come over here by your bed. We're all going to take a trip to Michigan today. To see Grandma and Grandpa."

"Yay!" Callie said.

"Do we have to?" Bella naturally reacted the opposite way.

"I want you guys to start packing some of your favorite things you'd like to take with you. Okay?"

"Like how much?" Bella asked.

"Just a few toys."

Callie wrapped her arms around her stuffed animals. "Like my stuffies!"

"Not all four hundred of them," he said. "Only your favorites."

Will and Amy had already packed enough to cover a few days. Will had also wanted to box up the "important" things, like the fireproof safe and family mementos and other personal artifacts. Just in case something prevented them from coming back. Just in case someone broke into their house or decided to burn it down. Even though Amy didn't fully understand his fears and his need to bring all these personal items, she didn't fight him on it. But the last thing they wanted the girls to think was that they were moving.

"When are we leaving?" Callie shouted.

"Tomorrow morning."

"But we have school!"

"You get to miss it," he said to her. The twins erupted in applause and screams. "Plus, we'll have some treats before we drive. Maybe ice cream or brownies." *Anything to get everybody out without drama.*

With the smell of spaghetti in the air and the sound of the girls looking through drawers and stuffing toys in their bags, Will looked around his office as he filled another box. He could hear the footsteps behind him.

"Daddy?"

He turned to see Shaye looking worried. "What is it?"

"What's going on? Why are we going to see Grandma and Grandpa tomorrow?"

"We haven't seen them in a while," he said, which was true.

"I know, but . . . you hate going to see Grandma and Grandpa."

"No I don't," he said with a frown.

"Yeah you do. Last time Mommy wanted to go, you guys argued, and she took just us."

"It was Christmastime. You know how busy the store can be then."

"You said you didn't want Grandpa offering you a job."

She can hear everything.

"And why are we going tomorrow?" she continued. "It's a school day."

"Maybe I'm going to ask Grandpa for a job," Will said.

"Are you serious?"

Will smiled and nodded.

"Is that why you and Mom are packing up everything?" She scanned the boxes in his office and then looked around at the bare bookshelves and the missing photos.

She was too smart to be only eleven. Or maybe she knew her father too well.

"Just get your stuff ready," he said.

"Daddy, are you—" Shaye suddenly covered her face with her hands and started to cry.

Will stood up and moved over to her and held her. "Shaye, what's wrong?"

"Daddy—are you leaving us?"

For a second he didn't understand what she was asking. When he realized, he clutched her harder. "No, sweetie. I'm not leaving you. I'd never leave you."

"But you and Mommy— All you guys do is fight. And you look sad all the time."

"No I don't," Will said. "And like I told you, things have been tough. But I don't want to argue with your mother. We shouldn't argue."

She looked up at him, wiping her wide, beautiful eyes. "You never make me laugh anymore."

Will stopped, not breathing for a moment, then gave her a big, sad smile. "I know," he admitted. "And that's gotta change. I need to change. Okay? But I'm not leaving you guys. *Ever.* You understand? Okay?"

She wiped her eyes again and sniffled, nodding and looking down at the ground.

"Shaye, look at me. This trip—it's good. We have to do this. If you've ever trusted Daddy in your life, you have to trust me now. Okay?"

"Okay."

The look on her face was reassuring. She did trust him. And even though Shaye resembled him more than Amy, for the first time in a long time, Will saw the same expression on her face that he had seen on Amy earlier that day.

5.

Will Stewart stood for a moment on the edge of the overlook and scanned sprawling Lake Michigan. A sailboat was gliding along, all alone on the blue waters and underneath the blue skies. It seemed early in the season for a boat to be on the water. Will studied the craft and felt as if it was a perfect reminder. All of this—the morning and the hilltop and the lake and the sailboat and the sky—was a gentle whisper from God.

He sat back on the bench and looked at the sky. "Lord, thank You. For getting my attention. For waking me up. For everything."

This morning as they left the house in their two cars, Will tried not to appear as emotional and sad and frustrated as he felt. He tried to show strength in front of Amy, but he wasn't sure how well he was doing. She was driving straight to her parents' house with the girls. Hutchence had told Will to meet him here at this park, so that's exactly what he was doing.

A gust of wind came from the lake below and caused Will to close his eyes for a moment. He shifted on the park bench, sipping the cup of coffee he'd just purchased. Since Hutchence was nowhere to be found, Will continued his prayer out loud.

"I know it was my dream to open the store, and maybe it wasn't Your will," Will said, looking back out to the waters in the distance. "But I know You allow things to happen for a reason, Lord. I thank You for Your protection and Your mercies, Lord. And whatever happens with our family and with my father, I pray You will continue to protect us."

He paused for a moment, letting the still settle around him like a heavy fog. He had intended to talk to God for only a few moments before Hutchence came. Will hadn't meant for all this to come pouring out of him.

"I know there's a war happening out there. A war happening now. Help me be the soldier You need me to be. Help that message of hope to be heard by the country in some way."

Will could feel his heart beating, trying to keep up with a hundred thoughts.

"I think—I know—my mistake has been thinking and feeling and trying to do it on my own. And I know I can't do anything without You, Lord. I—we—need to trust You. I'm willing to do anything." He thought of his father-in-law and could already hear the condescending tone. "I'll do anything, Lord. Just open the door to show me."

After a few more minutes passed, Will decided Hutchence wasn't coming. *I hope someone didn't get to him first.*

He knew he needed to get back on the road and get moving again. He needed to be with Amy and the girls. As he tossed his empty coffee cup into a garbage can, he began to read a sign that explained the history of this stretch of land called Lookout Park in St. Joseph, Michigan.

> In the early 1950s, at the point at which you now stand, nature was taking its toll along the shore of Lake Michigan. Erosion, caused by natural conditions, such as the disruption of currents caused by the dual piers just north of this site; was gradually occurring . . .

Will continued to read about the thirteen homeowners living here who took every precaution they could, building seawalls and placing boulders at the base of the bluff. The state highway department assured them their houses would safely stand for at least a hundred years. Yet in 1954, after eight days of rain that created massive mudslides, the homeowners needed to get out fast.

> Though 1954 brought much hardship for the homeowners in this area as they faced not just the loss of a house, but a family home full of memories, we can take solace that no one was hurt, and pride in the strength of the community as people reached out to do what was needed to help move families and houses.
>
> This plaque is dedicated to the people whose homes were lost to erosion, to those who faced the challenge of moving their homes.

Will looked out at the steadily moving lake water and couldn't help singling out this line:

> Time was running out, and families began to evacuate their homes.

He thought of the Reckoner. *Now I know why you told me to meet you here.* Hutchence wasn't coming. All he'd wanted was for Will to come here and read this sign. Perhaps this was a statement about what was to come or a picture of Christianity in America. Or maybe it was a metaphor for Will's life and what needed to happen next.

Will had so many questions, enough to fill this deep body of water in front of him. The problem was he had stopped bringing them to God some time ago, and it was hard to start doing that again. Will gazed up toward the heavens again, the blue horizon appearing endless.

"I'm doing what I need to do, Lord, what You want me to do."

TWENTY-THREE

While I'm Still Here

1.

He shouldn't be in New York City, but Dowland didn't care. Margaux told him to stay in Chicago, to let them sort things out and let everything settle down before figuring out their next move. Others left messages for him to call, for him to contact them, for him to meet them soon.

Mel Bohmer's old, cranky voice came to mind: *"These little messes you continue to make . . ."*

This was no longer one little mess but rather a gigantic one.

So far Dowland hadn't heard from Mel, and that wasn't good. It could mean multiple things, none of which would serve him well to contemplate.

The person assaulting him on the Chicago sidewalk was linked to Zander Stock, the dead man he'd disposed of somewhere outside of Nashville. Whether this meant Kamaria was responsible for it or someone else associated with Zander was coming for vengeance, Dowland didn't know. But that didn't concern him in the least.

Nor was he concerned with the rapper License and Cheyenne Burne. Dowland wanted Keith Burne. All he wanted was to finish things and stop all this chaos and insanity.

That was why he reacted the moment he got the message on the night of the SYNAPSYS hack. "It's done, Dowland. And what you need to do now is heed the warning we gave you and the rest of the country. There's no need to come find any of us. We've done what we could." The voice came through his SYNAPSYS, and once again it was the same person. The Reckoner.

Keith Burne.

He was the one.

This wasn't a theory anymore. This time the contact information on the other end came clearly from Keith Burne's very own SYNAPSYS.

"It could be a trap," Margaux said to him.

"It doesn't matter."

"We need to tell others."

"No we don't. This is my job, and I'm going to finish it and somehow salvage what I can of my reputation. To get out of this alive."

She argued for only a few moments. If he wanted to be stupid, she told him to go ahead. Her resistance to his chasing Keith Burne just urged him on.

It didn't matter if he was driving into a trap. These Christian radicals hadn't been violent, so Dowland didn't expect an ambush. That was more likely to happen if he stayed in Chicago. So Dowland tracked down the SYN-APSYS, all the way to New York. A city big enough to get lost inside. Easy to cover a killing. Easy to hide if you're wanted.

The cold rain fell as Dowland stood on the sidewalk and tapped the Beretta in its shoulder holster hidden underneath his overcoat. He felt the same as when he had arrived at the run-down motel in the middle of Indiana, moments before gunning down Senator Robert Vasquez. It hadn't mattered that Vasquez wasn't the Reckoner. He had been part of this underground network of fanatics and had been necessary to eliminate. Tonight he would finish what he had started. Tonight his job would be done. He could contact the powers that be and let them know the Reckoner had been dealt with. Whether that could save his life, Dowland didn't know.

The information had been easy to access, and the description of the man in room 1432 matched Keith Burne. Margaux would have said the information was too easy to track down. But considering the absolute insanity of what was happening in Chicago tonight, Dowland needed to follow every lead he could.

The doors to the elevator in this old hotel crackled like the bones of an elderly man. After walking past several doors to reach 1432, Dowland stood there for a moment to decide what to do next. He knocked on the door and waited for several minutes, but nobody answered. He took a small metal card out of his pocket and waved it over the handle, unlocking it immediately. This was old-school technology the FBI used for doors like this.

With his Beretta leading the way, Dowland stepped into the room. Instead of seeing Keith Burne sitting on the edge of his bed or hiding behind it, he saw a gold flask resting on the dresser. It was unmistakable with its white-and-yellow gold cap topped with the Russian imperial double-headed eagle encrusted with diamonds.

Russo-Baltique 2027, the vodka he named his artificial friend after.

After scanning the entire room, he rushed to the bathroom and searched it, but Dowland didn't find anybody. His first thought had been hasty and utterly foolish. *She's not here. This is a sick joke.*

He walked back to the bottle, picked it up, and removed the cap. He found a glass and tilted the bottle over it, but nothing came out.

"Empty," he said. "Classy."

How in the world could the Reckoner know about Kamaria? There was no way, not something as secretive as that. Then another frightening thought hit him. Maybe this was Mel's way of finally getting in touch with him. As fires raged through downtown Chicago and the streets flooded with protestors, maybe Mel and his secret group were sending Dowland a message. A warning? Or a threat?

I have to get in touch with Kamaria. She's in danger.

As he set the empty bottle down, he saw the Clicknote on the dresser. It was black and the size and shape of lip balm and held a single disposable digital message. Dowland picked it up and pressed the top to play.

Kamaria appeared in front of him, and he couldn't help gasping at her beauty. He hadn't seen her in person for a long time, and even the photos and videos of her lately didn't do justice. Virtual reality still wasn't the real thing, but it was close enough. She stood as tall as he, wearing jeans and a T-shirt that said LICENSE. She smiled, but not in the kind, loving way she once reserved for him.

"Surprised to see me?" she asked and paused for a second, making him believe this was live and real.

"Kam—listen, I can tell you—," he blurted out before realizing he couldn't communicate with her, that this was merely taped and not live.

"I hope this is the last message you'll ever receive from anybody," her message continued with her stare focused on him. "I hope these are the last words you think about before the end comes. And I really hope they scare you. I know it takes a lot to scare someone without a soul."

She moved as if she were in the room, looking down at the floor and then back at him. Dowland walked over to the wall, once again scanning the room with his handgun and making sure nobody else was there.

"I want to play you a recording I still have, thanks to the beauty of technology. Remember the earthquake of '28? Does that ring a bell? I still remember it. I was alone in the hotel room I was living in. A room like the one you're in. A much nicer room, of course, but I was there all alone. And I called you and begged you to come out and help me. I called the man I loved and who claimed to love me and begged for help. But none came. Instead, this is what I got."

Soon he heard his own voice, sounding young and full of himself and completely soused. *"Listen, Kam, you're gonna be fine. You're always fine. Don't worry about this. Okay? You know how busy I am, and everything's gonna be okay. They're making a big deal out of nothing. Just stay there and stay calm. You know I'd be there if I could. But just relax 'cause everything's gonna be cool."*

The words made him sick. He winced and didn't even want to watch the rest of this video Kamaria had made for him.

"That was all I ever needed to know about Jon Dowland. I should've stayed there, far away from you. It took me a long time to learn, but I learned, Jon."

He cursed at the image as she continued to talk.

"You were looking for someone named the Reckoner? Well, he sends his regards. Whoever this person is, he was kind enough to let me in on what's been happening. I don't care about what you're doing or the people you're working for. But I do know you've failed. And I know what that failure is going to mean."

She chuckled in a delirious and haunting manner. "But my advice to you, Jon, is to stay there and stay calm. Just relax 'cause everything's 'gonna be cool.'"

With that last word the image disappeared. Dowland stood there for a moment, the Beretta waiting for someone to arrive, but nobody came. He was on his own.

2.

It was past midnight but how long after Dowland wasn't sure. The diner he sat in didn't have any screens on the windows and no clocks displaying the time.

The walls were bare in this vintage establishment, the kind of diner that had barstools and a server behind the counter who took orders and wore a coat and matching cap. Dowland hadn't seen the name of the restaurant, which was a block from his hotel. All he had seen was the stark glow through the long windows.

He had wanted to find a bar and forget this night, but he knew he couldn't do that. He needed to be clear and focused. He needed to figure out a new plan, one that got him far away from everybody. Perhaps leaving the country. But every contact he could think of was probably being watched and monitored. He couldn't trust anybody. Not a soul. So he needed to fill himself with some coffee and food and figure out a plan.

For half an hour he sat in the diner, sipping one cup of burned coffee after another, then ordering some eggs and bacon that he had difficulty eating. In the middle of his meal, a couple had come and sat on the other side of the L-shaped counter. They seemed at first to be a couple, though the way they barely spoke to each other and their body language said they definitely weren't in love. There was a coldness and distance between them. They both ordered coffee but nothing to eat. The young server made small talk with them until he realized they didn't want to be bothered.

Giving up on the rest of his dinner or breakfast or whatever it could be called, Dowland got a fresh cup of coffee and sat there, watching the couple to see if they were doing the same to him. Neither of them looked his way, however, and that made him even more suspicious.

I'm done. He knew this. It was no big revelation, no sudden realization. It was the absolute truth.

The Reckoner was still out there after exposing Jackson Heyford and Acatour. The CEO was ruined. If someone didn't assassinate the man, he would divide the rest of his life between being in court and being in hiding. He was done. The religious freaks responsible for this had somehow done the impossible, not just by breaking into SYNAPSYSes but by avoiding capture.

Mel and the others in control would be looking for heads to roll. *Literal* heads to roll. With long hunting knives that took their precious time. He was surely at the top of their lists since they didn't have many others to blame.

Blame God. Oh, wait. That's right. You already got rid of Him, didn't you? You can't blame someone you don't believe in.

He took another sip of coffee, feeling the weight of his Beretta resting in his shoulder holster. The man across from him in the dark suit and blue shirt glanced at him for the first time, but it was quick and then off him again.

Dowland knew it had come down to this. Fate and karma and all those other mysterious things in life had finally caught up with him.

Or maybe it's God finally announcing His arrival.

For a moment he shut his eyes and felt his body shiver. He had tasted hopelessness in his life, but this was different. It was almost as if he couldn't taste anything at all.

If You're up there, then You win. You hear me? You win.

Dowland slipped his hand into his jacket, felt the barrel of his gun, and then took it out.

Almost.

The woman leaned over and said something to the man for the first time since sitting down. The man nodded and then looked straight ahead at the server.

Dowland let out a long breath, looking at the couple. He knew it was time. And it had been a very, very long time coming.

TWENTY-FOUR

How the Story Ends

1.

"I never told you what I used to do," Hutchence said, his face shaded under the baseball cap.

Will stood on the lawn between his in-laws' sprawling lake house and the water. The rest of the family was back at the place where they'd been living for the past seven days, the large condo Amy's parents owned. Hutchence had told Will to meet him at this cottage on Gun Lake this April afternoon, a week after what was now being labeled "The Day of Reckoning." After a week of not hearing a single thing from the man this pun referred to, Will had wondered if he'd ever see him again.

"You never told me a lot of things about yourself," Will said.

"True. Want to take a guess?"

"I don't know . . . Maybe an FBI agent? Or a computer tech? Or maybe a drug smuggler? I have no idea."

"I taught high school band."

Will smiled. "I wouldn't have thought of that."

"A normal, happy, content guy. But then one day I woke up to find my wife was leaving me. I had no idea. *None.* I thought we were still crazy and madly in love. I mean, it was devastating. A year after the divorce was final, she re-married. The court found in *my* favor. She had to pay me alimony. That's how bad it was."

"And did you have any—"

"No kids," he answered, "which now, so many years later, I'm grateful for. But you know something, Will? I'll be honest. If my ex-wife showed up this second and walked over to me and asked me to take her back, I would. In a heartbeat. After everything she did, I'd still take her back. Without question."

"You must have really loved her," Will said.

"But here's the thing. I was as much in the wrong as she was. In many ways I put my wife on a pedestal, making her the idol I worshipped. Making our wonderful little life this lie I bought into. The rude awakening came after she left me. Things became . . . *real.*"

"How so?"

"I'll just say I turned into a real big mess."

The sun made the above-average sixty-degree temperature feel even warmer. Will couldn't wait for summer. Then again, he couldn't wait for any glimmer of hope, no matter how miniscule it might be. As bright as it looked today, things felt very, very dark.

"So, then," Will said, "how did you suddenly start hearing messages from God?"

Hutchence gave a wistful smile. "Let's just say that God got my attention in a pretty big way."

"Care to elaborate?"

"All I'll tell you is that when God called me to do His work, I ran and hid." Hutchence laughed. "I didn't want to have a part in any of this. You know what character in the Bible I most resemble?"

"The apostle Paul?"

"Seriously? No one like that. I'm Gideon, a timid man from a weak family who was so skeptical that he needed God to show him signs before he would listen to God's call. I did the same thing in my own unique and stubborn way."

"Didn't Gideon lead an army of three hundred valiant men?"

"'Then all three groups blew their horns and broke their jars. They held the blazing torches in their left hands and the horns in their right hands, and they all shouted, "A sword for the LORD and for Gideon!"'"

"You have quite a gift for memorizing Scripture. And book quotes."

Hutchence only laughed. He walked to the edge of the water and picked up a rock and tried to skip it. The rock took two hops before dropping.

"Never could skip rocks," he said, then turned and noted Will's expression. "How are you feeling about everything?"

"Honestly? I'm frankly more than a little terrified to walk outside. I feel I'm being watched. I feel as if I could be one of those Christians who are suddenly abducted and never heard from again."

"Will, 'the Bible is not a script for a funeral service. It is the record of God bringing life where we expected to find death.'"

"That's pretty profound."

"Actually, that's Eugene Peterson."

Will laughed. This took him back to their first meeting at his old bookstore.

God didn't allow my bookstore to fail. He closed that door and opened another. A much bigger one.

"So what's next? How do we keep fighting?" Will asked.

"Brother, every single day is a fight. A battle. So? 'A final word: Be strong in the Lord and in his mighty power. Put on all of God's armor so that you'll be able to stand firm against all strategies of the devil. For we're not fighting against flesh-and-blood enemies, but against evil rulers and authorities of the unseen world, against mighty powers in this dark world, and against evil spirits in the heavenly places.'"

"Ephesians, right?"

"Yes."

"I get that, but practically. Small, minute picture."

Hutchence moved closer to Will and clasped his shoulder. "You go to bed tonight and ask God for forgiveness for all your failures throughout the day. Then you wake up tomorrow and ask God for all the strength He will provide."

"I wish I had your kind of faith," Will said. "What are you going to do now?"

"Remember the movie I told you to watch after we first met? *Stalker* by Tarkovsky? Near the end of the film, the Stalker sums up my life's mission. He admits he's a louse who hasn't done anything good in this world and never will. But he tells the other two men his purpose, that he brings people like himself—desperate and tormented and hopeless—to this place and he helps them. I relate to the Stalker. That's what I've been doing and will continue to do."

Hutchence didn't give Will any more instructions or advice or plans. All he seemed to have wanted to do was to connect again and encourage Will. The only encouragement Will could find in the shadow of the darkness of today.

Before climbing into his car to leave, Hutchence took out a flat, wrapped present and gave it to Will. "Here's a parting gift for you."

Will knew by the size and the weight that it was a book.

"Thanks," Will said as his strange and unique friend got into his small two-seater. "Will I see you again?"

"Yeah," Hutchence said. "Or at least you'll see me around. In the news."

"I can only imagine."

"You know, Will, you're one of the very few who've actually met me in person, face-to-face."

"Why's that?"

"I don't know," Hutchence said. "But consider this. Maybe God's got big plans for you."

He shut the door and started the engine. With the window down, the loud rock music could easily be heard. But before Will could recognize the song, Hutchence drove away.

Walking back to the edge of the lake, Will ripped off the gold wrapping paper to see the book he'd been given. Sure enough, the first thing he saw was the author's name: A. W. Tozer. Underneath the name was the title: *The Set of the Sail.*

Will grinned as he opened the paperback book. Hutchence had signed a note on the title page.

To Will: True Love Waits. Your Friend.

He turned a few pages, and at the end of the first chapter, the final paragraph was highlighted.

Let us, then, set our sails in the will of God. If we do this we will certainly find ourselves moving in the right direction, no matter which way the wind blows.

2.

Later that evening Will found Amy in the corner sunroom of her parents' four-thousand-square-foot condo, reading instead of watching a show, which was her usual nightly ritual.

"You can turn on the news or whatever," she said. "I had to turn it off. It's hard to watch all day long. More than a hundred people have died in the rioting."

The leather-bound Bible she'd been reading rested on her lap.

"I don't feel like watching anything either," he said. "At least it appears that my father isn't going to show up on our doorstep anytime soon."

As he sat in the armchair next to her, he knew there were a hundred thousand words he wanted and needed to say to her. Will just wasn't sure which ones to start with.

"How are you doing?" he asked.

Amy began to cry. Her tears surprised him, especially after her being so strong during the past week they'd spent with her parents.

"Sweetie, what's wrong?"

"I'm— I'm scared, Will. I'm really frightened about the future. About our family. About what's going to happen to our girls."

He nodded. "I know."

"I know we're supposed to have faith and all that. But I feel . . . lost."

"I've felt lost for a long time," he said, moving over to kneel at her side. He took her hand and gripped it gently. "Living with me for the last few years—I know it hasn't been easy. And I know I can't change, Amy. Not on my own. But I know God can change me. He can make me more of the husband you need. More of the father our girls need. I don't know what's going to happen tomorrow or next week or next month, but I know tonight that all I can do is begin. Okay? To try to let God do some things instead of trying to do all of them myself and getting nowhere. Including . . . including getting a job and working for your father."

"I know you don't want to—"

"It'll be fine. Moving up here around family will be great."

"You're giving up on your dreams," she said.

"No. Those dreams left me a long time ago. They were mine and mine alone. God has bigger and better things for us. Not for me, but for *us.*"

More tears came, so first Will wiped his own cheeks, and then he brushed them off Amy's soft skin.

"We know how this story ends," he said. "Right? We're still in the middle of it. We gotta remember that even when it looks like we've reached the very end, we haven't, Amy. Not yet."

3.

A couple of hours later in the shadows of the family room, he saw the silver moon through the picture window and stopped to admire it for a moment. It hung perfectly still, yet he knew it rotated, moving at the precise speed to keep its face always pointed to Earth. God's purity could be seen in His creation, while His grace could be seen in each coming day.

The heaviness he carried didn't feel like shame or regret, nor was it frustration or exhaustion. It was grief over the ignorance that had followed their message. So many refused even to listen to the gospel message they had shared. People couldn't see, nor did they want to see, their Maker and Creator. They not only didn't care, but they also fought to obliterate the very idea of God with a tsunami of hate.

Will talked to God for a few moments and then wiped the tears off his cheeks and headed downstairs to check on the girls. The soft, warm glow of the nightlight stood guard just outside their room. He stepped onto the soft carpet, hearing Shaye turn on the squeaky bed and Callie breathing softly and seeing Bella's scrunched-up figure underneath her blankets. He stayed in the bedroom a little longer than usual, just listening and thanking God for these girls. For their lives.

He knew he'd been called to serve and love God and to tell others about Him. But he also had a duty to be a father to these three amazing girls, not just to tell them about Jesus but to show Him to them by his words and actions. Will didn't know which responsibility was more daunting. He had failed at both time and time again.

Heading to the other bedroom where Amy slept, or where she probably tried to sleep without success, he knew there was hope to still be a hero in this tale. Just like Gideon and like Hutchence. To no longer be a spectator but to be a soldier. But first he had to do the basics. He had to have more than a mere belief that simply accepts the truth. He needed a faith that was confident in the truth.

"See how very much our Father loves us, for he calls us his children, and that is what we are!"

At the doorway of their temporary bedroom, in the middle of the black night, in the aftermath of Acatour's desolation, Will was starting to see.

TWENTY-FIVE

Rescued

1.

Cheyenne looked at the paintings again, all of them surrounding her like a ghastly army of dark giants with ominous names. *The Expulsion of Adam and Eve from Paradise* with two distraught figures walking down into darkness from the slit of piercing light streaming from the narrow entryway in the massive stone mountain. *The Destruction of Sodom and Gomorrah* with its mouth of destruction, with bloody lips dripping and a throat of bright lava swallowing everything in sight. The darkness of *Jonah Preaching Before Nineveh* and the raised hands reaching toward the light in *Joshua Commanding the Sun to Stand Still.*

"Starting a collection?" Jazz asked as he walked into the small guest bedroom of Pastor Brian's house and saw the lit-up screens on the wall in front of her.

"Look familiar?" she asked.

"All this time I was expecting to see an image like that of the Incen Tower."

There was no smile on his face or irony in his voice. Only the stern solemnness death brought. She looked at the raging skies and fire collapsing on the helpless bodies below in *The Great Day of His Wrath.*

"I'm afraid," she said. "Afraid of the ramifications of what we did."

"As a Christian, I'm instructed not to be afraid," Jazz said. "But if I'm being honest, I am. Not of what's to become of me, but of what's to become of the rest of the world."

"Screens off," she said, and they disappeared, leaving the room in a dim light. "Is everyone else asleep?"

Jazz nodded. "Yeah. And Malek sometimes snores, so I might crash on the couch in the basement."

All of them felt a bit stir-crazy, but they knew they still needed to lie low and not do anything for a while.

"I want to give you something," Jazz told her. "Your father said if after three weeks we hadn't heard from him, he wanted me to give you this."

Once again someone was giving her a folded note from her missing father.

"Thanks," she said to Jazz.

In a lot of ways, she already knew the truth. *He knew it himself. He basically knew what was going to happen to him.*

"I don't have any sort of wisdom or encouragement to offer," Jazz said.

"Sometimes there's none to give."

He nodded.

She reached out and gave him a hug. "Thank you. And thank you for continuing to keep watch over me the way he wanted you to."

"Sure thing. I'm billing by the hour."

Wishing her a good night, Jazz left the bedroom. She walked over and sat on the bed near the lamp. Then she opened the letter from her father.

My dearest Cheyenne,

If you haven't heard from me by now, there's a reason. But just as the first time I sent you a letter, I want to ask you to do something again. I want you to come find me.

I don't want you to be sad, okay? I believe I'm in a better place, Cheyenne.

I want you to consider this.

You believe that your father loves you, right? Despite my flaws. Then consider this: There is a God, and He is perfect and holy, and He loves you. Enough to send His own Son to die for you and everyone else.

All you have to do is believe, Cheyenne.

If you're reading this, I'm probably in a better place now. Know this.

I want you to see this place too.

I want you to see the power in faith.

It's not a fantasy. It's not scientific, and it's not computer generated.

There won't be algorithms in heaven. God doesn't need them.

Let that curiosity you shared with me lead you to something greater. Just like the work you did at PASK. You're on a much bigger quest than just solving riddles in algorithms.

I love you, Cheyenne. But you know something incredible? God loves you even more.

Daddy

The tears felt like the only real and living things on her. As one streamed slowly past her nose and onto her lip, she tried to taste it, but there was nothing inside it. Nothing but emptiness. Cheyenne wiped her face and finally folded the letter after reading it several times.

Her heart ached for her father and for the words he'd written to her. She still didn't understand why he had to leave them, why he needed to be a decoy for the Reckoner. Hadn't he—hadn't all of them—done enough?

Maybe all of this would never make sense, including the faith part. Maybe she would spend the rest of her life trying to figure it out like algorithms. Maybe the complexities would drive her to insanity or, worse, would force her to finally stop trying to figure them out. Perhaps she would give up seeking any sort of answers.

In the glow of the lamp in her room and the comfort of the bed she rested against, Cheyenne wondered what it would be like to have her father's sort of faith. A kind that didn't fear dying and didn't wrap itself in regret at the thought of losing everything, including her. What would it be like to have this sort of blind belief that made you do the unthinkable and improbable?

What would it be like to suddenly stop your vehicle as it was heading down the highway at ninety miles an hour? To not only stop, but to suddenly take a side road and begin heading down an entirely different road? One that was unknown and uncharted. One that you trusted would lead to something bigger and better.

It would be nice to have a soul believing in that.

2.

Stepping outside onto the gravel parking lot, Cheyenne felt numb but was navigating through this. Not long ago she assumed her father might never be found again. He had found her and given her a gift. A chance to say goodbye. And hope, at least in his eyes.

Cheyenne didn't see it yet. Her eyes were still too blurry from her tears. Yet days after reading that letter from her father, she refused to give up on her own hope, a kind that said he might still be out there. He might still be alive.

On Sunday Malek and Jazz urged her to come with them, so the three of them drove to this warehouse to meet with everybody else. Cheyenne went reluctantly, knowing the pastor whose home they were staying in was leading the service. She imagined it would be like the gathering the Parschauers went to. The thought was both comforting and haunting.

Every day for the past few weeks, more people had shown up, thanking them and telling them how brave they were for taking down Acatour and Jackson Heyford. Saying how amazing it was to share God's grace the way they did.

She didn't tell any of these people how wrong they happened to be, how she really didn't do anything, how she still didn't understand that grace they were talking about.

She didn't say any of that but rather stayed quiet.

Nobody needed to know that really, deep down, she just wanted to go back to her old apartment in Incen Tower and sleep in her old bed. But the PASK division had been shut down, and she would have been left without a job if she had stayed. Jackson Heyford and a dozen other leaders of Acatour had been arrested. After two weeks of riots, fires, and destruction, Chicago remained in a partial lockdown mode with a curfew and the National Guard securing the streets.

The shadow of Acatour hung over every single person on this earth. Cheyenne knew that.

After entering the building, she was greeted by the friendly-faced Pastor Brian, along with his wife, son, and daughter. In this warehouse they were surrounded by vintage furniture she might have shopped for in another life. About thirty people were there this morning, all of them people she had met at some point in the last few weeks. There seemed to be a buzz in the room for some reason, but she wasn't sure why.

Several minutes after they arrived, the door behind them opened, and another new face approached. He was older, maybe in his forties, with a somber expression and dark rings under heavy eyes. Following him was a pretty woman and three young girls, all of whom remained silent and looked apprehensive. The man leading them scanned the room with suspicion, and then Pastor Brian walked over to him and gave him a hug.

Is this the Reckoner? She couldn't help thinking that. Maybe everybody was thinking that.

The pastor turned to them with a smile on his face. "This is Will Stewart. His wife, Amy, and his daughters, Shaye, Bella, and Callie."

There was a pause, and Cheyenne could see that even Jazz and Malek weren't sure who this family was.

"Will was helping the Reckoner," Pastor Brian told them. "Personally helping him with getting the message to everybody."

Will nodded and looked down at the ground for a moment. Cheyenne could see the heaviness on his face. Will gave them a sad and weary smile.

Jazz, Malek, Cheyenne, and everybody else began to introduce themselves. She couldn't help watching the young girls, seeing how scared they looked, especially the younger twins. Cheyenne went up to them and tried to make them comfortable by telling them how she liked their cute outfits.

After they had talked for ten minutes, Pastor Brian asked everybody to sit down so they could start their meeting. While they sat on the sofas and chairs gathered in a half circle, the pastor asked one of the new guests to talk to them. Will stood and appeared nervous and unsure what to say.

"So," Will said, "here we are." He chuckled and paused for a minute to gather his thoughts.

Cheyenne looked around the room, seeing the variety of people here. Old and young, men and women, boys and girls. She couldn't help thinking about what Susan Parschauer told her about her husband, Tom. *"Sometimes he fancies himself one of the early disciples, like the ones he spoke about today."*

Then she thought about something else, something Tom told her, this statement even more poignant. *"Don't you think they spent the rest of their lives talking about being rescued? And that every single day they could still see that massive ship slowly sinking into the dark ocean?"*

The words stung. Cheyenne knew she'd been rescued but from what? For what?

"I don't have much to say, except to say thanks to those of you who have been a part of this rather miraculous thing," Will said, looking at her and Malek and Jazz. "It's nice to see people finally waking up to what's really happening in this world. In a lot of ways, I'm one of them. It's amazing our family ended up here." Will grinned and looked at his wife.

"The man all of you know as the Reckoner wanted me to tell you something. He said his work wasn't finished. That *our* work isn't finished. That it's only started. He wanted to thank all of you and to leave you with some encouragement. They're not his words but those of the King. The words Jesus told His disciples in John."

Will looked at all of them, wiping his eyes and giving them a relieved and tired smile.

"'I am leaving you with a gift—peace of mind and heart. And the peace I give is a gift the world cannot give. So don't be troubled or afraid.'"

Acknowledgments

Thanks to Shannon Marchese and Alex Field for this opportunity. They indicated that they were "looking for a particular kind of project" and graciously asked me to send them some ideas. It's rare to have a project you think will never happen actually turn into a wonderful book like this. I'm also grateful for the rest of the team at WaterBrook and Multnomah, as well as Penguin Random House. It's an honor to be published by you.

I appreciate the impact that both William Leonard Thrasher Jr. and Barry Smith each had on this book. William is my father, and I'm eternally grateful to him for not making me William Leonard Thrasher III and instead making me a William Travis. When I was in fourth grade, my parents became born-again believers, and ever since then I have witnessed my dad's desire to wake up those who don't have an authentic relationship with Jesus Christ and those who are nominal believers not living out their faith. My father has always approached the Christian walk in the way the apostle Paul did—direct and head-on, sometimes leaving you reeling from the collision. Over the years, my father's urgency to proclaim the message of Christ has grown inside of me, so it felt only natural to pour all of that into this novel. My father is a writer too and has written half a dozen nonfiction books, his latest called *Consider This*.

Barry Smith, a former colleague at Tyndale House Publishers, has remained my best friend since I left the company in 2007. He's like my father in two ways: first, he believes in me and is one of my biggest fans—despite not caring for the fiction genre; and second, his desire is to make God known (and yeah, if you didn't see the dedication, check that out again). When dealing with hardships in his life, Barry has clung to his faith and made Christ his most important focus. He's been a steady rock in my life, and I'm so thankful for him.

So does the fact that I'm married with three girls and we ended up moving to Michigan sound familiar? Hmmm. Here's the beauty of fiction: you can put parts of your life in it, but the most obvious ones aren't always factual. I'm indebted to my loving and patient wife, Sharon, who has endured living with a full-time artist and all that that means. Kylie, Mackenzie, and Brianna have all done so great with our big move, and I'm truly blessed to be their father. I'm so thankful for our new home, neighborhood, friends, and community.

There are many others I should probably acknowledge, but the orchestra has started to play. However, I absolutely need to thank my faithful readers. Some of you have been with me since the start of this publishing journey in 2000 when *The Promise Remains* was released. What a ride it's been. Fiction has been, and will always be, my true love, and I will never stop writing it. It's been a while since I had a novel like this published, so thank you for being patient. I've written this book to be a satisfying stand-alone novel, but I hope to be able to continue the *American Omens* saga because I've always imagined this to be a series with lots of characters and storylines. (Those of you who know me are thinking, *Of course you did . . .*)

One last thing: I'm thankful to be in a country where I'm still able to write a book like this, where faith isn't a feeling but rather is someone called Jesus Christ.

About the Author

Best-selling author Travis Thrasher has written more than fifty books, spanning genres in fiction, nonfiction, and children's literature. His inspirational stories have included collaborations with filmmakers, musicians, athletes, celebrities, and pastors.

Thrasher's childhood goal, starting in third grade, was to pursue a writing career. After graduating college, he worked at Tyndale House Publishers for thirteen years, and his experience working as an author relations manager allowed him to understand the writing life and learn how to work with a variety of personalities. This experience has proven to be invaluable in the decade that he's been a full-time writer.

His novels are as diverse as the people he's worked with, ranging from love stories to supernatural thrillers. *Publishers Weekly* said, "Sara and Ethan are two of the most real and sensitive lovers to grace the genre" when reviewing his first novel, *The Promise Remains*. They also stated that "Thrasher demonstrates a considerable talent for the horror genre" in a review for *Isolation* years later. His readers have enjoyed the unpredictability of his novels, whether it's due to a unique style or a twist they never saw coming.

Thrasher's storytelling ability has also allowed him to work with others on their books, from musicians such as country superstar Scotty McCreery and Journey keyboardist Jonathan Cain to the Robertsons of *Duck Dynasty*. He has also penned novels based on songs, such as *Paper Angels* with Jimmy Wayne, and novelizations for films including *Indivisible* and *God's Not Dead 2*. Upcoming projects continue to expand his talents, including *Olympic Pride, American Prejudice* that sheds light on the lives of the other seventeen American black athletes who competed alongside Jesse Owens in the 1936 Olympic Games in Berlin, and *Baby Don't Hurt Me* about comedian Chris Kattan's life and his time on *Saturday Night Live*.

Travis lives with his wife and three young daughters in the Grand Rapids, Michigan, area.